PRAISE FOR ROBERT WARD'S KING OF CARDS

"Genuinely funny and fresh. . . . Ward has concocted a touching and comic romp about Tom Fallon's time of 'sweet wildness and precious hope.' "
—*Washington Post Book World*

"*THE KING OF CARDS* is a sexy, funny, and unsentimental memoir of a macho kid's coming of age in early-sixties Baltimore."
—*Penthouse*

"Leaves the reader carried away (sometimes unwittingly) by the sheer creative energy involved. . . . the vital excesses of the '60s are wonderfully evoked, and there are some hilarious and touching scenes. . . . The book's pulsing vitality—as in the novels of Thomas Wolfe . . . carries the day."
—*Publishers Weekly*

"*THE KING OF CARDS* is a wild poem that unravels like a flying carpet ride over the lush and rocky hills of sexual delights, intellectual longings, and raw familial wounds. I laughed so hard at one point that I fell off the couch, and yet two pages later I was weeping into wads of tissue."
—Beth Henley, author of the Pulitzer Prize–winning play, *Crimes of the Heart*

"Wild and outrageous, by turns hilarious and heartbreaking, a tribute to the free spirit of the '60s. . . ."
—*The Annistan (AL) Star*

"Alternately hilarious and compassionate. . . ."
—*L.A. Village View*

"*THE KING OF CARDS* is part romp, part raw confession, and part rite-of-passage novel."
—New York *Daily News*

Also by Robert Ward

Red Baker
Cattle Annie and Little Britches
Shedding Skin

the King of Cards

Cards

Robert Ward

WASHINGTON SQUARE PRESS
PUBLISHED BY POCKET BOOKS

New York   London   Toronto   Sydney   Tokyo   Singapore

WSP

A Washington Square Press Publication of
POCKET BOOKS, a division of Simon & Schuster Inc.
1230 Avenue of the Americas, New York, NY 10020

Copyright © 1993 by Robert Ward

Ward, Robert, 1943–
    The king of cards / Robert Ward.
        p.   cm.
    ISBN 0-671-73741-4
    I. Title.
PS3573.A735K5   1993   813'.54—dc20   92-30129
                                          CIP

First Washington Square Press trade paperback printing
April 1994

10 9 8 7 6 5 4 3 2 1

WASHINGTON SQUARE PRESS and colophon are
registered trademarks of Simon & Schuster Inc.

Cover design by John Gall
Cover photos: Cindy Lewis (top)
              Caroline Greyshock (bottom)

Printed in the U.S.A.

"YAKETY YAK" (Jerry Leiber, Mike Stoller) © 1958 (Renewed)
CHAPPELL & CO., JERRY LEIBER MUSIC & MIKE STOLLER
MUSIC. All rights reserved. Used by permission.

"YOUNG BLOOD" (Jerry Leiber, Mike Stoller, Doc Pomus) ©
1957 JERRY LEIBER MUSIC, MIKE STOLLER MUSIC,
CHAPPELL & CO., UNICHAPPELL MUSIC, INC. (Renewed).
All rights reserved. Used by permission.

*This book is dedicated to my mother, Shirley Kauffman;
and to the memory of my father, Robert Alan Ward (1915–1990);
to my wife, Celeste Wesson;
and to my son, Robert Wesson Ward, with all my love.*

ACKNOWLEDGMENTS

Thanks to my wonderful editor Jane Rosenman, to my agents and friends Esther Newberg and Heather Schroeder, to my assistant and pal Jane DeVries, and to those dear friends from long ago who lived the fast, wild life down "The Hole" in wild old Baltimore: Richard, Jack, Scott, Sam, Ned, Mark, Kathy, and the two we all loved the most, now spirits but still alive in our hearts, Jesse Rossman and Michael Thomas.

the King of
Cards

I always get the shakes when I go back to Baltimore. I actually thought this last trip—a year ago next week—would be easier, but as soon as the smooth-talking southern pilot announced that we were "starting our gradual descent into the Baltimore–Washington Airport," my mouth turned to cotton and my fingers became as cold as those on any corpse. I took a couple of deep breaths, gripped the armrests, and told myself to chill out, that this time was different. I was returning home a "hero," a "celebrity," no reason to panic. But such talk had zero effect on my racing heart. I took a deep breath and stared down at the lush countryside that ran next to the Baltimore–Washington Parkway. There were tall green bushes that looked like they might pull out their roots and start walking around and great blotches of some cream-colored flower—probably honeysuckle. Of course, it *would* be honeysuckle. Maryland was covered with that sweet-smelling vine; the old house at Chateau Avenue had wild honeysuckle running up a broken lattice on its north side, and even the mere thought of *that* made me feel something had broken inside.

"The only problem is you're scared shitless," I said, trying a little lame wit on myself, which helped some. Better to be in touch with the melting, panicky center than trying to sound like some Allstate salesman of the soul.

I blew air from my cheeks, wiped the flight grime off my neck, and tried to figure it out. I'd suffered major panic attacks in past swings home, but I had chalked those up to the ugliness of the tasks at hand, burying my dear grandmother, Grace, and my aunt Ida (beautiful, independent Aunt Ida who died young from smoking her filterless Raleighs) and seeing my father through a couple of rough sur-

1

geries (he was not a model patient). But why panic on this particular morning when I was flying down to be honored by my old school, Calvert College, for my "achievements as a writer"? The dean of Humanities, one Dr. Moss, had gushed about my books over the phone, especially my Pulitzer nominee, *The Black Watch* (he was kind enough not to mention I'd lost). Oh, yes, this was a fine day. I was to be given an honorary Ph.D. Henceforth, I would be Thomas Fallon, Doctor of Humane Letters, and though I had laughed about it and told my New York friends that it was hardly like being honored by Harvard, I'd be lying if I said I was less than pleased. After all, the year before Calvert had seen fit to honor another graduate, Grady Wheat, the famous abstract painter, and it was nice to know they regarded me in Wheat's class.

Beyond pride of achievement, however, I have to confess to a nastier emotion in all of this. I wanted the honor as a means of revenge on all the boobs, cretins, and imbeciles who had populated both Calvert's faculty and student body during my years at the college. The place had formerly been a state teacher's institution, and during my four wild years there, the school was largely still run by educationalists, the kind of mothbrained, pinheaded idiots who mumble cliches about the "joys of learning" while systematically squeezing every drop of life out of the process. Consequently, I had spent much of my time at the school railing against them and their moronic building block mentality.

But my experience at Calvert wasn't all bad. After all, it was there that I met the professor who forged my intellectual life, Dr. Sylvester Spaulding, and of course, it was at dear old Calvert that I met the only true genius I've ever known, Mad Jeremy Raines, not to mention my first true love, Val, and all the rest of the wild boys and girls at the battered old shingled house on Chateau.

As the plane touched down, I laughed in a manic, lunatic way. Of course that was why I felt like a crooked man falling down a boiling, greased hill. From the very day Dean Moss had called me at my apartment in the Village to tell me of

2

the impending honor, I had known that there was going to be a serious price to pay for becoming *Dr. Thomas Fallon.* Oh, no, this little trip home could never be as simple as LOCAL BOY MAKES GOOD. To walk on that green campus again, to sit on the hard benches outside the moldy English offices, to see the old lacrosse field, was inevitably to be drawn back to a particularly painful part of my history. Indeed, I knew as soon as I climbed down the plane's portable steps and stepped on Maryland soil once again that what I truly feared were the memories of youth, a deep sweet wildness and precious hope that was gone from my world.

All of this flooded through my brain as I grabbed my bag, walked like a zombie through the mental hospital glare of the airport, rented the only car they had left, a midnight blue Mercury Cougar, and headed out toward Calvert. On the freeway, I chattered constantly to myself, playacting the Good Coach ("You're gonna be fine. You're getting a god-damned award for Chrissakes."), while around me the other drivers on the Baltimore Beltway looked into my dusty windows and shook their heads. I could nearly hear their nasally Baltimore voices as they drove through the killer humidity back to their redbrick row houses. "Saw a loon-a-tic onna road today, hon. Man talking to his self. I swear to Gawd. Loon-a-tics is everywhere!"

By the time I made the York Road exit, I had sweated right through my nice, predictable blue oxford broadcloth shirt and felt as though a swarm of dark gnats had entered my ears and were buzzing around inside my addled brain. I scarcely remember parking the car or walking up the foot-path toward Old Main. The next time I became fully conscious of my surroundings I was ushered into a room called the Calvert College Public Relations Suite by a big Irishman named Riley, who apologized for the flashbulbs and the microphones that were thrust into my face. I blinked, smiled at the press, and told myself that this was fine. I was here to be honored, and the truth was, I was grateful for the lights and the questions. They served as a diversion from the terrors of the past, which lay coiled in my heart.

As I answered questions about my novels and screenplays, I looked around nervously for Dr. Spaulding. Surely he wouldn't miss my big day at the college, but he was nowhere in sight. Instead, I found Dr. Gerald Lawson, a fat literature professor, in a 1930s double-breasted suit, replete with tobacco stains. He was a great bore in class, droning on about the "little golden truths" in his favorite work, *The Faerie Queen*, the dullest great poem ever written. Lawson was one of the many legions of people I've met whose only distinction in life was attending Harvard or Yale and who feel it necessary to mention the fact in every other sentence they utter. "While attending Harvard, I first came across the poetry of John Crowe Ransom, taught to me by Visiting Professor Allan Tate. I remember well asking Tate about Ransom's use of syntax as we strolled through Cambridge . . . blah, blah, blah." This method of teaching is designed to make the state school student feel even more hapless, and I had a mind to go over and poke him in the stomach, a temptation I just barely managed to resist.

Near fat Lawson was an educationalist named Professor Roger Touhy, a Man Without a Brain. Gray suited, gray crepe shoed, and gray faced, he had taught something called Lesson Plan I, in which he taught us prospective teachers how to outline our course material. "You start with a capital A," he used to mumble into his rooster tie, "and then after you go to number 1. Now that's not roman numeral I—oh, no, indeed, that's a small 1—under which you must think of your objective for the first five crucial minutes." Once, on a dare from Jeremy, I'd hit dear Professor Touhy in the head with a snowball from fifty yards away. Now he smiled at me as if I were his acolyte, his native son.

Even after I had been fielding questions for fifteen min-

4

utes, there was no sign of Dr. Spaulding and my mood started disintegrating. Could it really be possible that he still held a grudge against me after all these years? The thought made me sag a little, and I looked over at Riley to save me. The last thing I could afford was one of my panic attacks. I could see the headlines in the *Baltimore Sun* tomorrow: "Famous Baltimore Author Goes Screaming from Room." Luckily, Calvert was only minutes away from Larson-Payne Mental Hospital. Once they scooped me up, they could put the Big Shirt on me and hustle me right off to the good old A-3 ward, a place I knew so well I could almost call it home.

I held my breath and felt the flashbulbs go off. I mean *felt* them go off under my own itching skin. If Spaulding wasn't going to show, I wanted—no, *needed*—to go find *him*. In any case, I'd had enough, and I wanted out of here.

Then the great oak doors swung open and he was suddenly standing there staring at me, dressed in his perfectly tailored brown herringbone suit and I smiled and walked toward him, trying not to seem like an eager child racing toward his lost father. I mean, I had to literally slow my feet down, remind myself that "Yes, I was an adult, yes, I was successful. Yes, I deserved his respect."

Of course he was much older. I had expected that. Or, no, that's not quite true. I had attempted to prepare myself for that inevitable fact by saying over and over: "Well, naturally, he'll be older. What do you expect?" But preparation doesn't really always coincide with expectation. I was still shocked by the deep lines in his handsome square face, by his short-clipped snow white hair, by the cane that he held at his side, by his noticeable limp. Indeed, his presence— this sounds melodramatic, but I am trying to be accurate— his presence, so much older and clearly weaker, actually weakened *me* still further; I felt for a brief second (and I am ashamed of this) furious that he had aged. I wanted to grab him, shake him, say, "What in the hell are you doing, Dr. S.? Walking in here *old*? For Godssake?" Instead, of course, I shook his hand and said in a measured whisper: "Professor, it's good to see . . ."

I couldn't say anything else. Suddenly, I longed to be away from this maelstrom of flashbulbs and roaming eyes, the good little machines that send your image to the world but cut out your heart.

"Good to see you, Thomas," he said in his stiff, formal way. "Congratulations."

I started to hug him but remembered his horror of being touched and settled for a pat on his shoulder. Words and thoughts came rushing back to me with such a force that I felt like grabbing him by his old thin arm, pulling him away from the lights.

But, of course, I didn't do that. I'm a professional now, aren't we all?

There was a good-looking blond reporter in the front row with a name tag on her perfect tweed suit. It said Sally Harper, and I recalled seeing her byline on a couple of stories during the past year. She smiled and held up *The Black Watch*.

"Dr. Spaulding," she said, "Tom Fallon's novel is about police violence and cover-ups in the Latino community in New York City. When he was a student, did he have such a well-developed social conscience?"

Dr. Spaulding smiled slightly and answered in a dry, ironic voice: "No, I think not," he said. "When he was in my class, he was rather fond of Henry James."

I looked at him for signs that he was saying this with affection or irony, but he gave me no smile, no wink of an eye. It was as though he was describing the weather.

Harper finished scribbling in her notebook and looked at me: "What was your inspiration for *The Black Watch*, Mr. Fallon?"

"Anger," I said. "I don't like the way the cops kick people around."

I was surprised and slightly embarrassed by my own voice. It was overtough, almost a caricature of some hard-boiled private eye of the 1940s. It sounded so ridiculous to me that it nearly made me laugh out loud. Didn't they all know that inside I'd regressed to age nineteen?

There was a small murmur in the crowd, and I looked at

6

Dr. Spaulding, but he seemed a little nervous, anxious, I thought, to get away from here, maybe even to get away from me.

"That's not quite the truth," I said, taking off my glasses. "The truth is that Professor Spaulding is the inspiration for all my work."

Everyone smiled at that (except for Dr. Lawson, whose mouth hung open like he was waiting for someone to stuff a doughnut in it) and dutifully wrote it down. Of course, I'd sounded sentimental, but it was my own awkward way of apologizing. I looked back at the professor and he allowed himself a small smile, then stared down at the floor.

"When I came to Calvert," I said, "I knew very little about life or art, a shortcoming that Dr. S. quickly made clear to me. He reminded me that before I could write a great novel, or even a publishable short story, I would first have to suffer the minor inconvenience of being able to write a coherent sentence."

That got an affectionate laugh, and Spaulding allowed himself another slight smile of acknowledgment.

"Is that true, Dr. Spaulding?" Harper said.

He paused for a second, took off his glasses with his right hand, and tapped them on his left palm, a gesture I'd seen him make a thousand times in class.

"Thomas was always a student with great potential," he said and let it die there.

There was a small, respectful titter, and I couldn't help myself. Though he had barely acknowledged my presence, I put my arm around him.

He stiffened like a corpse but stayed there as the cameras clicked away. Still, I felt him shrinking from my touch. He was dying to get out of there, and I wondered if after all these years, he still hadn't forgiven me.

I wanted badly to speak to him again, but at the end of the press conference, he apologized, saying he had to attend a faculty meeting. I nodded as though I understood but thought it odd. Would the school schedule a faculty meeting the same time they were honoring one of their graduates?

That seemed unlikely, and I felt a stain bleach over what happiness I had taken from the morning. So I walked with big beef-faced Riley down the marble steps and out the great stone-arched entrance to the green fields that ringed Old Main.

"You're free until tomorrow morning at nine," Riley said. "Is there anything more I can do for you?"

"No," I said. "Thanks for everything. Guess I'll give my dad a call."

What I wanted to say was give me Sally Harper's number, for Chrissakes, don't let me go redneck and drown in memories.

But such impulsive tactics were really no longer my style. So I simply shook his hand and watched Riley walk away, a man with a schedule, a man with a place.

I should have gone directly to my car, gotten away from the school, but the truth is, the campus had so expanded that I wasn't exactly sure where the mighty Cougar was parked. So I started walking across the green sward of campus in front of Old Main. I looked up at the great Gothic spire, the stained windows, the cupolas, and black stone gargoyles that hovered over the high-arched entrance and remembered my first days here—1965, the year that the world cracked.

The pictures came back with a buzz, a great swarm of bright images, one overlapping the other, until they made me physically dizzy and I sat down under an oak, behind a surrealistically green hedge.

I lay my head back on the tree's trunk and tried to order the bright images, but they kept coming as though sent by some half-drunk projectionist behind my eyes, so I reached into my sport coat pocket and pulled out a half-pint of Jack Daniels.

I uncapped it and laughed. What would the press make of their hero now? The distinguished Dr. Thomas Fallon gets shitfaced on the College lawn. I took a long hit and said loudly and absurdly to myself: "What one needs here is a sense of order! Indeed! This above all else!"

8

THE KING OF CARDS

The booze hit me instantly, and I laughed at the sound of my ridiculous voice. Or, rather, the high and proper academic voice I had borrowed. For this was not Dr. Tom's voice, but rather Dr. Sylvester Spaulding's. Or, perhaps, that's not exactly true either, for in a real sense his voice *was* my voice, I think. I mean the liquor felt fine, and I was at last settling in, giving myself over to the House of Memories, as old Merle Haggard once called it. And I laughed a drunken cough of a laugh and thought of the irony of it. Here I was a professional writer, a man who lives through and for memory, afraid to recall my own past. All this time I had kept these years sacrosanct, built a temple around them, and watched it sit there glimmering on ancient hallowed ground, afraid what I would feel if I kicked open the battered doors.

But who was I kidding? The doors were going to fall in the end, the temple would collapse, and I had my Jack to keep me warm, so why not now? Why not here? On the very lawn where the great, stumbling adventure began?

It was the fall of 1965, my parents were fighting again, and I knew I had to leave home or risk some kind of violent reaction against them. What form it would take, I wasn't sure. All I really knew was that it was coming; there was a mounting fury in my heart and I feared its release. For they screamed at one another over breakfast, they glared and cursed and cried at one another at dinner, and they slammed their bedroom door shut at bedtime, still clawing and shouting as the lights went out. What was this endless battle all about? I wasn't really sure. Only that my father, James, harbored a vast resentment against my mother. In his eyes, he had fallen from grace, and she was the instrument of his collapse.

He had been an artist before they met, a watercolorist of

some talent. (Even now I had two of his early paintings on my apartment walls.) His dream had been to go to New York. My mother told me he talked of nothing else when they first met. But being poor and not well connected, he had no idea of how to go about getting himself into school there. Of course, he could have simply gone, roughed it, lived the Bohemian life in the Village, and at one point he was going to do just that. But his mother, Grace, wouldn't hear of it. She forbade him to go; she had an image that he was "frail" and was certain he would never survive such a life. There's no use in trying to make her out a villain for this decision. Indeed, with my grandfather either gone to sea or wasting the family's money in sailors' bars and whorehouses, Grace had slaved to keep the family afloat. In all ways she was a remarkable woman. Though her education had ended in the eighth grade, she played Mozart on the piano and her favorite book was *The Magic Mountain*.

It was beyond my father's will (or anyone else's in the family) to defy her, so he stayed home in Baltimore, accepting a scholarship to the Maryland Institute of Art. Here he was happy enough and spent two years painting his watercolors, taking field trips throughout the lushly vegetated city and down to the Eastern Shore to make nature studies. It was by all accounts one of the happiest times in his life.

In his second year at the Institute, he met my mother, Ruth, at a church dance. She was a beautiful red-haired girl, full-figured, with an appealing overbite, and a pageboy haircut. In old photographs she looked like Gene Tierney. On her side, my mother was from a farm family who had recently migrated to Baltimore when the crops failed in Mayo County. Bored by her provincial home life, she was thrilled to meet a sensitive boy, a real artist.

Now when I remember the terrible screaming, the endless fighting, I try to think what it must have been like in those first years of courtship, the two of them taking the old yellow No. 8 streetcar out the York Road to "the country" (only one mile past Calvert College there was once nothing but forest and streams and glowing, green Maryland fields), my

10

father with his easel and canvas, my mother, his lovely muse, holding his paintbrushes and colors. I see them walking over the old train trestle that bisects Towson, walking and talking philosophy. (My father, like my grandmother, was much taken with Bertrand Russell.) I think of the excitement they must have felt, their growing love for one another, my father's wonder that at last he had met a girl who understood him as his mother did. I picture them lying in one of those impossibly beautiful green fields, near a stand of oaks, my mother with a picnic basket, my father thin and muscular and tan. I watch them making love, feeling young and beautiful and strong. They must have felt that they were never going to get old, would never turn bitter, never turn away from the good, radiant world.

But their happiness lasted a short season. The Depression wiped out my father's hopes of becoming an artist and in short order he was put to work in a local CCC camp, building roads and planting trees in the reservoir by Druid Hill Park. My mother, meantime, worked as a secretary for the Relief Fund, the first of the terrible slavelike jobs she held all her life.

After Roosevelt got the country back on its feet again, my father tried to resume his painting career, but there was little outlet for his work in Baltimore. It was not only that people were too poor to purchase paintings. There is something else in the very fabric of Baltimoreans, and it is this thing that drove my father mad, I believe. The city has such a deep provinciality, such a profound inferiority complex, that it rarely recognizes its own.

To be blunt, my father's dreams were crushed, and he became a bitter and sarcastic man.

I remember him standing on the front porch looking at the neighbors coming home from their jobs. He would say to me, "Look at 'em, Tommy, a bunch of sheep. All living in their goddamned little row houses, all having their same little row thoughts. Who do the goddamned Orioles play tonight, wonder if there's any National Bohemian in the 'fridge, gotta get up to the moronic Catholic church and play their precious bingo. Never read a book. God knows, they would never look at a painting. Mencken had it right, son. Baltimorons, that's what old H. L. called them and that's what they are, a great, brutal horde, as dumb as any jungle animal. Believe me kid, get the hell out of here as soon as you can. 'Cause once you get married . . . you're in this craphole for life."

"But why don't we all leave, Dad?" I said, staring at his pinched face, silhouetted by the perfect evening blue light. "We could go. We could live in New York."

"Ha!" he would laugh, shaking his head as he leaned on the porch railing. "You don't know your mother, son. She can't leave wonderful Baltimore. Why, to her, New York is next to nothing and Paris is some city dump. Oh, no, son, to your mother, there is only one real place in the entire world, godforsaken old Baltimore."

The bitterness in his voice, the sound of defeat, frightened me even then and though I badly wanted to back him up, I felt torn apart, for I didn't really want to leave town either. Like my mother, I loved our redbrick row house neighborhood, loved the fact that just down the street were my friends all living in houses that looked just like mine and around the corner was Tom Mullin field where we would act out our fantasies of being major leaguers. I loved getting on my bike and heading down to Northwood Shopping Center to see the Saturday afternoon horror films, loved having my aunt and grandparents only five blocks away. On Sundays, I would call Pop and ride my bike over to Stonewood Road, where we would eat root beer ice cream floats and watch the Colts on TV, and he would tell me about the old-time players, Jim Thorpe and Red Grange and Bronco Nagurski. I miss him badly even today, dear old toothless, big-muscled Pop, who had started his life as a farmer and become a full-time carpenter at age forty-seven and could fix anything, a man who loved everyday life, the simple joy of the Colts game, or making a plate of stewed tomatoes and who himself thought Baltimore was the best place in the world. Indeed, once, when I was a tortured teenager, I said to him, "Pop, I want to go live in Washington," and he merely looked at me and said, "Don't know why you would want to do that, boy. Those people don't even live where they grew up." A sentiment my mother shared in spades.

So, I loved Baltimore, too, and yet I knew that it had crushed something special in my father, for it was a city that only valued the practical, the everyday, a city that was ruthlessly unforgiving of its dreamers and its artists. As my mother often said to my father when he would spend too much time reading: "Mr. Philosopher. He thinks who *he* is, hon!"

That was the city I grew up in—warm, nurturing, and mind-bogglingly provincial, a combination that proved deadly to my sensitive, bitter old man.

But I am getting ahead of my story (a habit of mine, like my father, I am impatient, eager for fireworks), for in 1965, I knew all this only dimly. Indeed, I would liken my own consciousness to that of a drunken pug fighter who has suffered so many blows he only wants to fall in his corner and get the seconds to plug his cuts.

Not that my parents fighting was a new situation. They had fought off and on for years. There would be a violent period followed by a couple of weeks (sometimes, even a month) of relative calm. Then the mad cycle of screaming and crying would begin again. Of course, given the lunacy in our house, I should have gone away to college, and I would have if I had planned things a little more carefully, but in those days the future was like some alien, uninhabitable planet and my parents were too wrapped in their own misery to worry about my higher education.

Indeed, to be fair, I had given them little reason to think of it. My high school years had been spent drinking National Bohemian beer, playing cards with friends, and chasing girls at Ameche's Drive-In. My three best friends were, like myself, drunken carousing boys, all bright underachievers and after graduation they had scattered, attending colleges out of state. As for me, I had convinced myself that I "hated school," when quite the opposite was true. The truth was, I had always been a torn child, rowdy *and* sensitive, bookish *and* athletic. This kind of complexity was no more tolerated by the children of my neighborhood than it was by the adults. One had to be a jock *or* a brain, and those of us who fell in between were highly suspect. Worse, we felt not quite right about ourselves. I remember stabbing myself with a fork in the hand once to prove I was a "real boy," not some fag intellectual.

Given all the tensions at home and my own ambivalence about my bookishness, I studied only sporadically. Needless to say, my grade-point average suffered, and when it came time to apply to colleges, I found that I had a very slim selection to choose from.

Finally, when the deadline was almost past, I applied to Calvert, telling myself that I didn't really want to go, that the only reason I was bothering at all was because it was near my house and I had seen a few cute girls walking across the campus. When Calvert surprised me and accepted my application, I felt no joy at all. After all, I had nearly convinced myself that I was not a scholar, not a reader, not a sensitive intellectual type. Nothing, in short, like my father, the failure.

But there was a surprise waiting for me at Calvert. Dr. Sylvester Spaulding. Like my father he was bookish, like my father he was brilliant, a lover of the arts. But unlike my father, Dr. Spaulding seemed a happy man. Rigorous, demanding, but essentially happy. Baltimore had not crushed him, for he didn't really live in Baltimore. He lived inside the books he read, he loved literature, and he transmitted that love to anyone in his class.

Having written this, however, I should say that he was not a Romantic. He didn't believe in motivational tricks to make students read. He was demanding, frighteningly so. The early days I spent in his Contemporary European Novel class were both exhilarating and humiliating. First, there was the matter of the man himself. Dr. S. was intimidating in the extreme. Small-boned, trim, and dressed inevitably

14

in a herringbone suit and a rep tie, he walked nervously back and forth as he lectured, tapping his glasses on his open palm. He had total recall of every poem, play, or novel that he had ever read, and he expected his students to understand his every reference.

"We are here," he said on the first day of class, "to discuss art, high art. If that makes me an elitist, then so be it. I believe art, true art, is always elitist in that it is complex rather than simple, in that it stands above the common fray, in that it transcends the mundane and often unpleasant facts of our lives. If it were not elitist, if it were to be what some misguided souls wish, an art 'of the people,' then it would lower its standards, become kitsch, and ironically lose its power to move and instruct people at all."

He stared at me like he was trying to see into my soul. I swallowed hard and tried to meet his gaze.

I had never been exposed to such seriousness of purpose, and although I was intimidated, I was also thrilled. I looked at Dr. Spaulding and said, through an embarrassed cough, "I . . . quite agree, sir."

He nodded as if he approved, tapped his glasses into his palm, and went on: "True art is demanding, complex, filled with multiple meanings. You don't enter into the worlds of Henry James, James Joyce, or Virginia Woolf lightly as you might casually turn on the television or listen to the banal confessional chatter of coffeehouse poets, like Allan Ginsberg. I know my attitude toward art seems like sacrilege to some of you, who have been raised to think that the Baltimore Colts are the highest achievement of Western civilization, but I believe that the rewards of art are far greater than our good crab cake–eating citizens know."

I knew from the second I heard him speak that I wanted to be his most serious student. As I left class that day, I heard some of the other kids moaning about how hard the course would be, but I felt a secret jubilation. I *wanted* it to be difficult. I wanted it to be arcane, complex, mysterious. I wanted to lose myself in the rich sensibilities, the aristocratic manners of Henry James, of Virginia Woolf.

15

I wanted to be lifted up on the wings of genius, with Dr. Sylvester Spaulding as my guide.

That night, as I headed home, I felt lighter than air. I couldn't wait to tell my father about Dr. S. I envisioned the three of us drinking beer, seriously discussing the subtleties of literature together. Perhaps, I thought giddily, meeting Dr. Spaulding might even inspire my father to resurrect his painting career. But, when I arrived, my father wasn't in the mood to listen. He had retreated, as he often did of late, into his temple of bliss, into his inner sanctum, into his secret garden of tile, the Great Bathroom.

This was his retreat, the last step in the great bitterness that had become his life. He walked down the hall in his navy shorts, shut the door, and was gone, gone into the land of steam and running water, acne creams, scalpels, cotton balls, Q-Tips, gauzy bandages, razors, special laxatives, back scratchers, and specially ordered Lufte sponges from Sweden. Gone, gone, gone from Baltimore into some narcissistic playland where a man could dream, as he endlessly worked on his thin, muscular, acne-covered body.

He would enter the Inner Sanctum at 6 A.M., stay in there shitting; pissing; tooth scrubbing; washing and rewashing his body, his face, his hands; slicing open the big red acne cysts that plagued his back, neck, and face until 7:30, at which time he would emerge, wrapped in towels, lanced boils bleeding from his chest like some acnefied versions of Roman Catholic bleeding hearts—James Fallon, the Baltimore Bathroom Job. On some mornings, like a Roman emperor, he would raise his scalpel high above his head, stare wide-eyed into my bedroom, and scream, "They thought they had Jim Fallon, Tom. The bastard cysts thought they were taking over, but I showed them, by God! I showed them." Then he would join thousands of other depressed and furious souls on the Baltimore Beltway in a nose-to-nose gridlocked drive across town to his hated civil servant's job at the Social Security Administration, from which he would return at six, snarl at my mother for a while over her nervously overcooked dinners, and once again enter the

16

Holy Toilet at around seven, from which he would not remove his oil-drained carcass until eleven at night. To this day I cannot think of my father without hearing a toilet flush.

Sometimes he would take in his purple Philco radio and play the classical music station for hours on end—Rachmaninoff, Beethoven, Mozart—while my mother would sit as though she had been poleaxed at the white kitchen table, under the golden sunburst clock. What did he do in there? That was the great mystery. The great unanswered question, though, of course, I knew part of it. He would wash, then wash again, place selected salves on his skin, brown salves, skin-toned salves, white creams, special acne soaps, magical oils from Formosa that promised to rejuvenate dead cells. And though he barely talked to me, he never stopped his dialogue with his pimples. Through the oaken door, I could hear him saying, "Yes, you little red creep. You think you've got old James Fallon licked, but I'll show you. I'll show you, you pus-filled bastard." Then he would hold high his mighty scalpel and lance the pimple with his sterling silver boil popper, as though he were a medieval knight on a white charger lancing Baltimore itself, the great pimple of a city that had kept him from reaching his artistic dreams.

This was nothing new to me. He had been behaving this way since I was twelve. Much of my life had been lived leaning against a bathroom door, trying to tell my father about a shot I made in basketball, what happened on our Boy Scout trip, a spectacular catch in an Oriole game, or the plot of a movie I'd just seen. Sometimes, when he had had a particularly good lancing session and had sufficiently screamed at my poor mother for a few hours, he would even be in a decent enough mood to answer.

So in the fall of 1965, hot with excitement from books and my heroic new teacher, Dr. S., I found myself once again leaning up against the Holy Bathroom door, saying, "Hey, Dad, I have this brilliant new professor over at Calvert. We're studying Kafka." After turning off the water, he answered, "Kafka, huh? Well, that's good, Tom, yeah that's

17

great. Read *The Trial* when I was sixteen and I can assure you that Kafka knew exactly what he was talking about. This whole city is one Kafkaesque nightmare, believe me. Big shots run your life, guys you never even see."

"I finished it today, Dad. You know, it's amazing. Dr. Spaulding told us that no one understood that Kafka was a genius except his pal, Brod."

"Nothing all that amazing about it, Tom," my father said, his voice rising so I could hear him through the roar of the shower. "The Baltimorons didn't understand Poe either. Left him in the gutter to die, but now, of course, they have the goddamned Edgar Allan Poe house fully restored. Oh, yeah, they love him now that he's good and dead, and the founding father assholes can sell tickets to see where he starved and froze. That's your Baltimoron, for you, Tom! Love their artists when they're dead. Can't *wait* for them to die!!!"

Though it was a sour, bitter answer, hardly the elevated conversation I had hoped for, I wasn't really discouraged. No, I was thrilled at the sound of my father's voice croaking over the roaring shower, ecstatic that I had gotten him to respond at all. "This Dr. Spaulding is a great guy, Dad. He really understands literature." I hoped that he would respond again. I had so much to tell him about Dr. S.

But suddenly my mother was leaning on the door next to me saying, "James Fallon, don't talk that way about your native city to your son. He doesn't need your bitterness." But I quickly cut her off: "No, Mom, it's all right, I don't mind," and felt an icy fear come over me. God, they were going to start at it again, just when I had gotten him to talk to me. Oh, Lord, don't let them do it. My fingers got cold, and I felt the panic starting to rise inside my chest. But there was no stopping her; she was flying now, soaring, "Well, I do mind. Okay, Bertrand Russell? You can't blame everything on Baltimore, James Fallon."

"Don't worry," my father's voice said, cutting like a switchblade through the bathroom door, "I don't blame it *all* on *Baltimore!*"

18

That was the end. She started beating on the door with her fists, her red face a mask of pain, a huge blue vein throbbing in her forehead.

"Oh, I see, then. It's all my fault is it? It's all my fault that you're so unhappy. Don't you say that, you liar. Don't you tell our only son that!"

"Mom," I pleaded, "Mom, we were just having a conversation. About books."

"Which she can't stand," my father boomed through the door. "Having never read any except those moronic romance novels!!"

"That's it," my mother said. "You bastard. You rotten liar. Let me in there. Let me in!"

Now she was beating and kicking and screaming, tears rolling down her cheeks, and I could hear my father's voice jacked up as he screamed back, "You want in? You want in? 'Cause if you come in here, if you come in here, you're gonna get it, Ruth. Get the picture?"

"Fine," my mother screamed, bashing and kicking the door until the wood splintered. "Beat me up in front of Tommy. Go ahead. I'd expect nothing less from you. Nothing at all! You cowardly bathroom-loving son of a bitch!!!"

And then I was holding onto her, pulling her from around the waist, saying, "Mom, Mom, you don't want to go in there. You don't." And she was crying and scraping at the door, flailing about like a madwoman, and it went on like that for five minutes before she finally let me take her into the living room, sit her down on the couch, where she broke into deep, moaning sobs.

Needless to say, with such a cozy home life, my studies suffered. Those first few months of school I would spend all day hanging out in the student union or reading in the library. As long as I was lost in the world of books I was fine, but as soon as I started the walk home—our house was only seven blocks away from Calvert—I would feel my stomach tighten, and a kind of numbing sensation would roll through my arms and head. It was as though I'd been in some kind of car accident and I felt as though I were falling through a whirlpool, like a battered gumshoe in some old noir flick.

Only Dr. Spaulding was tangible, real. He was still giving me C's, but he'd begun to speak to me outside of class—in the student union, in walks we took to his car. I wonder if he knew the importance of these little chats. Probably not. He was merely making small talk on the way to lunch, but as far as I was concerned, it was as though I was talking to God himself. Oh, how I lived for Dr. S.'s pearls of wisdom and hoped that he didn't feel he was dropping them before swine. Indeed, as the year rolled on, I decided that more than anything, I wanted to become a gentleman, an academic, not a fiction writer, but a Man of Letters, like, say, Edmund Wilson or Dr. S. himself. I had even begun to fall into Dr. S.'s speech rhythms and tried to *think* as I imagined he thought. Yes, I wanted not only his intellectual muscle and his gentlemanly stature, I wanted to *be* him. I wanted his posture, his brains, his suits. I wanted to transcend all that sweat and screaming and pimple popping with high-mindedness, rare sherry, herringbone suits, and great novels. Ah, the naked sadness of it. I remember driving to Ameche's (named after our Baltimore Colt hero, fullback Alan Ameche, of course) one day and saying to the pimple-faced boy who served out the swill: "One would like a malted, and one would like a bag of fries, and one would *very much* like a massive Powerhouse Double-Burger."

The kid looked at me as though I was an escapee from Larson-Payne, but I didn't mind in the slightest. Of course, I was aware of how ridiculous I sounded, but even though there was a large element of private parody in my speech, I felt a certain satisfaction, a certain frisson of aesthetic pleasure, in using such quaint, archaic phrases. Indeed, on one date I had later that year, while sitting through *It's a Mad*,

THE KING OF CARDS

Mad, Mad, Mad, Mad World at the Passion Pit, I said to a
fellow English major, a cute but chunky girl named Leslie
Walker, that "one would love to partake of a blow job,"
which she found so amusing, so truly Spauldingesque, that
she complied with one's request and for the next hour and
a half licked one's throbbing log until all the sacred juices
had run dry.

But even though I used such language with a sense of
irony, the truth was, I held out an almost unconscious hope
that I would be able to somehow, someday, transcend. But
transcend what? Everything, I suppose. Row-house Baltimore, my own crowded past. Transcend to some cool, well-
lit place where cultured people talked in lush tones about
the deeper things, the finer textures, art.

That first year I was a saint in the library. Nearly every
day I sat in my carrel and attempted to write papers in
the manner of my new heroes (and Spaulding's), Wilson,
F. R. Leavis, or Lionel Trilling. I remember these papers now
as endearingly ludicrous attempts of an eighteen-year-old
Baltimore boy to talk about "high culture" and "political
reality" and "levels of irony" as though he were some fifty-
five-year-old sophisticate who had been to the Finland Station; who had stood in breadlines in the 1930s; who had
read every word of Freud, Jung, Marx, when, in fact, I had
just barely scratched the surface. Indeed, only a few years
earlier my favorite author had been John R. Tunis, author
of boy's sports novels like *The Kid from Tomkinsville* and *World
Series*. Not that I was completely blind to my pretensions.
It occurred to me that I was becoming faintly ludicrous, that
I had taken on near foppish airs, and yet, there seemed no
other course. After all, I did truly love reading Henry James.
The Ambassadors seemed to me an altogether brilliant book,
wonderfully alive. I saw my own reflection in the American

21

businessman Strether as he attempted to cultivate his sensibility in Europe. Both he and I were undergoing our real education, the education of our hearts and souls, and when he faltered, made a fool of himself, I ached for him just the same as if it were I myself who had committed the boobish, American faux pas.

Needless to say, with my own spotty education and completely derivative prose style (not to mention that all my "critical judgments" merely aped Spaulding's own), my papers were at best earnest, lifeless bores. I still remember my first paper for which I received the mighty grade of C −. The grade was so pathetic, given the endless amount of hours I'd put in that I felt physically ill.

That afternoon, screwing up my courage, I went to see Spaulding during his office hours. Lord, what a sullen and uncommunicative sack of a person I was. I felt that I was barely fit to sit at his English pebble-grained feet.

"You see, Mr. Fallon," he said, as I slumped in my chair, "you have much to learn about using the English language. For one, you use the first person, but in a formal essay, one never does that."

I looked at him and shook my head.

"Why not, sir?" I said, "I mean, I'm doing the writing . . ."

"True," he said, "but it's a matter of literary convention. By saying 'one' you are able to achieve a more felicitous style. As I've told you before in matters of literature, style is all."

"Really?" I asked innocently. "I would think there is more to it than that."

"Well, of course, there is," Dr. Spaulding said as he tapped his glasses on his palm. "I was speaking ironically, elliptically. You've been taught many bad habits, Tom. You think that by blurting things out directly, by just saying what's on your mind, you're being bluntly honest. But what is unsaid, what is left out, what is said cleverly or cloaked in brilliant bursts of language, is where real art lies. That is what separates art from mere confession. Though, of course, there are some misguided souls, the so-called beat writers who think that by spilling their guts, they create a more vibrant art."

"Yes," I said quickly, "but I don't consider them artists at all."

"Good," Dr. S. said. "That shows there's some hope for you."

"Thanks," I said, feeling as though bugs were creeping under my skin. "I'll try and do better, sir. I really will."

"The thing is, Thomas," he went on after a considered pause. "You are not without talent. Occasionally, you *are* even capable of subtlety."

These words, so casually stated, sent a shock wave through me, nearly great enough to knock me off the chair.

"But, sir?" I said. "How can you tell? I mean I get lousy grades, and I obviously don't understand the first thing about art."

Dr. Spaulding got out of his chair and walked to the tall window that looked out on the southeast side of the campus. Outside, an oak tree's branches brushed lightly across the glass.

"One has a feeling for these things," he said with his back turned to me. "There is something in your work—wit, intelligence, a feel for language—that is trying to burst forth from beneath all your crudeness."

I felt a light sweat break out on my head. Oh, God, I thought, let it be true.

"You need to apply yourself strictly," Dr. Spaulding said. "You see, what we are all of us hoping for is to perfect a kind of inner vision, what James calls our sensibility. It is that sensibility that is the wellspring of any real, lasting art."

"And you think I might possess such a sensibility?" I said in a choked Victorian whisper.

"I think you have potential," Dr. Spaulding said. "But before you let your spirits soar, Thomas, you must understand that as rare as potential is, *realized* potential is many times rarer. In my many years of teaching I have seen quite a few people with a potential, but sadly only once or twice have I seen such potential result in palpable achievement."

23

God, I wanted to say something, something that would convince him, *assure* him, that I would not be a case of wasted potential (even if I had no idea what *palpable* meant). I started to speak. I intended to swear to him that I'd do anything necessary, drain the blood out of my veins, if it would help me achieve this rarified sensibility.

Then I farted.

Oh, the shame of it, the pain, and horror. I let rip a long, near pants-tearing fart, which sounded like my old bicycle wheel with my baseball cards stuck in it. The smell was violently sulfuric, like five cartons of ancient rotting eggs left in some weed-filled refrigerator on an abandoned Waverly lot. This was a majestic, jazz-scatting, gaseous, bilious fart.

Tears nearly sprang to my eyes, as the hideous smell engulfed the room. Dr. Spaulding gasped, held his throat, and then, when he was able to speak at all, said: "That will be all, Thomas. You must study harder and try to eat a more balanced diet. Good day."

Oh, Lord, the humiliation of it. I nodded like a zombie, got stiffly up, walked slowly out of his room, and staggered to the stairwell.

And as I walked down the English Department steps, my face burning with embarrassment, it occurred to me that the Terrible Fart itself was symbolic. Yes, the young literary scholar who saw Freudian signs and symbols in every coffee spoon now saw the Hideous, Horrific Fart as the intrusion of his home life into his perfectly ordered artistic world at Calvert, the world in which he had True Potential. And the source of the Fart Most Foul was home. Yes, home where his mad father and his beaten hysterical mother were locked in their melodramatic death grip.

At that moment, I knew I could no longer wait, even if my leaving somehow meant they would drown together in the great toilet that had become their lives. One had to get out of there, one had to find a retreat, a room of one's own, to borrow parlance from V. Woolf. One had to escape, race away in the lifeboat of high art. And never look back.

24

THE KING OF CARDS

It seemed to me, at the moment I walked down the steps, that it was a very simple thing. I had saved enough money from last summer's job—working on the old Port Welcome boat, carrying tourists up and down the Chesapeake Bay from Pier 1 to Tolchester. So I could at last move out from the fart-filled bathroom of a home to my own clean, modest place, a place where I could cultivate my sensibility and begin the long, arduous, and serious pilgrimage to find the one and only Holy Grail, my true artistic sensibility.

I squinted at the torn piece of paper in my hand and looked up through the branches of the huge evergreen tree at the tilted, warped house on Chateau Avenue. The number on the paper was 1529; therefore, this battered monstrosity of a house should be the place, but it was impossible to say for sure because there was only one deformed white numeral hanging off the brown shingles on the wide, shady front porch. The number was either a nine or a seven, and if indeed it was a nine, it looked as though wild animals (in this neighborhood, rats probably) had chewed through the loop.

There was an old patched tire for swinging hanging from a branch on a bent oak tree in the front yard, and when I walked farther down the sidewalk, where I could get a better look at the house, I noticed there were two large rolls of clear plastic sitting a few feet from the front door. One of them had become unfastened and had rolled down the rotting steps like a long white tongue.

I shook my head and laughed a little. Though I'd never met the person who owned the house, Jeremy Raines—we had talked only briefly on the telephone—I'd gotten the distinct impression that there was a certain playful, witty quality to his character, and the ramshackle outward appearance of the house did nothing to dispel this notion. The thought of living with such a person was unsettling, and yet, I had to confess that almost against my will I had been somewhat charmed by our brief conversation. Now, as I stood in front of the place, I reminded myself that the greatest writers often began their artistic lives in nothing more than humble rooming houses, and in fact, it was just such a place that might offer me the kind of privacy and solitude that real art required. As I walked up the front steps, I tried to imagine Dr. S.'s reaction to the place. I was sure he'd agree.

I walked to the collapsing screen door and looked inside. There was a long, old-fashioned, and dusty hallway that led out back to what looked like a big, comfortable-looking kitchen. A spiral oak staircase, battered but still somehow elegant, led up to the second floor, where I could hear music playing. The sound was that of a tenor saxophone wailing in some wild arpeggio of pain and desire. I listened for a second and realized I recognized the song, "My Favorite Things" by John Coltrane. In those days I was just beginning to listen to jazz and had only a small appetite for it. Of course, I had never spoken to Dr. Spaulding about my newly found enthusiasm; he was strictly a classical music lover, but I felt that he might possibly find it of artistic worth. As for myself, like everything else I encountered, I didn't know quite how to feel. Since I had come under Spaulding's tutelage, I was obsessed with the idea of authenticity. How was one to tell if something was truly artistic or not? After all, I certainly couldn't depend on my own inner feelings, crude and undeveloped as they were, for in spite of both my father and Spaulding's ravings I had always loved the Baltimore Colts. Indeed, in 1956 when they lost their last two games and with them the championship of the Western Division, I had been so inflamed that I had nearly kicked in our television set. And though I was not the kind of boy who idolized rock 'n' roll performers, I did have a nearly complete collection of Elvis Presley's records, the early ones anyway. I shuddered to think what my cultural hero, Dr. S., would say if he knew that at one time I had collected the Elvis oeuvre as seriously as some bibliophile might collect Proust. So that left me in a serious quandary. Was the music I was hearing now, so filled with longing and pain, really art or just some unshaped mass of musical glut by some undisciplined, half-talented Negro?

As absurd as such arguments seem now, they were the kinds of absurd thoughts I had even as I stood there on the front porch, deeply moved by Coltrane's genius. Moved actually so deeply that the very notes he played seemed to probe into my own acute loneliness and desire.

"Hello," I said unsteadily. "Hello in there . . ."

There was no answer. Whomever was upstairs probably had their bedroom door closed, so I tried the screen door and found it unlatched. Cautiously, I walked inside and turned right into the big, high-ceilinged living room.

The furniture was old, comfortable, and utterly mismatched. There was a huge red velvet couch, which looked like it had been purchased from a house of ill-repute (that is, it was formerly velvet, the surface had been worn down to a frazzle, and there were weird amoebalike stains all over it), a couple of overstuffed 1940s' chairs, and an Indian rug of a deep reddish hue, with some strange-looking Vishnu god dancing in a ring of fire. In the corner was a battered end table with a black-and-white television set with a crack that ran diagonally from one corner to the other and an ancient mahogany magazine rack with a copy of *Time* magazine that had a picture of President Lyndon Johnson looking nobly toward the horizon on the cover. If that wasn't seedy enough, lying next to the rack were three old balled-up formerly white shirts. They were covered with what looked like mustard, lettuce, ketchup, onions. It was as though some cosmic slob had made a sandwich using the shirts for bread. Yet, they had a curious effect on me; rather than being put off by such sloppiness I began to laugh. There was something liberating about the anarchic mess, though I doubt if my father or Dr. S. would have thought so. Finally, in the corner, was the pièce de résistance of the room, an elaborate old barber chair, with leather headrest, cracked leather armrests, and a great black steel footrest. The last shocked me, made me laugh out loud, a laugh I cut short lest someone overhear me. What kind of people would have such an idiotic-looking piece of furniture in their living room?

I shook my head, trying to imagine how Dr. Spaulding would react to all this. I could hear his words in my mind, "No, Tom, this looks like an extremely disordered universe. Perhaps you had better move on. Not the place for a serious student of literature. Not the place at all." I was about to turn and leave, when I again remembered Jeremy Raines's voice on the telephone.

"Tom Fallon?" the crisp voice had said. "Name's Jeremy Raines. Read your ad on the student union bulletin board. Listen, I have the room you are looking for. Yes, sir, know you're going to love the place, my boy."

"Really?" I had answered, somewhat too coldly. There was something playful and—what was the right word— mocking in his voice, and though I had half a mind to hang up on him, I kept on listening.

"Aha . . . well, how best to put this? I live in a group house, all wonderful people. We've got a great sense of community. Everyone is very heavily into their studies. Could be just the spot for you."

"Well, no offense, Raines, but . . ."

"Jeremy," came the instant reply.

"No offense, Jeremy, but I'm not looking to make friends or hang out. I just want to get some reading done. I've got a very tough course load."

"Absolutely," came the swift reply. "Oh, yes, absolutely. The work must come first. No one understands that better than we do. We are all serious students at good old Calvert College. What's your major?"

"Literature," I said proudly (with perhaps just a touch of arrogance).

"Wonderful. I'm a psychology major myself."

I felt a certain sense of smug satisfaction and thought of Dr. Spaulding's endless put-downs of the "educationalists and their little twin brothers, the psychologists." Indeed, the very fact that Raines was a psychology major nearly convinced me to hang up the phone on him. But before I could make the move, he preempted my unspoken criticism.

"Of course, psychology at Calvert is still in the Stone Age, but I'm working on some alternatives to the usual Freudian junk. Love to talk about it with you, get your feedback on it."

"You would? But you don't even know me," I said.

"Details, details," Raines said. "I can tell you're intelligent though. You're studying with Spaulding, aren't you?"

"Yes, but how did you know that?"

"Well, if you're a serious lit major you have to get Spauldingized," he said. "A good man, a bit old-fashioned, of course, but a good man, nonetheless."

"Oh, really," I said, offended. "Well, I'm glad you approve of him."

There was a brief silence on the other end of the line.

"Well, I can see you're deeply influenced by him. That's fine. Don't get me wrong. He's first rate. It's just that there's newer things under the old Bal'mere sun."

"I doubt it," I said, intensely annoyed by his offhand arrogance.

"Perhaps," Raines said, "we should discuss all this. Anyway, listen, we've got a great house. What better place to study than in a good house with congenial folks? So why don't you come down tomorrow about three and check us out?"

"Well," I said, "I suppose I could. But no promises."

"Of course not. Wouldn't think of it. We're at 1529 Chateau Avenue. Just a block off the conveniently located York Road. See you tomorrow, lad."

I hung up and shook my head. The nerve of the man, attacking Dr. Spaulding. And what of Raines's odd figures of speech (even stranger, it suddenly seemed to me, than Dr. S. himself). "See you tomorrow, lad?" There was a kind of irony in his voice that sounded like W.C. Fields. On the other hand, that "conveniently located" bit made him sound like some kind of local game show host, the kind of windbag who you might see interviewing people on "Duckpins for Dollars." Just who really lay behind all the verbal parody seemed a mystery to me, and though I once more told myself I didn't have time to play games, I was intrigued.

Now, I found myself wandering tensely around the living room of the strange house, debating whether I should go upstairs to the bedroom to find who was playing Coltrane.

On second thought, going upstairs didn't seem a good idea after all. It might be one of the other roommates, and he or she may not take it lightly that a stranger was intruding.

Then there was the possibility that Raines had forgotten our meeting, or even worse, maybe I'd gotten the wrong address. The thought made me a little panicky. Chateau Avenue was in Govans, the very neighborhood I'd been born in. But that was back in the 1940s when the neighborhood was still lily white and safe. In 1965, Govans was what social critics called a "changing neighborhood." Chateau Avenue still looked like a mostly white block—there had been a few old people watering their lawns when I'd walked down from the streetcar stop—but it was clearly heading in the other direction. It was even possible—given the wailing Coltrane saxophone—that I was this very minute standing in some Negro's house. The thought made my body stiffen in fear. Lord, if a huge and angry Negro came walking in and found this confused white boy pacing nervously in his living room, God only knew what kind of trouble I could be in.

With that in mind, I turned to beat a hasty retreat toward the door, but I hadn't gone three steps when the noise started. A horrible clanging, like the sound of a great metal robot's footsteps, began just beneath my feet. The living

room floor shook violently and even the dining room walls
vibrated to the hideous sound. I grabbed onto a sofa arm
and held on for dear life, as the infernal noise grew louder,
and the floor heaved up and down. It was not unlike standing in the middle of hell.

For a breathless few seconds I stood stock-still and debated whether I should find the source of the racket or if I
should escape now, while I was still in one piece.

I nearly staggered out of the door, but curiosity won out
over my own good sense, and I turned and headed toward
the back of the house. Slowly, I walked toward the kitchen,
which was shaking so violently that pots and pans hanging
on the walls shook up and down, setting off a further com-
motion. Even the refrigerator itself shook off its foundations,
and I thought of houses I'd read about, houses inhabited
by restless, furious ghosts. Good God, the place was right
out of *Turn of the Screw*.

I was about to give it up and head out the backdoor when
I saw a door open to the basement. I walked toward it,
grabbing onto rollicking chairbacks for support, and taking
a deep breath, I started down the ancient rotting steps. As
I descended into the damp basement, the noise became
unbearably loud, but by the time I was halfway down into
that damp hellhole, I became aware of yet another sound
—one even stranger than the metallic clang. Indeed, this
second sound was so eerie that it gave me chills in my arm
and chest. It was the sound of people chanting, a couple of
men's voices for certain and at least one girl's. I stopped,
trying to make out the two words they chanted over and
over again. It seemed impossible, but they were chanting
the words "Iron ore, iron ore, iron ore." What in God's
name could that mean?

And why did I go on? Indeed, that is something I have
asked myself many times since that fateful day and I think
the answer is simple. I was young and it was an adventure,
a true mystery, my own mystery that I had discovered on
my own. And in spite of all my efforts to seem and act like
Lionel Trilling or Dr. Spaulding, there was something else

that second being born in me, something that had its own needs, had to take its own risks, even at the risk of death (which occurred to me as a real possibility as the consequence of walking to the bottom of those steps).

Now as I descended toward the damp, musty-smelling cellar, the sound grew louder and this time it was almost as if the words were being sung in some twisted Hindulike harmony: "I-ron ore!! I-ron ore! I-ron ore!"

I took the rest of the steps in a leap and looked out into the old yellow-bulbed cellar.

Across the room was some kind of huge black steel machine as big as a church organ, but which, upon closer inspection, looked more like a giant typewriter of some kind. Sitting at it and banging away on the huge keys was an intense looking young man with eyes as blue as the Chesapeake Bay. He wasn't typing on paper, however, but on what looked like a roll of the plastic I'd seen hanging off the front porch.

I blinked and stared at the mad figure sitting behind the keyboard of the giant black typewriter. He wore a filthy once-white business shirt, much like the ones I'd seen discreetly balled up on the living room floor; wrinkled, stained, and baggy gray dress pants; and a pair of terminally scuffed cordovans. Though he was only a few years older than me, about twenty-five, he was already going bald, and what few strands of blond hair that were left stood up in a kind of wild, untamable cowlick. He had narrow, almost Oriental, eyes, and there was an idiotically happy lopsided grin on his face, which revealed a likable and sensual gap between his front teeth. I stood there astonished, unable to take my eyes off of him. Indeed, I had never seen such a complex, comical-looking man in my life. He looked like some kind of old movie comedian, a combination of wistful Chaplin, sour-faced Buster Keaton, with more than a little of the demented Moe Howard thrown in.

Next to the machine, a short, powerfully built boy and a very fleshy, sexy blond girl prostrated themselves, throwing

32

their arms wildly up in the air and then back down to the ground, as if they were slaves worshipping this weird, comical god and his monstrous typing machine. It was they who chanted the strange words again and again: "I-ron ore! I-ron ore! I-ron ore!"

The man seated at the infernal contraption brought his right hand down on it, dramatically punched a key, then lifted it off in a grand burlesque gesture as if he were a drunken concert pianist. As he did this, the two slaves laughed wildly and chanted again. Smiling maniacally, spittle flying from his crooked mouth, the madman smashed his left hand down on the machine and typed in yet another letter. The roll of plastic squirted another inch through the machine and came looping crazily from the top. And now I noticed that there seemed to be something embalmed inside that coiled mass of plastic. From my vantage point on the other side of the room they looked like baseball cards, the kind I had collected as a child.

I shook my head and tried clearing my throat, and moments later the seated man looked up.

"Ahhhh, my boy, Thomas Fallon, I presume. Welcome to the Hellhole."

The two chanters stopped and looked up. They seemed not at all embarrassed by their actions.

"Jeremy Raines?" I said.

"One and the same, lad," Raines said, smiling grandly. "Just worshipping the old embosser. Or as we Hellhole Dwellers call it, the old iron ore machine. 'Old Iron' gets kind of temperamental, and studies have shown that a certain amount of worship and praise makes it run smooth as silk."

"Oh, well, of course that explains the chanting then," I said.

Jeremy laughed a little, nodding his head up and down as if he were listening to some private joke. His wispy hair hung over his narrow blue eyes.

"No," he said, "that doesn't begin to explain it. All in due time, my boy. Meanwhile, you must meet some of the loyal employees of Identi-Card. This is Eddie Eckel and his traveling companion, Miss Babe McCallister."

I looked at the short wild-faced man. He was dark complexioned, handsome in a brutal, almost apelike way, and wore a jet-black T-shirt, black Levis, and black motorcycle boots. It was clear from his powerful arms that he was a person to be reckoned with, but his exceedingly short, bowed legs gave him a comical look. Holding his hand and smiling widely was a chubby but attractively buxom blonde with curly Shirley Temple ringlets on top of her head. She, too, was dressed completely in black.

"Nice to meet you," I said, giving them what I hoped would be taken as my cool, ironic smile.

The woman, Babe, smiled sweetly, but Eddie Eckel just shook his head.

"You thinking about moving in here, bud?" he said in a rough street voice. Though he dressed like a young Brando, his voice was that of a Glen Burnie redneck.

"Perhaps," I said, trying to look both friendly and sound formidable at the same time.

"Hmmm, ma-haps," Eddie said. There was a playful mockery in his voice, and I felt the tension growing in my back and neck.

"Now, my boy, let me show you around. There is much . . . a great deal you need to know," Raines said, gesturing broadly.

"Jeremy," Babe interrupted. "Don't forget your meeting at Hopkins. It's at three-thirty, and you have to change your shirt before you go, 'cause that one looks like somebody's science project."

Raines looked down at his sub-stained shirt. He picked off a piece of dried lettuce and popped it in his mouth.

"Tasty," he said. "Harry Little's makes a hell of a sub. Hope Sister Lulu's managed to find one that's a little more presentable."

"Sister who?" I asked.

"Another of our happy band," Raines said. "Look, Tom,

why don't you come with me? The meeting won't be long, and we can roll back here and see about the house later today."

"You want me to come with you while you do business?" I said, incredulous. "Look, I really have to get back to my studies, so I'm afraid that would be . . ."

"Well, of course you do, my boy," Jeremy interrupted. "You have things to do, people to see. On the other hand, you might find all this amusing."

I shook my head doubtfully. This was not at all what I had bargained for. If anything, this house seemed less suitable for serious scholarship than my parents'. I started to voice these objections, but when I looked up at Jeremy Raines, I found myself curiously unable to speak, paralyzed by his friendly, cockeyed smile.

What was it about that face—some openness, some charm, some boyish roguishness that I hadn't seen since I'd hung around with my lost friends from high school. Indeed, since I'd started college, I'd scarcely made any friends at all, so intent I was on seeming adult and full of high seriousness. Raines's impish smile promised something illicit, something I knew I should resist at once, which made it all the more attractive.

Now he opened both his palms as if he were inviting me to partake in some great adventure.

"Come on along, my friend," he said. "Why not?"

I stuttered and sputtered, fully intending to tell him exactly "why not," but for some reason I found myself hedging: "Well, I don't know if . . ."

Then he cocked his head to the left and winked at me. It was a wink that said that we both knew my objections were going to be swept away sooner or later, so why not give in at once and join in the fun. Still, I had no intention of letting him simply browbeat me into anything. As a budding gentleman and a scholar, I had learned from W. B. Yeats to "pass a cold eye on life and death." I made up my mind to say "forget it," but when I managed to speak, I instead said the fateful words: "Well, I suppose it wouldn't do any harm to take a few hours off . . ."

"That's the spirit," Jeremy interrupted. He turned, put a long, muscular arm around Babe, and smiled at Eddie.

"Ah, the Babe," he said. "We could not function around here without the lovely Babe."

Though she scowled, it was completely obvious that she adored him.

"Before you go, you should have your brown rice, Jeremy," she said in a motherly tone of voice.

Jeremy bowed to her in a parody of courtliness, then pulled me by the arm, and I found myself following him up the steps.

"Love the Babe," he said. "No one better. But she's a kind of a health food nut. What we need to do is get out on the old highway, eat giant death-ball burgers, and act like Americans. Why the hell not?"

He laughed wildly, and in spite of myself, I found myself laughing back, and seconds later I was racing after him up the rotting cellar steps.

We didn't quite make it out of the house before things became more complicated. Sitting in the living room in the outrageous barber chair (which she had jacked up, so that she was a good four feet off the living room floor) and having a drink was a stunning-looking woman of about thirty. She wore skin-tight midnight blue satin capri pants and a form-fitting, sleeveless fire engine red turtleneck sweater. Her hair was jet black and hung loosely around her shoulders. Her legs were long and muscular, and she had the largest, most perfectly shaped pair of breasts in North America (or at least in Baltimore). Upstairs, I could hear John Coltrane still wailing away.

"Sister Lulu," Jeremy said in his arch, amused way. "Having a little afternoon pick-me-up, are we?"

"Yes, we are," Sister Lulu said, running a long sensuous tongue around her lips as she rattled her ice cubes. "Scotch on the rocks, and we are enjoying it immensely. Might I fix you both a huge one?"

She spun around in the chair twice, lowered it quickly, and reached for a bottle and an ice bucket that sat next to the ancient gold-filigreed reading lamp, but Raines waved her off.

"Afraid not, Sister," Raines said. "Late for my business engagement."

"I ironed a shirt for you," Lulu said, smiling and pointing to the sofa.

There, hung neatly, was a freshly ironed shirt, with only one mustard stain on the sleeve.

"Sorry about that, Jeremy," Sister Lulu said. "You're such a pig though."

"It's true, I'm afraid," Jeremy said. "Thanks, Lulu, and let me introduce you to a new friend. This is Tommy Fallon. He's a fellow student at Calvert, a literature major, and he's thinking about becoming a member of our little family."

He crossed over to the couch and took his filthy shirt off. His body was muscular and hard, with a well-defined chest and rib cage. Given his sloppy nature, his build came as a surprise to me.

"You'll like it here, Tommy. We have our share of fun."

"Well, that's great," I said, watching as Raines wrinkled the old shirt into a ball and threw it into the corner with all the others. "But I'm looking for a place to study."

As I spoke, I was aware that I must have sounded like a pompous fool.

She tossed her head back in a mock-haughty way and took a long belt of her Scotch.

"Well, honey," she said. "Work hard, play harder. That's our motto."

"Gotta get rolling," Jeremy said.

He gave her a squeeze, and she rewarded him with a long kiss on the mouth.

"Knock 'em dead," Sister Lulu said, taking a long sip from her drink. "Nice meeting you, Tom. Hope you come back, honey, 'cause I like a serious man."

She laughed wickedly and spun around twice again, and her huge breasts shook like two perfect Jello molds.

Jeremy laughed, and I couldn't help smiling myself. Then we were out the door.

Though I probably wasn't aware of it at the time, I was in shock. The iron ore machine, chanting hipsters, and what appeared to be a very questionable alcoholic ex-nun were more "deviance"—to use a favorite word of the era—than I had experienced in a lifetime.

"*Sister* Lulu?" I said when I was able to formulate any words again. "Was she actually a nun?"

"Yes, of course she was," Raines said casually, as we walked up the block, "that is, she was right up to the day she was caught having sex with her mother superior."

That stopped me dead.

"What?" I said.

"Yes, afraid so," Raines said. "It's such a sad story. Tragic actually. It happened this way: Sister Lulu was confessing that she had unhealthy sexual desires. She'd had this dream that she was caressing the very white-skinned long leg of a faceless woman and then that caress became a lick, and the sister's tongue went higher and higher into the creamy thighs of the other woman. Once there she saw this little black beauty mark, and just seeing it sent her into a monster orgasm. All the while as she is telling this, she becomes aware of a kind of panting and sighing on the other side of the confessional booth, and when she describes the beauty mark . . . well, the mother superior starts moaning and she says, 'My child, those are *my* legs!' It seems that Sister Lulu had seen the mother superior in a state of undress during one of the convent's Christmas pageants and transposed those legs into her dream lesbo experience. Well, nature took its often-perverted course after that and somehow the two of them ended up *inside* the confessional booth. Sister Lulu was pulling up her habit and burying her face in the mother superior's sweet spot when another nun came along and saw the booth actually shaking up and down, and I'm afraid that was *it* for Sister Lulu. She was drummed out of the convent, excommunicated, actually."

"Jesus Christ," I said, floundering for words, "that's unbelievable."

Suddenly, I burst into laughter. Not because of the story exactly, but because for a fleeting second I had an image of Dr. Spaulding's horrified face as I told him this tale. Perhaps his glasses would fall off and he would make some horrible gagging sound. But my laughter was short-lived, for right behind this perverse fantasy came a wave of guilt. What in God's name was wrong with me? Why would I want to shock my mentor, my friend, the man who I most admired? It was terrible and cheap of me, and I felt low for it.

Raines shook his head sadly: "Ah, but the Church made a big mistake with Sister Lulu, for she is a deeply committed person. It's an honor to have her live with us. She gives our whole operation an elevated tone."

I assumed he was putting me on, but when I looked over at him, I saw that he had said this with no trace of irony. Finally, not knowing what else to say, I concurred lamely: "Yes," I said, "I'm sure she does."

He gave me a big smile and opened the door to his hideous huge green and white 1962 Nash, a massive tub of a car that looked like a striped tank.

I got in, shut the door tight, and locked it. I was about to comment that I hoped this would be a brief trip as I had work to do, when my head snapped back so violently I felt a bright pain in the back of my neck.

Raines had slammed the big Nash tank into reverse and

smashed into the car—a red Corvette—parked only inches behind us.

"Sorry," he said, then slammed the gear into forward and catapulted into the fender of the blue Ford Fairlane in front of us. There was a loud crunch of metal on metal, the smash of headlight glass, and my head whipped forward, causing me a bolt of pain in the front of my neck.

"Jesus Christ," I said. "What in God's name?"

"Sorry, my boy," Jeremy said. "These people have wedged me in, and we're having to blast our way out."

"Right," I said, grabbing the armrest and shoving my feet up on the dash for stability.

Once on the street, Raines drove like he was being pursued by the very hounds of hell. The car veered wildly from the right lane, went over the centerline, and headed for the parked cars on the other side of the York Road.

"Jesus, look out," I said. "Are you blind?"

"As a matter of fact, yes," Raines said. "Legally blind actually if I look at things straight on, but luckily my peripheral vision is superb."

"Which would explain why you are squinting and looking at me instead of the road," I said, terrified.

"Relax, Tom. I can see you're a worrier. You and good old Dr. Spaulding have that in common. Absolutely worthless trait. Anyway, it only *appears* I am looking at you, believe me. I've got this peripheral driving thing down to a science."

At that precise moment a small black dog darted across the road, and Raines gave a mad little laugh and swerved the wheel wildly to the left, barely missing him. I put my hands over my eyes, sucked in my breath, and mumbled a short prayer.

"Fast little bugger, isn't he?" Raines said.

"Raines," I said. "Slow this projectile down. I mean it!"

"If it will make you relax, Mr. Worrier, I will happily," Raines said, taking his foot off the gas petal.

We managed to drive a hundred yards without incident, and I caught my breath.

"Look, what in God's name is going on here anyway? Why are we going to Hopkins?"

"Well, my boy," Jeremy said, as we pulled into the wrong turn lane on the York Road. "It's all very simple, really. I have this small talent for inventing things. Nothing had really taken off until I came up with Identi-Card."

"Identi-Card?"

"Cards," Jeremy said. "Identity cards. Don't you see?"

"Not exactly," I said.

"Okay, you're a Calvert student. Take out your student activities card."

I pulled out my battered black wallet and did as he asked.

"Now look at it. It has your name, your social security number, your address, and your signature. That proves it's you, right?"

"Right."

"Wrong," he smiled. "What if I stole your card and wanted to cash a bad check on it? What would stop me?"

I wanted to answer the question, but we were headed directly into a National Bohemian beer truck, and I was forced to reach over and grab the wheel. I gave it a last-ditch desperation turn to the right, and we were clear—narrowly.

"Christ," I said. "How have you lived this long?"

Jeremy smiled and ran his left hand through his cowlick.

"Oh, I am here for a very definite reason," he said. "I have things to do. You see, my ultimate goal is to make people happy and to do that you need money, lots of it. Now, what if I wanted to bang a check on your card?"

"Well," I said, "I guess all you'd have to do is forge my signature."

"Exactly," Jeremy said, "But if you had your *picture* on your card, I couldn't do that, could I? You'd be protected."

"That's your invention?" I said. "Identity cards . . . with pictures?"

"Uh-huh. You're unimpressed? Well, dig this, my friend. There was a guy out in Los Angeles, name of Bott. He invented those little speed bumps they have on the freeway.

41

They're known as Bott's Dots, and they made him about a hundred million dollars."

"Come on."

"I'm serious. That machine you saw. The old iron ore machine. That machine is the embosser. When we've taken all the pictures for, say, the freshman class at Calvert, we run the card through the embosser, and we have the student's individual serial number indented in the card. That number and the picture make him secure. Neat, simple, and we're the first to think of it."

"Fantastic," I said. "And how many schools have bought this idea?"

"Only Calvert, the University of Baltimore, and Johns Hopkins so far," Jeremy said. "But there are fifty colleges in this area and many, many more in D.C. By this summer, my boy, Jeremy Raines is going to be the King of Cards and velly, velly rich. And by the way, I need partners, pals, guys and gals, to get mind-bogglingly wealthy with, so it's not lonely at the top. Interested?"

"I don't think so," I said. "I have enough trouble just getting my studies done. I intend to spend the next six months in what you would consider a very dull way. Locked up in my room reading novels."

"Ah, yes, Spaulding's influence," Raines said. "Well, that's a worthy pursuit. Which ones?"

"Well, for starters, I'm reading *The Ambassadors* by Henry James."

"Oh, Henry James," he said. "He's one of Spaulding's favorites. Always talking about James's rare sensibility. Well, I have to confess I never read much of him. He seems to go on and on, though I did like the *Turn of the Screw*, but I have read just about all of his brother, William. Now there was an amazing man. Still they were a great family, afraid of nothing. Just been reading a little Wilhelm Reich myself, you know him?"

"A psychologist?" I said with a certain distaste in my voice.

"Yes," Raines said. "And I don't blame you for sneering. I even agree with you. Most psychologists are moronic, bourgeois idiots. But Reich's different. Fearless. The man invented a box, orgones. Understands the power of orgasm, which, of course, has made him very unpopular in his profession. But he's a pioneer. That's the kind of shrink I want to be. Right now, I'm working on a new theory, motivation through hypnotism. You ought to let me put you under. Could improve your whole outlook."

Not on your life, I thought, though I smiled and said a noncommittal "hmmmm."

The man was mad I thought, part eccentric and part huckster, definitely not anyone for me to get involved with. What I should do, I thought, is politely tell him that I wasn't interested, ask him to drop me off near the streetcar line, head back to Calvert, and put up a new sign in the student union. But for some reason, I did none of these things. There was something exciting, nervy happening here, and suddenly I remembered high school when I'd played two years of lacrosse. I recalled the way I felt at the beginning of the game, just before the referee dropped the ball in the opening face-off. As I dug my stick into the hard winter ground and glowered at my opponent, my lips would go dry, time would stop, and I could hear the loud thumping of my own heart. It was pure adrenalin, wild and terrifying, and there was nothing else like it in the world. Until now.

These thoughts were quickly interrupted when Raines nearly ran into a sodium light that stood at Thirty-third and Greenmount. He jerked the wheel, dodging it at the last minute.

"How in God's name did you pass the eye test for your license?" I said, panting.

"As a matter of fact, I didn't," Jeremy said. "To be totally honest, Eddie E. took it for me."

"Come on," I said. "You can't get away with something like that. They have your social security number, and they make you sign your name."

43

"Yes," Raines said, "and that presented us with some difficulty. But you'd be surprised what a couple of hundred bucks can do down at the DMV."

"You bribed somebody to pass your driving test?" I said, astonished.

"I wouldn't call it bribery," Raines said. "I'd say we made a couple of new friends, guys who agree with me that the old vehicle laws are far too inflexible."

"Oh, yeah," I said. "Yes, indeed. A driver having to be able to actually *see* the road is practically a Fascist idea."

"My thoughts precisely," Raines said, smiling happily.

"God, look at the time," I said, looking at his dash clock. "It's two-fifty. We have to hurry."

"Yes, sir, a professional must always be punctual," Raines said, nodding gravely. "Though I have had certain . . . continuing problems in that department."

He smiled widely again in an attractively loopy way and jammed his foot to the pedal.

"Oh, God, no," I said. We took a screeching left at Charles Street and shot forward nearly clipping a Tip Top bread truck and hitting two ambulances that were turning into Union Memorial Hospital.

I held onto the door with all my might and looked at the madman, Raines, who was staring at me, a happy smile planted on his face.

"Never be late, that's my motto," he said.

We parked beneath some great shade trees on the Hopkins campus, and I felt my old shyness taking over. Though I had lived in Baltimore all my life, I had never been on this campus. Boys from my class didn't go to school here. It wasn't even an issue; the thought was as inconceivable as my father suddenly being recognized as the new Picasso.

"Coming in?" Raines asked.

"No," I answered, shocked that he would even suggest it. "I'll wait here."

He smiled and sighed.

"I'm going to be a while," he said as he opened the door and hopped out. "Why don't you come along?"

"No," I said. "No, really. Who are you going to visit in there anyway?"

"The president," Raines said. "A. Taft Manley. He's a great guy. Somebody you should get to know."

"Oh, right," I said, certain he was lying. "I'm sure you're very close friends with the president of Johns Hopkins University."

"Matter of fact," Jeremy said, "he and my father used to work together in city politics. 'Course that was a while back."

"Of course," I said.

"Doubting Tom," Raines laughed. "Well, then why don't you come in and find out?"

He looked at me with a challenging smile, and for a second I felt a little surge of anger. Did he think he could con me that easily?

"Okay," I said, "I will."

"Great. You're gonna love Taft. Real down-to-earth guy."

I followed along behind penguin-gaited Raines as he led me over the perfect Hopkins campus toward the white-domed president's building. Even to this day I recall my twisted emotions, a growing irritation with Raines. All this mad stuff about I.D. cards with pictures being worth a fortune and now telling me that he was meeting with A. Taft Manley. Did he think I was a total fool? And yet, it was exciting, promising. Was it possible that he wasn't kidding?

As I walked a step or two behind Raines, I remembered my high school friend Ned, who had once asked our counselor at City if he might apply to Hopkins. The counselor had patted him on the back in a patronizing way and said, "Sorry, son, you're not Hopkins material."

No, we were the boys who would go to the second-rate colleges (if we were that lucky) and end up in the second-rate jobs. The boys who would end up managers at the Acme or, like my father, in some horrible soul-killing job. Boys who lost the bloom of youth by the time they were twenty-five. Boys who married neighborhood girls who soon ran too fat and lived in redbrick row houses and had

unpromising kids and quickly forgot that they'd ever
dreamed of anything greater to begin with. Boys who soon
developed beer guts and sat on bar stools for thirty years
swilling down National Bohemian beer while they mumbled
about the glories of the old Baltimore Colts.

Until recently, I had never really questioned any of this.
Of course, I had my wild high school drinking nights with
Bobby Murphy and my other friends, and when we were
lying out under the stars at Loch Raven Dam, we would
say, "We're never going to work, we're never going to end
up like our old men. Hell, no!" But we didn't mean it. In
the backs of all of our minds lay the knowledge that of
course we were going to end up that way. What other way
was there to end up? Ironically, of all of my friends, only
Murphy had taken another route from his father, a house
painter. Bobby was a criminal, into drugs, hustling, betting
parlors, and I half-admired him for it, but that wasn't a real
alternative for me. No, the truth was until I had met Dr.
Spaulding, I didn't see another route. That is until today.
But, here ahead of me, was a Calvert College student who
had not only brought me onto the Hopkins campus, but
who strode across the green sward as though he owned the
place. Jeremy Raines, whoever or whatever else he was, was
not scared. And though I scarcely knew it at the time, I
wanted a piece of that assurance, that fearlessness. So in a
kind of delirium of confused and half-formed thoughts, I
ran on behind mad Raines, half expecting him to pull a fast
one on me, to try and lose me in a maze of hallways or lock
me in the janitor's room. But he did none of these things.
Instead, he did precisely what he said he would, he took
me through the great Colonial doors of the administration
building, up the deep-pile-carpeted stairs and into the outer
office of A. Taft Manley, president of Johns Hopkins University.

It was the last thing I expected, and I stood there stunned
and confused as the secretary, a thin mantis-faced woman
with red hair, a maroon dress, and a handsome pair of

buckteeth, greeted Jeremy as though they were old school chums.

"Jeremy Raines, my favorite con man," she said affably.

"How sweet of you, Margaret," he said. "Is Taft around?"

"He's in there waiting for you," she said. "And, ah, Jer, I ought to warn you. He's not in a very good mood."

"No?" Jeremy said. "Hmmm . . ."

"Maybe we should come back later," I said, half turning toward the door. But Raines grabbed me by the collar and yanked me back.

"Come along, Rog," he said, smiling at me.

"Rog?" I said. "What the hell?"

"My assistant," he said as she pushed open an oak door and led us into the president's office.

I had never been in such a place before. The president's desk was massive and made of ancient oak. There were brass lamps, and on the walls were a series of degrees, honorary and otherwise, and pictures of racing horses at Pimlico. A tall, well-bred-looking blond woman stood next to the horse. She had a long lean face, not unlike a thoroughbred herself. The office took my breath away, but it was nothing compared to the effect of the great man himself. He stood in profile in front of a floor-to-ceiling window and gazed out onto his campus. A. Taft Manley was just as I had seen him in pictures in the *Baltimore Sun*—a huge round man, dressed impeccably in a blue pinstripe suit. His head was extraordinarily gray, and his forehead was nobly high. His cheeks were extremely red, and his chins were countless in number. His eyes were round and huge behind his pince-nez.

"Hello, Jeremy," he said in a grave and gravelly voice. "Who do you have there with you?"

"Taft, this is Roger Whirley," Jeremy said. "Roger has just been sent down by the central office in Rochester to assist us in straightening out some of the little glitches in our operation."

I stood stock-still, stunned by the enormity of this lie. My first time on the Hopkins campus and I was using an assumed name. In my mind, both Dr. Spaulding and Henry James shook their heads at me.

"Pleased to meet you, Mr. Whirley."

I walked ahead and shook the great man's hand, convinced that at any moment he would discover Jeremy's hapless ruse.

"Well, I hope you'll help Jeremy out, Mr. Whirley," President A. Taft Manley said. "Because he has a very, very promising product here, and it would be a shame to see it go down the drain."

On that final phrase, A. Taft Manley's voice took on a stentorian gravity. I looked over at Jeremy and saw his Adam's apple jump.

"Surely there were no problems with the last batch of photos, was there, Taft?" Jeremy said. There was a little catch in his voice, the first sign of vulnerability I had seen in him.

"Yes, Jer," the great man said gravely as he walked toward an antique end table and picked up a box of cards. "I am afraid there was and there are."

He sighed a little to show how sad it was for him to impart this information, then he picked up the little box and let a pile of the cards fall into his great red hands.

"Take a look at these, Jer," he said. "You, too, Whirley."

I looked down at the cards, half expecting them to be out of focus or in some other way ruined, but to my surprise I saw a picture of a young student named Maurice Reskind. The picture wasn't what you would call memorable, but it was a very decent likeness.

"What do you think, Whirley?" President Manley said.

"Well, not bad," I said. "I mean it's not a picture to be hung in a photography exhibit but a thoroughly professional job. Let me see the others."

Jeremy quickly shuffled through the deck, and we looked at pictures of students named Billy Brandau and Terry Dearborn. Again, the photography seemed to be perfectly acceptable. But there *was* something wrong, terribly wrong, you could sense it from Manley's raised eyebrows and quickened, impatient breath. I looked at Jeremy, who smiled and looked up at the Hopkins's president.

"You're kidding, right, Taft?" he said. He turned to me and smiled. "That's how Taft is, Whirls, a great kidder."

"You think I'm kidding?" A. Taft Manley said. His voice was low and serious.

"Of course," Jeremy said. He tried out a wink and a smile, but A. Taft Manley took off his pince-nez and gave him his Great-Man Scowl. I felt myself sinking a few inches into the deep-pile carpet.

Jeremy shook his head and took another look at the cards.

"I don't know, Taft," he said. "I look down here at these cards and I see good pictures, the number embossed in neatly, the student's name and address."

"Yes," A. Taft Manley said, "but that is precisely the problem! Read me a card. Any card."

"Well, okay." Jeremy said. "The first name is John Westcott. He's a senior and he lives at 2335 Charles Street."

"Right," said the president. "Very good. The only problem is that isn't John Westcott's picture."

"No?" Jeremy Raines said, his voice cracking.

"No," said A. Taft Manley, "and this next picture isn't Bradford Karnes. You see this fat boy in the back, whom you have under Bill Dillon, *that's* Westcott. And this one here is Karnes. Every one of these cards has the wrong picture with the wrong identity. These cards are what I would call Anti-Identity cards. As in unusable!"

There was a long silence, and I saw Jeremy's knees buckle slightly. God, I thought, why have you led me here? Then, to my horror, Raines turned and, with a whiplike wraith, pointed an accusatory finger at me!

"Now listen here, Whirley," he said. "This was exactly the kind of thing you fellows in the processing plant assured me would never happen!"

"Huh?" I explained.

"No 'huhs,' Whirley. You said you had the new solutions, the whole new matching index," Raines said, pushing his face so close to mine that spittle flew into my eyes. "You assured me that the marsgale filters and the data-coded I.D. number nelds were all color sequenced so that none of this would happen. But look, just *look* at what you've done."

"I'm . . . I'm sorry," I said, both panicky and in a state of almost supernatural rage. "I'll make a memo of this and take it to . . . to . . ."

"To J.B." Jeremy said. "You take it to J.B. and you tell him that I cannot and I will not tolerate this kind of screwup. Really, Whirley, I thought when we joined up with you Rochester boys we had signed on with professionals. But apparently you only *talk* a good game. When it comes down to delivering product, you fall abysmally short. I must repeat again, this is simply unacceptable!"

I swallowed hard and looked up at the unflinching and damning gaze of A. Taft Manley. I had a sudden urge to rip Raines's heart out and eat it in front of the unforgiving president.

"I am extremely sorry, Mr. Raines," I said through clenched teeth. "Believe me, I will look into this at once."

Jeremy turned and shook his head at President A. Taft Manley.

"What can I say, sir?" he said. "It's completely my fault. I take full responsibility for the entire foul-up. I mean, I trusted Whirley here to do a professional job, but in the end I have to take the blame for hiring him. If you want a full refund, I'll be more than happy to . . ."

"Well," said A. Taft Manley, putting his glasses back on and shaking his head. "That won't be necessary, son. I'm certain we can work something out. *If* you have the cards straightened out by, say, Saturday two weeks."

"No problem," Jeremy said. "We'll reshoot everything at our expense. Don't you worry, sir. The cards will be done right next time through. Won't they, Whirley?"

Jeremy stared at me as though I were a very small piece of snail dropping.

"I'll certainly see that Spaulding in the front office hears

50

about this, sir," I said to Manley. "The next batch will be picture-perfect. You can count on that."

A. Taft Manley grumbled something that sounded like agreement and shook his head. Then he turned and stood in noble half profile against the window, and we hurried on out of his office.

Where are you going?" Raines asked as I walked away from him in the sun-baked parking lot. "The car is in the other direction."

"I know where it is," I hissed through clenched teeth. "Which is why I'm walking in *this* direction. Because I never, *ever* want to see you again!"

I picked up my pace and headed for Charles Street, but in a flash Raines caught up with me.

"If you don't want to get punched in the face," I said, "then I strongly suggest that you get the fuck away from me."

He stopped walking then and dropped his hands at his side.

"Okay," he said. "You're right. Punch me. Go right ahead. I deserve it. Give me your best shot."

I stopped and looked at him hard. I made my right hand into a fist. I held it up in front of my chest. Then I let it fall back to my side. He looked so helpless, so distraught standing there in the steaming heat.

"Look," he said. "I'm sorry, but I didn't know what else to do. I mean, the whole damned company could go down the tubes if we lose the Hopkins contract. I was desperate. And you pulled me out, Tom. Man, I owe you."

"Owe me?" I screamed. "Owe me? You asshole, you set me up as a whipping boy in front of the president of Johns Hopkins University? I know it doesn't mean anything at all to you, but just recently in my life I found out I have a goddamned brain, and I'd like to maybe become a teacher someday, and if a guy like A. Taft fucking Manley found out the truth, he could have me blackballed from all graduate schools in the Northern fucking Hemisphere!"

I shocked myself at the fury in my voice.

"I know, I know," Raines said, "and I'm sorry. I really am. I'm going to make it up to you. I swear."

"No," I said, "promise me that whatever you do, you won't try and make it up to me. I can't take anymore of your goodwill."

He looked hurt when I said that. His mouth curled down, and he frowned deeply.

I realized that I had wounded him and felt some of my furor fade, which irritated me even more.

"Look," I said, "you owe me nothing. Zero. *Nada.* Let's just shake hands, wish each other luck, and call it a day."

"Okay," Raines said, "but at least let me give you a ride home."

"No, thanks," I said. "I'd like to keep what's left of me together. Do you realize you're the worst driver in the known world?"

"Yeah, I guess I do," Raines said. And suddenly there was defeat in his voice. "Okay. Do what you want. I'm sorry, though. Really. Take it easy, my boy."

He turned and shuffled off toward his car, and I stood there looking at him go, at his drooping head and his sad penguin walk, and there seemed something terribly familiar about that gait, something I couldn't name then but know now without a doubt. That walk was the walk of defeat, the very same walk I had seen so many hundreds of times in my own home. The stoop-shouldered walk of my father, trudging from the bedroom to the bath, the walk that said, "Yeah, I could have done something. I had the talent, but the bastard Baltimorons slapped me down." In spite of all he had done to me in two short hours, I couldn't bear to see Raines dejected like that.

"Okay, okay," I said. "Wait a damned minute! I could use a ride after all."

He turned and smiled at me, but there was no happiness in his face.

"Sure," he said. "That's the least I can do."

I trotted after him, and sweat pouring freely off of me, I got once more into the Deathmobile.

We drove out Charles Street in stony silence. I was furious at Raines and tried my best to pretend I was simply being taken home in a cab. My God, he had made a fool of me, and I'd gone along with it. Hell, I had even dragged Dr. Spaulding's name into the sham. Now the paranoia machine went into high gear: What if A. Taft Manley knew Dr. Spaulding? What if Manley called him and they formed a cabal, burning my body at the academic stake?

This was no way to think. I had to shut down my brain.

Desperate, I stared gloomily out at the big houses in Roland Park, the palatial homes of the rich. I remembered that as a kid I had cut lawns for these people. Govans, the neighborhood I'd first grown up in, was just north of here. I still remembered the stone wall that separated our hillbilly, Hank Williams–playing neighborhood from these discreet houses, recalled pushing my old hand lawn mower door to door, asking the maids and butlers if the lady of the house was home. More often than not I got no farther than that, but sometimes the owners would come out and agree to pay me a dollar and a quarter to mow their front and back lawns. I recalled wanting to do the best job in the world to show them that I was somebody, too, somebody worth knowing. Oh, Lord, the fantasies I had. It's a steaming hot one hundred percent-humidity Baltimore day, one hundred degrees in the shade. The rich man's wife (young, beautiful) looks through the window and sees the honest craftsman tilling in her garden. She is drawn to his seriousness of intent, to the absolute conviction he brings to the job. She tries to turn away from the window, to go about her frivolous life, but there is something about him, something irresistible. Soon she is walking down the garden path, a glass of lemonade in her hand, and they are talking. In a very few minutes she realizes that this boy is special, sensitive, bright, an artist. He makes her feel more alive than her husband, a dull banker, ever could. They form a friendship, rebels in the eyes of the world.

Of course, nothing like this ever happened. Mostly, the ladies of the houses complained that they had to pay a whole dollar and a quarter to have their lawns cut, and not one of them ever even offered me even a drink of water.

But that didn't stop my fantasies. Oh, Lord, where did I get such romantic claptrap? From my father, of course. And, more importantly, from his mother, my grandmother Grace. She lived only three blocks away on Thirty-eighth Street. A brilliant, brook-clear woman, there was no one in the world I loved more. It was she who taught us all that though we were poor, we were as good as anyone, that we had to turn on the secret light that shined from within. Now, as I drove with Raines out leafy, shady Charles Street, it occurred to me how similar my grandmother's teachings were to Dr. Spaulding's. Indeed, both literature and religion taught that the inner life was the true life and that the life we could easily observe, the life of money and ambition and power, meant nothing. Yes, eventually the people in the big houses *would* offer you that drink, eventually they would introduce you to their daughters, for by associating with you, they would become more fully human, more alive themselves. Though they might not know it yet, they couldn't really live without you.

Was any of this true? I didn't know. At this time I still hoped it was, that much I was sure of. I still thought that if I refined my sensibility, became as great an artist or humanist as, say, James or my grandmother's hero, Dr. Albert Schweitzer, then the world would love me for it.

A naive and not very bright young man's fantasy? Perhaps. But it occurred to me that it wasn't out of the question. After all, look at the way my family loved my grandmother. Loved her for keeping them together while my drunken sea captain grandfather, Rob, hit the sailors' bars and strip joints down on Baltimore Street, the infamous Block. Loved her, because she stood up for Negroes by inviting interracial groups to her house on Sundays, though the hillbillies stood on their front porches in their sleeveless T-shirts and screamed, "Grace Fallon is a nigger lover." (To which my grandmother said, "They're trash, and we don't truck to trash.") Loved her for insisting that we learn to love Mozart and Bach and Hayden, even though the rest of our neighborhood believed only in Hank Williams and later Elvis Presley.

No one could have loved her more than me, for her home and her great, open heart were my sanctuary from the madness that was my own home life. When things had become so bad I could stand no more, I had often packed up my things into my old Baltimore Colts overnight bag and walked to Gracie's, where I was given hot chocolate and tollhouse cookies and where we sat on her old glider on the front porch, rocking gently back and forth, talking of Schweitzer and Kafka and Hans Castorp on his frozen sled of death.

Now all that was gone. First, my grandfather had died in a bar fight in a place called the Wishing Well Tavern on old rummy Pratt Street, and then Grace had become enfeebled and moved to Washington to spend her last days with my aunt, who had herself died soon after. I held tight to Raines's armrests and remembered the ordeal of their funerals. Only two years ago they were both still alive. Now they only lived in memory, stories. My mother, my miserable father, and I were all that was left of the Fallons, and as Raines and I drove up Charles Street, I felt my dead family's absence as though someone had amputated my left arm. I could not let them all die in vain. I had promised my dear grandmother that I would somehow distinguish my family. I had promised her and I had promised Dr. Spaulding, and I had to somehow show my father, too, that his life as a failed artist had not been for nothing. No, though Baltimore and his own weakness had beaten him down, his son would sail on and on, on brilliant plumed wings. If he could learn to write a decent sentence first and if he could find a place to live outside of the madhouse that had become his home.

Which brought my thoughts full circle back to Raines. I had hoped that moving in with him and his friends would be the answer, but clearly this idea was a bust. I would have to start all over again, seeing other houses, other furnished rooms, and that sad thought made me sag against the car door.

Raines seemed to notice my mood, for he turned and smiled at me: "Hey, it's not that bad," he said.

"Oh, shut up," I said.

"No, I mean it," he said in a sweet shy voice. "You really don't have anything to worry about with good old Manley."

"No?" I said. "Why's that?"

"Because," Raines smiled slightly, "he doesn't even know your real name. He thinks you're some guy named Roger Whirley!"

There was a brief silence during which I tried with all my might not to laugh. I sucked in my breath, I bit my lower lip until it bled, I threw my right hand over my mouth, but I failed miserably. The name Roger Whirley, the full-blown absurdity of it, struck me with gale force.

"Whirley," I blurted out. "Whirley? Where the hell did you get that name?"

"I don't know. It's something about you. Don't take this wrong now, but you look like you're in some kind of whirl. A massive state of confusion. You gotta admit, it's a killer name."

I suppose I should have been insulted, but Raines fell into a great howl of laughter, and in spite of everything I'd suffered, I couldn't help but join him. In a few seconds both

56

of us were pounding the dash and screaming out the name Whirley over and over again.

And then right in the middle of this hysteria, a funny thought occurred to me. I rarely laughed like this anymore. No, ever since I had become a literary person, I had perfected a kind of superior ironic sneer.

Raines, on the other hand, laughed, truly laughed, wildly, deeply, and in spite of what he had just pulled, he had me laughing with him in hysterical joy.

He shook his head and pushed his hair out of his eyes and said in a portentous voice: "All right, Mr. Roger Whirley! You *better* get those pictures right the next time or else, Mr. *Roger Whirley!*"

"Whirley, Whirley," I said, helpless. I found myself doubled over in my seat, my sides aching from the sheer joy of it.

It took a while before I could get control of myself and assume my newfound air of literary dignity. Finally Raines stopped laughing and shook his head.

"I don't see how it happened," he said, pulling out a white handkerchief and wiping his eyes. "I just don't get it. I thought we had everything perfect. God, now we'll have to reshoot. There goes the profit in this batch. Ah, but live and learn. The next batch we shoot . . ."

I turned to him and stared with great eyes.

"Don't say 'we,' " I said. "Don't ever say 'we' around me. I'm going home. I hate it there, but after seeing this nutso scheme of yours, it's looking better all the time."

Raines didn't answer me, and for a while we drove quietly down elegant leaf-strewn Charles Street, during which time he nearly hit a golden retriever, a cyclist, and a nun who crossed the street at St. Mary's Convent.

I sat still, afraid that if I moved, if I spoke at all, I would erupt in either a towering rage or begin laughing like a mental patient. After only one maniacal afternoon with this madman, my entire emotional center had been displaced.

➤

Finally, we pulled into my parent's gravel driveway in Towson. The house looked like a morose little pile of green shingles. My father, Happy Jim himself, sat on the front porch glider, a paperback novel in his hand. In his customary way, he looked up, saw that it was me, and immediately went back to reading his book. Though I feigned indifference to this slight, it was as though an arrow had stabbed my heart.

My stomach tightened as I started to get out of the car.

"Your father?" Jeremy said.

"Mr. Wonderful himself," I said, feeling the tightening spread to my chest.

Raines shook his head and his eyes took on a surprising compassion.

"Yes, he does look miserable. He has, if you don't mind me saying so, the same kind of pain in his face that you do, my friend."

That insight irritated me all over again, even more so because I recognized its truth.

"Yes," I said, "we're the Misery Guys. They're going to do a television series about us soon."

"It's sad," Jeremy said. "I see it all the time in my work out at Larson-Payne."

"Larson-Payne Mental Hospital?" I said. "What kind of work do you do there? Con the patients into buying I.D. cards?"

"Nasty, nasty," Jeremy said. "As a matter of fact, I work with schizophrenics, catatonics, the A-3 ward for the deeply distressed. Having a little luck with them too."

"Right," I said. I had heard just about enough of this whacko's jive. "You succeed where the mere doctors fail."

"Well, sometimes yes," Raines said. "See, I have this theory . . ."

"Spare me," I said.

"I'll give you the short version. Most modern psychology concentrates on early family life and the damage done there, which is all well and good."

"I'm sure Freud is relieved that you think so," I said.

"But *I'm* more interested in what makes the person happy right now. Take your father, for instance. What would make him happy right now? This second."

"News of my death for starters," I said, then wished I hadn't.

From the car window I looked up at my father and felt guilty talking about him. Indeed, for a second I felt that he had heard everything we were saying and the thought made me sick inside. But he was still sitting there reading his book as though I were a ghost in some old Topper movie.

"I'm serious," Raines said, and I had to confess that he seemed serious. The charming con man was gone, and there was a gravity and concern in his voice that I found moving in spite of my best efforts to resist him.

"He used to like to paint," I said. "But he gave it up and I think he's hated everything else ever since."

"Ahh," Raines said. "Well then in your father's case, all therapy, short or long term, should be aimed at getting him painting. Once he's doing that, chances are he'll be happy again."

"That sounds moronically simpleminded," I said, unwilling to give in to Raines's glibness again.

"Yes, doesn't it?" Raines said. "But I've had some fairly amazing results. Sometimes the answer *is* simple."

"I'm sure," I said. "Well, it's been interesting. Good luck with your quest for riches and happiness."

"Wish you were going to share it, partner," he said, offering me his hand.

Reluctantly, I reached across the seat and gripped his hand. Though his hands were small, he had a grip of steel.

I got out of the car, and he gave me a little wave, then pulled out into the traffic. I watched him go, driving in his loopy way down the street, nearly hitting three parked cars within a hundred feet of my house. Watched him and somehow already missed him, though I told myself that I was lucky to be rid of him. When he had disappeared from sight, I walked up to the porch, feeling like George Raft walking the last mile to the electric chair.

"Hi, Dad," I said.

"You didn't cut the lawn yet," he said, then looked back down at his book.

"Sorry," I said.

"So get going on it," my father said, "And don't forget to edge. Last time you didn't edge the front walk, and we had grass hanging over the cement."

"Gosh," I said, "that's terrible. Did the neighbors call the cops?"

My father looked up at me and narrowed his eyes. I narrowed mine back, but felt a terrible pain in my lower bowels.

"Funny," he said, "very, very funny. Listen, if you don't like it around here, you can move out."

"Which is exactly what I'm trying to do," I said.

We stared at each other some more. I wondered if his heart hurt as badly as mine.

"As long as you still grace us with your brilliant presence, you should edge," he said. "I edge and you should edge."

"Right, Dad," I said. "Edge. Got it."

I turned and headed for the door. He gave me a parting glower, then picked up his novel. It was Kipling's *Light That Failed*. About an artist who lost his sight. Absurdly obvious, I thought, then thought of Raines's absurdly obvious theory. In my domestic zombie daze, I went to my room and changed into my old Levis and headed out the back of the house to get the lawn mower. In a way, I thought, it would be a relief to lose myself in the mindlessness of lawn cutting. At least I would be out of reach of either of my parents. But I didn't make it past the kitchen. My mother was sitting at the Formica-topped table, listening to Bobby Vinton warbling on the old maroon portable Philco (my father's Philco, and seeing it, I felt another little sharp sense of panic, what if Big Jim came in from the front porch and saw her "running down his batteries," a crime in our house second only to "bothering me in the bathroom"). She was doing something odd with a bunch of small party-sized white paper napkins.

"Hi, hon," she said, smiling at me as she blotted the napkin on her red lips.

"What are you doing, Mom?" I said.

She smiled shyly; it was my favorite smile of hers. Often she was in a rage, and I would forget that just beneath the surface, she was a sweet, funny person.

"Well, your father thinks I'm crazy, hon," she said in a near whisper. "But what do I care what he thinks?"

She blotted her lips carefully and put the napkin down on the tabletop, along with six other napkins that she'd finished.

"Which one do you think looks most like my lips?" she asked with a slightly perplexed look.

"Mom, they all look like your lips, but this one is the cleanest."

I reached down and picked up a napkin, and she took it gently from my hand.

"That one? Let me ask you a question, Tom. Do you think that one is the most kissable?"

"Geez, I don't know," I said. "Kissable? What's going on here?"

"Well," she said, "Johnny Apollo, you know, the disc jockey on the radio? He's sponsoring this Miss Kissable Lips contest. You blot your lips on the napkin, and you send it in and if you're picked out of the first contestants, then you get to come down to the studio, and you get to be Miss Kissable Lips. Maybe. If you win, I mean."

"Miss Kissable Lips?" I said. "What's that? You get a prize?"

"Oh, yeah, hon," she said. "I mean I wouldn't do it if it was just for hubris. That's a word I learned last week out of my word power book. That means having too much pride."

"I know what it means, Mom," I said and immediately

wished I hadn't spoken with such a condescending edge.

"Well, Mr. Chips Goes to the University," she said. "As a matter of fact, there are a lotta surprises . . . clothes and kitchen stuff and best of all free tickets to the Lyric Theatre to see a Broadway show."

"Sounds good, Mom," I said.

I shook my head and headed out back, but she reached up and grabbed my wrist.

"I know what you think," she said. "You think I'm a dink for thinking I have a chance to win. Fat lady in a muumuu going down to see Johnny Apollo. Well, maybe my shape isn't what it used to be, but I have always been told, by more boys than your father I might add, that I have very kissable lips."

That melted my heart, and I stooped down and kissed her forehead.

"I know that, Mom," I said. "I think you have the most kissable lips in the world."

She smiled and kissed me back on the cheek.

"You know," she said, "You are a very, very nice boy when you aren't being a pretentious little intellectual."

She said it softly, though, and there was an adoring mother's smile on her face.

I patted her on the arm and said: "Keep blotting. And when they call you down there, I'll be the one who takes you."

"Uh-uh," she laughed. "That would be too embarrassing. There's some things us adults need to do on our own."

I started to laugh, then my father came walking into the room.

"You're wearing down the batteries on my radio," he said. "And why aren't *you* out back?"

"Edging," I said. My tone was less than respectful.

"That's right, Mr. Henry James," he said. "Edging. And I'll be out to check how neat a job you did, you can be sure of that."

I started to come back with a snappy, hate-filled line, but

my mother interrupted us: "How kissable do you think these lips are, James?" she said.

My father looked at her and shook his head.

"You and him," he said. "You're a couple of hopeless, foggy dreamers, I swear."

He shook his head, turned, and walked toward the bathroom.

"Have a nice wash," my mother said.

I laughed a little, but she sighed deeply, her eyes glazed over, and she returned to blotting her lips.

After cutting (and edging) the lawn and eating what my father called one of my mother's "bouncing meatball dinner" (so called because they were burned black and bounced on the plate when served), I went back to my room and lay on my bed. I heard my father wander into the bathroom and turn on the faucet. I thought again of what Raines had said. If my father could only somehow begin painting again, perhaps he *would* be happy. I remembered his early watercolors—scenes from the Chesapeake, haunted line drawings from the lime pits out at Texas, Maryland. There was a lonely nighthawk, Hopperesque feeling to those paintings. Of course, they were derivative, but they had soul, the first letters of his own signature.

I twisted and turned on the bed, remembering the time I had tried to put his work up on the wall. He'd forbid it, saying quietly that the paintings were second-rate, an embarrassment. But what he really meant, I thought as I lay there, listening to him gargle through the wall, was that seeing them, his only completed works, was too painful to bear. Better to lock them away, forget about what might have been.

If only he hadn't given up; if only he hadn't had a child.

That was the inescapable logic of it; I turned over on my belly, then back again to my side, like an insect pinned to a mat.

Why kid myself? He had given up his art, spoiled his promise, primarily for me. And what was I? A self-conscious, stick-in-the-mud intellectual. A literary poseur.

I thought of Raines then. He might be mad, he might be a con, but he was going to go out there and succeed in the fast-buck world. With a son like Raines, a man might be able to brag to other men, "Hell, yes, I gave up my art, but it was worth it. That boy might end up being governor."

But Tommy Fallon—ex-high school fuck-up—was now headed toward some kind of new folly. A barely middle-class Baltimore boy pretending he was going to end up a Man o' Letters. God, the sheer pathos of it all turned my stomach, and I suddenly wanted to rush into the bathroom and scream at him: "All right, I know I'm nothing. I know it. Just tell me what would make you happy, proud? Name it and I'll do it. A doctor, a lawyer? Is there anything in the goddamned world I can do to make you happy?"

Ah, but that wasn't me either. That was a scene from "Kraft Theatre," weekly middlebrow television plays that my mother faithfully watched. Of course, in these sterling melodramas, the father would at last see how he has maligned his sensitive son and would hold him in his arms as the scene faded and the melted cheese poured so warm and comforting down the screen.

But there would be no such easy resolution here. We were, it occurred to me as I lay there sweating from the overheated house, too much alike, too frail, too sensitive, too introverted, to ever make our mark on the world.

In the morning, eating my poached egg, I again found myself thinking of Raines, and again, to my surprise, I began to laugh. God, I thought, yesterday had been fun, even if it had been at my expense. Then I thought of Professor Spaulding, with whom I had a meeting in just an hour, and my stomach twisted into knots. I was going to discuss my paper for Contemporary Novel. I had an idea that I would write something comparing Kafka with Edgar Allan Poe. It was a thesis I'd been working up for some time, that they were both artists of paranoia and pain, that they both found psychic release in horror. In all my critical readings, I had never seen anything comparing the two men and I had felt that I was onto something unique, even—God help me—sophisticated.

I had fantasized that Dr. Spaulding would be dumbstruck by my ideas, that he would nod his head and give me a sliver of a smile. And both of us would know, at that exact moment, that I was on my way, headed up the yellow brick road to the suddenly wide-open doors of the Great Golden Palace of the Mind.

As I finished my breakfast that morning, however, I found it difficult to concentrate on my thesis. I kept seeing Raines striding across the Hopkins campus like he owned the place. I remembered his easy manner with the secretary, how he addressed the president of the great institution by his first name as if they were equals.

I also remembered his patronizing attitude toward Spaulding. He treated my intellectual hero as if he were nothing more than an interesting, lovable, but slightly dotty old eccentric, someone's faintly ludicrous uncle. I had detested his arrogance, and yet, I thought to myself as I showered and shaved, there was some truth to it. If one looked at it from a certain perspective, Dr. Spaulding was slightly absurd.

The thought both amused and startled me. For, logically, if Spaulding was absurd, then what was I? An *imitation* Spaulding?

I ran cold water over my face, combed my hair, and looked at my books. No, I couldn't afford such thoughts. To hell with Raines and his crazy notions. I had to stick to the straight and true. With some effort of will, I put Jeremy Raines out of my mind, grabbed my books, and headed out of the house toward my appointment with my mentor.

Ah, how I recall the pain of that meeting. To this day it remains engraved on my soul.

Professor Spaulding listened politely as I explained to him in hushed tones how Kafka and Poe were on parallel tracks on the Great Train of Literature. Then, when my fifteen minutes of halting, stammering "brilliance" were finished, he looked at me and said the words I most dreaded.

"Yes, Tom, somewhat interesting."

You must understand that this was the comment he made to students who wanted to write "Bravery and Cowardice in *The Red Badge of Courage*" or "The Short, Choppy Sentences of Ernest Hemingway." It meant that my ideas were obvious, hackneyed, tenth-rate.

"Then you don't like the idea?" I mumbled, blushing.

"It's not a matter of me liking it," Dr. Spaulding said, taking off his glasses and tapping them on his palm. "It's simply the kind of observation that doesn't bear close scrutiny."

I slapped my hand to my head and blew wind from my cheeks.

"Well, of course not," I said. "Of course not. I don't know what I was thinking."

"You see," Dr. Spaulding said, "that while there is a superficial similarity between the two writers in that they both deal with extreme mental states, Kafka is always cool, understated, whereas Poe is an hysteric, a melodramatist."

And here Dr. Spaulding's voice reached a new low as he whispered in my ear: "Poe is a sensation monger, the forerunner of Rimbaud and contemporary triflers like Allan Ginsberg, whereas Kafka comes out of a great modernist

European tradition. Of course, the two men have certain superficial similarities but only at the most obvious level."

"Oh, well, *of course*," I said, devastated. "I guess I didn't think it through. Look, I'm sorry I wasted your time. I'll have to work on something else. I mean, I have a lot more ideas. Better ideas."

"Fine," Dr. Spaulding said. Then he turned and picked up a pen.

"Come in again, Tom, when you've firmed up your thesis. Now I've got some Kafkaesque paperwork to attend to."

"Right," I said, backing out the door and bowing like a slave.

I gave him a little salute as I left and then turned and walked down the hallway. There were other students there, but I stumbled by them like a drunk. I felt as though I had been branded an idiot, a moron, one of the countless students who "betrayed their potential."

Oh, Lord, I was washed up at nineteen. I would never be a literary scholar. No, I would end up in a bathroom somewhere, a madman washing away the stink of failure, of mediocrity, from his skin. I vowed to race directly to the library and spend time there until I came up with an unassailable thesis, one so critically bold and yet so solid that Dr. S. would be flabbergasted. I would stay in there night and day if necessary, but I would, by God, be a serious scholar in the end.

Just walking into the library cheered me up. Since I was a small child, I have always lived in libraries. To me they were and still are mystical places, where deep magic reigns. Just walking through the great glass doors gave me a feeling of power and freedom. Somewhere, somewhere in this vast treasure trove of books and ideas, there was something that would spark off my intellect, something that would take me one step closer to being the man I intended to be—a scholar, a gentleman, a credit to Calvert and Dr. S.

I intended to get right down to serious research, hustling into the card catalog system, but instead I became hypnotized by the silent beauty of the place. I began walking around the aisles of the library with no fixed goal in mind. It was liberating just to be around so many books. They were and still are my friends, my benefactors, the father and big brother I never had. Just seeing their spines, their titles, their covers, sends me into a state of grace.

I glided through philosophy, touching the spines of books by Russell, Kierkegaard, and Kant. I cruised through history and promised myself that one day I would read all of Spengler and Wells's *Outline of History*. Then I arrived in the fiction section, the holiest of places.

I felt a kind of glow come over me, a glow that was completely irrational, I know, for only a few minutes ago, I had proven myself as yet unworthy of understanding real artists, but still the books called out to me in a voice that was beyond Dr. Spaulding's powers to discourage me, beyond even my own feelings of self-loathing.

Books, thoughts, words, powerful floating images, whole worlds imagined and described by great artists—and all of it sitting there silent but powerful, like some great sleeping giant—the colossus of the library.

Now I glided from row to row, running my hands across the spines of the volumes, like a native touching a talisman. When I came to an old favorite, Stevenson's *Treasure Island*, I took it out, opened it up, and smiled down on the illustrations of Jim Hawkins and Long John Silver. God, how I had loved that book as a child. I remembered sitting by the goldfish pond at the downtown Enoch Pratt Library, reading it while the light of a Saturday afternoon glanced off the sparkling water. And I remember offering a little prayer: Oh, Lord, do not let the library ever close. Let me stay here by the pond, lost in my adventures with Jim Hawkins and Blind Pugh and good Squire Trelawny.

I remembered being sick with rheumatic fever, my

mother, young and happy then, wearing a blue apron and reading to me, while she lay cold compresses on my head. I even recalled the lovely odor of that first copy of the book, the fresh smell of the ink and the new pages.

Suddenly, I was overwhelmed with a desire to do something crazy, foolish. I wanted to smell the book in my hand. Why, I wasn't sure. Surely it wouldn't smell like the old edition I had loved as a child, but even so it *was Treasure Island*. In my strange library trance, I began to entertain the idea that it was the great pirate story itself that gave off the odor of romance. Why not? It was entirely possible that stories had their own smells. *Catcher in the Rye* smelled like fresh chestnuts bought from some horsecart vendor near Central Park; *You Can't Go Home Again* smelled like old suits left in ancient closets, the sacred, heartbreaking smell of yesterday's lost Sundays; and *War and Peace* smelled like sulfur and smoke and the odor of dying men on a great blood-drenched field of Russian poppies.

I looked around, saw no one, and put the book up to my nose. I inhaled deeply, and to my surprise there *was* an odor. Not precisely the one I had remembered as a child, but one reminiscent of it, the dank smell of old pirate ships, rotted rafters, and unbathed men drinking down flagons of cold, foaming grog. Oh, yes, I could smell it—the odor of *Treasure Island* bore me back into the past so swiftly that it nearly made me dizzy. I could see my old bedroom; the cowboy curtains on the window; my "pet skeleton," Skelly, hanging off the door; my cedar chest with the mothball odor inside; my little orange bookcase with my Golden Books; my Mickey Mouse and Plastic Man comics; my coloring books lying in a pile next to the bed. And there was my red plastic radio sitting on the night table next to my bed, on which I could dial Jack Benny or Bob Hope or the Lone Ranger. Sniffing the book, I was again in my room and I was happy, and downstairs . . . downstairs there was laughter, my young parents' laughter, as they entertained other young couples. I remembered them eating Ritz crackers and onion dip off a blue plastic lazy Susan that my mother had

gotten from S & H green stamps. They were drinking mar-
tinis and dancing to a Prez Prado Mambo beat. Oh, Lord,
they had been carefree and happy once. But now all that
laughter and sweetness was swept away, gone, lost forever.
The memories came in a great wild rush, and I felt dizzy
and held on to the side of the bookcase to ballast myself.

Then, suddenly from behind me there was a sound, a
rustling, and when I turned there was a girl, a girl I had
seen once or twice on the campus, a most interesting girl
with short red hair, a small adorable pugnose, and a midnight blue turtleneck sweater. She wore a knee-length black
skirt, skintight, which revealed her tight little ass and terrific
pale white legs. I had seen her hanging around with the
arty crowd, poets and actors, and I'd wanted to say something to her but had been too shy to know how to proceed.
And now, astonishingly, here she was staring at me.

Me, with my nose stuck in the binding of a book.

I felt absurd, foolish beyond belief. God, how long had I
been standing here? Minutes probably. She may have been
watching me the entire time.

I slowly took the book away from my nose, though reluctantly, for now she could see my reddened face.

"I think there's a law against that," she said.

Her voice was unlike any voice I had ever heard. It was
deep, throaty, theatrical. I was so struck by the quality of
it that I felt my own embarrassment diminish.

I knew then, in ways you can only know when you are
young and trusting, that I could simply tell her what I had
been doing and she would understand.

"Did you ever . . . smell a book . . . I mean they do *have*
smells," I said.

She looked at me and smiled. A smile that was pure
innocence and yet promised something else entirely.

"Of course," she said. "And different books have *different*
smells. I have some poetry here, smell this one . . ."

She reached down to a large Spanish leather handbag and
pulled out a small volume of poetry.

Then she walked toward me (and, God, that walk, that same incalculable mixture of schoolgirl innocence and full-grown woman) and laid it in my hand. The book was none other than the City Lights paperback edition of Allen Ginsberg's *Howl and Other Poems.* I nearly recoiled from it and suddenly feared that Dr. Spaulding would come around the corner and catch me reading this "ersatz sensation monger."

"Take a whiff," she said.

I hesitated for about a half second and then, smiling like a complete fool, put the book up to my nose.

"It smells like old wine, some coffeehouse out West somewhere, smoke, jazz," I said, feeling every bit both a fool and a liar. This book had only the smell of her perfume on it, something like fresh roses, and I felt dizzy, breathless.

"That's what I smell in it," she said. "God, I didn't know anybody like you went to Calvert. My name is Val Jackson."

"Tommy," I said, offering my hand. "Tommy Fallon."

We stopped and looked at each other for what must have been a full ten seconds. I looked at her face; her prominent, almost masculine cheekbones; her huge blue eyes; her red hair; and her thick, sensual lips. I could have stayed there all day.

"Well," she said, "I've got to go. I work downtown as a waitress and I'm doing a paper on Ginsberg."

Ginsberg, I thought. Dr. Spaulding again appeared in my mind shaking his head, but I suddenly found it extraordinarily easy to ignore him.

"You're an English major then?" I asked, feeling my heart racing.

"Of course," she smiled. "Do you like poetry?"

"Sure," I said. This wasn't entirely true. I was much more a prose man, but just then it seemed as though I could learn to like it.

"Then why don't you come downtown tonight," she said, smiling in a way that made me feel weak in the knees. "Monty's Bar. Eight o'clock. I'm reading there."

"Eight?" I said. "Well, I'm supposed to be doing some

research, but maybe." This was a patent lie. I had nothing at all on my plate, but I had to do something to slow myself down.

She reached out and touched my hand, and I felt an electric shock go up my arm.

"I hope you will come," she said in a low buzz of a voice. "I want you to come."

Then she was gone, into the elevator, riding up into the stacks.

I stood there numbed and felt my heart beating wildly in my chest.

"Val Jackson," I said once and then again. "Val Jackson."

I scarcely remember how I made it through the rest of the day. It seemed as though I were in some kind of waking dream or that I had inhaled laughing gas. I went to class but had no idea what any of my professors said. I vaguely remember having lunch in the student union, but there was an air of unreality to all my doings. I felt as though somehow my real life, the one that I was meant to live, would begin that night.

I should add that I did not allow these feelings to run unchecked inside my skin. Quite the contrary, I fought the impulse with all my diminished might. I told myself that this woman, this apparition of a woman, Val Jackson, was clearly another impediment to my becoming a scholar and a gentleman. As I walked (or rather floated several feet above the ground) around the campus, I harangued myself for letting a pretty face and a sexy voice dissuade me from my appointed tasks. I sternly told myself that I was again acting like a bloody fool, that it was clear, eminently clear, that this woman was nothing more than some kind of sloppy beatnik. After all, she admired the poetry of Allen Ginsberg! That said reams about her lack of character. And I reminded myself (out loud, and several times I noticed students staring at me as I walked by mumbling to myself) that only this morning Professor Spaulding, who stood for all that I truly valued in literature, had upbraided me for my lack of focus, for the softness of my critical perspective! My God, time was wasting; in another five months I would be twenty years old—barely a teenager. I simply had to start acting like an adult.

I sighed, deeply disappointed with myself. I wasn't going to her poetry reading and that was that. Saying it made me feel strong, sure of myself. I took a deep breath of the warm fall air. I knew who I was and I knew what I wanted. With an air of satisfaction that comes from making the correct, definitive decision, I went to the library for the remainder of the afternoon.

From where I stood at the corner of Park Avenue and Eager Street I could hear the sounds of a vibraphone. The music tinkled out into the night air, music so cool and lilting that it made me (against my scholarly will) tap my feet on the unseasonably hot sidewalk. Now I headed toward it like a lemming heading for the sea. All my resolve, discipline, and fortitude had been washed away by seven-thirty.

Though I knew I was a ridiculous figure, though I still firmly believed that heading to this coffeehouse was a disastrous idea and made me practically a card-carrying member of the great army of the second-rate, it seemed I had no choice. I had to see her again, even if just to assure myself that I wasn't really obsessed by her (by her smell, by her walk, by her voice.)

The coffeehouse was right next to a dark alley. The building had glass doors with a floral design in them and the word *Monty's* written in some obvious copy of Victorian lettering.

I pushed open the door gingerly like a child sneaking into his parent's bedroom and walked inside.

There was no question about it, this was the Baltimore version of some beatnik joint. I felt my stomach tense as I looked around. Though I had never been in such a place, I had seen so many pictures in magazines about North Beach joints in San Francisco that I felt I had already been here. In front of me were the compulsory little black wire tables and chairs. Standing at the old oak bar were negroes and white men with long beards and longer hair and two women with black sweaters and black leotards. The women were both attractive but I told myself that they were attractive in a predictable way, a coffeehouse way. After all, there was nothing new here, nothing new at all. (And yet, that was only the academic part of myself talking, mumbling, for I was excited by it all, excited and a little apprehensive that they would not accept me.) I looked to the back of the place and saw an elevated dining room and a bandstand on which were three Negroes dressed in elegant suits playing the cool jazz that had summoned me into the place against my will.

I looked at the vibraphone man, dressed so coolly in his two-button green satin suit. I watched his hands bang the mallets on the keys, hitting them lightly, skimming over them, and saw the happy blissed-out look on his long, elegant face, and I felt something melting inside me, something mere rhetoric and academic fussiness couldn't touch.

He was cool and he was there in the moment, in love with his own body, his own music, and uptight white boy that I was, I envied him.

Now I walked in a little farther toward the bar, my heart beating fast, my miserable self-consciousness in full bloom. I tried looking around in a blasé fashion, hoping that no one would realize I was the enemy. But Val Jackson was nowhere in sight.

The bartender, a huge Negro man with a scar across his left eye, looked at me and grunted: "What you have?"

"Ah, beer," I said. "National Bohemian."

"Check," he said.

He smiled and reached into the freezer just below the bar and pulled out a cold beer for me. I felt a small sense of triumph. I was only nineteen years old and the drinking age in Maryland was twenty-one. Yet he hadn't carded me.

I stood there, drinking my beer, pretending to listen to the music, but my heart was racing. One of the Negro men at the bar was staring at me.

Finally, I could stand it no longer. I turned and looked at him.

"Great music," I said. "Those guys really . . . know how to, ah, blow . . ."

I immediately blushed and felt as though I should cut out my tongue. Where had I ever picked up such absurd talk? Probably from watching movies like *High School Confidential*, in which Hollywood screen hacks did their own lame version of beatnik patter.

The Negro looked at me and smiled. He wore a handsome brown leather vest and had a little gold star in his front tooth.

"I get it," he said.

Then he smiled and looked at the blond-headed white girl standing next to him, one of the black leotard twins.

"You get what?" I said, having no choice but to play this out.

"I get what you're putting down," he said.

"You do?" I said. My voice had risen to near falsetto.

"Yeah, I do," he said in a voice rich with sarcasm. "You a white boy, you probably ain't even drinking age, and you coming in here trying to come on like a hip nigger from 'de streets.' How am I doing?"

I felt my heart literally sink into my stomach. I had made a complete and utter fool of myself. He smiled at me now, which softened his attack a little.

"I'd say you're doing pretty well, Sam," a voice said.

I turned, startled, and looked into the eyes of Val Jackson.

"But you should go easy on Mr. Fallon. This is his first time down here, and we don't want to scare him away. After all the man is a poet."

"Yeah, right," I said, blushing as I stared at the floor.

"A great poet," she said, putting her arm around my waist and pulling me away. She wore a red turtleneck sweater and tight-fitting black Levis. Casual dress and she looked casually sensational. I looked into Sam's eyes and saw them soften a little.

Val said, "Tommy, this is Sam Washington. Sam's an artist."

The big Negro man put out his hand and squeezed mine. Now he smiled, and I was stunned by the warmth in his face.

"Well, you ain't ever gonna be a nigger," Sam said, "but you could maybe become a nice loose white boy. And I dig poetry."

The Leotard Twins smiled behind him, and I couldn't help but laugh myself.

"Come on back, Tommy," Val said. "We're about to start."

I nodded to Sam Washington, who nodded back and then followed Val to the back of the bar and up the little steps. We sat down at a table just a few feet from the musicians who were now working their way through a wonderful version of a tune that I would identify later as "Green Dolphin Street."

"I didn't think you'd come," she said, smiling through the candlelight.

"No?" I said, breathless as I stared at her pale white skin and red hair. "Why not?"

"Oh, I don't know," she said. "I thought I detected a faint air of disapproval."

I swallowed hard.

"No. No way," I said. "I couldn't wait to get here."

"Really?" she said. "Well, I hope you'll enjoy it. I have a feeling you don't much like beat poetry."

"I like anything, that is, if it's good," I said and immediately felt like I was a sixty-year-old prig.

"Oh, I see," she said, laughing. "I bet you're strictly a Pound and Eliot man."

THE KING OF CARDS

"No, not at all," I said, lying through my teeth. My God, Pound and Eliot were my heroes, and I had sold them out in a snap simply to curry her favor. The serious, unflinching eyes of Dr. Spaulding bored into the back of my head.

Val laughed at me and her eyes flashed.

"Maybe you do have some potential after all. I had kind of crossed you off as one of those pipe-smoking liberals."

I looked down at the table on that one. It hurt to hear myself portrayed this way. Especially since, not three weeks earlier, I had just bought a briar pipe. She must have sensed she'd hit a raw nerve, because a second later she was up and walking around behind me.

She put both her hands on my shoulders and squeezed. I was surprised by the strength of her fingers.

"You just need to loosen up a little," she said. "You should try yoga."

"Only if you'll teach me," I said, turning and smiling at her.

She made a face—"naughty, naughty"—and said: "Maybe you aren't as uptight as you seem. Anyway, whether you like it or not, you have to stay and hear my poetry."

"I wouldn't miss it for the world. When do you read?"

"Right now, I hope," said a voice, a faintly familiar voice, from behind us. I turned and looked into the lopsided grin of Jeremy Raines. He wore his same filthy business shirt and battered gray suit. And his hair was mussed in the same endearing cowlick. In spite of myself, I couldn't help but smile at him.

"You made it!" Val yelled. She left me at once and threw herself into Raines's arms.

He picked her up effortlessly and spun her around like a dancer. There was something immediately appealing about this move; he was grace personified.

I felt a pang of ridiculous jealousy shoot through my chest. Of course he would be here and she would know him. They were both outcasts, and he would be at home in this world in a way that I never could be.

When he had set her back down on the floor, he offered me his hand, and I reluctantly accepted.

"I didn't know you were a fan of poetry and jazz, Raines," I said.

"Oh, yes, my boy," he said. "A great fan, one of *the* greatest fans. You should have come back to the house and taken a look at my record collection. All the biggest names . . ."

"And all hot," Val said, poking a finger at his ribs. "Jeremy used to work at the Music Mart up in Govans, where he permanently 'borrowed' half the jazz bins. Remember the night it was raining and we grabbed about ninety albums and took them down to the Hellhole?"

"Only too well, my dear," Raines said, and then both of them cracked up. "That was indeed a night to remember."

What had he meant by that? I tried hard not to think about it. But she smiled happily at him, the same adoring look that had graced the faces of Eddie and the Babe the day before.

Val looked up at the bandstand, where one of the black jazz musicians was waving to her. She kissed Jeremy on the cheek, squeezed my hand, and grabbed her little black notebook, then headed up to the podium. A waitress in a short black lace skirt, black fishnet stockings, and red pumps came by our table. I started to order a beer, but Raines shook his head.

"For poetry you need something with a little more bite," he said. "Try some tequila."

"Right," I said. "That's exactly what I need."

I had never had a shot of tequila before. I thought of the Champs old tune, bullfight posters, and dusty Mexican towns. The drink seemed exotic, romantic. Naturally, Raines would know all about it.

Then, as Sam Washington stepped up to the microphone, it occurred to me: Jeremy Raines was some kind of hybrid, businessman-beatnik. He didn't wear the long beard or the sandals, but he was clearly as mad as any angel-headed hipster in some Allen Ginsberg epic. That was the connec-

78

tion between himself and Val. But was that all? It was all too easy to imagine them both naked and rolling across some great unmade bed, and I literally shook my head to get the image out of my mind.

I sighed and listened to Sam Washington on the stage: "Welcome to Monty's Poetry Festival," he said. "We got all kinds of cats reading tonight, big cats and small, short cats and tall, every kinda cat to entertain and enlighten ya all."

The crowd went crazy over that bit of doggerel. At least sixty people clapped and whistled and, in some cases, snapped their fingers to show their pleasure. Out by the bar, I could make out two other members of the Raines clan. Short-legged Eddie and the sexpot, Babe. Tonight both of them were wearing hats: Eddie, a rakish black beret, and the Babe, a floppy purple sunhat with a long goose feather. As absurdly Bohemian as ever, I thought, yet I felt a twinge of affection for the two of them and found myself waving their way. And lo and behold, they smiled and waved back. They even seemed happy to see me.

"Now the first of the cats we have for you tonight," Sam Washington said, "is the swingingist and sexiest alley cat we have seen in many a night—Miss Val Jackson."

The place erupted in applause and whistles.

She stepped up on the stage and when the spotlight lit up her face, I felt a chill move down my arms and legs. God, she was beautiful.

She put her hands over her eyes, shielding them from the hot lights and smiled.

"A nice crowd of Baltimorons," she said. "Here's a little love poem for you."

There was a ripple of knowing laughter, and I strained forward in my seat. I saw Jeremy Raines's eyes on me. He was obviously waiting for my reaction, but I ignored him and gave my full attention to Val.

"This one is called 'Summer Boy Blues,' " she said.

She began in a low, purring voice, the unmistakable voice of sex, and as she read, she moved around, wiggling her shoulders and her ass, almost as if she were dancing naked

in front of a mirror in the privacy of her own bedroom. I
felt my stomach twist into a knot, and my mouth went dry.
The only other poetry reading I'd been to had been at Calvert
my first year. For Senior Week we heard Marianne Moore,
who was about ninety-eight years old and dressed like a
witch. She whispered and posed and tried to look like a
pixie, and everyone found her lovable but me. I couldn't
wait for her to leave and head back to her iron lung or
wherever it was she lived when they didn't drag her out in
front of the public. But this was something different. All of
my earlier academic caveats disappeared in one flash of that
body and in the sound of her voice. I could not take my
eyes off of her.

"So it was another killer hot day in Crabtown,
and so I had nothing to do,
and no one to do it to,
and I wanted to scream a little,
break a few windows,
and say soft, ironic feminine words, like Emily D.
"heard a fly buzz when I died,"
but instead found Nikos, the sweet Greek sailor boy,
burned out and lonely,
sitting at the bar at the Acropolis,
drinking cheap Ouzo,
watching a belly dancer with a Moby Dick gut,
black-haired Nikos talking about some little dark-haired
village girl he left behind,
and I said,
"Don't cry sweetheart . . . I'll be her . . . only better 'cause
I'm a Baltimore girl, and we aim to please,"
Oh I scared myself saying those words,
But he was kind and sweet and sad,
And put his fingers inside me,
On the docks sitting beside an old abandoned anchor,
Overlooking the sad ships,
and said over and over again, "Elena, Elena . . ."
And I dug being Elena,

And rubbed his cock for him,
Something I would never ever do as burned, dead,
Catholic Val,
And he cried again,
And I kissed his face,
And opened my legs,
Right there on the steaming cobblestoned streets,
And fucked him to rid him of his homeland blues,
And for dear sweet Elena,
And for my own ragged ass self,
And for Francis Scott Key,
And the Star Spangled Banana,
And for all the Catholic dead-faced nuns who never got to
make love to anybody,
'cept each other in the lilac hours after Vespers,
And he came rockets red glare,
And stopped his crying,
And laughed with me,
As we sat there,
All reborn on the shining, oil slick Holy
Baltimore docks . . ."

When she stopped, the place went crazy. There was hooting and screaming and cheering. Behind her the black jazzmen played a hot little blues riff, and Val nodded coolly and gave her perfect killer smile, then walked off the bandstand nonchalant and so very cool.

I found myself in a torment of conflicting emotions. I was clapping wildly, knocked out by her bravery and the power of her writing, but at the same time feeling jealous and shocked. God, did she really do these kinds of things? Screw sailors down at the docks? Guys named Nikos? My cheeks burned, and when I looked at Raines, he was smiling at me and I wanted to hide my face. Damn, I didn't want to look like any square. And then Val was walking toward us, touching hands with her admirers all the way to our table.

"That was amazing," I said, hoping to God I wasn't blushing. "Absolutely terrific."

"You liked it?" she asked.

"Oh, yeah. Too much."

Val smiled shyly and sat down. Now there was almost no trace of the hypnotic figure who had held the entire café spellbound only minutes before.

"Wonderfully done, my dear," Jeremy said, handing her tequila on the rocks.

She gave him the sweetest smile I'd ever seen, almost, it seemed, the smile of a grateful and loving daughter to a wise and beloved father. Then she drained the glass in one gulp and said in a Mae West voice: "That's my only new poem. Before the next poet comes on, I think maybe we should retire to your study, J.R."

Jeremy nodded his head and looked at me.

"Shall we take our new acquaintance, Miss Jackson?"

"Oh, I *do* think so," she said, patting my hand. "By all means. He should see the study, and he should hear the music."

"What are you two talking about?" I said, but they were already up and Val had taken my hand. We were heading through the crowd, past the bandstand, and out a back exit to the dark alley behind the bar.

Once out there in the black night, I found myself with the others as well, Eddie Eckel and the Babe. Someone was lighting a hash pipe, and they began to smoke and pass it around. I watched Jeremy lean on the club's brick wall and draw heavily on the pipe. He held the smoke in and comically bugged his eyes out. Then he passed the pipe to Val.

"Oh, this hash," she said, as she cut off a piece and put it on the pipe. "I love it. You'll see, Tommy. It's gold. Nice and light, makes your dreams all Arabian."

She took a long drag, then passed it to me.

"I think I'll pass," I said.

That stopped the party cold, they all looked at me as if I were a sniveling weasel.

"I just don't like drugs that well," I said. "I mean they make me nervous."

82

"Hey, man," Eddie Eckel said, "you're making *me* nervous. You the heat or something?"

"Cool it, Eddie," Jeremy said. "It's all right if Tommy doesn't want to smoke deadly drugs."

"Of course it is. But I wish you'd try it," Val said, smiling at me. "Bet you've never had gold before."

"Well, no . . ." I said. "No, I haven't . . ."

"Oh, it's great," she said. "It's not threatening at all. No great black body rush but to hear poetry and to listen to music behind it. Fantastic."

"I don't know," I said.

"Try it," she said. "I won't *let* it make you nervous."

The others laughed at that, but she put her hand in mine and squeezed my fingers and suddenly I had the hash pipe to my lips.

I sucked in the drug. It did have a pleasant, light taste to it, not at all like the dark, heavily opiated hash I'd smoked a few years ago with my high school friend, Bobby Murphy. Bobby had connections with the Merchant Marine smugglers down on old Pier 1, and we used to smoke the black hash at his little apartment down on Pratt Street. Those were wild scary times, because Bobby had already started moving into the nighttime world of drugs, thievery, and making book, a world he had now successfully entered. Inevitably, my own literary dreams had taken me in another path, but I missed him and always associated hashish with dark waterfront nights.

Now I stopped and waited for the pipe to go around, waited for the drug to come on, waiting for the first signs of disorder and night strangeness, the dry mouth, the thumping heart, the feeling that my toes were curling up inside my shoes.

But none of this happened.

No, instead, much to my delight—dismay (or to Tommy's dismay, for suddenly "I" no longer identified with this uptight would-be scholarly twit, Tommy Fallon), I began to feel as though I were floating in that dark black alley, floating over it and glowing slightly, and in fact when I now looked around, I realized that I was no longer actually standing next to the exit door, but was twenty feet away leaning on a parked car with Val pressed up against me.

That is, my right arm was around Val. And it seemed I was sort of tapping my foot in rhythm to what I felt must literally be the music of the spheres. Inside Monty's, a poet was reading his work while being backed by some blues music, and it seemed to me that I had never heard music with such a stupendous complexity, such a fantastic density, music that was light and yet killer bluesy, as in darkest midnight blue as in back alley blue as in Claude Monet blue as in blue on blue as in blue boy as in blue lights in blue alleys in blue guitars in blue studios on blue-cobblestoned Baltimore streets as in falling down some perfect blue-leaf-clogged drain of blue love . . .

And it seemed that I was saying these things, as it were, to Miss Val Jackson, whom (oh, God, help me why can't I shut the hell up) I was actually *calling* Miss Jackson: "This, ah, combination of music and words, Miss Jackson," I said, "it has this contrapuntal quality. It seems to actually have some kind of physical density as in some kind of light projection, well, not exactly light, no, Miss Jackson, I wouldn't call it light, I would call it a kind of simultaneous . . ."

"Orgasm?"

She looked up at me and smiled. I began to laugh a bit. A bit too much.

"Am I that amusing?" she said.

"No, no, no, no, no, no," I said. "Not at all. It's just that when you said that word . . ."

"The O word?" she said, rubbing my cheek with the palm of her hand.

"That's the one," I said. "Well, when you said it, I was suddenly aware that your head started to shimmer. I mean actually light up, so to speak, Miss Jackson. I mean your head looked like a light bulb, as it were, Miss Jackson. Just a hallucination, I'm sure, Miss Jackson."

"No," she said. "Uh-uh-uh-uh."

"Uh-uh-uh-uh?" I countered.

"No," she said. "It wasn't a hallucination. When I say the word *orgasm*, my head *does* light up. But that's nothing compared to what happens when I actually *experience* an orgasm. I've been known to, well, you heard about the fire down at Pier 1 last year. I have an apartment down there, and it was a *very* wild night."

She put her arms around me. I hesitated for a second, waiting to feel a great surge of embarrassment and self-consciousness—in short the emergence of my usual self. But this didn't happen. Indeed, I felt no self at all. And yet I felt no fear at the loss of himself.

I was happy to lose old Tom. Who was he anyway?

I wanted himself to go away, stay away, don't ever come back. Screw himself.

I kissed her, leaning on that great black Buick.

Then I stopped kissing her and I laughed.

"What what?" she said.

"One question," I said. "When we started this conversation we were standing over there by the exit of the erstwhile beatnik café, isn't that correct?"

"Yes," she said, "we were. Indeed. This is so."

"Fine," I said. "Then riddle me this. How did we get over here? 'Cause I know we didn't walk."

"We flew on time's winged chariot," Val said. "We were like angels flying over the redbrick Baltimore rooftops and all the little kids who are supposed to be asleep were looking out of their windows with great eyes as we sailed over, both of us wearing bright, red robes, and trailing fragments o' stars. Don't you remember that, Tom?"

"Yes, yes, yes," I said. "It begins to come back to me, Miss Jackson."

"And by the way, Tom," she said, "I love kissing you and I want to stay with you tonight. Does that sound like a good idea?"

"Nah," I said. "I hate the idea, Miss Jackson."

Then I kissed her again, and there was one sensation that cut through the wonderful haziness and that was the pure sensation of God-help-me-i'm-going-to-die-if-I'm-this-happy-for-more-than-fifteen-minutes love.

I was deep deep oh so stoned deep in love with Miss Val Jackson. (Even so, there behind me for the briefest of seconds were the surrealistically lit eyes of Dr. Spaulding, who was shaking his precise head in his precise way and saying "How unfortunate, Tom. How unfortunate, indeed!")

I might have doomed myself forever by telling her then and there, but something else happened, some star–space time displacement, and we were suddenly not in the alley anymore at all but were in a car, Mad Jeremy Raines's car, and were driving ninety-five miles per midnight hour toward Baltimore's Friendship Airport.

Cars squealed and nearly ran off the road. Dogs barked in trash-filled alleys, while old women in flowered-print muumuus stood in their Westport backyards safety pinning up sheets in the fall night winds. While a half mile away stock cars raced around the eternal Westport raceway as thousands of hypnotized redneck fans waited for the one final lap and the one amazing crash that would send them all over the edge of the Jehovah's Witness *Watchtower* black suit–wearing West Baltimore reality into the greatest golden bowl of demented car explosion happiness, which, unbeknownst to them, I was now already living for Miss Val Jackson with her perfect ass, pure Baltimore poetry, was sitting on my lap in the massive backseat of the huge Nash, crushed up against great cardboard boxes of I.D. cards.

In the front seat were Babe and Eddie E., who were chattering like crazed black magpies, while Jeremy Raines drove the great Nash bomber through the dark night.

And somehow we were all singing songs of our youth:

> Take out the papers and the trash
> Or you don't get no spending cash
> And when you finish doing that
> Bring in the dog
> And put out the cat,

THE KING OF CARDS

Yakety yak,
Don't talk back!!!

And Jeremy Raines was discoursing on the true meaning of this song, which he explained in some strange W. C. Fieldsian voice, saying, "Don't talk back and don't look around and don't do nothing that'll lead to any ecstasy . . . oh Lord no no no . . ." and I thought to myself, this is only some kind of drugged-out thing, this is only some kind of wild night, some kind of one-time aberration, nothing for a sensible man to, say, stage a life from, but it didn't feel that way, didn't feel that way to him at all. Because Tommy wanted this very, very badly, oh, yes, indeed. Wanted, needed, loved riding with these people he barely knew but nonetheless now felt were somehow his soul companions.

And how badly he needed soul companions, how often he had been left alone, so alone that he felt someone had stuck a carving knife into his bowels. He felt that too intensely now on his golden hashish high.

And he also needed this strange girl, this lovely girl, wanted her for her bold poetry and her beauty and her anger and her kisses and her breasts that were touching his chest and her legs, ass, oh, God, her perfect ass.

"Hey," I said, as we drove another car nearly to their death on the Baltimore Beltway. "Just where are we going at a hundred miles an hour here?"

"To Friendship International Airport," Jeremy Raines said.

"Yes," I said, "and that is charming, but why? Since all the friends are already here?"

That got a long appreciative laugh, and Val kissed my neck.

"Did you like the hash you just smoked?" Eddie Eckel asked as he hugged the Babe.

"Ah, well, I would have to say affirmative to that," I said. (Did I say that? Who said that? Who made me say that? It sounded like Raines talking. Was Raines somehow throwing his voice through me? It was possible, entirely possible. Yes, I was a hand puppet. That, I thought, was possible too, and one day, yes, one day, Dr. Spaulding has his hand in my neck and arms and is throwing his voice, as in "One feels such and such" and now, the very next day, Raines is throwing his voice and saying, "Yes, my boy," and if this is so, then who is it inside this brain, these strong arms, this fast-beating heart?)

"Yes, well said, my boy," Jeremy said. "Well, you see that's the point. We love this hashish, too, and therefore we are sending Eddie Eckel to Tangier to buy five hundred pounds of it."

"What?" I said.

I looked around the car. There were great looming sets of smiling white teeth (Happy Happy Big Teeth!!) and equally happy, if slightly red and lost, eyes.

"You are going to Tangier *now* to buy drugs?" I screamed.

"Yes, isn't it wonderful?" said the Babe.

I looked around. More happy, happy smiles. The smiles of saints or morons.

"I will stay at the Aegean Hotel," Eddie Eckel said. "I've heard about a couple of contacts there. I'll get the drugs and send them back and then we won't have to ever worry about running out of hashish again for, say, five years."

"Wonderful," said a voice.

"Very wonderful," said another voice, or was it possibly the same voice saying things in a different manner, with a different tone, maybe even with a different set of lips?

"I think it is a wonderful plan," Val said. "Don't you think so, Tom?"

She smiled and kissed me full on the mouth. Somebody else handed me the pipe. A few seconds later I lacked a certain critical perspective.

That is, everything seemed entirely wonderful.

And then the strange spatial time displacement took over, and we were all in the airport, walking six abreast through the wide neon-lit hallways, and we were in lockstep like people in some old 1940s' musical, singing the Coaster's "Young Blood."

> I saw her standing on the corner,
> A yellow ribbon in her hair,
> I couldn't keep myself from shoutin'
> Looka there,
> Looka there,
> Looka there,
> Looka there!!!

And now for reasons unknown to yours truly we were all walking *backward* in lockstep toward the exit gate, and Jeremy Raines was explaining to Eddie the importance of the mission.

"You see, Edward, my boy, if you get this hashish brought back in two weeks, we can sell some of it off and have money to pay people we owe for reshooting and for new film and for the rental on the iron ore machine."

"Check," Eddie said. "But you're forgetting one thing, Jeremy, I need my buy money to get the drugs."

"Of course you do," Jeremy said as we all walked sideways toward the terminal, "but I have to wire it to you first thing on Friday, soon as the check clears from University of Baltimore, which is coming tomorrow."

"You are one hundred percent certain on that?" asked Eddie, picking up the Babe and swirling her around in a tender arc.

"Dead certain of it," Jeremy said. "You don't need to worry about a thing."

"That's beautiful, Jer," Eddie said. "Then we'll have a lifetime supply of hashish and money to run our company with as well."

"I think we are geniuses," the Babe said, kissing Eddie on the mouth.

"Most certainly geniuses," Jeremy said.

He hugged Eddie too and then Val hugged Eddie. Then

for some reason even I hugged Eddie, and he was smiling his dark never-brushed teeth at me and saying: "I wasn't so sure of you, professor, but now I think you're going to make one hell of an outlaw. Hope you're going to move in with us soon."

And with that everyone was cheering and pounding me on the back, and I felt tears come to my eyes and told myself it was just drugs, just the hashish working its golden magic, but it didn't feel that way. It felt like friendship and romance and true youthful love . . . Oh, Lord, this friendship, this excitement I was feeling inside me was something all *too* real, and I saw my defenses crumbling or rather saw that they had altogether crumbled and disintegrated, blown away like old crab claws down at the tin roof Baltimore docks, for why did I want to go back to my parents' house or look for some other place to live when I was surrounded by my friends, my buddies, *mis compadres, mis amigos*, the Identi-Card Magicians (and in my addled, wasted, visionary mind was Dr. Spaulding, only this time he looked very, very small, and his voice was that of a burning locust on an Eastern Shore fall leaf fire, "Most unfortunate, Tom, oh, most unfortunate . . .").

"Well, I have to consider it," I said. "I have to think this thing through very carefully."

"Of course," Val said, laughing out loud.

"I'm quite serious," I said, laughing with her. "Quite serious."

"Aren't we all, professor?" Eddie said.

"Yes," Raines said. "Here's to seriousness. Here's to the seriousness of love, laughter, and adventure. Hip, hip, hooray!!"

As he cheered, all of them followed suit, and I stood there smiling at them, at their mad, wigged out, joyful faces. Then suddenly I was cheering, too, cheering and smoking hash right in the Friendship International Airport, which felt as though it was about a hundred feet off the ground. And I was hugging Val and saying: "After long and careful consideration I've decided: Hell, yes, I'm moving in," and everyone cheered again, and Val jumped into my arms, and the Babe hugged me from behind, and I was standing there in a breast-and-legs sandwich and I heard Jeremy Raines say: "The Identi-army finds its newest warrior. Here's to the mad professor!" And we all laughed at that, and hell, I didn't even mind being called professor. It sounded to me like some 1960s version of cool Doc Holiday (all I needed was a vest, a terminal cough, and a gambler's boot Derringer) and Jeremy was some jazzed-out wasted Wyatt Earp.

Then Eddie took out the little hash pipe again and looked around for about one-tenth of a second and seeing only, say, half a dozen people lit right up, fearless and crazy, and all of us had a few more wispy golden angel tokes as we waited for Eddie's plane to Tangier.

I remember the rest of that night like the brilliant topography of a dream: the dark drive back over the streets of Baltimore, as Val and I sang and kissed and pressed ourselves upon each other in the giant old Nash backseat. The way the Chateau Avenue house loomed up against the brilliant midnight sky, all cupolas and jagged shingled abutments, like a true haunted house, and yet there was no fear inside of me. No, that night the prissy and frightened Tommy Fallon was wiped away and yet "I" was still there, but the "I" was some stronger and better version of myself, not the terrified little academic, cautiously passing judgment on books and stories and his friends as if each of them had to be measured by some high critical yardstick, but instead someone else was moving inside of me, someone strong and confident and joyous, someone who laughed, fell down on his knees laughing, as we entered the basement and Jeremy began to pound comically on the old iron ore machine, while the Babe and Val sang their doo-wop slave song to him. And then we were running outside to the backyard, which

I had not yet seen, with its wild holly trees and elms with
ninety-year-old branches reaching up eerily beautiful to the
yellow star-rimmed moon. And there was a bottle of tequila
and another hash pipe, only this one was a huge hookah
and the Babe was pouring wine in it, chanting "Hubbly
Bubbly, Hubbly Bubbly, man's got to smoke dat Hubbly
Bubbly," and I sat on the back porch steps and pulled on
the giant hookah and the stars themselves were twinkling
and darting and shooting and calling my name, and then I
saw that—oh, amazing moment—there was a swimming
pool in the backyard under the twisted vines. How could I
have not seen it before? We were all taking off our clothes
and falling into the cold, cold water, and I had never felt
such a thrill of wetness since the first time I had fallen in
the mighty blue Atlantic at Ocean City, Maryland, age four
with my grandmother and father and mother, back when
they were all still optimistic and happy and we were still a
family and loved one another with no questions asked, or
that's how it had seemed. And now, as if my own mind
conjured it up, there was a beach ball, and we were playing
some whacked-out game of water polo, and we batted the
ball higher and higher into the cloudy night, and we laughed
and splashed and then . . . then miraculously, there on the
side of the pool was a completely naked and wild-looking
Sister Lulu Hardwell, and everyone stopped in perfect awe
at the size of her two unbelievable breasts. She looked down
into the pool at all of us and for a second I felt embarrassed
and ashamed that I was staring, but she ended that promptly
by throwing back her head and giving a wild, wild laugh;
then she stopped and sweetly fondled her two breasts, and
she yelled into the night: "What's wrong with all of you
guys anyway? Doncha like my two wonderful Ripleys?"

Ripleys?!! Calling her own breasts Ripleys! Yes, Lord, that
was true crazed, ex-nun whacked-out poetry, and she dove
wildly into the pool, and we all cheered, "Hip, hip, hooray!!" And Jeremy began his own separate cheer, "Ripleys
ripleys yeah yeah yeah," and we joined right in behind him
as she came floating up to the top, like some holy religious

Lady Godiva, Good Sister Lulu Hardwell and her two floating fantastic Ripleys. And we worshipped them, floating
there like two fantastic balloon fish from the briny, unfath-
omable hashish deep.

And then she was out of the water and up on the diving
board, everything moving like strange loving little cartoon
blips and Sister Lulu Hardwell made the sign of the cross
and said in sweet, clear tones: "Oh, Lord, let this magic
night be blessed. Let these friends be blessed. Let the stars
and the trees and the moon be blessed. Let naked as jaybird
water polo be blessed, and let the blessed chips fall where
they blessed may!" And then, with no more blessings to be
given, Sister Lulu Hardwell dove into the cool dark pool,
and my mouth dropped open. Miss Val Jackson saw my
look of pure amazement and came over and kissed me hard.

And then like someone had flicked a channel in the sky,
the picture changed again, and they were all gone except
Miss Val Jackson, and she in some impossibly tender and
sexual way wrapped her legs around my waist and I was
entering her right there in the moon-dappled water and we
sank to the bottom of the dark pool, and I moved inside
her, both of us like moonglow fishes in the deep, deep end,
and, oh, Lord, I was long, long gone down the deep blue
drain of serious love.

The rest of that night was spent in a great double bed in
what became my room at the Chateau Avenue house. Truth
be told I had only been to bed with one other girl before
Val Jackson, and that experience was memorable only as a
textbook example of ineptitude and hopelessness. That poor
first girl was a sallow blonde named Maggie, whom I made
love to on the beach at Ocean City, Maryland, three years
earlier. I had gone down to that charming little beach town
with my parents for our dreaded family vacation. We had

a funky little apartment that overlooked the beach, but this didn't make my father happy. He complained bitterly that our rented bathroom was (1) too small, (2) had dirt in its corners, (3) didn't have neon lighting. "What's a matter?" my mother quipped as we sat in the straw-mat-rugged living room waiting for his majesty to come from his toilet: "The old-fashioned light bulbs make it harder to see your zits?" This cracked me up, and my mother took one look at me and began to giggle like a school girl, holding her hand over her mouth so that the King of Misery couldn't hear her insolent happiness, which didn't work, of course. My father came out of the bathroom and bellowed at her: "You think it's funny, huh? You think it's funny I have the goddamn Curse, do you? Well, you won't think it's so funny when I . . . I . . . walk the hell out of this door and keep walking, right into the sea!" As a threat, this failed miserably. My mother and I began to scream with laughter. I fell down on the floor, holding my stomach, as I imagined my father headed across the old boardwalk and out past the innocent vacationing Marylanders sitting on their Baltimore Colt beach towels. Yes, I could see it clearly: He'd be wearing his Mexican sandals, his Hawaiian aloha shorts, his face covered with acne creams, his cysts bleeding from his chest, and as the happy sun lovers gawked in horror, this ultimate beach nerd would head right into the Atlantic Ocean, like Norman Maine from *A Star Is Born.* Nothing Dad ever said struck me as funny as this, and I pounded my mother on the back, who was now choking from sheer hysterics. Finally, when breath returned to my chest, I looked up at my father, who stood there staring down at both of us, a blank expression on his face.

Suddenly, a little shot of fear wormed its way into my heart. Both Mother and I could pay for this for a long, long time. I expected one of his monster rages, but suddenly he cracked up along with us. He began to laugh, a little at first, but soon the hopeless bathos of it struck him full force, and he was howling and pounding a deck chair. "God," he said, "God, God, God! How did I ever come to this?" And that self-consciousness, that moment of vulnerability struck me full force, for I suddenly saw my father in all his naked confusion. And my mother saw it, too, and hugged him, and he looked surprised, like a kid who's received an unexpected gift. And something gave way inside of him. For that week he lost his fear; he seemed to understand that we knew he was driven, that he had no control over the nattering demons within, and we loved him anyway. At least for that one week my father and mother relaxed. He stopped screaming about the bathroom, and by the time my grandmother and aunt had joined us, we had a real vacation together. What was most memorable about it was that when he relaxed, my father could be a loving and happy person. Every night that week he would read one of the great English ghost writer M. R. James's stories to us. Sitting on our little screened porch, drinking root beer floats, eating crabs on newspaper, seeing my grandmother's sweet and kind smile as she looked at the roaring surf ("It calms me, honey. I feel closest to God when I stare into the sea."), hearing my aunt singing "I Can't Get Started" as she put on her sunglasses and tied her jet black hair back in a red bow, these are the trivial and eternal family details I remember; each of them became all the more poignant because this was the last good vacation our family ever had. As the week came near its end, I began to feel a small panic inside because I didn't want it to end, as I knew it must. I didn't want to go back to our house in Baltimore, with its Curse waiting for us at the door. I didn't want to go back to screaming and fighting and cries in the night. I didn't want to see my grandmother go home with my aunt, back to their lonely life near Washington. I wanted it to stay this way, all of us at the beach, in harmony, loving one another quietly, consistently. I felt that I would have given my right arm if only that were possible.

But, of course, I knew it wasn't. By the next to last night, my father was grumbling again. Someone had "moved his acne cream." He began to rave on about how "they" moved everything around. "I'm telling you, Tommy, *they* come in

at night and *they* move your things!" "Who's *they*, Dad?" I
asked lightly, trying to smooth over his mood. "Who's *they*,
son? Who's *they*? Well, you'll find out soon enough who
THEY are, believe you me." I could stand no more of this.
I wanted to hang on to the kind and silent stream of affection
we'd established during the past week, so that last night I
went out alone, forsaking our final meal together, and found
a girl. She was a blonde named Maggie, and she was standing in front of the pinball casino, Al's Place, on Ninth Street.
Most of my horny adolescent life I'd struggled with my few
dates in the backseats of cars, getting nowhere. I'd invented
an elaborate and ridiculous line of patter with women, based
on mumbling and trying to look furtive and sensitive like
James Dean. I even had the red windbreaker Dean had worn
in *Rebel Without a Cause*. But this night was different. I had
barely begun my line, "Not much happening at the ocean,
huh?" when Maggie turned to me and said, "I think you're
cute . . . Why don't we go walk on the beach?" I was fairly
flabbergasted by this offer and didn't know what to say but
went with her down near Nineteenth Street, past the place
where the hotels stopped (they no longer stop at all anymore, they stretch like a gaudy carnival necklace all the way
to Delaware). Minutes later, I found myself lying on top of
her, à la Burt Lancaster in *From Here to Eternity*. The only
difference was that Burt and Deborah Kerr looked like they
were really enjoying themselves, whereas I suffered one of
the small humiliations of my life. Beach sex may look and
sound romantic, but what I recalled was sand seriously chaf-
ing my balls and two blue point crabs attempting to enter
Maggie at the same moment I did. This frantic and painful
copulation ended approximately forty-five seconds after it
had begun, and afterward both of us spoke not a word as
I walked her down the boardwalk toward the crumbling
porch and ripped yellow awning of the Magellan Hotel.

She was staying with her aunt, said she had to go right
in, but then as I turned to walk away, she suddenly pulled
me to her and cried in my ear: "Was I any good at all?"
"Yeah, sure," I said. "You were fine . . . really fine."

"Good," she said, "Cause I want to be a good lover for my husband . . . I'm going to get married in three weeks." "Great," I said. "I think you'll do just fine." She smiled when I said that, then kissed me in a dismissive way, so I turned and walked down the dark boardwalk. *Great,* I thought, *my first sexual experience and I'm a warmup fuck.*

As I headed down the warped boardwalk, feeling the cool ocean breeze, I pretended that my parents and my grandmother and aunt all lived in a big hotel near the ocean, that we were some kind of Italian family who ate huge meals together, who drank wine and argued and fought, but who loved each other in a sentimental, earthy way. Single guests and divorced people registered at our hotel because we were so kind, so warm . . . so *family.*

When I got back to our house, it was eleven o' clock and the lights were out, but my grandmother was sitting on the front porch.

"Hi, honey," she said. "You look a little messed up."

I looked down at my pants. They were wrinkled badly, covered with sand and the cuffs were wet.

"Went for a walk down on the beach," I said.

"You're going to be all right, you know," my grandmother said.

She didn't smile when she said something serious and personal, like people do to try and take the edge off, but looked at me in her steadfast way.

"I know," I said, embarrassed.

"Your father loves you," she said. "He doesn't know how to show it, but he tells me. When he came over to visit us last month he cried because he can't reach you."

"Yeah, well that's wonderful," I said in a harsher voice than I felt.

"He wants you to do all the things he never did," my grandmother said. "He thinks . . . I think . . . you can be great at whatever you try to do."

"Whatever that is," I said.

"Whatever that is," my grandmother said. "You don't have to be in a big hurry to decide."

She reached out and put her hand on my cheek, and I had to pull away for fear of crying right then. I didn't want her to go, I didn't want her to get old, I didn't ever want that summer to end.

But the next morning we saw them off, my aunt smoking her Raleighs and laughing about a sailor who whistled at her as she packed the trunk in her red short shorts. These were my people, I remember thinking as they pulled away. These are my real people, and I will never love anyone as much as them again.

And I never did until that first night at Raines's house. After we came from the pool, Val and I found ourselves in what she said was her bedroom. I was surprised by this, for she had already mentioned that she kept an apartment downtown. But she didn't bother to explain and I never asked. Indeed, there was barely any talk at all; what had happened in the pool was for me too profound for words. I felt stoned and connected to the world in a way I never had since our family fell apart, though I didn't know that then, of course. All I knew for sure was that I had met people who seemed alive in some new way; they were guerrilla fighters of the psyche heading into new territory without any maps. And yet they seemed to be led by Raines's mad, brave, vision. Never mind that Raines might be insane. It occurred to me now that a little insanity was exactly what I needed. That and Val Jackson. There had never been such a woman for me—her perfect, smooth but muscular body, her small but beautiful breasts, her long white legs, the patch of red pubic hair that looked like a flame. I fell on her and kissed her, licked her body, her pussy, her ass. I wanted to know her beyond syntax, beyond even sensation itself. We made love in the bed, then in a wicker chair, slamming up against the wall so hard that plaster rained down on our stoned heads. Then I was facing her lovely, perfect ass as she leaned out the window and screamed "William Carlos Williams" to the entire neighborhood.

Of course, to this day, I remember the sex. Who can ever forget their first really great sex, the sense that when you enter into another person you know them, become them, and then, beyond that, that you both become something else, that you are transported out of your selves completely to become some nonself, a nonbeing, like some force of nature, pure sensation. And yet, beyond that as well, for one is aware of the consummate tenderness of love. One doesn't want only sensation because one wants to reflect on the beauty and perfection of one's lover. One wants to engage her mind as well as her cunt. And so we talked. Fucked and talked and drank and smoked again until dawn. I found my own voice with her that night, found myself able to talk to her about anything, about my dreams of someday becoming a writer, my terrible pains with my father and Miss Kissable Lips, and I had the delicious sense that I was being understood, truly understood by a woman for the first time. She sat up in the bed, her face in her hands, her elbows resting on her knees, naked and unashamed, and she listened, laughing, nodding, comparing my story with her own.

She said that she understood my mother's desire to stay in Baltimore, for her own parents were army people. Her father was known as the Colonel and she had already lived in South Carolina; Japan; London; Fort Collins, Colorado; and Bethesda, Maryland. The Colonel, it seemed, was now working for the CIA, having something to do with Intelligence in Vietnam. I told her about my own father's small part in World War II, his code-cracking unit, and she smiled and said, "So you're an Intelligence orphan, too? It figures we would meet like we did." I smiled, not understanding. So she boxed my ear and said, "Well, think of it. You feel most at home all by yourself in secret in the library and your father feels best all by himself either in the bathroom or staked out at some data-processing machine. You're both intelligence junkies, secret freaks. What else would an intelligence officer's son or daughter become but a writer, a person who knows the secrets."

I smiled and kissed her on the neck.

"Don't tell me I'm like my father," I said, laughing. "I don't want to be anything at all like him."

"Of course not," Val said. "And I don't want to be anything like my parents either, but believe me, it's hopeless. Genes are destiny."

"Obviously he hasn't read any of your poetry," I said.

"He thinks I'll end up marrying a military man and having nine little cadets."

"Not if I have anything to say about it," I said, kissing her again. "I just can't believe you're here . . . in Baltimore."

"I love Baltimore," she said.

"Why?"

"Everything your father hates is what I like about it. People grow up in neighborhoods. They meet the girl down the street. They get married, have kids, stay put. I'm going to make a million dollars with Jeremy, get myself a row house in Bolton Hill, and never leave the city for the rest of my life."

"You?" I laughed, playing with her beautiful red hair. "Come on . . ."

"Why do you laugh?" she asked.

"Because you're not the Baltimore type. I don't see you wearing a muumuu and getting down and washing your three ivory steps or playing bingo twice a week up at the Catholic church."

"You're wrong," she said, tracing her finger over the head of my cock. "I am the greatest three-card bingo player in the United States. Listen, what I want is to have all my friends stop in anytime and go to the Lexington Market for crab cakes and watch Oriole games and go see fireworks at Fort McHenry every year."

"And skate on the ponds at Homeland in the winter?"

"Is that a Baltimore tradition, too?" she asked.

"It is for the rich. That and the Hunt Cup every year."

"Are you very rich?" she asked, smiling and kissing my nose.

"What do you think?"

"I think . . . not very. You're far too nice."

"Right again," I laughed, stroking her back (oh, the sheer loveliness of it). "But I have some rich friends, so sometimes I get invitations."

"I don't suppose you'd take me. I don't guess they like girl poets out there in fashionable Homeland."

"They don't know any," I said. "Rich people don't read books you know. Well, some of the women do when they get bored with charity works, but none of the men, ever. They play golf and tennis and drink."

"Well, that sounds boring, so the hell with them," she said. "When I get bored I like to read poetry and have sex. I especially like oral sex. Would you care to partake?"

"Anything to please you," I said, trying to keep the genial light tone going. But my heart was racing and seconds later I saw her perfect head in between my legs and I was in love all over again.

All I have told you came streaming back to me in a wild rush of images, hundreds of them, some painful, some so sweet that I could almost touch and taste them again, but all filtered through a scrim of nostalgia and loss so heavy that tears sprang to my eyes. Which upon reflection now was not exactly the appropriate emotion to have sitting and drinking bourbon under a tree in midafternoon on the campus of the school you attended over twenty years ago. For suddenly and with no warning, there was hovering above me a campus rent-a-cop, a man with a faded blue uniform, a walkie-talkie, a shelflike forehead, a dumb, predatory look in his eyes, a large nightstick, and a small but lethal-looking gun.

"Hey, you," he said, in an East Baltimore accent (which sounds to a non-Baltimorean remarkably like a mildly retarded cockney). "'Es ain't some refuge for da homeless, ya knaow. 'Es here is Calvert College. Maybe you oughta go uppa shelter in Towson."

Hearing this vast ignorance delivered in the classic Baltimore accent, I immediately made another mistake: I laughed. The rent-a-cop squinched up his eyes until they looked like frozen peas and assumed the posture of all irate gendarmes since the first centurion glowered down at the first harmless beggar. That is, he stuck out his belly and rocked his weight back on his hind foot while reaching for his truncheon.

"Something funny, mister?" he said. "Maybe you'd like a little taste o' dis?"

He took out his sap and smacked it into his huge red palm three times.

"Wonderful," I said. "I'm here to get a Ph.D., and you're threatening to cave my skull in."

"Ph.D.?" he said. "*You?* Now that's a laugh. I seen you over here drinking and I have a mind to whack you one uppa side a head and then run you in to 'ah state boys!!!"

I don't know what possessed me . . . no, that's a lie. I know precisely what possessed me. All these thoughts of Jeremy and our wild, lawless, dope-filled days. That and the voices of the blacks and the Puerto Ricans and the El Salvadoreans I'd interviewed for *The Black Watch* as they told me one tale after another of the police running riots in their neighborhoods, beating and shooting and stun-gunning their sons.

"You know," I said. "You're real fat and real dumb." His eyes opened wide as he raised the truncheon.

"Good," I said, "let's do it. You hit me a few times and then haul my ass in. We can have the Ph.D. conferred from jail. I'd like that. Calvert College would like that."

That stopped him, and he looked at me sideways.

"You're not kidding?" he said. "They're giving *you* a Ph.D.?"

I said nothing more but got up and brushed the leaves from my clothes.

He looked like he dearly wanted to swing his club, but then begrudgingly, he put the nightstick back in his belt loop.

"Damn," he said. "Damn world's falling apart atta seams. Get outta here now, mister, before I loose my temper!!"

I glowered back at him, dusted my pants off, and started walking toward where I hoped my car was. This was the world of our cities now, even here on this green little campus in Baltimore. No, more and more it seemed that the old prognostications of the Left and the hippies of the 1960s were coming true. We lived, just as people like Eddie and the Babe had foretold, in a world that was fast becoming a police state, cops bashed in the heads of the poor anytime they liked and the middle class turned their collective heads away. What did they care as long as they had their VCRs, as long as they didn't have to step over the filthy, stench-filled bodies of the homeless as they lay on the city streets, as long as they didn't have to be bothered by embarrassing, slobbering beggars who might rob their precious sailboats down at Harbourplace? No, I had seen it again and again, even heard it from the lips of my own father on my last visit—the middle class was "tired of the poor"—it had been fashionable to care about them for a few years, but the filthy raving hallucinating bastards simply wouldn't go away, so now if you had to have a few police to round them up and ship them off (Where? Anywhere! Just get them the fuck out of our sight!), then so be it. And if the poor and the homeless and the mad happened to resent or even, God help them, resist being treated like cattle, then what was there to do but have the cops kick the bloody shit out of them, pummel the filthy bastards into submission but, at all costs, get the sons of bitches out of our sight! That was what really mattered in the end.

I staggered across the campus and suddenly felt panicky again. Oh, God, it was beautiful here, just as it had been when I first walked these hills in the mid-sixties, and I thought for a second that I had been wrong, wrong all along to ever leave Maryland for the concrete towers of New York, though I knew with my rational mind that this was all sentimental bullshit. I couldn't have stayed. How could I have ever stayed? And yet . . .

Oh, that way was no good at all. I had to get out of this spiral, like some cornball noir movie where the tough but sentimental detective falls down a spiral web into the terrifying gossamer past.

Finally, I found my car, got in, and just sat there in a daze. I had lived in the world of the past so intensely that I could barely return to the present. I stared at the students walking across the parking lot, short haired, earnest students trudging to class. I watched them, and I told myself not to give in to despair. No matter how melancholy I became, I refused to subscribe to the idea so fashionable among many of my sophisticated friends that each successive generation was de-evolving, moving backward toward some Paleolithic dawn, where the only winner had the cleanest nuclear clubs. That was stupid, self-serving. We were as selfish, as arrogant, as wasteful, and as just plain crazy as any generation that ever lived. Yet, there did seem to me to be something missing in the kids now, some wild spark, some sense of possibility. They seemed afraid (even more afraid than myself), almost eager to let others make their decisions for them.

In that, they were very different from us. We believed we could remake the world.

Yes, in the beginning down at Chateau Avenue, there *was*

a hunger for the full bore American dream, with all its idealism and all its perversity all wrapped into one great bleeding flag with stars and stripes and, yes—I admit it— dollar signs, but not *only* dollar signs, even Jeremy who wanted money as much as any yuppie ever born was torn. Oh, yes, it was obvious from that first day. He wanted power, he wanted money but not badly enough to buy the clean shirt that would make the proper impression on his customers. And there was, I found soon afterward, another side to him entirely, a side that endeared him to me and to all those who knew and loved him.

I drove down the York Road and looked at the maple trees in full bloom on the side of the road. I had hours to kill, and I wanted to get over to see my father at his apartment, but there was time for that. No, though I knew it would take a good piece out of me, I wanted to see Chateau Avenue again. So I drove through Stoneleigh and saw the old sub shop where we used to stop when we were stoned and eat giant fried oyster subs, Harry Little's. I laughed and thought, *Yeah, Tom, you are really middle-aged now,* because when you remember a giant grease-filled sandwich with such overwhelming nostalgia, there's no hope for you at all. I kept driving down past what used to be Stewart's Department Store, the oldest and best in town. Now it was gone and in its place was a giant cheap-looking Caldron, the kind of store that sold inferior primary-color clothes and tenth-rate power tools and was built for future riots with absolutely no windows. I kept driving past Belvedere and York Road where the Yorkshire Restaurant used to stand, the place where my mother and father and I went to eat perfect imperial crab on humid Baltimore Sundays, but it, too, was gone. Instead, there was a chain pizza place, with a grotesque corporate cartoon, an Italian Gepetto hanging out over the street, his huge cartoon mouth wide open so that he could stuff in another piece of their tasteless trash. A half a block down the street, the old Senator Movie Theatre was still hanging on, but Frank Leonard's, where I'd bought my first decent dress shirt, was gone and I drove on, with my hands squeezing the steering wheel, feeling my spirits sag again.

This was what I had feared about coming home, falling down the great memory hole, drowning myself in the vanished world. Why put myself through all this again? Why not just shut it all down? Move on, go to some motel, take one of the forgiving downers in my suitcase, and turn on an afternoon movie. Soon I would be blissed out, not really in Baltimore at all anymore, but floating in the pleasant vacuum of dope and television, buzzing through a soft chemical cloud.

It was tempting, but I knew the price one paid for those loose, easy escapes. No, I had to ride the Memory Train all the way down into the burned-out places that lay in waiting, the deserted train stations of the heart.

Maybe, I thought now as I drove by the Old Trail Bar, where my grandfather had spent many an afternoon drinking with his hunting buddies, maybe I had known all along I would have to risk writing about Jeremy and Val and those first not-so-innocent magical days, even if no one wanted to hear it anymore, no one but myself. For I suspected that without taking that risk, the risk of fully understanding one's own heartbreak, one could never really write from one's deepest tangled self, and beyond that (and infinitely more important), one would never be fully alive.

And I thought again of Jeremy, who burned to live faster, deeper, who risked everything on his own wild ride.

And when had I last risked so much or felt such crazy joy?

I turned left at Chateau Avenue and drove slowly down the leafy street. It looked almost as it had twenty years ago. The great Victorian houses sat back off the narrow sidewalks, their wide, wraparound front porches like an invitation to come and sit and talk. In front of one, I saw a young black man and a white woman walking with their child. When they heard my car come slowly idling by, they turned and looked out at me, not in any obvious way, but there was concern in the man's eyes. Not wanting him to think I was some cruising redneck, I stepped on the gas a little and headed downhill to the bottom of the black cracked macadam street. Then, suddenly, I was there, pulling into an open parking space right in front of 1529.

Of course, the house had been rebuilt. Now, instead of the old shingled place there was a huge white clapboard mansion, restored and picture perfect, with white wicker chairs sitting on the old veranda. Someone had put a gold American eagle out front on the newly seeded lawn, and in the driveway, there was a black Cherokee Jeep. When I rolled down the windows of my car, I could hear a power mower humming away out back. The owner would be around front to finish the job soon, probably some Baltimore yuppie homesteader. I knew these people too well, having done a magazine piece on them for *The New York Times.* I had spent weeks with their babies, their boats, their ersatz Greco-Roman tapestries painted on their Bolton Hill dining room walls, and I'd heard, until I nearly choked, their endless smug conversations about their new kitchens, their country houses on the Eastern Shore, and their absolutely favorite subject—How Much More Value for Their Money They Got Living in Baltimore Instead of Awful New York!! They were a group of smug, terrible bores, and the thought that one of them now owned our old commune made me sick with jealousy and loathing.

But before I worked myself up into a wolverinelike snarl, I had to stop myself. Wasn't some of this a fantasy? And weren't at least part of my feelings simply a result of my own guilt for leaving my hometown to begin with? After all, what did I actually know of this guy? Why should I judge him so harshly? Hell, he would probably like me, maybe he even read my books. The truth was that there was a harshness in my heart, a foulness. I'd never really forgiven myself for the things that happened so long ago.

A second later the owner did come around the side of the house, an overweight man with a pink alligator Izod shirt on and a pair of baggy khakis. He looked down at me, and I smiled back at him. He gave a little wave, but there was confusion, even fear, in his face, and I have to admit that seeing it gave me a kind of twisted guilty pleasure.

I knew I should go at once, before my riotous, drunken feelings took over completely, before I got out of the car and said or did something stupid and ugly. But I didn't leave. Instead I sat there with my lousy attitude, sat there listening to the death drone of the power mower and dreamed my sweet, bad dreams.

After that first wild night with Val, I didn't quite make it to class. In fact, I didn't get out of bed at all until three in the afternoon. Sweet Val was long gone by that time. She had a modeling job at Maryland Institute, and in the morning she reached down and kissed me on the lips and disappeared. In some kind of doped-up alcohol stupor I remained unconscious until Jeremy knocked on my door and entered, smiling at me.

"Ooooh, the beast arises," he said.

"Oh, God, my head is swollen," I said. "I'll be fucking dead soon."

"Here drink this," he said and handed me a brown potion.

"What in God's name is this horror?" I said.

"It's just a little Coke syrup in some soda water. We've used it in my family for over a thousand years. Don't worry, I won't poison you. I need you to do me a little favor."

I drank the stuff—it was sweet tasting, like candy—and I doubted if it would relieve my headache. But there was something reassuring about it.

"What favor?" I said doubtfully.

"Well, you see I mentioned to you that I got the University of Baltimore to buy my cards?"

The cards again. I had become so sentimental the night before, had convinced myself through dope and sex and blind-only-child-dad-goes-berserk-in-the-bathroom need that Jeremy was my friend, my mentor, but now all this gab about the cards reminded me that he was first and foremost an operator. And he was obviously operating on me right now.

"So?" I said.

"Well?" he said. "Tonight at six, I am supposed to be at that venerable institution with cameras in hand and take the pictures of all three hundred members of their freshman class."

"Good luck," I said, falling back in the bed, as he slashed back the curtains and unwelcome blinding sunlight flooded the room.

"Well, my boy, you see, I have this little problem," Jeremy said. "Thing is, I'm slightly understaffed. I have to be off selling our product to yet another school. So, I was wondering if you and the Babe and maybe Val could go down there and take the pictures? There's nothing to it, really. I can show you how to use the camera in five minutes. Then you just snap away, flirt with the pretty girls, and it's all done. Oh, and one more thing, you'll be paid handsomely. A hundred bucks for the three of you."

I scratched my head and looked through the gauze over my eyes at him.

"A hundred? That's pretty good money. Can you afford it?"

"I can, my boy. See, this business is very, very lucrative. Each one of these contracts is worth ten thousand dollars. Now imagine that we get all the schools in the Baltimore–Washington area and just think how much money we're going to rake in."

"But can you get all the schools?" I asked, wondering how I could get out of this.

"Of course we can. While you were sleeping I was over at Hopkins. We reshoot there tomorrow. I just got Morgan College to sign up. And by tomorrow I think I'll have Goucher."

I laughed and shook my head, which was a mistake, as pain flooded my temples.

"This damned thing just might work," I said. "You could get rich."

"Yes, I can and I will. But not just to become another of those Hunt Cup bores, believe me. What we are going to do here is finance our own plans to become miraculous."

His reference to the Hunt Cup sent a little warning bolt through my stomach. Only hours before, Val and I had had our conversation and suddenly I felt spied upon and wondered if she had reported to him what I had said.

"You're familiar with the horsey set?" I asked, pulling my aching body from the bed.

"God, yes," Jeremy said. "My family used to have a little shack out there in Calvert. They play polo. They get drunk. God, what a boring way to waste one's life. The whole world's changing, my boy, and all my relatives want to do is have a perfect, unbruised martini."

"Yeah, right," I said with my usual irony, but secretly hoping he was right.

"There are even some people I've been in touch with," Jeremy said, "a small movement out in San Francisco. They think you can drop out of society altogether, without any money, some kind of saintly Zen trip. But while I admire their courage, I know they're dead wrong. No matter what kind of new ideas you get behind, they all take money. That you can bet your proverbial ass on. Take rock 'n roll, that's all about money, of course. No reason why it shouldn't be. Well, these little I.D. cards are going to be our meal ticket, so that we can finance our experiments."

"God, you talk like a lunatic," I said, using one of my mother's favorite Baltimorisms. But I didn't mean it; I was intrigued, greatly so, and I suddenly thought of Dr. Spaulding and it seemed (and I felt an intense creeping shame in

110

my guts for feeling this) that when I talked to him I was in a stuffy museum somewhere, but when I talked to Jeremy, I was talking to a man from the future.

"Yes, I expect I do," he said. "But just the same, how about humoring me a little and taking the pictures for me tonight. Val's going to be there."

"Look," I said, "I like you. I had a great time last night, but I don't know about getting involved in your card games. I need to read, study . . ."

I expected him to give me a hard sell, but instead he merely threw open his palms and smiled.

"Your call," he said. "I just thought I would give you a chance to make some easy money as a way of paying you back for that mess we got into the other day."

He turned and started out the door. I immediately felt like a prude and a bad sport. He was a new friend after all, and I could use the money.

"Wait up," I said. "All right. Let me get a shower and some food in my stomach, then show me how to use the camera."

He turned and smiled at me, then gave me a conspiratorial wink.

"Super, my boy," he said. "You won't regret it. The King of Cards never forgets a friend. See you downstairs."

Then he disappeared out the door. And as I started to put on my clothes, I wondered if he hadn't somehow hypnotized me after all.

At six that evening I started my career as one of the King's Identi-Card minions, though at the time I was convinced that this was simply a one-shot attempt to help a strapped friend. The very next morning, I would lock myself in my room and start on my serious reading of Henry James's *The Golden Bowl*. That was precisely the book I needed to im-

merse myself in to get back on the right track with Dr.
Spaulding; then something occurred to me. Though I had
shared most of my life with Val the night before, I had
neglected to mention my mentor. The truth was that I
dreaded them meeting, for they seemed like two completely
disparate elements in my crazy quilt of a personality, the
Academic and the Outlaw. Two warring elements that were
struggling for possession of my soul. Such thoughts caused
me to shake my head, blush. What melodrama . . . what
corn. If anyone else had told me such stuff about their lives
I would have been unmercifully satirical, and yet wasn't it
true? Wasn't I as turned on by the wildness and the craziness
at Chateau Avenue as I was by reading Great Literature?
Indeed, wasn't I a little *more* turned on by the outlaw world?
I mean, did dear old Henry James ever stop thinking long
enough to fuck a black-clad girl up the ass while the great
moon sent down its wild yellow rays? Lord, I was losing
my way. I had to maintain a sense of balance, keep my cool,
detached perspective.

The thought sent chills down my back and I cursed myself
for wanting too much. Why couldn't I be a good little English
major, reading my books, going to the right faculty parties,
paying attention to the politics of the department, moving
smoothly ahead, or for that matter why couldn't I be a
simple-minded Bohemian like the Babe and Eddie? Doing
drugs, walking the wild life outside of all bourgeois con-
straints. Instead, I wanted everything at once—High Seriousness and Deep Thoughts and Beatnik Drugs and Crazy
Poetry and Wild Throbbing Sex—the thought made me
dizzy. Suddenly I had a flash of insight into myself that I
didn't want to have. All along, I had felt weak, small,
helpless—in my own house I couldn't even get into the
bathroom to take a piss, for Godssake—but suddenly, it
occurred to me that I was not this little helpless waif after
all. No, underneath the smallness and the little boy lost
feelings, there was something else—*someone* else—born of
a thousand hours of lonely only-child fantasies, some *thing*
that *was* weird, wild, some thing that was maybe not even

a "boy" at all, something more like an open mouth, yes, a great open mouth that wanted to swallow the great Slimy Chesapeake Bay Oyster of Experience whole, and that thought was so frightening to me, so unlike any image of myself that I had ever entertained before, that in a panic I instantly put it aside, shoved it at once under the piles of both literary plans (read, read, take notes, and read) and plans to help Jeremy in his University of Baltimore job (do good, be a pal, make money).

But the image of the open mouth was still there just below the surface, smiling, like some floating pair of lips, under piles of dark, glistening seaweed.

Jeremy spent the afternoon showing me how to use the camera. It seemed simplicity itself, but when I arrived in the University of Baltimore student union, I felt like running away. I was already twenty minutes late, and there, waiting for me, was a huge line of angry students waiting for their picture to be taken.

And right in the front of the line were three huge hulking guys with massive muscles. I recognized one of them, Buddy Biddleman, formerly a leading wrestler from Patterson Park High School. Though he was a freshman, he was already twenty-one years old. At one time, every college in Maryland wanted to give him an athletic scholarship, but he had been mixed up in some trouble with a girl—for a while it looked as though he might go to jail for rape. Although the charges had eventually been dismissed (rumor had it that he and his family had threatened to break the girl's kneecaps if she continued with her complaint), most of the schools had reneged on the offers of a free ride. Only the University of Baltimore, a pathetic school filled with the flotsam and jetsam of the Baltimore high school system, had kept its doors open.

Now he stared at me as I carried the big Rolliflex thirty-five-millimeter camera in and sat it up on its tripod. As I tacked a sheet of blue contact paper up on the wall, I heard him make a crack: "Asshole don't look like no professional, does he?"

With him were a couple of his gooney-looking Drape friends with their leftover DA haircuts, white T-shirts with the sleeves rolled up, and packs of Luckies in them. They brayed at me along with him. I kept working, trying to ignore them when someone touched my back. I must have jumped an inch off the ground, which sent a scream of delight from Buddy and his friends. But when I turned around, I saw not one of the hoodlum crowd but a fat blond boy with pinched eyes: "My name is Randy Roberts," he said. "Your colleagues, Babe McCallister and somebody named Val, called and said they'd gotten hung up, so Ted Hawkins, our activities coordinator, sent me over to assist you. You shouldn't have been late, you know. The students are getting very restless."

He turned and looked at Biddleman, and there was fear in his eyes.

Great, I thought, the Babe and Val don't make it, probably down at Monty's smoking hash and drinking wine, and I'm left here facing this psycho on my own.

"Well, thanks for the help," I said. "I'll shoot the pictures and you get their names."

I tried to steady my already frazzled nerves by looking through the camera, but that only sent a wilder panic through me: Everything I looked at was black. Nothing but total darkness.

"Jesus," I said, "this thing might be broken . . ."

"It would help if you took off the lens cap," Randy Roberts said.

This brought howls of execration from Biddleman and his buddies.

"You believe this guy?" Buddy said. "Hey pal, how'd you get the job . . . blow somebody?"

I felt a helpless anger rising up inside me. I wanted to

turn and tear into him, but, of course, I knew how that would turn out, so I said nothing.

"Guy's a real pro, Randy," Buddy said. "He's looking good, by the way so are you, slobberino!"

He moved forward and gave Randy a hard little snap of his index finger on the earlobe. Randy fell backward with a yowl and smashed into the camera, knocking me backward and sending both of us sprawling on the floor.

Biddleman and friends screamed, and I felt the anger rise inside of me again.

"You guys are beautiful," Biddleman said. "Just beautiful!"

I couldn't help myself any longer. I looked up and smiled at him.

"Feel tough today, do you, Buddy?" I said. "Why don't you go rape somebody?"

That brought things to a grinding halt. There was the kind of silence one associates with the second before a firing squad sends off their volley into a quivering blindfolded man.

Buddy moved toward me slowly.

"You shouldn't have said that," he said. "That was unwise."

Then he kicked me as hard as he could in the right shin. The pain was indescribable. I saw a little shower of meteors cross in front of his gorilla face.

He reached down to hit me again. I wanted to resist, but there was nothing I could do. I was literally paralyzed by his first kick.

Then I saw a black hand reach in and grab his wrist.

I looked up and saw a huge black man push him away from me. Then another black hand came out and helped me up off of the floor.

"He said I was a rapist, Mr. Hawkins," Buddy said. "You know I couldn't let him get away with that."

"Get out of here, Buddy," Mr. Hawkins said in a deep, angry voice. "Are you all right, son?"

"Yes, I'm fine," I said, though it did not sound like my own voice at all.

"I ain't leaving till I get my picture takin," Biddleman said.

"Take his picture," Hawkins said to me. "Then get on with your job. And, Buddy, you get to practice. Fast."

I felt my hands shake as I got behind the camera.

"You're a menace, Biddleman," Mr. Hawkins said. "I'm reporting you."

"For what?" Buddy said. "I didn't do nuffin. This asshole started the trouble. Ast any of the guys here."

The others agreed with him loudly, and Hawkins turned to me.

"Come with me," he said.

I followed him away from the crowd, around the corner of the student union near a men's room. Fat Randy Robert's tagged along with us and tried to take up for me.

"Buddy started it," he said. "Really, Mr. Hawkins . . ."

Mr. Hawkins nodded his head but still gazed at me sternly.

"I have no doubt that he did," he said, "Buddy's a monster, but the truth is Mr. Fallon you were late, and you couldn't deal with the situation. You and your friend, Raines, strike me as amateurs. I heard what happened over at Hopkins, and I warn you if any such mess occurs here, we won't be so forgiving. Your contract will be canceled, and there's a good chance we'll hit you with a lawsuit. So I suggest you get your act together, at once!"

"Yessir," I said, flexing my leg so that I could get some semblance of feeling back in it. Worse than the physical pain, however, was the fact that I knew he was dead right. A professional would have defused the situation, and a man would have fought back. I had done neither, and I felt a kind of film spreading over my skin, the slimy ectoplasm of cowardice.

Humiliated and barely able to stand, I went back to the camera and took Buddy's picture. He smiled like a gargoyle, then blew me a kiss on his way out.

THE KING OF CARDS

➤

Somehow I managed to fake my way through the rest of that long uneasy evening, though I didn't get back to Chateau Avenue until 1 A.M. Depressed and with my leg aching (there was a black-and-blue bruise on my right calf that looked like Italy), I hoped that Val might show up and surprise me, but there was no sign of her. Only Sister Lulu sat on the wide front porch, swinging moodily to and fro on the glider. She was dressed in her tight black capri pants, pink flats, and red halter top, which showed a generous amount of her two fabulous Ripleys. In her hand was a Howdy Doody jelly tumbler filled with her inevitable Scotch and ice. She looked a little worse for wear. There were deep bags under her eyes, and it occurred to me that she wasn't nearly as young as I had assumed. Indeed, tonight she seemed ancient—at least thirty-two.

"Your first big night," she said. "How did it go?"

"My *last* big night," I said. "Believe me, I am no photographer. Where is that madman Raines anyway?"

"Upstairs. He passed out hours ago," Sister Lulu said, taking a sip of her drink. "Care for a drink and a joint?"

"Not right this minute," I said, sitting down gingerly on the top step and leaning against the old shingled column. "You know, Sister, you're a first for me. I mean a drinking, dope-smoking ex-nun?"

"Well, Tom," she said, batting her eyes in a comic way, "you have to remember . . . the spirit moves in mysterious ways."

"Yeah," I said, "I suppose so . . ."

"What's wrong with your leg?" she said.

"Nothing, I just, ah, fell down trying to carry the camera in from the parking lot tonight. Just a little bruise."

"Let me see that," she said, sliding down from the glider.

"No, it's all right, really," I said.

117

But it was too late. She had already slid up next to me and was pulling up my pant leg.

"Oooh, that's a bad one," she said. "You need to get some ice on it."

She reached into her jelly tumbler, grabbed a piece of ice, then began rubbing it back and forth on the bruise. I felt weird, embarrassed, and, absurdly, guilty. Suddenly, I imagined Val catching us here and thinking all the wrong things . . . Sister Lulu looked at me and smiled. It was as though she could read my mind.

"Don't worry," she said. "Val's staying downtown at her place tonight. Besides, she wouldn't mind, she's no square."

"No?" I said. "She wouldn't?"

"I don't think so," Lulu said, rubbing the ice around in a circular motion and smiling at me in a way that was spectacularly un-nurselike.

"Why," she said, "does that bother you?"

"No," I lied. "Not really."

Lulu smiled and took the ice away from my leg. She put it to her mouth and licked it with her tongue, and I felt my cock harden in my pants.

"You're adorable, Tom," she said, "you really are. I don't blame Val for eating you right up. I wouldn't mind a little myself. You want to go upstairs and play a few records?"

She was running her fingers through my hair, and I felt dizzy, hot, and confused. I wanted her then but imagined Val walking in on us.

"I'm a little tired," I said, as Allen Ginsberg shook his head and said, "What a square."

"It's okay," Lulu said, taking her hands away and continuing her massage of my bruised leg, this time without the ice. "I know how you feel, really."

"You do?" I said.

"Sure. This is all new to you. You still believe in purity and one girl and true love. I mean you still have some kind of Ricky Nelson thing in your head, right?"

I laughed in spite of myself.

"Maybe," I said.

I managed a sheepish smile and again felt like a fool, but she moved closer and put her arm around me.

"It's okay, Tom, I believed in purity, too, I mean real one-hundred percent purity. I believed I was married to God."

"What happened?" I said as she rubbed my thigh.

"Well, let's just say that other urges began to present themselves, and I saw myself getting older, with only my thin little faith to sustain me, but worse, with all that time on my hands in the nunnery, I began to think . . . and you know what, I came up with, my own little theory. A theory of love."

"You did?" I said. She was running her hand through my hair now, and I found myself putting my own arm around her shoulders. It was like we were brother and sister, almost.

"Yes, well, the Church is always talking about the mortification of the flesh, how this body is only transitory, how we will eventually be in our heavenly bodies. Know what I mean?"

"I think so," I said, as she began rubbing my leg again.

"Well, they're right, I mean, as the body gets older, it breaks down and you lose your natural sexual desire."

Now Sister Lulu did a very unnunlike thing. She stopped rubbing the ice on my bruise and started licking it.

"But you see, Tom, it doesn't have to happen that way."

"No?" I said as I started stroking her hair.

"Definitely not. The flesh can be renewed through constant sexual contact. Sex sets up a life-enhancing energy field that restores dying cells. Don't you kind of feel that your cells are getting renewed right now, for instance?"

"Definitely," I said. "They feel a lot younger."

"I'm so glad, Tom," she said. "I just want to be the agent of your healing process."

"You're succeeding beyond your wildest dreams," I said as she put her face up to mine, kissed my lips, while simultaneously squeezing my cock. I rubbed my hands across her fabulous, pendulous Ripleys and felt as though my bruise was healed by some higher being.

"I feel all healed, Sister," I said.

"I love doing God's work," she said, pulling down my fly.

Then I heard a voice: "Lulu! You up there, Lulu?"

Before I could say another word, she had pulled me down on the porch behind our shingled rail.

"Who the hell's that?" I said.

"Dan the Trucker," Lulu said, quickly zipping up my pants. "Good Lord, he's out there in the street."

"Dan the Trucker?" I said, out of breath. "Who the hell is he?"

"My ex," she said. "When I got out of the nunnery, I spent a couple of weeks on the wild side up the Kent Lounge in Towson. I wanted to try out my theories, so to speak, to store up my new sexual faith in my cells so I wouldn't let my batteries run down."

"Of course," I said. "So you . . . fucked a lot of guys."

"Well, yeah," she said. "About thirty . . . or so. They even tried to put me in jail for prostitution. But that wasn't true. I never charged anybody. I mean, okay, I took a few drinks, then I met Dan."

"Sister Lulu Hardwell, you up 'ere?" Dan screamed in his East Baltimore accent. " 'Cause I'm coming up to take you home and if any of them hep cat friends o yours tries to stop me . . . I'm gonna break 'ere little heads, unnerstan?"

"Oh, shit," I said.

"Don't let him take me back," Lulu said. "He's a jealous maniac. And he wants to marry me."

"God," I said. I thought of my cowardice only hours before, how I'd sat there on the floor and let Biddleman kick me, and I knew I'd rather die than act that way again.

Therefore, I heard myself say the noble and absurd words: "Don't worry, Sister. I'll save you."

She looked at me doubtfully but managed a small smile of gratitude. Then she said in a very tiny voice: "Ah, Tom, Dan has this thing about . . . crowbars. So you be careful, honey."

I felt my knees knock together, but I stood up anyway

120

and looked down at the street. There was a huge truck with the words *Oriole Movers* on it, and standing outside the cabin was a uniformed man of considerable size. On his wide chest was a Baltimore Oriole and in his hand was a very large crowbar.

"You bring her down here this minute pal, or I'm gonna cave in your skull, you hear?"

"Drop dead," I said and started moving toward him.

He gripped the bar tightly and whacked it a couple of times in his palm, but I still kept moving forward. Then from behind me I heard a voice: "You call yourself a man?" the voice said in thunderous tones.

I turned and looked and saw Jeremy Raines, dressed in a priest's vestments. He wore a black coat, a white shirt, with a black turned collar. In his hand was a Bible. He walked past me, down the steps toward the irate, crowbar-wielding trucker.

I glanced at Lulu, whose eyes were now nearly as big as her breasts. Then I walked behind him, imitating his purposeful gait.

Finally, the two of us were only three feet away from Dan, who up close was not a pretty sight. He was about six feet seven inches tall, looked as though he were made of pure muscle, and had cheeks, lips, and eyes that would have been fashionable in Cro-Magnon circles. His giant square head was stuck into his barrel chest without the impediment of a neck. In his right hand was the black steel crowbar, which he swung up and down, hitting his left palm in much the same way Dr. Spaulding tapped his glasses.

"Who the hell are you?" he said.

"I am Father Jeremy S. Raines," Raines said. "And this is the Holy Covenant Halfway House for Fallen Nuns. If you have business here, sir, then you have business with God."

A great swirl of confusion entered Dan's eyes.

"And who is 'es guy?" Dan said. There was more than a little doubt in his voice.

"This man, sir, is Father Henry James," Jeremy said. "Like

121

your friend, Sister Lulu, Father James has lost his faith, and both he and she have come here to our spiritual mission to work with me so that the fire of commitment might again burn in their breasts."

"Huh?" Dan said. "You serious or what?"

"Never have I been more serious," Raines said. "Now why are you standing here in the middle of this street in the middle of the night interrupting our spiritual work?"

Dan looked around furtively. A blush came over his face.

"'Ere must be some mistake," he said. "I was told by some of the guys uppa Kent Lounge that Lulu had joined up wif a house fulla hippie dope takers, and I come to save her from 'at."

"Well, you were misinformed, sir," Jeremy said. "I suggest you get in your truck and go home before you endanger your mortal soul!"

"All right, Fodder, but what about Lulu?"

He looked up on toward the porch, and there was a terrible pain in his voice.

"What about it, honey? You gonna give up all our good times and go back to become a nun?"

"I don't know, Dan," she said. "I'll call you when I make up my mind."

"I miss you, baby," he said. "I miss you so much I can't even sleep no more."

A tear rolled down his eye, and I suddenly felt an unexpected tenderness for the big guy.

Raines must have felt it, too, for he put his arm around Dan's shoulders as he turned him back toward his truck.

"We must trust in the Lord, son," Raines said. "He knows what's right."

Dan nodded sorrowfully and got inside.

He looked down at us as he switched on the engine.

"I'm real sorry, Fodder," he said. "I sure don't want to get in wrong wif Jesus. I got me enough troubles already."

"Godspeed, my boy," Raines said.

I almost burst into a howling laugh on that one but managed to contain myself as Dan pulled up the hill toward the lights of the York Road.

When he was out of sight, I turned and shook my head.

"Good God almighty," I said. "You are the biggest bullshit artist the world has ever known."

"I knew this priest's costume was gonna come in handy someday," he said. "You know I was thinking about asking him for a tithe to help protect his mortal soul, but I thought that might be stretching our luck a little."

I broke into a laugh and Sister Lulu ran down from the porch and threw herself into Jeremy's arms.

"My hero," she said. "Raines, you are one of a kind. Truly."

"Thank you, my dear," he said.

"I thought the 'Godspeed' was a little much though," I said, roaring as we headed up the steps. "Where'd you get that?"

"Robin Hood," Raines said. "You know Friar Tuck is always saying it to Erroll Flynn when he goes off to fight Prince John, 'Godspeed, Robin.' I thought it was a nice touch."

We all laughed again, and then I recalled just where I had been with Sister Lulu before Dan The Trucker came by, but when I looked over at her, I saw that she was staring deeply and passionately into Raines's eyes.

"Time for bed, Jeremy," she said.

He smiled sleepily, ripped off his collar, and picked her up in his arms.

"Yes," he said, "I believe it is . . ."

Then he turned, winked at me, and carried her over the threshold into the house.

"Godspeed," I said, then sat back down on the porch, alone and a little jealous.

I didn't sleep well that night. Dreams of Sister Lulu's fantastic body were interwoven with strange images of a hooded skull-faced specter with a giant brass-plated machine gun. I awoke twice in the dark ready to scream out but caught myself in time and gripped the bed tightly. Then, when I thought about the meaning of the dream, it was so transparent, so patently square that I felt foolish. What a patently obvious dream. I wanted to screw a nun and a hooded figure, obviously Val, had shown up to kill me for my desires.

The thought disgusted me at first. Lulu was right, of course, Val and I weren't engaged. I was a free agent—like Lulu, like Raines, like Val herself—so why didn't I feel free? *Had* I swallowed whole the idea of a wife and a Suburban Squire station wagon? God knows, I had railed against that pathetic image of middle-class mediocrity, but deep down wasn't it stamped in my soul?

Worse, didn't I even kind of relish the idea? Yeah, Val and I living out in Timonium somewhere, with a great split-level house, three cute red-headed kids riding back and forth to Little League games, dinners and dances at the country clubs, like people in John O' Hara novels (desperate people who eventually committed suicide, but somehow I'd forgotten all that).

My God, what was I thinking? Last night I had been playing with the stiff nipple of a dope-smoking ex-nun and now I was ready to become Ozzie and Harriet.

And what of my work? Yes, my work, my thesis. I remembered my humiliation at the hands of Dr. Spaulding, the pain I had felt walking out of his office, knowing he thought I had wasted my potential.

Then I thought of Val sucking my cock and Lulu putting her hand between my legs and I felt dizzy and fell back on the bed. Things were happening too fast. There was only one hope for me. I had to read. I had to study. Reading had always been my salvation. When I read, my internal thermostat went down, and I was able to make intelligent decisions again.

Yes, I told myself, leaping out of bed and throwing on my clothes, today would be a day devoted monklike to reading. I would go downstairs, eat a little breakfast, make a big pot of coffee, and come back to my room and read, read, read.

I rushed out of the room and bounded down the steps. Already I felt sharper, clearer, filled with purpose. Yes, the asceticism of my day to come made me feel spiritually cleansed.

But when I got to the kitchen, Raines had another surprise for me. He was dressed in a white hospital orderly's suit— he looked like a bedraggled, hung-over version of young Dr. Kildaire—and as usual he was hugely energetic.

"Young Tom. Listen, I forgot to thank you for what you did last night at B.U. I heard you had a little unpleasantness but that you came through in style."

"Only too glad to be of help," I said.

He walked over and put a friendly arm around me.

"Anytime you want to get more involved in our business, let me know," he said. "There's even a couple of new opportunities today."

"Save your breath, Jeremy," I said. "I'm heading right back up to my room to do some serious reading before I flunk out of school."

Raines smiled and nodded his head.

"That sounds like a good and sensible plan. Of course, I might be able to make you a counteroffer."

"Absolutely not," I said, smiling, "no card business today."

"Who said anything about the card business," Raines said, smiling. "I've got to do some work with a patient out at Larson-Payne. Just thought you might want to observe."

I looked at him and shook my head.

"Thanks, but no, I have work to do."

I picked up my copy of *The Golden Bowl* and waved it at him.

"Ah, good old Henry James. Well, you get on with it. Just thought as a writer yourself, you might really benefit from seeing this patient. It's a unique experience, believe me. But no bother. See you around."

He smiled in such a charming way that the room itself seemed to light up. Then he turned and headed for the door. I sighed, shook my head, looked down at my novel, opened it, and tried to read. Then I thought of Larson-Payne's Gothic, redbrick buildings out by Towson. There was a road that cut through the grounds, and only a few years ago, my high school friends and I had driven madly down it while drinking beers, scaring each other with stories about crazed escaped inmates. It was juvenile stuff, jokes with fear and ignorance at their base. The truth was, we knew nothing about the place, and I had always wondered and dreaded what the reality would be inside. Now Raines was offering me the chance to see first hand.

There was no resisting the offer. I shut my book and threw it on top of the old metal breadbox.

"Wait up, Jeremy," I said, running after him again. "Just wait a damned minute. I'm coming."

Now I recall that drive toward Larson-Payne as if it were yesterday. Jeremy chattered on about the card business, all our potential clients, and, as usual, nearly crashed into a bus, but I paid little attention to any of this. I was too nervous about going to a mental hospital. The truth was that I had often thought of my own family life as some kind of mental hospital in miniature. My father, with his endless salves, lotions, pills, needles, scalpels, seemed to me like a man who had turned himself into a perfect mental patient. And my own mood changes and massive confusion as to who or what I was often made me fear for my sanity. The truth was that during those midnight drunken runs through Larson-Payne I had more than once thought of a scenario in which I ended up inside the hospital, but not as a visitor.

In short, the place unnerved me, and as we turned up the black gravel driveway and I could see the first of the redbrick spires that made up the old hospital, I felt a cold fear in my wrists and legs, and my stomach turned into a twisted mass of snakes.

Jeremy chatted on amiably, while I stared out the window and tried to regulate my breathing. Suddenly, I thought of the old horror tale in which an observer is mistaken for a patient and is locked in a steel cage, and it took all my nerve not to jump out of the car and head back to the gate.

Not that the place looked like a madhouse. Far from it.

On the outside, at least, things seemed completely serene. Sitting in some big comfortable white wooden chairs out on the endless green lawn were three patients and two white-coated attendants. One of the attendants had a pitcher full of what looked like lemonade and was pouring a glass for a red-haired middle-aged woman who smiled at him with the worshipping face of a trusting child. Another man threw a ball up in the air, caught it, and repeated the process. He looked harmless, happy.

Too harmless and too happy, and I knew that under this pleasant tableau was madness pure and simple. Everyone was moving too slowly, things looked *too* normal, as though imitating normalcy might hold some transforming magic for the patients' tortured hearts.

I heard my breath come quicker, and my own heart raced double-time.

Inside the great oak doors, things were equally pleasant. Equally quiet. The hallways were perfectly clean, spacious, and cool, the furnishings charmingly Victorian and beautifully kept up. There was a bronze statue of the god Pan just before we got to the first caged and locked door. The little imp was smiling and I was sure some well-meaning therapist thought it would be just the thing to lighten the burdens of the patients, but there was a devilish, nearly sadistic glint in his eye as if he was mocking the mental contortions of those lost souls locked inside. Jeremy reached into his pocket and took out a large ring of keys, and I got scared all over again. This man, this hustler, this all-American maniac was a keeper of the insane? The thought made me giggle uncontrollably, until two bearded doctors came walking briskly by and greeted my friend in surprisingly collegial voices.

We walked on farther, down a long, wide tile hall, on one side of which were twenty-five-foot-high iron-grate-covered windows. The place, I thought, was exactly like a haunted house out of Poe, and I felt goose bumps appear on my forearms. Finally, we came to a massive steel-mesh door, which Jeremy had to open with his keys:

"This is the male A-3 ward," he said. "It's for patients who are diagnosed as incurable schizophrenics, paranoids, catatonics. It's where I'm doing my field work for my psych courses."

I said nothing in reply but managed a nod. I felt as though I had swallowed a glass of sand.

Jeremy turned the key, and we went inside.

"You sure I can just walk in here with you?" I croaked.

"Of course, they trust me in here. Besides, I've already had you cleared."

"You what?" I said, at once outraged, but starting to smile in spite of myself.

"Well, I figured you'd want to come out with me some-day, so I just had you cleared as a matter of course."

"I see," I said. Not the cleverest rejoinder, but what else could I say? I suppose the truth of the situation is I admired his absolute belief in himself, even as I was made furious by his manipulations.

I sucked in my breath as we started into the A-3 ward. The hallway was long and wide, with white, white tiles, white paint on the walls, white sunlight pouring through the white-painted iron bars. It was as though some hospital architect had tried to combat the blackness of the patients' minds with an endless splash of white optimism and that alone was enough to make me feel depressed. Everywhere on the ward, beaten, miserable men were huddled together. Two of them held hands and rocked slowly to some unheard music. A gnarled-looking man, his hair a tangle of snakes, sat in a rocking chair, his fierce crow's eyes staring at his feet as he rocked furiously back and forth and said the words "G'monza, G'monza, G'monza," over and over again. He seemed locked in some private hell, and when we walked by, he stared up at us for the briefest of seconds before heading back into his endless rocking.

I wanted to give him a wide berth, but Jeremy stopped in front of his chair, knelt down, and smiled at him kindly.

"Hello, Larry," he said softly. "G'monza."

"G'monza," Larry said again, a little drool bubbling from his lips.

"Why, thank you, Larry," Jeremy said. "I agree. It is a very good morning."

A light went on in my head. So that's what this poor, twisted little gnome was saying, "Good morning."

"This is Larry Thompson," Jeremy said. "Larry, this is my friend and assistant, Tommy Fallon."

I managed a weak smile, then moved forward gingerly and bent down near him.

"Good morning, Larry," I said.

Larry smiled at me and cocked his head to one side exactly like a dog when he's heard a noise that has caught his curiosity. It was an endearing childlike gesture, and I was flooded with a feeling of compassion for the poor, tortured man. Then he lashed out with his left foot and kicked me squarely in the nuts. The pain was like an electric bolt, and I fell backward howling. For a few seconds I could see nothing but brightly colored lights.

When I could breathe again, I became aware of Jeremy's hand on my arm as he effortlessly pulled me to my feet.

"You okay?" he asked.

"Yeah, great."

I looked back down at drooling, rocking Thompson, but his eyes had clouded over, and he looked at a fixed point somewhere just to the right of my head. It was clear that as far as he was concerned the incident had never happened.

"He's testing you. That's something you can expect the first few times," Jeremy said.

"Looks like I flunked," I groaned.

Jeremy looked down at Thompson and shook his head.

"Very naughty, Larry, Tom is a friend," Jeremy said, pulling me rubber kneed down the hall.

As I staggered along behind Jeremy, I saw a middle-aged man, graying at the temples and dressed in a handsome Italian silk suit. He paced back and forth along the hallway, taking long, elegant strides as if he were a boulevadier out on a fashionable Sunday stroll. And all the while he walked, he talked: "Yes," he said, staring at an invisible walker on his right. "You say that's where you were . . . You tell me that's what you did . . . But how can I know? How can I know for sure? How can I know, you fucking jerk? You fucking idiot? You fucking cunt? How can I know, huh?"

He flailed at the air as though he were slapping some invisible spook.

"Jesus," I said. "What's happening?"

"That's Epstein," Jeremy said. "He's having autohalluci-
nations, acting out scenes from his marriage. His wife killed
herself."

The man stopped and looked at us fiercely. I tried to meet
his gaze but felt the madness and torture in his eyes boring
through me. Then he walked toward us, taking large, heavy
steps, like a warrior about to do battle.

But when he came within inches of Jeremy, he smiled
and put out his hand: "Dr. Raines?" he said. "This is indeed
a rare pleasure."

"Yes, it is, Dr. Epstein," Jeremy said. "Allow me to introduce you to my associate, Mr. Fallon."

"Pleased to meet you Mr. Fallon," Epstein said in as civil
and polite a tone as I had ever heard.

"Likewise," I said, feeling the creepiness settling on my
shoulder like a vulture. It was all too calm, too genteel.
Then, without saying another word, Epstein turned and
walked off, resuming his argument with his nonexistent
partner.

"You bitch, you cunt. You lied to me, you lied . . ."

I looked at Jeremy and shook my head. I was fascinated
and terrified in equal portions.

We walked on and a woman in a white lab coat came to
meet us at the nurses' station, which was housed behind a
glass window, with chicken wiring inside of it.

She was about fifty-five years old, but well proportioned,
with short graying hair. She had a lined, kind face and thick
glasses with clear plastic frames.

"Dr. Hergenroeder," Jeremy said. "This is Tommy Fallon,
a roommate and writer. He's come to observe our work with
Billy McConnell."

"If he is a friend of yours, he can look on. But you mustn't
interfere in any way, Mr. Fallon."

"I won't," I said. "Thanks for having me."

She smiled curtly and turned to Jeremy as we walked into
another wing of the A-3 ward.

"Billy has been having a difficult time today," Dr. Hergenroeder said. "He hasn't moved in over a week."

Jeremy nodded, then turned to me: "Billy McConnell saw both his parents get killed in a freak boating accident out on the Chesapeake. That was over a year ago. He hasn't spoken to anyone since then. But one of these days we are going to get him to come out, I swear it."

He squeezed my arm in a comradely way and went into a room marked 302. Dr. Hergenroeder guided me into an adjoining room and turned on the lights.

"Keep your voice down," she said.

She walked to the far wall, where there was a brown muslin curtain. She pulled a sash, and the curtain opened on a one-way mirror, from which we could see into the room. Jeremy stood next to an adorable brown-haired boy of about nine. The child had fine, even features and bright green eyes. He sat supernaturally still, as though he were a wax figure. Though he was very handsome, it was obvious that he had not had enough nutrition, for there were deep circles under his eyes, and his skin had a yellowish hue.

I was struck at once by the kindness in Raines's eyes. This was no longer the smiling hustler who slashed his way through life like a pirate. He looked at the boy with such tenderness, such a depth of feeling, that I felt a lump come into my throat.

"Well, Billy my friend, how have you been? And what mischief have you been up to?"

The child did not move at all. There was not even a flicker of recognition. He sat so still that it was difficult to believe that he was real at all. Indeed, I got the eerie sensation that he was a puppet and that Raines had staged this whole thing.

I looked at Dr. Hergenroeder, who shook her head and whispered: "This is a most difficult case."

I looked back at Raines. He reached down and took the boy's limp hands tenderly in his own. He stared at him and gave a smile warm enough to sell fifty schools on his infernal cards. And yet the boy showed not the slightest response. His eyes looked like two cloudy marbles.

Then suddenly, Raines began a little dance in front of the

child—a tap dance, done surprisingly well, elegant and funky at the same time. He seemed the very essence of an old-fashioned minstrel man. And as he danced he sang a little song:

"Gimme the old soft shoe . . .
Can't cha gimme that old soft shoe?"

As I watched, tears came to my eyes. Never had I seen one human being so desperate to make contact with another. All of Jeremy Raines's powers and charms seemed to have magnified tenfold in order to bring Billy McConnell out of whatever deep and abysmal web of darkness he was lost in, and yet, this, too, failed. The boy did not make a move of any kind, and I had to turn my head.

"I see you're a sentimental man, Mr. Fallon," Dr. Hergenroeder said.

"Yeah," I said, choking back tears.

"That is not anything to be ashamed of. When I began this work thirty years ago, I would go home and cry myself to sleep every night. During my first year of residency, I nearly quit because I felt I couldn't take it, but then I realized that my own unhappiness was unimportant. The patients needed me to be strong. They needed me to care and keep on caring; that is why I stayed. And it's why your friend Mr. Raines is going to be a great psychologist someday. He has compassion and insight, and he is spiritually tough. But don't tell him I said this. Jeremy doesn't need any more praise. In case you haven't already guessed, he's the star student around here."

"Don't worry," I said. "If he got any more confident, his head would blow up."

I looked through the window. Jeremy was down on all fours, crawling in front of Billy McConnell. He made barking noises and pawed at the air, and still there was no response. Finally, he got back to his feet, dusted himself off, patted the kid on the head, and walked out of the room.

"Ah, I thought this was the day," he said as he entered the observation room. "I just had this feeling that today I would get to him, in one Zenlike swoop I'd hone in on him, and he'd snap out of it. Then I could talk to him and find out what the hell is going on in that sweet little head of his. But, of course, it's not going to be that easy."

"No," Dr. Hergenroeder, "it seldom is."

Jeremy turned to me and looked apologetic.

"I'm sorry," he said. "Look, I know you want to get back to your work. So why don't you take my car and just get the Babe to come back and pick me up in, say, three hours."

"It's okay," I said, "I'll stay if there's any way I can help."

"No," Jeremy said. "It's just going to take some new approach. You like to think that with the sheer power of your personality you can will somebody out of these things, at least get them talking, but talk therapy just doesn't work that easily. He's locked in there, and he's watching himself. It's as though one part of him is a cop, and that cop is holding the rest of Billy prisoner. Somewhere along the line he's said to himself, 'Never, never again. I never get caught feeling anything again.' What I have to do is come up with something new, a diversion, something that will catch Billy's guard *off* guard."

He paced the room and ran his fingers through his tufts of hair, like some manic Stan Laurel. I felt a flood of warmth for him. It was obvious that he was deeply serious about his patients here, and it occurred to me once again that I had judged him too quickly, made my easy little literary assumption. He wasn't a person who read books, he wasn't one of Dr. Spaulding's cognoscenti, so he must be shallow, when it was precisely the opposite. I was the one who had to deal with reality through a scrim of books and polished aesthetic dictates, whereas Raines grabbed the world by his two hands and forced it into his own likeness.

Watching him there that morning, fighting for Billy McConnell's soul, I felt a chill run down my back, and tears

134

rolled down my cheeks. Standing there helplessly, I felt something akin to love.

The rest of the day passed as if I were in a dream. I brewed a cup of coffee, found myself a cozy chair in my room and tried to lose myself in the denseness of *The Golden Bowl*, but my mind inevitably drifted off to my new friends, to my new life. I told myself to stop being melodramatic, that these were just students like myself, but it didn't feel that way to me. Val and Eddie and the Babe and especially Raines seemed almost an entirely new breed of people. I had known rebels before—drapes as they were called in Baltimore—the wild juvenile delinquents from the Harford Road and Hampden, who combed their hair in DAs and took part in chain wars and rod races, guys like Biddleman, but their rebellion was doomed to die out once they hit the work force. I always knew they would eventually replace their parents in the Baltimore working class. Likewise, at City High School, I had come to know bright middle-class rebels who were brilliantly funny and cynical, but I was separated from them by their conventional ambitions. Though this group despised, feared, and mocked the drapes, they, too, were only "going through a stage." Eventually, they would become professionals like their parents—doctors, lawyers, and dentists.

But my new friends were harder to pin down. I had tried unsuccessfully to dismiss them as mere sloppy Bohemians, but my few days on the scene didn't seem to support that case. Led by Raines, they were both practical and Bohemian at the same time. Like Raines himself, they were completely self-indulgent, wildly crazy, and yet deeply humanistic. There was something touching about all of them—something deeply hopeful and romantic in a way that I had never seen before.

I sipped my coffee and thought of Raines with Billy McConnell and then with the president of Johns Hopkins University. It was as though he were two different selves locked in a struggle in one body. The idealist versus the con man. Or perhaps, I thought, that was too simple by far. Perhaps it was the fact that Jeremy Raines believed in the American dream in a complex and energetic way. Raines seemed to believe in *both* business and art; he thought that a man could have it both ways, keep his innocence, save souls, and still be a wheeling, dealing millionaire as well.

I looked out the windows at the elm trees. My thoughts gave me a sense of fear and foreboding. I knew where these feelings came from, my own Methodist background. Practically the first church lesson I had ever learned as a child was that it was easier for a camel to go through the eye of a needle than for a rich man to get into heaven. My father had never shown the slightest material ambition and heaped disdain and mockery on the "power merchants" and "phony ad men who made a sham of American democracy." My mother's favorite stories were the ones she read in the women's magazines about miserable movie stars and unhappy rich folks in New York and Hollywood. Indeed, as I sat there in my comfortable room on that bright afternoon, it occurred to me that Raines challenged all the moral lessons I had learned as a child. Maybe the Methodist church only preached genteel poverty, because most of its parishioners were poor and moral superiority was their only balm.

And it seemed obvious to me—now that Raines and company had shaken me up enough to think about it at all— that in spite of their highly touted problems, the rich were infinitely happier than we were. A simple enough fact and obvious you might think, but not so obvious to me. Though I had mocked both my parents' pieties, I had never really questioned them deeply before. Somehow Raines had not only seen through all this pious sham, but he was actively fighting to change it on the business front, where he was about to parlay a simple idea into a fortune, and on the consciousness level as well. He wanted to reach Billy

McConnell I was sure, not just for the hell of it, but because he had a message of consciousness to impart to the lost boy—"You're not alone, and with your friends, the world can be pure joy."

I stopped and wiped off my sweating brow.

I was coming very close to bald hero worship and I knew it, and I stopped and sucked in my breath. I told myself that Raines was no great hero. He was interested most of all in his own comfort and success. Witness his card business, in which he wouldn't hesitate to lie or hustle someone in order to get over. "Keep a critical perspective," I said out loud to myself, but when I shut my eyes, I kept seeing him dancing around Billy McConnell, trying to connect with him with every cell in his body. When I fell off into a dream, I thought of someone else, too, a child who kept banging on a bathroom door, trying to reach a father who couldn't hear him because of the sound of a shower blasting out scalding steam or a toilet that never stopped flushing.

Of course, it is so easy to see it now. Raines was becoming the brother I never had, the father I never knew, but how could I know that then? No, I only knew that I was fascinated, entranced by him. He was part con, part idealist, but one-hundred-percent magician and I felt as if he'd hypnotized me after all.

I left the house around six and headed out to my parents' for dinner. I had scarcely seen them since I had moved into the house on Chateau, and I figured that I owed them a visit if for no other reason than to explain myself and assure them that things were fine.

But when I arrived, I found them both in a foul mood. My mother had overcooked the hamburgers even more than usual, until they were as black as lumps of coal. As my father and I tensely waited, she dropped one each on our plates. In both cases the burgers bounced on the cheap porcelain, sending my father into one of his familiar tirades: "Same old thing again," he said. "Burned to a crisp, Ruth."

"They aren't burned," my mother said. "They're only well done. Would you want to eat meat with worms in it?"

"I'd risk it rather than eat pure charcoal," he said.

"Tastes good to me, Mom," I said, trying to push the hard, juiceless black meat down my throat without gagging.

"Bet you don't get homecooking like this where you're living now," she said. "Wherever that is. I think it's awful that you moved out of the house and didn't even tell us where you're going. Nobody should do a thing like that to people they love."

"It's not that far, Ma," I said. "It's only down on Chateau Avenue. I'm living with some really interesting people, too."

I was about to tell them all about Jeremy, but my mother just shook her head and did her "despair eyes" at me.

"You remember Mr. and Mrs. Hargrove from Northwood Appold church, hon?" she asked.

"Yes," I said, though I barely did recall them.

"Well, all their lives they wanted to go to Africa, though I don't know why," my mother said.

"Probably because Mr. Hargrove was such a great liberal," my father said.

"Don't start that now," my mother said. "Besides, you're a liberal yourself, so you don't have to pretend you're a racist just to annoy me."

I smiled at that one. My mother was easily as complex a person as my father. She saw through his childish, attention-getting ploys beautifully, though she had similar ones herself. He would pretend to be a Baltimore racist (like many of the real racists on the block). It made him feel somehow less alienated from the rest of the neighborhood, and she would pretend to be folksy and "simple," though nothing could have been farther from the truth.

"So what happened to the Hargroves in Africa?" I said.

"Oh, they had a wonderful time at first, hon," my mother said. "They went out in the bushes with the natives and saw ceremonial native dances, and Mrs. Hargrove said they drank some kind of guava juice out of a native gourd, and they sat by the fire and they took an airplane ride over the veld and saw great herds of lions."

"That's *prides* of lions," my father said in an exasperated tone. "Not herds, for Godssake."

"Well, excuse me, Mr. National Geographic," my mother said. "And then they went out on a safari. Can you imagine the Hargroves on a safari? I mean Mr. Hargrove who works repairing washing machines over at Bendix out on the Joppa Road wearing a pith helmet? Have you ever heard of anything like that before?"

"Pass the peas," my father said, shooting us his I Can Barely Stand Anymore of This Ignorance expression.

"Anyway, they're having a great old time but Mrs. Hargrove was very, very nervous, you know out there in the bushes."

"Jesus God, Ruth," my father said. "Bush, not bushes."

"Do not take the Lord's name in vain in this house in front of your only son," my mother said.

My father sighed and stared down at his plate. Tension leaked from him like radioactivity from a hot canister.

"Anyway," my mother said, "Finally, finally just when Mrs. Hargrove is starting to relax and enjoy herself, they go out to shoot the lions, which I think is awful and wrong, but they go out there with guides and they get near this clump of bushes and the guide goes into the clump and Mr. Hargrove has his gun and follows him in, and they tell Mrs. Hargrove to wait by the jeep, and suddenly she hears a terrible, ominous growl, and then all of a sudden a couple of shots and a scream, and she walks toward the bush and somebody tries to pull her back, and the lion comes falling from the bush dead. But in his mouth is Mr. Hargrove's arm."

"Ah, Jesus," my father said. "Rather eat Hargrove's arm than this goddamned charburger."

"Do not take the Lord's name in vain," my mother said again.

"Not his arm?" I said, astonished. "You're kidding?"

"I only wish I was, hon," my mother said. "I only wish I was. It was his arm all right, cause the wrist had his Timex on it."

"Takes a licking and keeps on ticking," my father said.

I laughed at that, but my mother was holding her head and shaking it sorrowfully.

"He died right there, hon. Mr. Hargrove, who I have known for thirty years, from bake sales uppa church, eaten up by a lion on safari. You see the terrible things that can happen to a person when they leave their home and go off traipsing around the world."

"Ahhhh," I said, giving up on the hideous black burger, "now I see the moral of this sad tale. I go off and get a new home and I end up eaten by lions. Is that it?"

"Well, I don't know why you have to leave anyway," my mother said. "You have a perfectly good room right here."

"Mom," I said, "for God's sake, I just need a little room to breathe. Besides, I'm not that far away. Just down in the old neighborhood on Chateau Avenue. And I'm living with really good people, especially this one guy, Jeremy Raines. He works with mental patients over at Larson-Payne."

"That's a rich person's *private* hospital," my father said, obsessively stirring his iced tea. "People like us don't have time for nervous breakdowns."

I felt my throat tighten. My father had many voices, many selves, and this one was one of the most familiar to me, the bitter populist.

"I was over there just today with Jeremy, Dad. I saw people with really bad problems, and Jeremy is trying to help them."

"A lot of rich people end up in asylums, hon," my mother said as she passed me the stewed tomatoes. "Just proves that money doesn't make a person happy. I remember when Mamie Eisenhower was in that place. That was when Ike was still president and she got to drinking something awful."

"Gee, poor Mamie," my father said sarcastically as

140

he looked with distaste down at his burned meat and mayonnaise-drenched cole slaw.

"Well, I think she was a nice lady," my mother said. "She just didn't want to be a first lady. Sitting around and waiting for her husband to give speeches all a time. No wonder she took to drink."

"Ruth, you kill me," my father said. "She *loved* being first lady, doing her brave little Mamie routine while he played the great general. Meanwhile, the two of them together had the combined I.Q. of a flatworm."

"Always say something nasty if you can't think of anything original to say, hon. That's his motto," my mother said, looking down at her plate.

"Yes," said my father, "and you should certainly know, master of invective and sarcasm that you are."

"Oh, well," my mother said. "Why don't you just go into the bathroom and spend the whole night washing your pathetic little body?"

She stood up and threw down her apron on the chair and, to my surprise, walked out of the kitchen. My father's mouth dropped at this. This kind of self-righteous exit was usually his meat.

"Where do you think you're going?" he said.

My mother popped her head back in the dining room. She had a scarf on her head.

"I am getting dressed, and then I'm going to wood-carving class," she said. "You have fun sitting around and feeling sorry for yourself."

With that said, she disappeared and I heard her clomp across the living room floor and slam the door to her bedroom.

My father sighed heavily.

"I'm going to have a sign put over the door of this house," he said.

"I know," I said, "and it's going to read 'House of Pain.' "

That was his favorite expression; he'd gotten it from an old H. G. Wells story, *The Island of Dr. Moreau*. And though he said it now with obvious bitterness, just hearing the words sent a small shiver of tenderness to my heart. There had been a time, a time that seemed part of another century now, when he had read the old ghost and horror stories to me. I remember him sitting on the edge of my bed; when he read to me he became another person entirely—not the neurotic, obsessive ranter who lived in the bathroom, but calm, focused, whole. His favorite writer was H. G. Wells, and he had often read *The Island of Dr. Moreau* to me, the story about a mad doctor who hides on his own lost island and turns animals into humans. His laboratory was called the House of Pain, and it was there that the revolting animals killed him in an orgy of revenge at the story's end. For a long time, when we were happy, my father had made a joke about his bathroom being the House of Pain. Indeed, it was our own little private joke, for he would often go into the "House" and then, when I was nearly asleep in my bedroom next door, he would emerge, a towel wrapped around his head, and push my door open, which made me scream in terror. Then he would walk stiff armed toward my bed, reciting in a brutish monotone Claude Raines's soliloquy from the movie version of his other favorite Well's story, *The Invisible Man*. "All right you fools," he would say, as he came ever closer, walking stiff and zombielike toward the bed, "you're dying to know who I am, aren't you? Never giving me any rest, prying and peeking into keyholes . . ." "No, Dad," I would scream, half-afraid and half-ecstatic, "don't . . . no!" But that only encouraged him further. "You want to know who I am, do you?" he would say, unwrapping the towel. "Well, I'll show you who I am!!!" With that he would give a wild and cruel laugh—a perfect imitation of old Claude himself—and then grab me, tickling me wildly, causing me to scream in fear and joy. Oh, Lord, how I looked forward to those attacks, the one strange way we were like father and son. But that was long ago, before he had become a bureaucratic drone, pissed off at the world and especially his ball and chain, Mother and myself. Now our home really was the House of Pain. It was no joke at all, and I suddenly felt such a stab of loss and such a blazing fury of anger toward him for throwing me away that I had to push myself away from the table before I went into my own bitter tirade.

"Wiseguy," my father said as I left the room. "Thinks he's heard it all."

I started to go into my old room, just to lie on the bed and try to calm my aching heart when my mother came out of her bedroom and signaled to me to come outside. She put her index finger over her mouth, and I followed her to the front porch, amazed that she had dressed up in her fancy Sunday clothes, a blue dress with pleats and a Peter Pan collar and her black leather pumps.

Once outside, she began whispering to me: "Can you give me a ride downtown, hon?"

"I guess . . ." I said. (I had borrowed Val's Volkswagen, which sat in the driveway.) "But where are you going?"

"It's a secret. I'll tell you onna way. But I don't want your father to find out. So you just pull out and I'll start walking uppa street toward the bus stop, then you can pick me up."

"That seems silly, Ma," I said. "You can just get in the car here."

"But what if he sees?"

She actually looked frightened, and under her makeup, she was blushing.

"Who the hell cares?" I said. "You're a grown woman. You can do whatever the hell you want."

"Okay, hon," she said. "Let's go then."

She hurried off the porch, looking back furtively to see if he was watching, and I followed quickly behind her and opened the door for her, and a second later we were headed down Burke Avenue.

Okay," I said, as we drove down Charles Street, under the beautiful oaks and elms, past the homes of the rich. "Why don't you tell me what you're up to?"

"Well, hon," she said. "Remember the Miss Kissable Lips contest? Offa' radio? Well, you won't belief it but Johnny Apollo has chosen my lips as one of the finalists inna contest. And they're gonna have the Big Kissoff tonight down the radio station."

I scarcely knew what to say.

"That's great," I finally came out with, though I didn't sound very convincing. "So that's where I'm taking you, down to the radio station?"

"That's right, hon, and the winner gets all kinds of prizes."

She smiled at me with such innocence, such sweetness, that I reached across the seat and held her hand.

"Of course, I know you think I'm silly," she said under her breath. "An old fat lady like me."

"No," I said, "I don't think so at all. And don't call yourself names like that."

"But it's true, hon," she said. "Back when I met your father, I was real pretty though. At least all the boys at the dances used to think so. They all wanted to dance with me up at St. Ann's, hon. We would go round and round . . . there was Herbert and there was Larry Johnson, and there was Edward . . . he became a missionary and went all over the world. You know he even asked me to marry him once."

"Why didn't you?" I said, feeling choked up, almost unable to speak.

"Because I met your father," my mother said, taking out her lipstick and applying it gingerly to her lips.

"He was so much brighter than the other boys and better looking, too. He seemed sophisticated, the way he talked about the world. He read books, and he understood politics. I was just a neighborhood girl. I didn't know anyone who could talk like that. Of course he got it all from Gracie, your grandmother, and when I met her, I thought she was the most wonderful person in the world."

"She was," I said.

"There was only one difference between them. I mean they were both smart, but Gracie had love in her heart. I know you think it's corny, Mr. College Boy, but it was true nonetheless. Your father uses his intelligence to lash out at the world, at everyone around him, but with your grandmother, she mixed it with love, so it was like everyone could share in her brains. She made us all feel smarter and happier just being around her."

I nodded my head and tried to catch my breath. There was a pain so deep inside me that I wanted to take a knife and gouge it out.

"I don't think it's stupid, Mother," I said. "I don't think you're stupid either. I want you to know that. I don't care what he says, you understand. I don't think you're stupid at all."

My mother shook her head and patted my hand.

"I'm not very bright," she said. "Not like your father. But I know a few things they don't teach you in books."

She looked at me and smiled then. How to describe that smile? It was as though it came from beneath the skin, a smile that was filled with maturity, wisdom, as if her real self had burst from under the endless masks she felt she must wear, the dumb girl, the neighborhood girl, Miss Helpless.

And I thought, she really is smart. She really is a wonderful woman and what in God's name is she doing going to the Miss Kissable Lips contest?

"Ma," I said. "You sure you want to go through with this?"

"I know it's stupid, hon," she said, falling back into her helpless voice. "I know it's silly, but I just wanta see if I have a chance."

"Okay, Ma," I said, leaning over and kissing her on the cheek. "Sure."

The parking lot at WOAX radio was jammed with cars and Mother gripped the armrest as we found a space.

"I know it's silly," she said for about the tenth time. "But I just think it'll be fun. You don't have to come in . . ."

"Are you kidding?" I said. "I wouldn't miss this for the world."

We hurried across the windblown parking lot. Old Baltimore Sun papers wrapped themselves like snakes around my mother's leg, and she reached down and cast them off with a furious motion, and it occurred to me then, she really wants this, she wants to be Miss Kissable Lips. I thought of that shy, sweet girl at her Methodist's dance party, where she was popular, and of all the intervening years putting up with my father's madness, and, yes, I knew that this was pathetic, absurd, but by God, I wanted it for her, too.

But when we got inside, my heart sank.

There were five other contestants—five young girls, either in their late teens or early twenties—and they were dressed to kill, tight skirts, push-out bras, and tighter sweaters. My mother looked around, then turned and looked at me, and I started to say, "Ma, come on. You don't need this." But she only gave me a brave little smile and sat down, while the five girls stared at her and traded condescending looks.

I felt a panic coursing through my stomach. God, she was going to be humiliated and she knew it, but she wasn't going to chicken out. No, she'd stay until the bitter end, when sleazebag Johnny Apollo gave the award to one of the young beauties.

I slumped down in a chair near her while a curly-haired woman made her little announcement in a voice that sounded as though it came from a carnival Cupie Doll: "We are certainly glad to have each and every one of you, the final finalists in the Miss Kissable Lips contest, with us at the studio! Our master of ceremonies, Johnny Apollo, will see you all very soon. Meanwhile, you'll see on that big table to your right a box filled with special Kissable Lips blotting paper. Now, I want you all to blot your lips and drop them into the Miss Kissable Lips box. I will take it away and Johnny will look at your lips for one last time and then make his announcement. One of you will then become Miss Kissable Lips!"

The young girls twittered and shifted in their seats, and one of them, a sexy blonde with a poodle on her pink sweater, looked over at me with a certain malicious confidence in her eyes.

Slowly, each of the girls got up, walked toward the table, and began blotting their lips.

I looked at my mother. She was gripping the chair arms as if she were on a rocket ride at Gwyn Oak Amusement Park. How she wanted this!

I felt the tension building in me and something else, a kind of fury, which caught me completely by surprise. All of her life she had been cheated, robbed of her rightful share of joy and happiness. She hadn't always been a worry wart, a party-killing nag. My grandmother had told me that when my mother was young, she really was the life of the party. I remembered something my aunt had told me before she died. "Tommy," she said, "If your mother had had an education, she could have been a writer, because she is a natural-born storyteller. It's just a shame she has so little confidence." And I began to feel a kind of nausea, for I knew that of course she wouldn't win, that once more she would go home in defeat.

Then I thought of Raines—I don't know why—but his voice popped into my head. It was as though he were communing with me from across town, and I heard him say: "Don't just sit here, my boy. Kick some ass!"

The voice was so clear that it startled me. I got up out of my seat and walked out of the room.

Outside, I found myself in a hallway, and I looked down at the studio adjacent to the room with the contestants. I walked quickly down the hall and went inside.

The room was dark, except for one small light in the back. There, sitting alone, was a small middle-aged man in a maroon velour shirt, tight black leather pants, and ankle-high black Beatle boots. I recognized him at once as Johnny Apollo, for his picture had been featured on dance posters on billboards and telephone poles all over the city.

I walked toward him and saw the curly-headed woman leaving by a side door. It was just the two of us. Now was my chance, but what could I do?

And then, like in the old Mandrake the Magician comics, it was as though I was no longer in the real world, but in some swirling fog, and I clearly heard Raines's voice inside my head. It wasn't a matter of me thinking "here's what Raines would do." No, it felt as though he had literally taken over my body, my mind, my speech, and he was saying to me, "Listen Tommy, there are no rules except what we make. Everybody who has ever gotten anything knows that. So what are you waiting for, a miracle?" His voice was so clear inside my head that I felt startled and even turned around to see if somehow he had magically entered the room behind me. But there was no one else there. Then it was as if Raines himself were reaching into my pocket, pulling out a comb, and combing my hair straight back on my head, like a Harford Road Hot Shoppe Drape. I shrugged my shoulders a couple of times and walked slowly and with a certain measured bad-assed dignity toward Johnny Apollo, who slumped in a canvas director's chair, with his short little legs up on a radiator. He was older than I had suspected, about thirty-five, and he was already losing his greasy black hair, which he attempted to hide by parting it from ear to ear. He had spent too much time in the sun, and his face was creased like a shrunken walnut. Then I saw what he was up to, looking through the darkened one-way mirror, as the Miss Kissable Lips contestants finished blotting their lips on the paper and deposited them in the tin-foil-covered box.

I must have startled him, for he jerked back in his seat, nearly tipping himself over. I stared down hard at him.

"Who the hell are you?" he said.

"My name is Eddie Moriarity," I said. This was not my voice and not Raines's voice either, but the husky, raspy voice of a hundred gangsters from a hundred tough-guy movies. Inside me there was another little voice screaming to get out, the Mr. Panic Voice, who was saying "What in the fuck are you doing, Tom? You're going to get thrown in jail. Your mother will die of embarrassment." But it was a voice I couldn't use, so I ignored it.

"So what's that to me?" Johnny Apollo said. "I mean what are you doing in my studio, kid?"

"Just visiting, pal," I said. "You see I brought my aunt down here today. That's her right there through the glass, the rather big, mature lady in the blue dress. She's a finalist in the Miss Kissable Lips contest."

His face kind of relaxed after that.

"So you brought her down. That's very nice of you, kid. Now why don't you go back in there and wait with her, 'cause I'll be announcing the winners real soon."

"I don't think you understand, Johnny," I said. "I want my aunt to win the contest."

That stopped him cold. He looked up at me in complete astonishment.

"You're putting me on," he said.

"No, sir," I said. "And there's some other people who would very much like her to win, too, like Bobby Murphy, maybe you heard about him. He runs the gang down in the Tenth Ward called the Shamrocks. You see that lady, Ruth Fallon, she's Bobby's second aunt. She practically raised him, you unnerstan me?"

Johnny Apollo looked as though I had put an axe through the middle of his head. He swung out of the chair and started toward me.

149

"You little Irish fuck," he said. "You think you can come in here and fucking intimidate me?"

I felt a sudden desire to piss in my pants. How had I ever gotten into this? Then, I swear, it was as if Raines took over the show.

I reached down to my left. There was a turntable there, and with one quick swoop I pushed it off the edge of the table onto the floor. It smashed on the tile and the arm dangled off and quivered a little.

"What the fuck are you doing?" the little man said.

"I'm real sorry," I said. "That was very, very clumsy of me. But things like that happen all the time when I get mad. I mean I seem to lose control of my fucking muscles or something and everything around me gets all fucked up. Weird, huh?"

He started to say something else, but suddenly there was fear in his eyes.

"The Shamrocks, huh?" he said.

"Uh-huh," I said. "That is correct. Bobby Murphy sent me personally. He also told me to tell you he is your biggest fan, and the Shamrocks are gonna make a sizeable contribution to your Mercy Hospital fund later this year. Just remember her name, Ruth Fallon."

I turned and walked out then as cool as any movie idol. It wasn't until I got out into the hall that I started shaking. I found the men's room just down the hall, went inside, and shut the stall.

My arms and legs were literally trembling, and I felt like I was going to puke. So I held my head over the toilet bowl, but then a strange thing happened. I didn't get sick. No, I didn't feel sick at all, but something else, something akin to sex, swept through me and I shut my eyes and I saw that huge mouth that I'd seen in the dream only nights before and I felt strong and powerful and there was a kind of wild electricity zapping through my veins. Only this time I wasn't afraid, not at all, and I saw little pathetic Tommy —Little-Terrified-Waiting-by-the-Bathroom-Door Tommy— fall away, like a snake shedding his skin, and instead there

THE KING OF CARDS

was somebody else there, somebody young and strong and
unafraid and ready to meet the hustling, lying, conniving
world on its own terms, and I began to laugh—Oh, God, I
laughed—tears ran down my face as I stood in that bathroom stall, because I suddenly understood what I had done.
I had used Raines's voice and style to give myself courage.
But it really was me and only me who had just pulled off
that outrageous hoax.

For a second I felt guilty for using my old friendship with
bad Bobby Murphy to terrify Johnny Apollo, but then I
realized that Bobby would have loved it. Besides, he owed
me one. Bobby and I had met a long time ago in Govans,
on Winston Avenue, just a block away from our house at
Chateau. He was already a legendary battler in the neighborhood, famous for taking on three hardasses from Hampden at Ameche's one night and sending two of them to the
hospital (the third showed some uncommon good sense,
leapt into his 1949 Ford and got the hell out of there). At
the time, however, I was better friends with his younger
brother Terry. What endeared me to the Murphys was that
I had once "saved" Terry from being thrown down a sewer
by three ducktailed bullies in a Waverly gang called the Four
Aces. (This was not bravery on the Murphy scale. They had
jumped us outside of Govans Bowling Alley, and when a
lizard-faced boy named Minsner had tried to grab Terry, I
kicked him in the shins, grabbed Terry, and made a run for
it. The Aces had nearly caught us, but we lost them in the
Govans woods behind our houses, a woods completely gone
now, covered over with more redbrick row houses.) That
small piece of bravery, bravery I'd almost forgotten, made
Murphy a friend of mine for life. Even though we had long
ago gone down different paths, I would see him now and
again in Baltimore Street corner bars and he would come
over and hug me and say: "Tommy, you ever need anything, you know where to come. And fuck the Wops, huh?"

I leaned on the bathroom door so long, lost in a thousand
reveries of my past, a past I had almost stomped out in my
headlong rush to become an aristocratic little scholar. Sud-

denly, I looked around at the toilet stall and laughed out loud. It struck me that I was having all these thoughts in the goddamned bathroom, the place where my father escaped the narrow, claustrophobic realities of his life. But for me, on this day, the old tile Mecca had become the Room of Recognition, the place where I understood my deepest strengths came from the past I had tried so hard to repress. The thought excited me, made me want to race home and start writing in my journal, but then I suddenly panicked thinking that Johnny Apollo might not have fallen for my little sham after all. Christ, he could right this second have the cops coming down on me and my mother, and I thought of my father's fury if he had to bail me out of jail.

So I crept out of the bathroom and down the hall, and I looked through a little square window in the big studio door and tears came to my eyes. For there, in the studio, black leather-suited Johnny Apollo was presenting my mother with the big silver Fun Box. The look on her face was worth ten thousand dollars, there were tears of joy rolling down her cheeks, while the young girls looked shocked in total disbelief (two of them were crying quietly), and I opened the door and went inside.

She saw me and smiled and called me over. She said, "Mr. Apollo, this is my . . ."

I cut her off then and looked coldly into the slimy little DJ's eyes: "Johnny, I'm your biggest fan," I said.

He looked at me as if he wanted to tear my throat out, but I merely smiled, looked at my mother, and said: "You won! That's terrific. But then I always knew you had the most kissable lips. I mean it was obvious, huh, Mr. Apollo?"

"Yeah, obvious," he said, staring holes through me.

"Well, this is truly terrific. So show me your prizes, Ruth!"

That set her back a little. We were not the kind of family that called each other by our first names.

"Oh, they're wonderful," she said. "I got this beautiful costume jewelry."

She held up a pair of vintage earrings and modeled them

a little. They were gold and orange half-moons, cheap junk, but they didn't look bad on her.

"And I got a year's subscription to *Good Housekeeping* and *Photoplay*—you know I love to read both of those—and I got some wonderful new lipsticks, pink, just like Jackie Kennedy, hon, and a gift certificate to Ameche's Drive-In—isn't that great—and, best of all, theatre tickets to the Lyric to see two shows. It's just wonderful, hon. I really want to thank you, Mr. Apollo."

She threw her arms around the little sleazebag, and though he looked as though he wanted to run, he squeezed her back, while Miss Curley Hair took pictures. I laughed out loud and said in as "street" a voice as I could muster, "Hey, you've done the right thing, Mr. Apollo. She's a very happy lady!" Then I watched my mother show all the other "girls" the rest of her prizes. They all tried to be good sports, but you could tell they were dying inside.

A few minutes later Johnny accompanied my mother and myself down the long gray hallway toward the windblown, wet parking lot. My mother walked a few feet ahead of us, chatting in an excited voice with Miss Curly Top. Johnny leaned in next to me, and I could smell whiskey on his breath.

"You tell Murphy I want a really big contribution this year for this," he said. "I'm fucking serious."

"Don't worry, John," I said, "The Shamrocks never forget a friend."

When we left, I gave him a Judas hug, just like Cagney in *Public Enemy*. My mother cried with joy all the way home.

All my life I have used melodrama, action, wildness to protect me from the brutal facts. High Doctors of the Mind I have known call it acting out, and maybe it's true. But I prefer to think of it as a creative battling against the odds, finding some kind of victory in the midst of the hard, shitty facts. All I know is that day I conned Johnny Apollo into giving my mother the Miss Kissable Lips award, I felt good for hours. After I dropped my mother off, I rode around town higher than I could be from twenty tokes of gold hash, reliving the crazy moment when I tapped into my old rough self, a self that I had nearly forgotten. As I prowled the streets, it occurred to me that whatever good things studying with Dr. Spaulding had done for me—and there were many to be sure—that I had somehow paid too high a price. School had made me feel ashamed of my old friends like the Murphys, boys I had loved since I was five years old. Now I was an apprentice aesthete, and what contact did I have with my old buddies? None. Oh, I dropped in at the Hollow Bar now and again to see Murph and the old boys, but the gulf was too wide between us now. The old boys hadn't gone to college; though Bobby was brilliant, he had barely finished City. His attitude had once fiercely been my own. College was for "pinheads," "fairies," and though I disliked his anti-intellectualism, his willed stupidity (the same kind of willed stupidity that my mother and much of the city practiced), now I thought about it all again, thought about it all in light of Raines and the house on Chateau Avenue.

Of course, the Murphy family had long ago moved out of our old neighborhood; they'd fled to the suburbs with all the rest of the Irish. Now Bobby made headlines for his gambling hustles, his series of restaurants that were reputedly just fronts for money-laundering operations. He was, I suppose, merely a thug. Still, when I thought of him I felt a deep tenderness and respect, and as I drove the streets I saw now that moving in to the house at Chateau had put me in touch with some spirit of community, of real neighbors and a real neighborhood that we had lost when we moved near Calvert. Hell, out there, no one spoke to their neighbors, much less watched out for them, and as I drove moodily through the dark streets of Rodgers Forge, I thought that it wasn't any accident that my parents had become even more estranged in the country. Yes, my father was embittered from giving up his art and by the terrible obsessions with his body and cleanliness, but it seemed to me now, all those obsessions grew wilder and faster, like some vicious cancer, in the isolation of the suburbs.

I stopped in front of an Amy Joy doughnut shop and looked inside at the blue neon, the trays of surreal doughnuts, and one lone gray-clad state trooper who leaned wearily over his coffee cup, and I remembered how it was in Govans after the war, the bustling streets, young mothers in flower-print dresses, their hair pulled back with safety pins, and guys in striped polo shirts walking down the block with baseball bats and gloves taking their kids to the parks to shag flies. At twilight everyone was out on the corner of Winston and Craig Avenue, in front of Pop's Grocery Store, listening to the old International League Orioles, muscular, bald, Mr. Bond kidding dark-skinned Mr. Mitchell about his new Indian motorcycle, and Mr. Mitchell taking all of us kids for fast rides around the block. And the girls, girls like beautiful Ruth Anne Muir who smiled and flirted with the older boys, while we younger kids sat under a mulberry tree playing marbles in old man Snyder's front yard. And Danny Snyder would buy a Nehi soda, and Eddie Richardson would put three blue gumballs in it and take the soda cap off the bottle and take out the cork with a penknife and use it to backup the bottle top as he put it in his felt-crown cap. Then we'd shake the soda up and fizz it all over one of the kids, and they would scream and fizz it back, and everybody laughed, and old man Snyder, in his undershirt and with his black lung cough (he'd emigrated from the coal mines of West Virginia), would get out a garden hose and bucktoothed, but kind Mrs. Snyder would squirt all of us kids and we would run around in that artificial rain, me and the Murphys and the Snyder boys, and it was like we were all one person or so it seemed, all one person, in one sweet little redbrick neighborhood in dear old Baltimore. And as the summer sun went down and a little cool breeze came sifting through the honeysuckle vine, even my disappointed father seemed happy. He'd walk with my mother down to the corner store and look at us and smile and say, "Just like young savages, aren't they, honey?" but there was pride and love in his voice, and my mother would lean into his arms and he would hold her, and I would see them watching me and feel such pride that it made me want to burst inside. It was as though I was truly home and I wanted it to stay that way (and thought it would) forever.

But now . . . now . . . our house was truly a House of Pain, and only this new house, the house on Chateau, felt alive to me. I had found friends, other outlaws who were heading out for some strange new world, but who were also, in their own wiggy way, taking the best of the old world, too, or at least I hoped they were. Yes, Raines reminded me in his own way of Bobby Murphy. He was smarter than Bobby, and he hadn't fallen prey to the Baltimore curse of hating anyone who didn't come from your neighborhood, but unlike the academics, he hadn't cut himself off from the real world, like (and even thinking this, I felt like a criminal, a betrayer, an ingrate) Dr. Spaulding.

As soon as I had those thoughts, I was tortured. I had to be careful and I dimly knew it. I did love books, I did love reading, discussing them, and I couldn't throw the baby out with the bathwater, but I had to know my own world, the world of down and dirty Baltimore. It occurred to me that night as I finally circled back toward Chateau Avenue that I couldn't "transcend Baltimore" (as Dr. Spaulding always preached we must), but rather I would have to love it, as Raines truly loved it, love it for all its brashness, its stupidity, its down-home friendliness, its crab cakes, its marble stoops, its fat women in muumuus saying, "Hiya, hon . . . How bout Johnny U., in't he the greatest?" Yes, I had to embrace it all if I were ever going to write about it well, and more importantly than that, I would have to love it if I was ever going to really be a man.

THE KING OF CARDS

I roamed around for three or four hours and didn't get back to Chateau Avenue until after ten o'clock. The place was quiet, and when I walked up the dusty Victorian steps to the second floor, I saw that Jeremy's door was closed. From inside, I could hear the sound of John Coltrane playing "My Favorite Things." Raines played that song night and day now. I started to rap on the door, but then I heard a low giggling coming from inside, the sound of Sister Lulu Hardwell's voice saying, "Jeremy . . . Jeremy . . . baby . . ." and I just smiled and moved on down the hall. It was good to be home. I had grown to love everything about the old house, the scarred furniture, the ridiculous barber chair, the musty smell of dustballs. It was all funky and Bohemian, and I told myself as I crept down the hall that I would never live any other way. Still, I worried a little about Lulu and Jeremy's relationship. What if she really fell for Jeremy? He surely didn't take her seriously, but it was possible on her side, all too possible it seemed to me. And on the more practical level, what if Dan the Trucker showed up again after finding out Jeremy had lied to him? That seemed more than a little likely. Good God, half the time we didn't even bother locking the front door. What if the lunatic decided to storm the house with his nice little crowbar? I decided I would have to mention something about this to Jeremy first thing in the morning.

But meanwhile, I badly needed sleep. I was deeply exhausted. Nothing takes it out of you more than reinventing yourself on a daily basis, and I half staggered to my door and pushed it open, longing for my bed.

But my room wasn't empty. It was pitch dark except for one candle and the exotic smell of incense. And there in my bed was Val sitting stark naked, holding a book of poems by William Carlos Williams.

157

I felt my heart pump wildly. God, she was as beautiful as some romantic cliche. Her skin *was* literally like alabaster, her breasts were so perfectly shaped, her mouth was a bow of desire and playfulness. The red hair that framed her face looked like an arc of fire and her red pubic hair made an enticing V to her perfect, muscular thighs.

"I thought you'd never get here," she said in a purr.

"Val?" I said. I wanted to add something else, something suave and hip and memorable, but my lips couldn't form any words. I moved to the bed quickly, shedding clothes on the floor, and then I was there with her, holding her, kissing her face, rubbing my hands across her perfect back, and I wanted to cry out I was so happy. I kissed her nipples and put my finger into her satiny cunt. Lord, let it stay like this forever and ever, and then I started to penetrate her, but she pulled away: "I have this little problem," she said. "I should have told you the other night."

"What is it?" I said. Though I hated myself for feeling this way, images of Greek sailors swarmed through my mind.

"Well," she said, nuzzling next to me. "The problem is I like you a lot. I really like you. I don't usually like to fuck guys I like this much. It leads to tragedy and pain and heartbreak and crying jags and broken records."

I rubbed my fingers through her hair and laughed. I had no idea what to say, how to handle this, or at least, the old Tommy (of, say, a week ago) wouldn't have, but having won the Miss Kissable Lips contest for my mother, it seemed easier to deal with the whole problem by becoming someone else again. I smiled and stroked an imaginary black moustache.

"You wish I was Greek sailor named Nikos?" I asked in some kind of terrible Zorba the Greek accent. "Okay, I be Nikos. I so glad you here to velcome me to your country. Thank you so much. Now how bout sex, American wild thing?"

"You're terrible. You act like a scholar, but underneath you're like all the rest. You only want pussy."

THE KING OF CARDS

"Nikos cannot help self," I said. "Nikos is peasant. Peasant love only to dance and drink Retsina and eat pussy."

"You're a horrible man," she said. But she was laughing.

"You laugh, Nikos laugh. You dance, Nikos dance, too." I leaped up on the bed and started to dance. My cock and balls sprang around doing their own folk dance.

Val laughed wildly and leaped on the bed with me. We held hands and jumped up and down and yelled, "Hayo, hayo, hayo," like cornball Hollywood Greeks.

"Nikos love you."

"Val love Nikos," she said.

Then we screamed and threw each other down on the bed and started fucking like Greek gods.

"I do love you," she said as I went inside her. "That is the problem."

"No problem for Nikos," I said.

She shut her legs and pulled her ass and perfect moist pussy away from me.

"Don't be Nikos," she said like a little girl. "Be Tommy."

"But you don't like Tommy," I said. "He pipe-smoking liberal. He like T. S. Eliot. He a drag. I be Nikos. We dive for clams."

"No," she said, putting her hand under my chin and pushing my head up. "Nikos is an idiot. I want Tommy back. I demand Tommy, and I'll only give my throbbing wet cunt to Tommy."

"Tommy here, Miss Lane," I said, smiling at her like innocent sweet Jimmie Olson.

"Be Superman, and fuck me until I cry," she said.

"Golly, yes, ma'am," I said. Then I put on my cape and bit her lip until blood came, and we fucked in lust in love, and I was dead gone, gone, gone . . . Oh, Lord, sweet Miss Val Jackson.

159

In the morning I propped my head up on one elbow and stared at her sleeping. Long-lashed, pug-nosed, she looked like a veritable angel. I kissed her gently on the eyes, and she smiled and curled closer to me.

"My own poetic angel," I said. Then I thought of her screwing Nikos down by the docks. I pushed that thought from my mind. I was a bona fide Bohemian now. I had left the safe straight world forever, and in this new life people were braver, which is what I wanted, and yet the very thought that this perfect being, this saint, could be down on the docks with some Greek sailor. . . .

No, I would not let myself think it. I was going to be a new, improved Tommy, yes, yes, I was going to love sex and love the fact that she had had sex. I was going to purge myself of all Father Knows Best, Doris Day, *Good House-keeping*, "Leave It to Beaver," Methodist Girl Next Door fantasies.

I patted her sweet head. I kissed her eyes again.

Only a fool questions good luck on this order. Only an idiot ruins a good thing.

I put one innocent arm around her shoulders and with my other hand reached in between her legs. Oh, Lord, the softness, the wetness. I felt my cock harden, and I rolled over on top of her. She put her arms around me and began to lift her perfect flat stomach up toward me.

Then I heard a crash and a scream and what sounded like a gunshot.

I leapt from the bed. Val's eyes opened in blue panic.

"What the hell?"

"It came from Jeremy's room!"

We both leapt from the bed and found our tangled clothes lying in great heaps on the floor. Then, still half-dressed, we raced from the room and down the dark hallway toward

Jeremy's. My mind was filled with a bloody tableau. Dan standing with a smoking gun over the bloody fallen body of my friend. Seconds later as we got into the hall, we heard another shot, and I pulled Val back and leaned on the door, my heart beating wildly. It slowly opened and I looked inside. Jeremy was sitting in his bed, naked to the waist, but at the foot of the bed stood a man whose back was to me.

"You are gonna die, Raines," the man said. "You are gonna fucking die for *this!!!*"

He held up his right arm, and I gasped audibly as I looked at a stump where the desperate man's hand should have been. The man heard my shocked gasp and turned quickly before I could make a move. When I saw his face, I gasped again.

The crazed, stump-armed man was not Trucker Dan after all, but none other than our friend Eddie Eckel.

"Come in here you two. You are going to be witness to a murder!"

I did what I was told, my heart quaking. Val moved slowly in behind me. No one had ever held a gun on me before, and I was no Philip Marlowe. I remember my back muscles tightening in a spasm and a cold sweat breaking out on my chest.

"Now, Eddie," I said in a surprisingly calm voice, "it seems there's been some misunderstanding. We're all good friends here."

"No!" Eddie screamed. "That's history! Do you see this stump? Do you?"

I could have scarcely missed it. He had put the terrifying thing right in my face and was running it back and forth under my nose.

"Do you know how I got this? Do you?"

He was screaming very loudly now.

"No," I said. "No, I do not know."

Jeremy moved a little on the bed, and Eddie turned and waved the gun menacingly at him. Then he pulled the trigger and the gun roared.

"No!" Val screamed.

"Jesus Christ," I said.

Jeremy fell backward and didn't move.

"Oh, Christ, you've shot him!" Val screamed. "Oh, Jesus . . ."

"No, I haven't. Get up you son of a bitch."

Slowly, Jeremy sat up. Then I saw that the bullet had lodged in the wall to the right of the bed.

"No, I haven't shot him yet," Eddie said, grimacing like a madman. "But I am going to. I am going to shoot him piece by fucking piece for what he did to me, man."

"What did he do?" I said, my knees knocking together.

Now Jeremy spoke for the first time. And he seemed calm, even bemused by the whole thing. Indeed, I don't know what shocked me more—Eddie's gun or Jeremy's reaction to it.

"He has a case, I'm afraid, Tom," Jeremy said in an amiable tone, as if he were discussing whether we should eat hard or soft crabs for dinner. "You see, if you recall, we had an arrangement. Eddie went to Tangier to buy hashish and I was to wire him the buy money. Then he was going to purchase as many pounds as he could get and we were going to have a lifetime supply and still be able to sell some of it off and . . ."

"Only he didn't send me any money!" Eddie screamed. "He didn't send me a dime, and I had to live on the rooftop of a horrible hotel in Tangier and I had to drink piss!"

"Drink piss?" I said. My knees had stopped shaking. I was becoming interested.

I held onto Val's waist and could feel her heart thumping through her black silken blouse. I turned and looked at her and realized she was standing here in black bikini panties, and I thought, "God, if he kills us, someone will write a headline in the *News American*, 'Three Slain in Hipster Lovenest,' but I lost interest in the thought pretty quickly as Eddie turned, waved the gun at me again, and started babbling wildly:

THE KING OF CARDS

"In fucking Tangier, the rooftop was the only place to sleep if you didn't have any goddamned money, and it was covered with junkies and dopers from England and Amsterdam. Them and batshit-crazy Africans who played fucking cowbells and chanted all fucking day and night. Not to mention faggots who screwed each other up the ass and screamed out their little love cries in French and 105-pound speed-shooting hookers. Yeah, and there was this fountain up there, this old tile fountain with a big fucking goldfish in the middle of it. I mean this water was foul and horrible, but this great goldfish stayed alive in it somehow, after all the other fish had died. The British junkies called him Superfish, and I had to drink water from this fountain for two days because I didn't know where else to get any. But it turned out that these junkies and other scum up there, they pissed in the fountain every night, so I was drinking piss. Well, I couldn't stand it any longer, and I called here every goddamned day to find out when the money was coming, but I never got any fucking answer from my great friend Jeremy."

"Well, that's because the phones were temporarily out, my boy!" Jeremy said, smiling affably.

"Bullshit!" Eddie said. "Man, I trusted you, I trusted you and got the shit beat out of me, and I lost my fucking hand!"

There was a long silence after he said that.

"How *did* you lose your hand?" Val said coolly.

"Because I didn't have any money—because *he* didn't send me any money—I decided to steal. It was the only thing to do. How else would I ever get home? There was a guy on the roof. His name was Hadji, and he was a drug dealer. A great fat wasted pig of a man. He used his own opium, and he was always wasted so I thought I could steal his money, which he kept in a little sack tied around his waist. I waited until he was asleep and crept across the roof and I moved inch by inch up to him and then slowly, slowly I opened the sack . . . and I reached inside . . ."

"Oh, Jesus," I said.

163

"And the money was in there all right," Eddie said. "It was fucking in there. But there was also something else in there."

"What?" I said, sitting down on the end of the bed.

"A snake!" Eddie said. "A poisonous coral snake. It bit me. Because you fucking didn't send the money."

Now Eddie remembered the gun. He aimed it at Jeremy Raines and shot again.

This time the bullet was much nearer to the mark. It hit the headboard, just to the right of Jeremy's ear, violently splitting the wood. Jeremy, however, barely flinched.

"Eddie," I said. "Put down the gun. Really, man."

"I lost my fucking hand because of him," he screamed. "You want me to forget that? The venom hit me so fast, man. I thought I was done. But the fat dealer, Hadji, he woke up, and he looked at me and he shook his head and he said, "I should let you die for stealing, but I feel generous tonight. I feel benevolent, like the gods, so I am going to save your life."

"Oh, Jesus," I said.

"Four of them grabbed me, and they took me over to the fountain and put my hand on the tiles, and another guy got an ax and—Christ, I thought at first it was some kind of joke—I mean this could not be happening to me, but then I saw the looks on their faces, they were fucking laughing man, I mean they loved it, man, they chopped off my fucking hand! I passed out and woke up on the street with it all bandaged up. I still don't know who saved me."

I began to feel a little faint. Everything had started to look like watercolors.

"How did you get home?" I said.

"I finally got through to my parents, man, and they got me the money. But I lost my hand. And now you gotta die, Jeremy."

He squinched up his face and aimed the gun again, but then stopped and brought it down to his side.

"There's one more fucking thing I want to know before I

kill your lying ass," Eddie said. "Why didn't you send me the money, man?"

Jeremy looked hard at Eddie and then an extraordinary thing happened—a tear came down his face. But it wasn't as if he was begging for his life, not at all. It was as if he had somehow taken Eddie's pain—the pain of losing his hand—into his own body, into his own soul. His face had taken on an almost saintly pallor.

"I won't lie to you, Ed," he said in a low grave voice. "I did not send you the money because I became so involved in my work with the cards at Hopkins and the other accounts and . . . with our new deal with Kodak."

That stopped everyone in their tracks.

"Kodak?" Eddie said in spite of himself. "What deal with Kodak?"

"The deal I became obsessed with. I told a Mr. Harvey Spence, a vice president of Kodak, about our I.D. cards and he said the company has become more than a little interested in bankrolling our whole venture."

"Jesus," Val said.

"Well, that's too bad," Eddie said quickly. "'Cause you aren't going to live to ever get their dough!"

He waved the gun around a little. He was trying to look menacing, but the barrel sagged a little, making him look like a substitute teacher with a pointer in his hand.

"I do not blame you at all," Jeremy said. "Not at all. Because you are right. I have a disease. Believe me, I know it. I mean, God, listen to me, going on about the business right here and now, while you are holding a gun on me and telling me it's my last minute on earth. You see? It's a goddamned disease. What I am telling you is that I forgot, I forgot that you, my brother, a man I love and care about deeply, I forgot that you were even *in* Tangier. I got so goddamn involved in selling cards that I put all human feeling behind me and got into a complete capitalist business hustle, like a goddamned pariah. I became a fucking, sniveling, greed-mongering piece of shit. There's nothing more to say about it, though of course, your share of the company with Kodak behind us will be worth considerably more, much more, than we could have ever dreamed of in the past."

"Yeah," Eddie said in a weaker voice. "Fine. Maybe with all that money I can buy a new fucking hand. You asshole!"

That charged him up a little, and he waved the gun again.

Jeremy slapped himself in the forehead.

"Listen to me," he said. "I'm doing it again, trying to seduce you the same moment I am confessing, which tells you how far I am from the man I believe myself to be. 'Cause I like to think of myself as a guy who is building a family here, a real family, just the opposite of the ones we inherited, a family based on love and trusting. But at the same time, I see this disease in myself, I recognize it in my guts, eating at me like a cancer, this greed, this need to expand, to be Mr. Big Big Big. Which in no way excuses me from execution at your hand if you so wish to go through with this. I was wrong. It's on my head. So go ahead, Eddie, shoot!"

Jeremy folded his legs and his arms in front of his chest like Buddha and shut his eyes as if he were prepared to die.

Eddie squinted his eyes until they looked like little black baitworms.

"You think, you think you can just forget me? Let me lose my goddamned hand and get out of it because you're the goddamned King of Cards or something?" Eddie said. "Well, forget it man."

He aimed carefully at Jeremy's head and fired. But just before pulling the trigger he turned the barrel to the ceiling. Sawdust and wallpaper floated down on us like confetti. Then Eddie tossed the gun on the bed, turned, and pushed me out of the way as he stalked out of the room.

"Holy shit," I said, my heart pounding through my shirt.

Jeremy crossed himself and fell back on the bed, arms spread open in supplication to the God of Bullshit, who had just saved his life.

"Are you all right, Jeremy?" Val said.

166

Jeremy let out a long, long sigh.

"Oh, you almost lost it, pal," I said. "You came that close!"

"You think he'll try it again?" Val said.

"Find the Babe and apprise her of the situation," Jeremy said in what sounded like a death rattle.

Val went over to the bed and stroked Jeremy's head. He sighed deeply again and held onto her hand.

"You know, there's one thing I don't understand," Val said. "I don't see how cutting off Eddie's hand saved his life."

"This is true," Jeremy said, sitting up and running a shaky hand through his cowlick. "If that had been a true coral snake, Eddie would be planted somewhere in the Mideast right now. No, it sounds to me like it was a harmless milk snake. Looks exactly like a coral snake, but wouldn't harm a fly."

"Then they just cut off his hand for laughs?" I said.

"'Fraid so," Jeremy said. "But for Christ's sake, whatever you do, don't tell him."

Having averted Jeremy Raines's premature death and calmed the amputated Eddie, we were, of course, all anxious to know of the new "relationship with Kodak."

"The answer is our relationship is, at this point, tenuous," Raines said as we had our lunch—crab cakes expertly cooked by Babe—sitting in the Hellhole basement by the embosser and the endless rows of plastic cards. "They are eventually going to send a man down to chat with me. Which brings us to a few stumbling blocks. Nothing we can't overcome, of course, but they could prove a little troublesome. For one, the Kodak rep can never, ever, *ever* be let into the house. I had to, well, fudge things a bit in that department."

"Meaning what?" the Babe said as she fondled Eddie's stump.

"Meaning in my desire to make the business sound attractive, I kind of hinted that we had our own building," Raines said.

"Oh, Christ, you didn't," Val said.

"I'm afraid so," Raines said. "Well, I told him that I was *buying* a building for us right now. That by the time they sent their rep down to talk things over with us we'd be fully installed."

"Great," I said. "When he gets here he'll see the Hellhole and realize that we're rank amateurs."

"You worry far too much, my friend," Raines said, flipping me a beer. "Worry will make you old before your time. Believe me, I've got a little plan all set up for our friends from Kodak. Which brings me to a second part of the plan. There's a man some of you may have read about in the Sunpapers. Mr. Rudy Antonelli. He's going to be calling from time to time, and he'll help us with the Kodak situation. Old friend of my dad's."

"Rudy Antonelli?" I said. "As in the *gangster* Rudy Antonelli?"

Jeremy Raines put his strong arm on my shoulder and shook his head. "The things you don't understand could fill an encyclopedia," he said. "Baltimore doesn't have gangsters. That kind of crude stuff happens in New York and Chicago. Rudy is a businessman, owner of Soft Shell Limited, the most successful real estate company in the city, also owner of the most successful Italian restaurant—Antonelli's—of Little Italy. Not to mention various prize-winning racehorses."

"Also not to mention that he's currently being investigated by a federal anticrime task force," I said angrily, "and the Maryland State Police *and* the Baltimore city boys as well. Jesus, Jeremy, we're not going into business with the likes of him, are we?"

"Of course not, my boy," Jeremy said. "You see many years ago before my father got sick, he did certain favors for Rudy, all legitimate. The problem was a racial thing. Rudy wanted to get into the Maryland Country Club, and they didn't accept people of his persuasion. My father talked to a few of the club's board members, and Rudy has been forever grateful. He's actually going to help us find the building."

"And give it to us?" I said, unable to stop playing the devil's advocate. "Because it's not like we're rolling in assets."

"Worry, worry, worry," Raines said. "Relax my friend. Anyway, if Rudy calls, just be cool. Now I've got to go see a charming nun over at St. Mary's School for Young Women. Good old Sister Lulu has turned me on to her. Meanwhile, when do we get the University of Baltimore cards?"

"Today," I said. "I'm going down to the lab to pick them up this afternoon."

I felt a tremor of anxiety about that and prayed they'd turned out well.

"Fine," Raines said. "I'm certain they will be of the highest professional caliber, my boy." He patted me on the shoulder, and I felt warmth shoot through me. There was something so kind in his manner, he had such confidence in me, that I badly wanted to succeed for him.

"Mind if I tag along?" Val said. "I'll get lonely out here all afternoon by myself."

"Oh, I guess I can handle that," I said, smiling.

"Ah, young love," Raines smiled. "Remember, once you get the cards, you have to bring them back here so the Babe and Edward can emboss them and slip our fine high-grade plastic on them. If we work round the clock, we can get the whole set back there by tomorrow and be paid by this weekend. Then we can have a long, serious party. See you all later."

He waved good-bye and headed up the steps.

"What a madman," I said to Val.

"Yes," she smiled, "but ain't it fun?"

I must confess that bright fall afternoon seemed filled with promise. Though theoretically I *hated* business, I had to admit that actually *doing* business—at least this kind of business—seemed like a great adventure. Here we were, a lit guy and gal, cruising beneath the flame-colored fall trees on historic row house Charles Street, headed down to the photo lab to pick up a great stack of I.D. photos for which we would eventually be paid fifteen thousand dollars. It seemed a small miracle—nearly impossible—and if it worked (and why shouldn't it?), we could do the same at school after school. Driving with beautiful sexy Val, I succumbed to the I.D. card fever. Soon we would all be young millionaires, and then I would have plenty of time to devote myself more fully to my literary studies. After all, I told myself, even Dr. Spaulding once said that it was easier for a writer to get to the heart of life if he or she wasn't burdened by the mundane worries and crushing anxieties of making a living.

What's more, I had other thoughts about writing, new and exciting thoughts that Jeremy and Val had inspired in me.

"You know," I said to Val as we rolled happily along, "I really want to start writing more. I really know it now."

"You're kidding," Val said, grabbing my hand and looking at me with complete admiration. "That's wonderful. We can write poems together, help one another."

"No, you're the poet," I said. "I just want to start keeping notes on all this. Maybe I'm nuts, but I think we're living out a great adventure and I want to document it all."

She smiled and kissed my neck, sending goose bumps down my back.

"But you're capable of so much more than just a documentary," she said. "You could write a great novel."

"I doubt that," I said. "I'm no Henry James."

"The hell with him," Val laughed. "I know you think he's the king of subtlety and all, but on some level he just told stories about the rich fops he hung around with in London. So you'll do the same thing for Baltimore, only it'll be more alive, wild, and sweeter 'cause you're wilder and sweeter."

I started to blush, but she squeezed my cock for emphasis and such literary nit-picking seemed beside the point.

THE KING OF CARDS

I parked the car in an old abandoned lot, and Val and I walked inside the long gray halls of the photo lab. As we entered the door, I gave her a conspiratorial pinch on her bottom. And she turned and ran her long, sexy tongue around her thick, sensual lips.

We strolled hand in hand to the pick-up depot, where we were met by a gnomish-looking man in a gray lab jacket. He had thick glasses, a pocket protector, crepe soles, and a name tag that said, "Hi, I'm Marty."

"Good day, Marty," I said in an expansive Rainesian way. "Are our cards ready?"

He looked furtively at the ground and then, without uttering a word, shoved the box into my hands.

"They're a little, ah, weird," he said.

He tried covering himself with a grin, but he had the kind of mouth that was all gums.

I looked down at the box, then holding my breath, pulled out a card.

The girl's name was Jane DeVries, age nineteen. More than that about her, it was impossible to say, for all that I could see of her was one nostril floating in an inky black sea.

"Oh, God," Val said. "We are in deep trouble."

Frantic, I pulled out two more cards. This one was of a boy named Mark Reynolds, but all that was visible of Mark was a thick blond eyebrow. And the second card was of a woman named Celeste West, but all we got to see of her was a thick upper lip.

"It looks like a Magritte," Val said.

"Not funny," I said. "How could this happen?"

"Crummy photography?" Marty said, repressing a giggle.

It was all I could do not to throttle him on the spot.

"Let me use your phone, Marty," I said. "Now."

171

"Sure," he said. "Guess you got some explaining to do, huh?"

"Fuck you, Marty," Val said. "Go back to your cage."

He looked at her, panted a little, then handed me the bill.

"You gotta pay today," he said. "That's the contract."

"Yeah, sure," I said, handing him the check. "Now show me the phone."

I won't bother to record the entire conversation with Mr. Hawkins of Baltimore University. Suffice it to say that he (1) threatened legal action, (2) threatened bodily harm, (3) called us names that I had never heard before, one of which was "unprofessional, shit-faced, daddy-jacking, lame . . . third-rate con men."

But even so, I finally calmed him down by agreeing to reshoot the photos in one day at our expense. By the time the conversation was over, I slammed down the phone and collapsed on an old stool in that gray, dust-filled hallway. Sweat poured down my neck and back.

"I can't take it," I said. "Just when things were looking up."

Val put her hand on my neck and gave me a massage.

"Come on," she said. "Let's go do something smart."

"Which would be what?" I sighed.

"Let's go get very, very drunk and cry our eyes out," she said.

"I like the way you think," I said.

I got up and picked up the box of surrealist postcards and together we staggered down the hall.

We spent the rest of that afternoon and a good part of the night at the Mount Royal Tavern, drinking, playing darts, and dreading giving the news to Jeremy. Finally though, we had to stop drinking; we were out of money.

So bobbing and weaving on the slippery wet roads, we ended up back at the house around ten.

"He had such confidence in me," I wailed as we pulled up to the curb.

"Yes, and I'm afraid it's worse than you know. He's just about tapped out. I mean completely broke."

"Oh, no," I said. "You have to be kidding. Well, he's a legit businessman, sort of. Couldn't he go to a bank and get a business loan?"

"You don't understand," she said, patting my leg as though I were a hopeless case. "Jeremy's already up to his eyeballs in debts for the embosser and the lamination machine. He can barely pay those loans back as it is."

"Good Lord, and I failed him," I said. My head sagged heavily against the window.

"Not if we can make the reshoot tomorrow," she said. "We'll just have to give it a try. Hey, who's that?"

She pointed toward the front porch of the house. Someone was on the porch all right. Someone big and burly. Crouching down and peering into the windows. I couldn't quite make him out, but I was pretty sure who he was.

"It's Lulu's boyfriend, that crazy bastard Dan," I said.

"Well, he's not going to bother anybody tonight, I can promise you that. I may have flunked as a photographer, but I'll be damned if I'm going to let that asshole bug us."

"Be careful, Tom. You've had a lot to drink!" Val said. But it was too late. I was already out of the car and headed for the porch, which in my drunken haze looked like a shining beacon of sanity, some mythical Norman Rockwell front-porch America that was now being threatened by the forces of unreason.

Slowly, I crept up the hill, past the evergreens and the old swinging tire. As I crept along, I mumbled to myself, "Screw you, Dan." I thought of his crowbar, but somehow it didn't frighten me. All I knew was I could not fail again.

I hid behind the evergreen and watched him creep close to the window. From my vantage point, I couldn't see his face, but upon closer inspection it appeared he had a camera with him. Probably trying to get proof that Lulu Hardwell was having sexcapades with Jeremy.

This, I told my drunken self, was never going to happen!

So saying, I leapt from the front yard grass to the porch, directly onto his back. He gave out a loud cry as I firmly lodged my forearm under his chin and squeezed as hard as I could. He began to spin around, like some crazed Apache dancer, but I kept my grip there and cracked him on the top of the head with my other hand for emphasis.

Finally, he made a last wild spin and fell off the porch. Now it was my turn to yell, for we landed in a giant green sticker bush that had grown in the unkept flower garden just beneath the porch. The stickers were like a hundred tiny darts in my side, legs, and ass. Screaming and howling, I fell off into the lawn.

He leapt to his feet, frantically pulling stickers out of his arms, legs, hands.

"What in bloody hell are you doing?" he screamed at me.

I finally got a face-to-face look at the culprit. He had a big square face and was dressed in a herringbone suit and a blue and red rep tie. On his feet were a pair of Oxford wing tips. He looked more like a lawyer than a truck driver.

"You're not Dan," I said.

"Dan?" he said in an English accent. "Who in God's name is bloody Dan?"

"Dan, the trucker, that's who!" Val said, running up from the street. "But Sister Lulu's not coming with you!"

That stopped him. He scratched his head and rubbed his chin.

"Sister Lulu? You are both crazed," he said. "I was merely doing my job. Looking over this house for my employer."

I turned and looked slowly at Val.

"You're not from, ah, Kodak?" I said, my voice breaking.

"I most certainly am," he said. "My name is Alan Saxon-Hogg, and I was told that this address was the home office of the Identi-Card system. But . . . this place . . ."

174

I was stunned, unable to speak. Oh, we were in deep, deep shit.

"Delighted, Mr. Hogg," Val said, smoothly switching gears, dusting him off and helping him pull out his briars. "I'm Val Jackson, Mr. Raines's personal assistant. This abysmal place is simply our temporary lodgings. We are very, very cost-conscious at Identi-Card. The money we make we plow right back into the business so that we can offer the highest-quality cards."

"Yes, I see. And do you and this ruffian always make it a habit to manhandle visiting business associates?"

"Absolutely not," Val said. "But this neighborhood has seen a small crime wave of late and given the secret nature of our product, we can't be too careful now can we?"

She smiled her 360-watt smile and took his arm in hers. Then, with a wink to me, she walked him into the house.

A few minutes later, Val had Hogg seated comfortably on the old maroon couch, a Scotch and soda in his hand. As he sipped, she gave me the high sign and excused herself for a second. I followed suit and met her in the kitchen, which was cluttered with last night's dirty dishes. She handed me a piece of paper with two phone numbers on it.

"Call Jeremy," she said. "We've got to keep Hogg here and happy, or he'll report back to Kodak that we're just crazies."

"Right," I said. "But what if he wants to go downstairs?"

"Don't worry," she said. "I'll make *sure* that never happens." Suddenly the Val I had spent the night with—the warm vulnerable, poetic girl whom I had fallen head over heels with—was gone and in her place was a tough businesswoman, the kind of person whom you see wandering around Towson, Maryland, in tweeds with a sign that says Houses for Sale in her hand. A sharp-eyed, flinty-voiced business sharkette.

She had already turned and was heading back into the living room and the clutches of Alan Saxon-Hogg, but I grabbed her arm and pulled her to me.

"Just a sec," I said. "What do you mean by that?"

She looked at me with an almost pitiable gaze and patted my arm. But her voice was rock solid.

"I mean I'll do whatever's necessary. Leave me alone, Tom. You're drunk and you've almost blown us out of the water with that John Wayne act."

She pulled herself away from me and headed back into the room. I reached up and grabbed the telephone. Now more than ever it was imperative to get a hold of Jeremy. I dialed the number Val had given me, but there was no answer. Then, before dialing the second number, I peered from the kitchen into the living room. Everything seemed in order. Hogg was sitting back on the couch, and Val was three or four feet away from him. Both of them were laughing and talking, but it was all very civilized, until one second later, as I watched in horror, she slithered toward him.

"You look very tired Alan," (ALAN!) she said. "You really should relax."

I watched in disbelief as she knelt down in front of him and started untying his shoes.

I jumped back into the kitchen and dialed the second number. A woman with a voice like a trash compactor answered.

"Irma's Greek Acropolis," she said.

"I'm looking for Jeremy Raines," I said.

"You and the IRS," the woman said. "I'll see if he's here. Who's this, anyhow?"

"Tommy Fallon," I said, "and it's serious."

"It always is, honey," Irma said.

A second later Raines came on the phone.

"Tommy," he said, "that you?"

176

THE KING OF CARDS

"Afraid so."

"Good," he laughed. "I thought it might be Dan the Trucker. Lulu and I are just having dinner."

"You wish it was Dan the Trucker," I said. "The jig is up. The Kodak rep is here."

"In the house?" he asked. I was amazed at the coolness in his voice. It was as though he were asking whether the sun was shining or not.

"Yes, in the house. You had better get back here. Val's trying to divert him. He hasn't seen the Hole yet."

"And he must never see it," Jeremy said. "Let me talk to Val."

I put the phone down and walked out to the living room. To my complete horror, Val was cozying up to Saxon-Hogg. She leaned on his shoulder and looked up into his eyes as though she were some worshipful bimbette.

"You must get to travel all over, Alan," she said, purring. "You're so lucky."

"Well, yes, I do get around quite a bit, luv," Saxon-Hogg said. He put his arm around her, and she ran her tongue around her lips.

"Phone for you," I said in my happiest and bitterest voice.

She got up slowly, letting him get a full view of her terrific torso, and she shook her derriere like Bardot as she sauntered into the kitchen.

"Overdoing it a bit, aren't you?" I said through clenched teeth.

"No, I am not," she said, baring her teeth at me, "but *you* are acting like a jealous square."

She turned her back to me as she picked up the phone.

"Jeremy, I suppose Tom told you the worst," she said. "But don't worry, I've thought of something."

"Thought of what?" I wanted to yell but said nothing. Then, seeing that I was hanging on her every word, she took the phone into the little alcove next to the refrigerator.

Minutes later, she was off the phone and headed right by me, back to the living room. But I grabbed her arm as she marched by.

"Did Raines tell you to . . . did he tell you to . . . did he instruct you to . . ."

I am afraid the rest of the sentence was a terrible gagging sound.

"No," she said. "Nobody tells me what to do. I do what I think is appropriate. Now let me get back in there before Hogg flies out of here and makes a full report to Kodak." She rolled her eyes at me, pulled her arm from my grasp, and headed back into the living room.

My heart raced madly. She was right, so damned right. I *was* a complete square. She was only going to tease him a little. I was acting like a fool. I took a deep breath, felt my blood pressure drop, then looked around the kitchen door into the living room.

But there was another small problem. They were no longer in the living room.

"Not to worry," I said to myself, "just out for a walk."

Then I heard laughter, sexual giggling, there was no doubt about it, and it came from above me. They had gone upstairs.

I ran through the living room, turned to go up the steps, just in time to see them disappear into Raines's bedroom.

I started up the steps, then sat down hard midway up. What would I say? I would merely look like a bigger fool. I shook my head and made a weird moaning sound, like a turtle who has just had his shell pulled off by steel tongs.

She couldn't be . . . it was impossible. She wouldn't, couldn't. Then I thought of her poems. Hell, she had made love to old Nikos just for the fun of it. For dear old Jeremy, there was probably no sexual variation that she wouldn't perform, ropes, pulleys, bananas, anything to keep the Kodak contract.

I didn't know her at all. But I had to find out. I had to see with my own agonized eyes, just what treachery she was capable of.

I threw open the front door, raced out to the porch, tripped over the glider, and ran down the porch steps and around the side of the house.

THE KING OF CARDS

There above me was Raines's window and a warming light. I saw the thick ivy growing right up to the narrow little rooftop. I knew, yes knew, as the Apostle Paul knew when he was thrown off his ass by a burning Godly sunbeam, that this vine had been divinely placed here in order for me to climb.

I grabbed onto the ivy and dug in a right heel. I started to climb, right heel, left heel, grasping and grabbing. Upstairs, I could hear laughter. My hair was on fire with jealousy.

Oh, I was no hipster. But I *was* capable of hideous, square-guy sexual revenge.

Saxon-Hogg would pay, pay, pay. I would cut off his British cock and throw it to the Chesapeake Bay crabs.

I kept climbing, climbing. I could see my way brilliantly. They were going to be so very surprised. Val was going to be thrilled by my fury.

I was climbing assuredly, stability provided by the jet-fueled rage inside of me.

Then the bedroom light went out. I was in the dark, trapped on the side of a very large house, fifty feet above terra firma.

Upstairs I was certain I could hear springs bouncing. I could hear Hogg hogging her.

I had to push on. I reached my right hand up another notch and grasped into the dark ivy. Something large with nasty insect teeth bit my right hand.

I screamed "Traitor" as I fell.

When I awoke, the insect had crawled into my eyes and was busy eating away portions of my brain. I said, "Oh, Lord." The sound echoed through the dark hallways inside my head.

Then there was light and something cool on my brow and Val was staring lovingly down at me.

"How do you feel?" she said as tenderly as Florence Nightingale.

"Like Brer Rabbit," I said. "Zippety do-dah."

"You poor driven creature," she said.

I sat up and looked around. Hogg, Jeremy, and Lulu Hardwell stood a few feet away. They held drinks and smiled at me. Hogg was smoking a joint. His shirt hung out of his pants. He had his hand around Lulu—who smiled at him with her big sexual teeth.

"Lump on the head and you've got a nasty bruise on your back, old man," Hogg said. "Other than that, you look fine. Just fine. Nasty business though, wall climbing. I expect you were going to play a little joke on us."

"No," I said, "I was going to kill you for fucking my girl-friend."

"Oh," Hogg said, "well, here's to passion, then!"

He lifted his glass and drained it. Jeremy smiled, poured him another, then brought a drink to me.

"Looking much better, my boy," he said.

"I'm not going to die yet," I said. Val put a hand on my arm. For a second I wanted to knock it away, but it was a warm hand, a concerned hand.

"Going downtown for a little ride," Jeremy said. "Thought you might want to come along."

"I don't know," I said.

"Oh come on, sweety," Lulu said. "It's going to be fun."

"Really?" I asked Val. "Fun for who?"

"As a student of literature you owe it to yourself to come," Val said.

"Right," I said. She helped me up. The insects were still eating my cerebellum so I had another drink.

As we left, Hogg gave Lulu a little kiss and she reached around and rubbed his ass. I looked over at Raines, who smiled like a choirboy and walked to the car.

We drove through the black Baltimore night. There was singing from Lulu Hardwell—she had a surprisingly won-derful country voice—and there was harmony from Hogg, who looked like a decent guy to me, but I was still in a foul mood. As Raines drove in and out of traffic, I found myself hoping that we would crash and there would be massive damage to Hogg's penis.

But there was no such luck, only Lulu's sweet voice and Hogg's drunken confessions: "Could have been a Romantic poet. Yes, wrote like Shelley they told me at Oxford, but there came this corporate opportunity and I took it and yet . . . yet . . . one never knows, and one never will know if one doesn't risk all. Isn't that right, Jeremy?"

And Jeremy only smiled and said, "There's time to do it all my friend. Time for money and time for poems."

I turned to Val, who sat cozied up to me. She smiled and gave me a little kiss on the cheek.

"I do love you, you know," she whispered.

And I felt she was telling me the truth, but I wasn't yet ready to forgive her, so I turned and stared moodily out the window.

She smiled sadly and held my hand.

"There is so much you don't understand," she said.

And I looked down at her and back up at Raines and saw him nodding and laughing and Lulu Hardwell kissing Hogg in the front seat, and it seemed to me then that Raines was a spider, yes, some smiling tarantula who had trapped us all into his sticky little web, and where oh where was he taking us—down St. Paul, past the B and O railroad with their old dead engines standing out under the Baltimore moon. Down past wino streets and ghosty Poe-like doorways, down along Pratt Street past old Pier 1, where my grandfather Cap Fallon shipped out on the old tanker the SS *Barnacle* and sailed down that blackbird buoy line to Tolchester, and Betterton and Salisbury, and I was thinking perhaps that's what I needed to do: get on a boat and sail away from all of this. The whole life had become too fast, too confusing, and I was shedding too many skins at once. Who the hell was I? Lit man, con man, new man, old man, all of them undulating under the same squirming skin. Suddenly my reveries were broken by a tremendous thud, for right there at Pratt and Charles Street, Jeremy smashed into a telephone pole, and we all rolled around like rats in Raines's cage. Then we opened the doors and tumbled out onto the redbrick street, in front of some old ghost tankers tied up on the tin can docks of the rusted, bombed-out Baltimore pier.

I looked over at Raines, who smiled at me, and lifted his head toward the sky. I did likewise and gave out a gasp of pure surprise. For there above us was a huge fifty-story black obelisk-shaped office building on the very top of which was a huge red pulsating neon sign with but one word that glowed triumphantly in the night—RAINES!!!

At that moment I was so astonished by the sheer audacity of it all that I forgot my bitterness and doubt and let out a cheer, along with everyone else.

Then Jeremy said: "Well, Mr. Hogg, how do you like our new building?"

Hogg pulled himself from the long blue fingernails of Lulu Hardwell and opened his arms as if he wanted to make love to the place.

"Amazing, amazing," he said. "When do I get the full tour of the plant?"

"Afraid that's got to be on a later trip," Raines said. "We are just getting situated in there. But don't you think Kodak will approve of our newest acquisition?"

"Absolutely!" Hogg said. He smiled and looked back at the building.

"All this with bloody I.D. cards," he added. "America is a great fucking place."

"True," Lulu said. Then she put her arms around him and squeezed. Hogg's eyes lit up like the cardboard fat lady in front of the fun house tunnel.

I looked at the amazing, impossible Jeremy Raines, and he gave me an almost imperceptible wink.

THE KING OF CARDS

The rest of that evening was devoted to entertaining Hogg, for which the ex-nun, Miss Lulu Hardwell, was sublimely equipped. As for myself I waited for a decent interval, then went upstairs to my room, leaving Val to revel with the revelers.

I fell asleep and had a strange dream. There was a giant building, much like Raines's skyscraper, but the sign on top didn't say Raines. Rather, there was a huge puppet of Raines himself; he was dressed in a court jester's uniform with foolscap and bells and green pointy felt shoes. His face was painted black and white, except for the lips, which were clown red. His other features were indefinable, stretching like old Plastic Man's from my comic books days: now short and stubby, like some old Mick cop, and now long and wrinkled, like a sweet potato with hair. Pasted all over his body were identification cards, cards with giant nostrils and huge blinking eyes. Suddenly I was up on the roof with him and we were looking down on all that finny traffic, cars swimming by like great metallic fish, and he was smiling and beckoning to me to come to the edge. Oh, Lord, it was the most reassuring smile in the world, and yet, yet I knew that he wasn't to be trusted. Still, I felt compelled to walk toward him. There didn't seem to be any alternative. And I felt a wild and exhilarating fear and walked like a zombie to the precipice, watching his face changing again. It seemed to be the face of an old woman now, some kindly old grandmother, then it changed again, some sweet baby face, so pink and trusting only the hardest heart could resist. Once at the edge, he smiled and opened his palm and pointed to the street below and the winking lights of the passing cars and then he handed me a shimmering, silver I.D. card, and I looked at it like a child looks at his first bauble, with wonder and pure pleasure. For the shining card had my own picture on it. I looked young and happy; I was beaming. But then suddenly, I began to fade; my eyes and nose disappeared like old watercolors in the rain. All that was left was my mouth, the mouth of some retard escapee from the nut farm, open and drooling, and it terrified me that this was my real mouth, the mouth beneath the smiling mouth that the bright world saw, and I felt such a fear in my heart that I turned to Raines for reassurance, but he was laughing at me now. Oh, Lord, he laughed and laughed and I started to laugh with him, the mouth of an idiot drool baby, and then suddenly we were both screeching, and I was doubled over with rib pain. Then in a lightning gesture, he flicked the card out of my hand, and I blinked in astonished fear (but deep down knew, had always known) and tried to grasp it back. But his hand was gone. In its place was a bony skeleton, and he threw my card out into the sweltering, humid black air.

Then, as I watched it go, Jeremy Raines the jester, pushed me off the edge.

I screamed as I fell into open yawning space. And looked back up to see his smiling clown face and his long rubber fingers waving good-bye.

And then I awoke, and Val was there above me holding a cold towel on the big hot bump on my head.

We said nothing for a time, but then I put my arms around her and held her to me.

"I was nuts tonight," I said. "I'm sorry."

"No, you were jealous," she said. "I don't blame you, but there's a couple things you should know. One, I didn't screw him. I was just giving him a massage in the dark." She looked at me with such sweetness, such innocence in her face, that I had no choice but to believe her.

"What's two?" I said.

"Two," she said, looking down at the tangled sheets. "Well, two is harder. There's something you must understand. I *would* do anything for Jeremy."

"Well, I *don't* understand that," I said, propping myself up on my elbows.

She sighed and pushed me away from her and got out of the bed. When she walked next to the window I could see her in silhouette, her perfect gymnast's body illuminated by the great yellow moon.

"I didn't quite tell you the whole story the other day. There's more to it, I'm afraid."

"You mean about your past?"

"Yes. I didn't tell you because I was afraid how you would respond. You see, I met Jeremy when I was a patient at Larson-Payne."

"What?"

She turned and spoke to me in a low, smoky voice, a voice from a dream.

"It's true," she said. "When I met Jeremy, I was a patient at the hospital. I had what is known in our parents' circles as a total breakdown."

"What triggered it?" I asked in a voice that was not my own.

"I don't know. . . . I mean, what are the usual answers to that question. The Colonel? Screaming at me for my life-style, spying on me to find out who I was sleeping with?"

"The bastard."

She smiled sadly and ran her fingers through my hair.

"He thought he was helping," she said. "He's military, Tom. He believes in attacking the opposition."

"Even if the enemy is his own daughter."

"But it wasn't all his fault. Mother didn't help much either. She's an old-fashioned southern girl. For my twenty-first birthday, she sent me a single pair of white panties."

"Jesus, talk about right out of the Freudian textbook!"

"And there were the drugs," Val said in a dreamy voice. "I was taking quite a bit of peyote in those days. It helped for a while, made things dreamy, a bit too dreamy. I was at a party down at Bolton Hill, at the Marlboro Hotel. I took a couple peyote buttons, and I began to see this figure over in the corner. It was a woman. She looked like a gargoyle, all hunched over and hollow eyed with a strange little wooden staff. Something right out of the fairy books. I was terrified of her face, all ancient and cronelike, until I realized that she was me, and I followed her out of the Marlboro, down onto the street. I saw her go past Maryland Institute and into the train station, and I followed her in there, right out onto the tracks, and I sat down and waited and I realized then that this beaten, mishappened little gnome was really me, and all her fury and sadness were really inside my soul and that seemed too sad to me, so sad and so hopeless and small, that I just sat there waiting for the long black train to come and carry us both home."

"Jesus," I said.

"It was Jeremy who found me. About three minutes before the train was due. He got me into Larson-Payne, and he kept the Colonel off my back."

"How did he manage that?"

"He told the Colonel that if he bothered me, he would go to the Sun with the story . . . of how he hit me, beat me."

"You didn't tell me that. Your father beat you?"

I held her close. She had started to cry a little, and I cupped her cheeks with my hand.

"Yeah," Val said. "Yeah, he did . . . not all the time. Only when he was upset and drinking."

"Decent of him," I said.

"I was in Larson-Payne for two months. There were voices, fragments of faces, but that was all. The only face I trusted, the only one I could see whole was Jeremy's. And that was enough. Gradually, I came out of it, but I felt like a piece of crystal. I was so afraid that if I broke again, I would be finished. But Jeremy didn't let that happen. He kept me going, even after I got out of the place. Helped me get my little place downtown. Got me working for Identi-Card. Turned me on to the poetry scene."

I didn't say anything. I had always known, known that there was some subterranean pull between the two of them. But this?

"If you're wondering if we were lovers, the answer is yes. But you mustn't think it was because he took advantage of me. It was months after I got out of the hospital. And *I* wanted to make love to *him*. I needed to . . . to make it real; I lived in fantasy for so long—broken little pipedreams. I needed to be with someone physically, someone I could trust. After a few times we both realized that there wasn't that kind of magic between us."

"No, he'd rather just control you. Get you to sleep with anyone he wants you to as long as it helps the business."

Anger flashed in her eyes, and for a second I thought she was going to slap me.

"Jeremy's not Dr. Caligari," she said. "You should trust him."

"Look," I said, "I love the guy. Really. But he's a con artist. I mean . . . he . . ."

I caught myself before I went on. I was about to say something absurd like Jeremy had made some pact with the devil—something I didn't even believe—and yet, it felt that way tonight. There was some new, dark side to him, beyond all the charm and boyish fumbling. But I could see that there was no point in criticizing him to Val.

"Tell me more about your father," I said.

"He's pure army. Every single thing in his life is a battle plan. Do you realize once when I was a kid on the girls' soccer team, he came to a few practices, which I liked, but then he sat me down one night with a chart he'd rigged up, which had on it every single girl's name and her weakness as a player. He told me how I could win the wing position I wanted by beating out this other girl. More than that, he *expected* me to do it. I thought it was horrible of him. I was trying to make friends for Godssake, and he said that the other girls weren't friends. They were competitors and the object was to whip them all. Finally, I rebelled. Rather than do it his way, I just quit the team. He beat me, called me a coward, locked me in my room, from which I escaped by climbing out onto the roof. I ran away seven times before I was fifteen. They'd come and find me and take me to their shrink friend."

I held her tighter and kissed her forehead.

She turned and put her hand on my cheek.

"So how do you like your little rebel poet now, Tom? Pretty fucking pathetic, huh?"

"I love you," I said. "Don't doubt that."

"You love Jeremy, too," she said. "I can see it in your eyes."

"I don't know about that," I said. "I'm not sure I understand anything anymore. I only know that I love you and that I want you to love me."

I buried my head in her arms, and she rubbed my neck with her long white fingers.

"I do love you, Tommy," she said, "but we're not going to live like our parents. We're not going to see love as some little bank account. If you take too much out, you'll be broke. We're just starting on a journey to become completely new people. Jealousy, holding onto things, in the end we're going to sweep all that way. I know you understand all this, or why else would you be here?"

"You're assuming too much, Val," I said. "I don't know why I'm here. I mean you're talking about some new breed of man. Jesus, I don't even barely know who the *old* me is yet. I only know I need you. I *want* you."

"You've got me," she said, putting my fingers into her wet cunt. "Right now, you've got me."

I wanted to argue, to say, "But right now . . . isn't enough." But her mouth was on mine, my cock was hard again, and my words were drowned in her kisses.

Still, there *was* much more that I wanted to say to Raines himself, but I had to wait again, because in the morning we all gave Hogg a great send-off. Raines mixed the strongest Bloody Marys I had ever tasted, we smoked gold hash, and Lulu Hardwell dressed in her black lacy nightgown, which revealed most of her two fabulous Ripleys. By the time Hogg was ready to leave, he had a very large smile on his face.

"Absolutely nothing to worry about, my boy," he said to Raines as the hallucinatory yellow cab pulled up in front of the house. "I'll get you a temporary grant. It's a two-week loan-out, enough to bail you out of existing difficulties. And once you've shown that you can cut it there, we'll talk about getting you more substantial financing."

"Dr. Hogg, my friend, you are a gentleman and a genius," Raines said, hugging him.

Hogg hugged him back, then gave Lulu Hardwell a long, serious kiss and collapsed into the cab. I stood on the front porch with Val, Eddie, and the Babe in utter silence.

As soon as Hogg's cab had disappeared, the three of them rushed down the steps to embrace Raines.

"Congratulations," Babe said, hugging him. "We've got the backing we need."

"It does look that way," Raines said, smiling craftily. "It most certainly does."

"Thanks to the good deeds of Miss Lulu Hardwell," I said with serious, square disapproval in my voice.

This stopped the celebration a little, and Raines gave me a sharp little glance from the side of his eye.

The others started humming to him again as if nothing had happened. But Val looked at me and shook her head slightly as if to say "pathetic" or "take it easy," I didn't know which.

"I'd say this calls for a little celebration," Eddie said. "I think I'll go downtown and get fitted for my hand today."

"An excellent idea," Raines said. "You'll look distinguished in the extreme."

"Excuse me," I said, "but am I the only one that thinks we might have bitten off a little more than . . ."

"Doubting Thomas," Raines interrupted.

"Yeah, hon," the Babe said. "You need a little gold hash, and you'll feel better about the whole used car lot."

She handed me a small pipe right out there in the street, and I was so confused, so torn, I thought she might be right. Why not fly a little, put myself above the whole damned struggle. So I took three long tokes, sat down on the old cracked cement steps, and felt my head spin off my shoulders.

A second later, I stood up and announced to them all that I was headed off to class.

"What I need," I said, "is to read. Get back on the old high-lit track."

Everyone smiled and agreed and looking at their beatific faces, I felt like a spoilsport and a cur. They were decent and happy, and just because they weren't as conflicted and neurotic and confused as me was no reason for me to go around judging them.

I walked over to Jeremy and offered him my hand.

"Congratulations on the Kodak deal," I said. "I have only one question. How the hell did you buy a goddamned building in one day?"

"Hey, who said anything about buying it?" Jeremy said. "I just rented the roof."

At that, Eddie smashed his stump into his own forehead.

"What?" we all screamed.

"Yeah, from my good friend Mr. Antonelli. Leased the sign, installed it, turned on the juice. Only thing we own is the rooftop and our lease up there expires in a month. But by that time we'll have the Kodak deal sewed up, and then we can really rent office space."

This killed everybody, and I found my resistance to mad Raines had once again disintegrated.

"You rented the roof," I said. "Jesus, Mary, and Joseph!"

"Hail Jeremy, full of gas," Sister Lulu said as she threw her arms around him.

The subject in class that day was point of view in Henry James's *The Ambassadors*. As usual Dr. Spaulding was brilliant. He explained to us James's center of consciousness technique: Though the novel was written in third person, James wrote every scene through Strether's point of view.

"Thus, by limiting us to knowing only what Strether himself can know, the novel takes on a density of psychological impact. The aesthetic excitement of the book is not so much on *what* happens next, but rather upon a gradual unfolding of Strether's maturing sensibility."

Yes, I thought, this is undoubtedly true, and ordinarily, I, as a budding young scholar, would have been thrilled by the good doctor's words, but stoned as I was, it occurred to me suddenly that Dr. Spaulding was not actually in control of the situation (AS IT FUCKING WERE). No, in my hash-addled mind, it seemed to me that Dr. Spaulding was nothing more than a bright parrot: Oh, Lord, I knew this was wrong—very, very wrong—and yet the very idea of a Jamesian point of view (POV) seemed to bisect, as it were, with my New Understanding, which was that the aforementioned and highly touted POV could be highly misleading. Yes, misleading in the extreme, because in order to have a bona fide POV, as it were, one first had to have a BFS, that is a bona fide self; this seemed absolutely a necessity. But what if one had a "self in transition," or to put it more negatively, what if one's self had been Blown Down to Zero by Dad in the Bathroom, Mom in the Kitchen blotting her Kissable Lips, by deep-seated confusion about women, friends, Jeremy Raines, what one wanted to do with one's life in the (ha, ha) future, more and more pictures of American soldiers marching, marching, marching through some jungle called Vietnam, and, let us not forget, by this gold hash that was sending whispy shimmering waves of sweet paranoia over every single molecule of air? On top of all that, what if one wasn't sure if the voice of one's formerly idolized teacher was not actually his voice at all but was in all actuality the voice of some monstrous fat-cheeked English aristocrat who was throwing said voice into the frail body of Dr. S? Yes, that was a distinct possibility. What if . . . Oh, Lord, Dr. Spaulding was right this second being played for a fool by none other than some Evil Hand Puppet? And what if the Evil Hand Puppet had made sensibility slaves out of everyone who ever read old fake Englishman Henry James?

Sitting there, stoned and worried and confused, I thought, yes, yes, yes, it could happen. The Evil Hand Puppet might have his giant fingers this very second stuck up the asshole of good, kind, gentle Dr. Spaulding, making him walk that walk and talk that talk and tap his glasses. What if the fact that his voice was coming out of his mouth just a millisecond after the words were formed by his oh so refined lips? What if that little glitch was the only dead giveaway clue that he wasn't master of his own destiny nonono, but a victim of the VILE and EVIL ARISTOCRATIC HAND PUPPET Who Secretly Controlled the WHOLE LITERARY WORLD?

And what if . . . what if (open window, bird on window sill, leaves blowing right by the dusty glass, tits of women in alpaca sweaters looming like snowballs on dripping wet Baltimore back alley cherry snowball summer afternoons) . . . what if I *was* myself a Hand Puppet? Yes, first to my parents and now to Jeremy, and who can know for sure but that we aren't all some hand puppets? somebody's fingers up our ass, the dad who isn't there (but his fingers still are), the mom who lives in Fantasyville, the invisible government in the night washed away.

I shook my head, and the room seemed to swim back into focus. I was gone, wasted, whacked out. Then, to my horror, I realized that the entire class was staring at me, like the burning children's eyes in *The Village of the Damned*, and at first I thought, with the logic of pure, doped-out madness, that somehow the class had heard my thoughts, though perhaps we shouldn't dignify such rampant paranoia with the classy title "thoughts." No, perhaps, we would have to call it a mass of swarming, paranoic, but maybe also even profound impressions. For even now, as a man in my forties with an identity established, I still often feel that someone else has their finger up my ass and is making me move here and move there, and only the cushion of money and the ravages of time make it more bearable, but how far, how far indeed we still are from freedom.

Then, in my blinking, bright confusion, I realized that Dr. Spaulding was calling on me, and I looked up at him, like a newborn babe, so confused and unable to make out a human face, but heard him say, nonetheless, "So, Thomas, I wondered if you would like to explain to the class the role of the confidante in *The Ambassadors.*"

And I smiled and smiled and thought of the Evil Hand Puppet (EHP) walking and talking and acting like he was running the show and thought that in the end the EHP gets us all. But not wanting to be incarcerated in nearby Larson-Payne Mental Hospital, I didn't say any of that, but instead answered: "The role of the confidante is, technically speaking, a way to enter the hero's mind . . . learn his thoughts. Since James isn't telling the story in first person, he can't have the protagonist, Strether, talk directly to the audience . . . but by Strether confiding in the confidante, James is able to advance the plot and advance Strether's moral awareness at the same time."

"Very good," Dr. Spaulding said. He began to say something else, something about Conrad and *Nostromo,* but the bell went off and the class silently packed up their books and their pencils and trundled off out to the hall. I tried to follow suit, wanting to finish my drug-induced "insights" outside on the great green sward of grass, but Dr. Spaulding, who never spoke to me unless spoken to first, picked this very day (to my sweaty horror) to call me aside: "Thomas," he said, "may I see you for a second?"

"Yes, certainly," I said, falling into our old literary nineteenth-century formality (which now, now that I was out and about and acting bad in the world, seemed silly and pretentious).

"Thomas, I don't know quite how to ask this, but are you all right?"

"Yes," I said. "Yes, I'm fine, fine, fine."

"You're sure?" he said, and his eyes bore into me, like two hollow point bullets.

"Yes," I said. "Was my answer wrong or what?"

"No, your answer was fine," he said. "And it's none of my business, but you seem distracted of late. *Very* distracted."

My heart beat rapidly, and I felt my stomach lurch a little.

"I'm sorry," I said. "I had a rather long night."

"I would imagine, Thomas, that you have had quite a few long nights where you're living."

He stared at me with an almost unbearable intensity. I looked down at the floor, but then suddenly, without knowing why exactly, his remark began to irritate me.

"What does that mean?" I said.

"It means," he said, "that I've heard you've moved in with Jeremy Raines and his crowd."

The written word will not capture the amount of disgust in his manner when he said "Raines and his crowd." It was as if he was talking about a pack of filthy road beggars.

I felt something ugly rising in my throat.

"Yes," I said, trying to keep the rage bottled inside. "I *am* living there. That's true."

Dr. Spaulding sighed and tapped his glasses in his palm. He got up stiffly from his chair and did his usual dramatic walk toward the window (and I thought, uh-uh, this don't work so well anymore, I've seen it before, my boy).

"You remember, don't you, Thomas, our talk about your potential?"

"Yes," I said, staring at the swirling dust motes by his head.

"I'll reiterate. I happen to think you have real potential as a thinker, and I hate to see you squandering your efforts on a bunch of, well, you know what I mean, I'm sure."

"No," I said, feeling suddenly as though I wanted to scream at him. "I *don't* know. Apparently, you disapprove of Raines. I mean, how do you know so much about him?"

"I had him as a student," he said. "Last year."

"So?" I said, "What did he do, flunk out or something?"

"No," Dr. Spaulding said, "he got an A. Raines is a brilliant student. But he has already gone down another path, he and those sloppy pseudo-Bohemian friends of his."

I waited a full second before I spoke, but finally I couldn't stand it any longer.

"I resent that," I said. "Those people are friends of mine."

"All the sadder," Dr. Spaulding said. "Tom, I don't generally interfere with my students' lives and I debated long and hard whether to say anything about this to you. But those people. I know they're experimenting with drugs. No good can come of it, Thomas. It's all so second-rate. I mean, Raines and his friends think they're so avant-garde, but what they're doing has already been tried. The Dadaists tried it, and it led to second-rate art and a lot of suicides, and Rimbaud believed in stripping away the senses and it led to his giving up poetry and an early death. Not to mention the surrealists who created nothing of value, and then, of course, there are the beatniks, who are a pathetic crew of *third*-raters. Thomas, I know what it's like to be young, smart, and overly sensitive and be stuck on a campus where most of the people are, well, small-minded little educationalists, but believe me you are better off standing alone for now than going on with those hopeless, confused . . ."

I could stand no more.

"Oh, really," I said, standing up from my chair, though to this day I have no idea where I got the nerve to defy him like this. "Well, what should I do? Pretend I'm, ah, European aristocracy, sit around with my tea and my madeleine? No, make that my beer and crab cakes, remembering Oriole and Colts games from golden days past. Or maybe I should choose among my thousands of invitations to all the 'best homes' and play croquet and titter about the symphony and the love affairs of the countesses and dukes. I don't know where you're from, Dr. Spaulding, but me, I'm from around the corner in good old Baltimore. My old man lives in the bathroom night and day, and my mother lives in a fantasy world made up from soap operas and the *Reader's Digest*, and we don't get invited to the fucking Hunt Cup and we don't get to go on 'crew sails' down on the Chesapeake, and I didn't get to go to Harvard, because I didn't have the right connections or the right sensibility either, I suppose. The truth is I love living with Raines. He doesn't sit around worrying about what would be considered propitious or correct or which action would best reflect his 'highest species potential,' he just gets out there and makes the world listen to him. He's the first person I've met in this goddamned city who's not shaking in his boots, and if he's a con man and a lunatic, well, that's okay, too. At least he's not some quivering academic, hiding behind his bound volumes of the Great Masters while the real world passes him by."

Oh, I was filled with myself that day. The second I finished the speech I realized how much of it was pure falsity, how sorry for myself I'd been, how I'd had many of the same ambivalent feelings toward Raines. It was just that I couldn't bare to hear them coming from Dr. Spaulding.

Yes, I had been melodramatic and corny in my rage, and yet I also knew that much of the anger that had come out of me was real, and not only that, it was the very first time in my life that I had recognized it as such.

I was shocked by my fury, my resentment of the rich, and my own anti-intellectualism.

Still, even though much of what I had said was not only true but liberating, I felt nothing at that moment but a stunning and instant remorse.

Dr. Spaulding turned and stared at me as though he were seeing me for the first time, and I hated and feared what I saw in his eyes.

"You've made yourself clear, Thomas," he said. "You may leave."

Feeling numb and fearing I might burst into unmanly tears, I fled from the room.

I staggered to my car and drove down the York Road. The hashish had worn off, and my head throbbed so badly that I felt it might explode. I had no idea where to go.

Certainly not to my parents' home. Who knew what kind of insanity I might lay on my father? And not to Chateau either, for though I had denounced Dr. Spaulding in classic B-movie fashion and was aware now, to my huge embarrassment, how much my Great and Heroic Speech had sounded like some Warner Brothers late-1940s anti-Nazi movie. ("You see, Spaulding, it doesn't really matter what happens to me, 'cause there will be a million more beatniks marching through the streets and you European Aristocracy-Loving Sensibility-Selling Nazis will be slaughtered in your caviar, pal.") Still, I told myself, what did he know? It wasn't as if we were stoned night and day, and it wasn't as if Raines didn't have a plan, and it wasn't as if I had committed myself whole cloth to him, like he was some goddamned Svengali and I had fallen for his every line. Or had I?

Oh, if ever there was a confused youth, it was I. I found myself pulling over at the Hollow Bar 'n' Grill, with its wonderfully comforting sign of a huge blinking swallow and the words *Swallow at the Hollow* underneath. I walked inside that dark bar, pulled up a stool, and ordered a crab cake and National Bohemian beer. There was a bartender with one glass eye named Eric and he handed me the cake and smiled kindly, and I looked around the place at the rough-hewed men in plaid workshirts, having their morning beers, and I felt sad but somehow at home. Hank Williams was on the jukebox, and I remembered hearing him for the first time when we lived down on Winston Avenue in the late 1940s and my father screaming from the bathroom (even then the bathroom), "Turn that hillbilly music off, mister!" but I had liked it and thought Hank was the real, raw thing. Even now as he sang "Hey Good Looking," I thought this *is* Baltimore, this is my home and where I'm comfortable, and then that thought was canceled out by blushing embarrassment and remorse for I knew I'd been a class A fool and probably thrown away my future with Dr. Spaulding.

So I sipped my beer in that dark place and watched the men talk about the prospect for the Colts this year, and I thought about the team and how much I loved them, how

I'd waited once for three hours outside Memorial Stadium to get Johnny Unitas's autograph, and what foolishness Dr. Spaulding would make of that. The door opened and a few other truckers came in and shook hands, and there was real warmth in the way they greeted each other and I thought I like them, they're the guys I've grown up with all my life. Aren't they worth writing about? Doesn't anyone care about their lives? And I thought of old Dreiser and how Spaulding had laughed at his "clumsy writing," but I remembered reading *Sister Carrie* and being knocked out by it in high school. And was that wrong? Was it just because I was some second-rater? And what of all my friends? Eddie and the Babe and Val? Was it true? Were we all just a bunch of second-raters? And then I remembered Spaulding saying to me one day, "I intended to write more books myself, but after I got out of the army, I got into teaching and I never had the time," and I thought, it wasn't the lack of time, Dr. S., because teaching college you have nothing but time; no, it was the fact that you painted yourself into the Snob's Corner, that everything vital and interesting and alive was terrifying to you, so you called it sloppy and unwashed and stupid, and you x-ed it out, and now you want me to make the same fucking mistake.

But as soon as I came to these thoughts, I wanted to push them out of my mind, for I was as yet too frightened of them to really believe in them. After all, how did I know that *any* of what I was feeling was really true?

Maybe I was just making up excuses for myself because I hadn't been studying . . . elaborate rationales from the BRIGHT BOY WHO SQUANDERED HIS POTENTIAL . . .

And maybe when I was forty-five and still sitting on these very same bar stools mumbling inanities about the Colts and the Orioles, maybe then I would wish to God I had listened to Dr. Spaulding and chosen the road that would lead to being an English professor, a High Priest of Rarified Sensibility.

Oh, my mind was on fire from all the insights, half-insights, lies, truths, half-truths that were buzzing through my synapses. I couldn't take any more of it, so I drank three more beers and ate another cold crab cake.

Finally, drunk and confused, I was about to leave, when I felt a hand on my shoulder. I was so startled that I nearly spilled my beer.

But when I turned and looked up, there was the huge red-faced, gap-toothed, and squinty-eyed Bobby Murphy from my old neighborhood. He was dressed in a dark silk suit and an expensive black Chesterfield overcoat with a silk collar, and now he stared down at me with a mocking but not unaffectionate smile.

"Doctor," he said. "You look a little under the weather. College life too rough for you?"

"Murph!" I said. And without speaking another word, we embraced unashamedly at the bar. It was then that I saw he had two goons behind him. They were also dressed in black but not quite as elegantly. Neither of them looked at me but were busy casing the Hollow, their eyes roaming nervously around like pinballs.

"Christ, it's good to see you," I said.

"You too, Doctor, though our meetings are too rare now that you've become a college type. You write that big book about Baltimore yet?"

"No," I said, smiling and feeling a great rush of affection for him. "Not yet, but one of these days."

"Well, what are you waiting for, wisdom to strike you dead or something?"

Murphy laughed then, a great, warm laugh from his belly, and the thought made me laugh, too, for I saw at once that he was right. What the hell was I waiting for?

"I been reading about you a lot in the papers, Murph," I said.

Murphy nodded slowly, took out a gold cigarette case, and waved to Eric, who instantly brought him three beers. One of the goons behind him reached into his wallet and got out some table money.

"Yeah," Murphy said. "I thought that little piece they did on me inna Sunpapers . . . 'at was pretty good. You see it, Tommy?"

"Yeah, I saw it," I said. I was smiling now. I couldn't help it. Murph basked in his own semigangster celebrity, and yet there was a generosity to him, the sentimental Irishman who believed in watching out for the little guy.

"So what'd you think?" he said. "I mean was the writing any fucking good or what?"

"Yeah," I said. "It was good, but I don't think she knew you that well. I mean she made you out to be a tough guy, and all of us from the old neighborhood, we know you're a pushover."

Murph sighed and put his huge fingers on my arm and squeezed it until the pain was almost unbelievable, but I showed no signs whatsoever of discomfort.

"Ah, remember the old days, down in Govans," I said. "Playing cowboys and Indians and stuff."

I was now seeing stars, but that was par for the course. Murphy and I had played this game since we met as kids. He squeezed a little harder, and I gasped a little but kept on talking.

"Yeah, you were always Hopalong Cassidy, Bobby. I been meaning to ask you about that. I mean this guy was a white-haired, fifty-five-year-old homo and yet you wanted to . . ."

I couldn't finish the sentence, because I was now on the verge of a heart attack. Murphy saw I was turning blue and eased off the pressure a little.

"Pretty good, Doctor," he said, laughing. "You're still pretty tough for a college dweeb. Hey, but that's not right about Hoppy, is it? William Boyd wasn't no pillow biter was he?"

"I don't know," I said, "but Johnny Unitas . . ."

Both of the goons behind Murph snapped to attention on that one, as if I'd slapped them in the face.

"Oooh, that's cold," Murph said. "That what they teach you in college? Lose all respect for your childhood heroes?"

"You're right," I said. "Johnny U. is pushing it too far. I stand corrected, Murph."

"Johnny U. and Jesus H. Christ," Murphy said, "though I would bet money only on the former. Remember that pass he threw to save old Ewbank's job? Who was it caught that one?"

"Jim Mutschellar," I said, remembering it as though it were yesterday. "Away game against the Redskins, the ball bounces offa' Redskins defensive back named Norb Hecker."

"Norb," Murphy said thoughtfully, "he musta' been a Welchman. They all got bad hands."

"It bounces offa' Norb, and Jim Mutschellar catches it," I said. "Colts win in the last second, and old Weeb's still in there as coach."

"'N' the rest, as they say, is fucking history," Bobby said, draining his second beer. "Remember that guy who was quarterback before Unitas, George, ah, what was his last name, anyway?"

"Shaw," I said. "George Shaw from Oregon. He was good, too, but he got hurt, Unitas came in, and that was all she wrote for George."

"Wonder where the fuck he is now," Murphy said.

"You didn't hear?" I said.

"What?"

"He and Hopalong Cassidy are living down by the Chesapeake Bay in this little tin-roof love hut!"

"You crazy little fuck," Murphy said.

He swiped out his hand at me, but I easily ducked under it. When I came up he tousled my hair, like he did to his kid brother.

"Hey, I gotta go," Murphy said. "I got people to do. Why don't you call me onna phone sometime? You don't want to get too far from your own, Tom."

"I'll do it," I said.

"Good. My little brother, he still remembers you. You ever need anything—I mean *any*thing—you call Murph, okay?"

201

He turned and cruised out, his two goons in front of him. They stopped at the door and looked around outside, but Murph pushed them on from behind.

I sat at the bar and finished my beer, awash in the glow of old friendship and remembered our cowboy and Indian games down in the old neighborhood. Murphy and I sitting up in the Mulberry tree at Craig Avenue waiting to ambush Danny Snyder and Eddie Livingston as they crept down by the green hedges and I remembered Johnny Unitas throwing the ball to Raymond Berry in the 1958 Giants game, and all of us in every block in Baltimore racing from our houses when the Colts won the NFL championship. The Murphys and I were one big pile on their row house front lawn. I looked around at the Hollow Bar, at the cigarette smoke and the amber reflections on the beer bottles, and I thought the place was like a church, that coming here had reconnected me to my own past and maybe Dr. S. wouldn't understand it, but something in my soul once again felt healed and fine and whole.

Unfortunately, the next morning I had all my usual ambivalence about Raines plus a monstrous hangover. My head pulsed, my limbs ached, and I had the humiliating feeling that I had to go back and apologize to Dr. S at once. Even in my extreme state of confusion, I knew, deep down, that he was trying to help me. Still, I wasn't ready for that, not quite yet. First, I wanted to talk to Raines about his little bag of tricks and just where Val and I fit in. With that in mind, I went down to breakfast early and caught him just as he was finishing a phone call, but before I could say a word, he smiled, grabbed me by the arm, and started pulling me out of the house.

"I think you and I need to take a little ride," he said. "How about it?"

"Fine," I said with a certain coldness in my voice. "There's nothing I'd like better."

Minutes later, we were swerving directly into the path of a milk truck and Raines was shaking his head: "I'm worried about your attitude," he said, turning at the last possible second, thus avoiding certain death for both of us.

"Yes, I suppose you're going to say I'm not a team player," I said after I'd taken my hands away from my eyes.

"Well, you're right. I happen to be in love with Val and I don't dig it at all that she's ready to fuck some English jerk to save your company."

"Beyond that, how do you feel?" he said smiling.

"Lousy," I said, holding my head. "And no lame jokes are going to make me feel better. And if I'm not hip enough for you, then I'll pay up my month's rent and get out now."

Raines smiled and shook his head. His cowlick blew back and forth from the air conditioner's false breeze.

"Who said anything about hip? I hate the word *hip*. We just do what is necessary, my boy."

"And it is necessary that Val fucks Hogg so she can save your ass?"

"No, of course not. I wouldn't think of it," he said, nearly smashing into Mister Softee.

In spite of myself, I thought of Dr. S.'s warning. If Raines and I were going to have a friendship, I would have to demand a lot more out of it. I wasn't going to be fooled by his sweet smile. Not anymore.

"Oh, you are so clever," I snorted. "You pretend that you had nothing to do with it, but we both know that you control Val. She owes you her sanity, or at least you've made her think she does, so she'll do anything you like. That's just wonderful."

"What is it you think I had her do, my friend?" he said as we ran the red light at Charles Street and Eager.

"I don't know, only that she assumed you would expect her to fuck that British guy's lights out if *necessary*. She certainly didn't come to that conclusion on her own."

"So you've decided that I'm a manipulative, scheming rat?" Raines said. "Dr. Caligari? Is that it?"

I said nothing but looked morosely out the window at the dilapidated redbrick row houses, which leaned out into the street like an ugly child's crooked teeth.

"Well, it's true," Raines said. "I do manipulate things. As a matter of fact, I have a confession to make. I've sort of manipulated you and Val from the start."

"What?" A kind of electric shock went through me. He'd outflanked me again, the bastard.

Raines smiled mysteriously and looked over at me.

"Well," he said, "as you can well imagine, Val has endless guys hitting on her. I mean she only has to walk down the street and the guys fall all over her but since she got out of the B-3, that's the women's schizophrenic wing of Larson-Payne, I've been keeping tabs on her a little to make sure she doesn't make any bad decisions about people."

"How kind of you," I said, not ready to give an inch.

He shook his head and sighed deeply.

"No, it's not because I'm so kind. I just love Val and I don't want to see her fuck herself up, so when I met you, I thought, here's the guy for her, honest, sensitive, a student of literature."

"What?" I said, completely incredulous. "You're trying to tell me you set us up?"

"Exactly," Raines said, smiling at me openly now, but it wasn't a gloating smile. No, he looked sweet, happy to have been of assistance. Still, I didn't believe a word of it.

"But that doesn't make any sense at all," I said. "I met Val in the stacks over at the Calvert library, and you weren't anywhere around."

"You mean the day you were sniffing the books?" Raines said, smiling again in his most charming manner.

"No!" I shouted, my head swimming. "You weren't there. She told you about it and now you're just pretending that . . ."

"*Treasure Island* was my favorite book, too," Raines interrupted, pulling the car next to the sidewalk, across from the Washington Monument. "When you picked it up and sniffed it, I was sure I had made the right decision. Only a man who thinks for himself, only a man who loves and values books, would do something so foolish and so endearing."

I felt a flush of tenderness for my friend. And yet, I simply couldn't accept it. If he was telling the truth, he had been playing me like a harp since the day I first spoke to him on the phone.

"She could have told you about *Treasure Island*, too," I said. "You could have told her to remember everything and . . ."

"You're right," he interrupted. "It's true, I could have, but what reason would I have? *Why* would I do it?"

As I sat there staring out the window at the children running around the great white marble fountain in the square, I actually felt the seat beneath me grow hotter.

"Well," I stuttered. "Because . . . you're mad and you have to control everyone around you and . . . I don't know why . . ."

He shook his head and banged his big fist on the dashboard.

"Paranoia," he said. "Suspicion and pain and paranoia. My boy, these are the true diseases of our age. You're acting as though you were caught in some evil design of mine. I can understand that. And it's true, I did manipulate you . . . a little. I waited until you left your house that morning, then I sent Val over to see you in the library. I had her invite you to the poetry reading. That is all extremely manipulative, and I apologize for it. But it seemed to me that the ends justified the means. After all, if you and Val hit it off, then I had found her a charming and worthy companion, and if not, well, you go your way, she goes hers. What harm's been done?"

Everything he said was rational and perfectly well-meaning. I saw that then. But for some reason, I still wanted to give him a shot to the jaw.

"Yes, but a person doesn't want to think that his romantic chance encounters are all part of somebody else's design," I said. "That takes all the romance out of it."

"Really?" he said, smiling at me in that damned knowing manner of his.

"Really," I said.

But, of course, I wasn't sure of that. After all, in some way that I couldn't articulate at the time, Raines's whole wild tale made my meeting Val somehow *more* romantic.

"Well, I apologize," Raines said, starting the car and lurching forward a little. "I hope you'll come to forgive me in time. But you have to admit, it's not exactly a Machiavellian scheme."

"Jesus," I said, so stunned that I scarcely knew what to say at all. "You're impossible. I mean I don't know how I feel about all of this, whether to thank you or punch your lights out."

"You'll figure it all out in due time, my boy," he said. "That's the beauty of being young. We have all the time in the world."

"Well," I said. "Since we're making confessions, I have one of my own to lay on you."

"I already know," Raines said, "The University of Baltimore pictures look like modern art."

"I'm sorry," I said. "I just didn't get the camera stuff right, the exposures and all. You know, we have got to be a lot more professional than this. You should hire some pros."

"I know," he said, sighing sadly. "I had hoped we could keep the whole business strictly among friends, but it looks like we're going to have to make some concessions to the real world. That's why I'm adding a new man to the staff today, a friend of Eddie and Babe's, supposed to be an ace photographer. He'll keep us going until the Kodak funds come through. Then we'll take stock of our situation."

He smiled sweetly at me and bashed the car into a gasoline truck directly in front of us. I saw the word *Flammable* in great red print and shut my eyes.

THE KING OF CARDS

> ⮞

For the next few days, there was almost an air of professionalism about the home on Chateau Avenue. Hogg's promise of a grant from Kodak had made us all rather proud of ourselves, and over breakfast there was a kind of confident, buzzing chatter. Handless Eddie even started using the word *account*, as in, "Yes, I think we just about have the Morgan College account sewed up." He was answered by the Babe, who said, "Yes, there was no doubt about it we were headed up the ladder and in a couple of weeks we would be out of the red." I was faintly surprised and embarrassed by this sudden conversion to the cocky language of salesmanship. How had these beatnik weirdos who lived on the margins of polite society even learned of such things? It was almost as if the language of business was some secret, mythic, subconscious poetry that flowed in the hearts of all Americans, straight or bent, a somehow sobering and near tragic thought. I had always assumed that the subconscious life was one of Freudian weirdness, a swamp of wild incest and strange primeval longings. But what if this was not so? What if the real secret language of tongues under every American's heart was some kind of lame business chatter?

But at the time, these were not thoughts I wanted to have. And so I thrust them down down down into the great gaping hole of unwanted observations. At any rate, our new seriousness seemed to manifest itself most obviously in our newest business partner, Timothy Donnolly, Eddie's friend, the "ace photographer." A tall, handsome quiet man in his late twenties, he seemed the very essence of professionalism. His clothes were pure Ivy League, purchased downtown at Eddie Jacobs, the finest men's clothing store in the city, and he smoked a very handsome pipe. Indeed, Donnolly looked like a country squire, relaxed, judicious, the kind of man who inspires confidence in his co-workers. On a tour of the Hole, he looked over the huge embosser (iron ore) machine, the laminator, and the cameras and took out a small pad of paper on which he made copious notes. Having done this, he rubbed his chin, nodded to himself, and silently gave the notes to Raines.

Then he nodded sagely and said as much to himself as anyone else in the room: "Do-able, very, very do-able. Yes, indeed."

Whereupon he took out the pipe, a leather pouch of tobacco, filled up, and struck a match.

We all stood around staring at him, and it seemed to me then that Tim Donnolly was the answer to our ragtag group's prayers.

And for a week it seemed we would make it all come true. The reshoot at the University of Baltimore went well, and Eddie and the Babe managed to get them all embossed and sealed in their little laminated covers without making one mistake. Meanwhile, Donnolly was bringing in new equipment (paid for on the King's already bloated credit cards) and conferring with Jeremy Raines in his quiet and consummately professional way.

And by the end of that week, we had finally done it, handed the cards to a smiling Hawkins, who in turn handed me a check for fifteen thousand dollars. By God, we were learning how to make this thing work.

That night, after a wild party and an even wilder love-making bout with Val, I dreamed of Jeremy Raines wearing a crown of I.D. cards and conferring with none other than Benjamin Franklin himself, that original inventor of the American dream. Yes, I thought, smiling as I awoke and looked at Val's breast glowing in the Baltimore moonlight. Yes, it was true, Jeremy was some drugged-out hipsterized version of that old American gentleman, and I thought of him in his bedroom with Miss Lulu Hardwell, the crazy queen slut nun, and I remembered old Benjamin F., his very own bad self in France, taking those powdered wigs off the wives of the frog dukes and duchesses and lifting their silken dresses and I said, "Yes, yes, yes, score one for America, score one for the true democracy of blood and muscle and ambition and wild screaming eyeball-popping ejaculations in the black Baltimore night."

All of these memories flooded through me as I sat there in front of what had been our old house on Chateau Avenue, but now I stopped and looked up at the fat man with the pink alligator shirt. He was peeping at me in a curious way, and now he lay down his lawn rake and walked to my car.

"'Cuse me, buddy," he said, "but you got some reason for staring up at my house for the past three hours?"

"No," I said. "Sorry."

He gave me a look that said he wasn't fooled.

"Look, you may as well just admit it," he said. "You're one of them goddamned speculators from over in Washington, D fucking C, isn't that it? Well, I can tell you, pal, we don't got no intention of selling 'es here place. We are not the kinda people that cares about living with a few niggers."

"That's good," I said. "Because I don't want to buy the place, okay?"

"Yeah, 'at's what you say now. But I seen you staring up at it. But you can kiss 'es place good-bye, 'cause we like living here. Niggers or no niggers. Truf is I get along wif 'em fine."

"That's great," I said.

He looked at me hard, then kicked the side of the rented car.

"Now get the fuck outta here," he said. "Go back to the nation's capital, where youse belong."

"Right," I said. "Will do."

I turned on the key, hit the gas, and shot forward into the street.

I had been dead wrong about him. He wasn't a yuppie, but a Baltimore redneck trying to become a yuppie and, in his own confused way, a liberal. He was probably up from hillbilly Glen Burnie, and in his own set, he was a radical who would dare live "with the niggers."

The thought made me smile. It was the kind of complicated irony Jeremy would have appreciated.

I drove down the block, took a right and then a quick left into the old alley just behind Craig Avenue. There in front of me was the old softball field Val and I had found one stoned night, a night we'd smoked hash and lay out on second base, and as we made love, she'd screamed out "Safe," and we'd fallen into hysterical laughter.

I got out of the car and smelled the sweet odor of the honeysuckle, which grew wildly over the black tar garages, and I walked down behind the garage and looked out at the old field, half-covered with weeds and wild vines now. I thought how lush Maryland was and how, though I had never been a nature lover, I had come to take the wild smells of flowers and vines for granted and missed them in New York.

I sat down now on an old log, knowing that eventually someone else would come and tell me to move. That was the world we were in now, here and everywhere else, strangers were trouble, dangerous, and it seemed to me like a memory from another world that we slept at Winston Avenue, and even later at Chateau, with our screen doors unlocked.

Yeah, soon they'd be coming to move me again, but I sat there anyway and smelled the flowers and watched the black kids bouncing the ball off the old garage doors and dreamed on.

Those few weeks after we had hired Donnolly were full with promise. We were on our way, going up, up, up, into the wild blue yonder of fast greenbacks and comradely love.

THE KING OF CARDS

I remember it all now, like some movie montage: Eddie handing a tray of perfect cards to Donnolly, who smiled and passed them up the steps to a radiant Babe, who took them to the car. Jeremy clanging out the numbers on the old iron ore machine, as we all laughed and shared beers and joints, Val and Sister Lulu swinging like sisters on the tire swing, the two of them trading stories about where they would travel when the big money started coming in. And Jeremy telling me late one night that what he wanted to do most of all with his part of the dough was to start building a clinic, a place that would allow for new, radical treatments for the mentally ill. "By the time I'm through my postgraduate work, it'll already be built and we can attack these diseases in a new way, get to the patients before the goddamned hack therapists make them worse." Yes, the old house on Chateau was positively abuzz with the promise of success and money. There was no stopping us.

Then Hogg called.

As it so happened I was down in the smoking Hole overseeing a lamination job, a tricky business actually, because the lamination machine tended to overheat. When that happened, the graphite rollers, which spit out the long rolls of plastic-enclosed cards, would begin sending the cards through at some monstrous temperature, burning holes in the plastic, twisting them into some kind of strange plastic origami. Faces and noses were burned beyond recognition. That had already happened once a week ago, but luckily Tim Donnolly had been on the scene and quickly fixed the temperamental machine.

On this bright day, however, things were running smoothly, and I was sitting in the great new overstuffed armchair we had managed to get from a yard sale just down the block. Indeed, with money in my pocket, and the cards oozing out of the laminator in one long continuous flow, I was able at long last to get back to my reading of Henry James. In fact, as the call came in, I was thinking how old Hank James would approve of the I.D. King's quest. After all, many of his own heroes, Lambert Strether of *The Am-*

bassadors, for example, were none other than self-made men who, having made their fortunes, strived for more, for a touch of the higher spiritual and artistic life in Europe. But I had decided I was not interested in Europe. If I ever dared talk to Dr. Spaulding again, I would tell him that when I had money, I would try and really discover our own culture right here in funky old Bal'mere, and I would do it with my visionary company of poets, lovers, friends. Oh, yes, that day I was in a pure Utopian mood, and as I saw the faces of the happy students rolling smoothly inside the plastic, I began to smile back at them. It seemed to me then that each and every identity in those little cards was a potential friend, all of them part of myself, and I thought suddenly that all cards were one card and that God himself was the great wise Photographer in the sky.

Then the phone rang. I picked it up and answered cheerily: "Identi-Card Systems."

"Hello, Jeremy?"

"No," I said. "Mr. Raines is out on an important call. Can I help you?"

"Oh, I know who this is. It's wild and jealous Tommy Fallon, right?"

"Hogg," I said, my good mood not disturbed one whit by his crack. "Good to speak to you. Coming to town?"

"Not exactly," he said. Then I noticed it: There was something in his voice, something strained and tentative beneath the forced English bonhomie.

"No?"

"No. Well, I don't know exactly how to tell you this, so I'll just give you the good news first."

"Yes?"

"I'm moving to San Francisco. Isn't that just knockers?"

"Yes," I said. "I suppose . . ."

"Oh, it is, old son, believe you me. Haven't you heard? There's wild things happening there in a section of town called Haight-Ashbury. You know I was upset for a while when I got the news, but then I got to thinking, I'm not really made for business. I mean, buying and selling one

212

another, I don't think that can be good in the end. Hell, I may not even be a capitalist."

"I see," I said, shifting in my seat. "You were fired then?"

"Ah, you Americans," Hogg said, "masters of understatement and diplomacy. But why not call a spade a spade? I'm afraid yes, I was, but only technically. I've simply been doing things so assed backwards because I hoped they *would* fire me, you understand, Tommy? They say I was self-destructive. I say I am on the very first leg of a journey to free myself from all of the business hustle and bustle. I mean, who needs it?"

"We need it," I said bluntly. "We've made purchases on credit. We have to have that grant. It's still coming, isn't it?"

There was a long pause, and I heard him suck in a breath.

"You son of a bitch," I said.

"You don't understand, Thomas," he said. "You're into the old capitalist mind set. You just have to step outside of it and . . ."

"Fuck you, Hogg," I said. "We have to have that grant. Can't whoever is taking your job get it for us?"

"I'm afraid not, old boy," he said. "You know how it is, the new man doesn't want any of my projects to succeed. It wouldn't reflect well on him."

"Don't come to Baltimore," I said to him, "unless you want me to kick you a new asshole."

"Hadn't intended to," Hogg said. "Give my best to Jeremy. And kisses and hugs to Val, friend."

Furious, I slammed down the phone and watched the plastic cards curl up like a live twisting snake in front of my feet.

That night we all waited on the front porch—silent, glum, forlornly sipping iced tea like a band of abandoned children, waiting for our foster father to take us back to the stone cold walls of the Orphans' Home.

Finally, somewhere around nine, Raines drove up in his battered Nash. Indeed, the car now seemed to be some otherworldly vehicle, something designed by a race of post-nuclear radioactive mutants who only vaguely remembered what cars of the twentieth century must have looked like. There was only one front headlight, and the right front bumper was peeled back to reveal the balding right front tire itself, a strangely unsettling sight, like a man who had lost his lips in a fire and now walks around with his naked incisors fanged loose at the world.

Out of this steaming mass of junk stepped Raines, looking as boyishly happy and buoyant as ever. Though there were what looked like Polish Johnnie Hotdog stains on his unpressed cord suit, and his cowlick was standing straight up, like some weird exclamation point on his head, he somehow gave the impression of perfectly innocent happiness. He may as well have been a smiling five-year-old running up the steps toward a group of loving relatives. Such sweet happy trust lit up his face that it was impossible for me to do as I had planned, which was to tell him straight away. Instead, like Lulu and Val and the Babe and Eddie, I stared down at the front porch.

On the top step, Raines looked down at us all and cleared his throat in his ironical comical manner: "Ahem, ahem, what is all this? Somebody get cancer around here?"

"No," I managed to croak out. "That is not it."

"Oh, and nobody's parents died or anything. Nuclear war has not been declared, have I got that right?"

"Worse. Hogg called," I said.

"And there's no grant and he thinks we should all move to San Francisco and live on the streets and pretend we're moonbeams and we are flat broke with mucho bills to pay. Is that all that's bothering you, troops?"

Raines smiled his most charming smile and ran his fingers through his cowlick as if he were trying to flatten it, a useless task.

214

THE KING OF CARDS

"Jesus," I said. "Isn't that enough? Have you seen the invoices? Identi-Card is beyond bankruptcy. If there were still poorhouses, we'd all be shipped there tomorrow."

"It really does look bad, Jeremy," Val said, leaving my side to go hug him.

Never one to be outdone in the nurturing department, Lulu Hardwell jumped from her rocker and joined him at the hip on the other side.

"Well, at least if I have to go," Raines said, "it will be with two beautiful women at my side."

"Looks like the end of the line, King," Eddie said, rubbing his stump across his face.

There was a general mumble of tortured agreement with this assessment, but suddenly Raines unhitched himself from his two voluptuous pallbearers and jumped up on the old porch railing. Holding himself by one of the thick white columns, he swung toward me like some kind of frayed-suited Robin Hood: "You all are so damned hopeless. You see how easily you cave in. That, my dear friends, worries me much more than our temporary lack of funds. It's not our lot to give in to mistrust and despair. In fact, my buckos, it occurred to me just tonight that we are not just selling cards here at all. No, what we are doing is remaking our own selves, if you will, taking time-lapse pictures of our identities that don't even exist yet. You see that, don't you? I believe that once our true pictures are developed we'll no longer think or feel or walk or talk or fuck the same, and surely our photos will never look the same. Mistrust will disappear from our eyes, and fear and paranoia will be vanquished from our mouths. We'll be walking, talking angels, dear friends, shining so bright we burn out the lens of any camera known to this sad and dreary world."

His speech left me spellbound. I couldn't resist such a combination of vision and jive. Nor did I want to, and yet, it seemed that someone had to interject this poetry with a little hardscrabble reality.

"That's all well and good," I said in a voice too sharp

215

with sarcasm, "but how will we reach this visionary state without the aid of good old-fashioned dinero."

Raines leaped from the railing and grabbed me by the shirtfront. He stared at me with his coal-black eyes, and I felt fear suck through my chest.

"Money?" he said. "I am talking about your mortal soul, and you keep riffing about goddamned money. Haven't you heard? Money is shit. Let me ask you a question: How easy is it to take a shit? Well, that's how easy it is to get money. *Comprendez?* So do not worry your overheated head, my boy."

He pushed me away then and walked into the middle of the group, and we stared at him with fear and awe in our hearts, but something else, too, some love that was so deep and so wide and so powerful that it seemed to pour from my body like camera light. We all reached out to one another like some band of wigged-out apostles and held hands, and Raines beamed in on us like the eye of the ultimate fiery lens. I heard a click and saw a flash of white light and each of us then knew that we had been seen and known and that there was only one picture, one smiling face, and it was Raines's face and my own and Babe's and Eddie's and Val's and Lulu's, and we all dissolved into one huge, watchful tender eye.

In the morning I found myself once again driving downtown in Raines's nearly destroyed Nash. The day was black, the streets filled with blowing newspapers, as we drove by the abandoned ice-skating rink at North and Charles.

"Who are we hustling today, Jeremy?" I said, using the cynical tone I affected when I felt myself too overwhelmed by admiration for him.

"Here's the deal, my boy. When we go in for this interview, you make certain that you smile and agree with everything I say. But try not to talk if possible. Mr. A. doesn't much go for talk. Nothing personal, it's just his style."

"Mr. A?" I said. "As in Rudy Antonelli?"

But Raines only smiled and ran into a parking meter down at crumbling, ramshackled Pier 2. After I had removed my forehead from the windshield, I stepped out of the car and was immediately struck by an overwhelmingly powerful odor of spices, and I realized we were just across from the old McCormick Spice Factory. The richness of the smell made me dizzy, as though I were enmeshed in an Arabian dream. As we walked over the old condoms, candy wrappers, and wine bottles, I felt giddy with burning spices—paprika, marjoram, basil, mint—in my nose, eyes, and mouth.

We walked by the old tugs tied up at Pier 1 and the old *Port Welcome*, the funky and charming little tourist boat that my grandfather and I sailed on so many years before. Then we crossed Pratt Street and walked directly toward the spice factory, and every step of the way I got dizzier and dizzier. It seemed as though we were going to walk into the factory itself, but instead Raines led us down a redbrick alley in between two tin-roofed warehouses.

Soon we came to old faded redbrick steps that led down to a basement restaurant with a bright blue doorway. But we didn't ever get to the steps. From the alley behind us, two men quickly moved in on us, and I found, to my horror, a gun in my back.

"Move," said a harsh voice.

"Just a minute," Jeremy said, but this was a mistake.

"Shut the fuck up, you Shamrock scum," the other voice said.

We were pushed down the steps so hard that I lost my balance and my head crashed into the bar door. I half fell inside the place and found myself being shoved again, so much so that I fell onto the floor in a heap and Jeremy came sliding in behind me. When I looked up I saw two darkly burnished faces holding guns to our heads.

"Hey, we're not Shamrocks," I said. I thought of Johnny Apollo. Was this possibly his bizarre revenge?

"Right, you Irish fuck," the bigger of the two men said, kicking me in the ribs.

I groaned heavily and held my burning side.

"Be calm," Jeremy said. "Be very calm. We're not Shamrocks, believe me. We're just businessmen here to see Mr. A."

"Right, and I'm fucking Jackie Kennedy," the fat one said. He had three distinct fat ridges in his forehead, so that it looked like a pink accordion.

The thinner one with him made appreciative laughing noises that sounded like a man drowning in his own blood.

"You two little fucks are Shamrocks, sure as shit," the fat man said.

"I assure you we're not," Jeremy said.

"He fucking assures us," the smaller man said, waving the pistol around.

"That makes me feel a lot better," the fat man said.

"Let's take these two assholes for a ride out to Fort McHenry," the thin one said. "You look like a couple a patriotic Irishmen. You can sing the Star Spangled fucking Banner while we ventilate your Mick faces for you."

"No," Jeremy and I said.

"Yes," the thin one said. "Right now."

"No, no, no," said a voice behind us.

I thought for a second it was a voice I had hallucinated. But slowly I turned and looked, and there standing behind us was a man so big that he made the fatter of the two gunmen seem like a dwarf by comparison. He stood in the shadows and rocked back and forth on his heels, swaying to some unheard beat. His face was lost in shadow; all I could see were his huge hands, which he clasped together in front of him like an opera star about to sing an aria.

"Mr. A.," Jeremy said. "Great to see you."

"You know these two fucks, Mr. A.?" the fat one asked. There was real disappointment in his voice.

"Of course. Now *you two* fucks take off and try and find some of our real enemies, okay?"

"The Shamrocks?" Jeremy said as he scrambled to his feet.

"You got it," Mr. A. said. "Nasty Irish boys from out inna county. Bobby Murphy cut one of our boys, Tony De Luca, up real bad last week. They're real cute, too. When they ice somebody, they always leave one of these as a souvenir."

He reached his huge hand into his suit pocket and pulled out a four-leaf clover, which he dangled and twirled in his fingers.

"I'm getting quite a collection of these, believe me. Those Mick bastards are getting real bold. Word is they might gonna try and hit us."

"Here?" I said as I got to my feet. I couldn't imagine Bobby Murphy doing anything so dumb, but I kept my mouth shut.

"Could be." Mr. A. said, opening a door to a back room. "You know the Irish. They're prone to doing wild, dumb shit. They fucking love drama. Come on, you two, I gotta finish my lunch."

In the yellow light of the back office I could get a better look at Mr. A. He was twice as large as huge. His thick fingers looked like tongs, and his neck was as big as a fire plug. He walked royally to his desk and only took five minutes to sit down. On the desk was a gigantic crab cake submarine sandwich, which vanished when he picked it up.

On his ten fingers were eight diamond rings, which twinkled pink and blue in the half-light. On the knotty pine wall behind him was a swordfish with a disappointed look on his face, and off to one side of the room was a pinball machine called Aces High. The desk was littered with papers and pickles. The juice from the latter ran over the former.

"Jeremy Raines," he said in a voice that was a near whisper. "You want to have one of these subs. They got all kinds, babe. Your cappicola, your Danish ham, your Italian salami, your cheese. Thing is about these though is the sub juice; sub ain't worf dick hard if it ain't got juice on it, which you would think these goombahs would get right after I tell them, what nine hundred times?"

He signaled to somebody in the corner and a skinny man with a nose like a greyhound stepped forward. The man wore a black silk suit that shimmered like crude oil in the sun.

"Hey, Sonny," Mr. A. said. "Lay em down, all right?"

Sonny got an extremely reluctant look on his face but slowly put his left hand on the desk.

Mr. A. picked up a paper weight, smiled at Jeremy, and smashed it down on Sonny's hand. Sonny groaned, and I turned away.

"Now, Sonner," Mr. A. said. "I tole you once, I tole you a thousand fucking times, your sub needs pickle juice. So go over there with these pickles, and squeeze 'em on here and don't drench the fucker. I want a hint of pickle flavor, you follow me. Nothing fucking more."

Sonny had tears in his eyes, but he simply nodded, picked up the submarine sandwich and the pickles, and walked over to the jukebox.

"And don't get the shit onna records," Mr. A. said. "Last week you fucked up 'It Only Hurts for a Little While,' which happens to be my favorite song. Had to really rap him over that."

He licked off one of his huge, crooked fingers and stared hard at Jeremy.

"So, Jeremy Raines, boy genius. Hope the roof sign worked for you."

"It worked beautifully," Raines said. "By the way, this is my associate in Identi-Card, Thomas Fallon."

"Really?" Mr. A. said. "Pleased to meet you, Fallon. Hey, that's an Irish name. You sure you aren't some Shamrock fuck?"

"Believe me, sir, I'm not."

"No, you look like lace curtain Irish. Anyway boys, state your business. My time is wasting."

"I don't want to bother you, Mr. A.," Jeremy said. "But well, as you know my business has unlimited potential . . ."

"That's one man's opinion," Mr. A. said. "I'm afraid every business has its own built-in limits."

"True. But we haven't even come close to reaching ours," Jeremy said. "I won't bug you but I need, well, temporary funds."

Before Mr. A. could speak, the dog-nosed man was back with the sub. It dripped pickle juice, and Mr. A. looked at it cryptically.

"Soaks the fucking bread all the way through," he said. "I oughta hire niggers for this job. Niggers are the best fucking submen."

Mr. A. took a huge bite of his sub, then sighed.

"This is almost it, almost, Sonny, but not quite."

He reached up fast then and slapped Sonny with the back of his pinkie ring. Sonny tried to jerk out of the way, but the ring left a deep gash in his cheek, from which a small stream of blood began to flow. I felt my stomach turn like a washing machine and my knees felt weak.

"Maybe next time you'll get it right, Son. Now how much money you need, Jer?"

"Thirty grand," Jeremy said. "That would just about do it."

Mr. A. wiped some mayonnaise off of his lip and shook his huge head. Little beads of sweat flew off his neck ridges.

"I don't know, Jeremy. You're a fucking genius, no doubt about it, but you got bad organizational problems. I just don't know if it's good business."

"Mr. A., this will be the best investment you ever made. We're almost there, sir," Jeremy said.

Mr. A. shook his head.

"Remind me of your old man. A born salesman. You oughta come work for me. You'd make a fortune."

"We'll make a fortune on Identi-Card," Jeremy said. "But I need this cash transfusion. Fast."

Mr. A. took another bite of his sub, and the juice ran down his triple chins.

"Okay. I tell you what. Just for old time's sake, I'm gonna give you money, but for it I get fifty percent of the business and my associate, Johnny Martello, comes by and helps you get organized. He's a business whiz; he'll help set things straight."

Raines looked as though he had been shot in the knees. His entire body sagged.

"Thirty percent," he said, and there was great pain in his voice. "And with all due respect, sir, we don't need any help."

"Thirty-five then," Mr. A. said. "'Cause I'm feeling generous, but Johnny has to be part of the deal. You'll love him anyway. The kid's a pro."

Raines looked at me and shrugged.

"Okay," he said. "But I still retain control."

"Wouldn't have it any other way," Mr. A. said. "After all, you're the man. Johnny will just come around and offer some hints. It'll be good experience for him, and maybe he can streamline your operation."

Jeremy started to answer him, but it was too late. Mr. Antonelli picked up the huge sandwich, opened his cave mouth, and took a massive bite.

When we were back outside, walking along cobblestoned old Pratt Street in front of the big Greek ocean tankers, I couldn't contain myself any longer. I stopped walking and grabbed Jeremy by the collar.

"Listen to me," I said. "You can't fucking do this. This guy is a hoodlum, a killer. I mean, this is crazy."

But Jeremy simply took both my hands and pulled them gently away from his throat.

"What would you have me do?" he asked. "Give it all up? When we are this goddamned close? Don't you think I've already been to all the banks? They don't make loans on new inventions. Believe me, Tom, this is the only way."

"No," I said. "Look at what's already happened. I mean they thought we were fucking in with Bobby Murphy. I know that fucking guy, and he means business."

Jeremy smiled at me then as if he were pleased.

"You know Bobby Murphy?" he said. "Well, well, the innocent scholar."

"Look, we'll talk about my identity problems at some other time," I said. "But, Jeremy, you can't do this."

He shook his head at me and kept walking toward his car.

"You know?" he said. "You're starting to piss me off. I mean, I'm beginning to think you're the kind of guy who wants to have all the fun without taking any of the risk. And that's not how I play."

That hurt. It hurt because I sometimes suspected it was true, and it was the single trait I most despised in myself.

"That's not true," I said. "But if we get in with these guys, we'll never get out."

Jeremy out and out snorted at that one.

"You've seen too many mob movies, Tom," he said. "What makes you think these guys want to be in with us for good? Look, Mr. A. and my family go back a long way in politics. Hell, he was even instrumental in getting me into Harvard."

"Harvard?" I said. "When did you go there?"

"For a couple of weeks," Jeremy said. "But there was this nonsense about, well, my trying out my hypnotic experiments without consent. Nothing actually happened. I mean a girl got slightly hysterical, unfortunately she was a senator's daughter, and I'm afraid I found myself bounced out of there. Which was fine with me because I hated all that

Cambridge Square crap, anyway. But it was a real disappointment to Mr. A. He'd made so many donations there to get his own son Dominick through law school, he thought he had the place wired. Just goes to show you, you never know what's going on at the highest levels. Ever read any of that in old Henry James?"

He smiled at me then in a way that really scared me, and I thought, There's something wrong here, something that I'll never understand. As we got into his car, I felt a chill come over me, and I thought that if I had any sense at all, I would grab Val, and both of us would get out now before the ax fell.

That night I went to the library. But it was impossible to study. James's words wouldn't form on the page. All I could think of was how little I knew of life. Raines had been to Harvard. Mr. A. had helped him get in there with his donations. As common as such stories are now, they were to me then like electric bolts into the brain. Harvard, like Hopkins, had seemed the very embodiment of the Higher Purity. The idea that some gangster's money could in any way influence . . .

I could scarcely believe it, and yet, it seemed so fantastic to me, so beyond anyone's mere imagination (who could make up such a thing?), that it must be true.

Finally, at nine-thirty, I gave up even attempting to study and headed home.

Once back at Chateau, I felt the tension lying inside my stomach like a dark pool. I wanted to cry out a warning, tell them all that we had to turn back from this path before it was too late. Maybe Raines was right and I was being a naive idiot, but I didn't think so. I thought of Mr. A.'s casual brutality and could only imagine his wrath if we fouled up an order of cards.

I walked up the concrete steps, pushed the old swinging tire for luck, then took the last three wooden steps to the front porch with a single leap.

Without missing a beat, I swung open the screen door to the living room. There in front of me was the entire group,

Babe, Eddie, Lulu, Tim Donnolly, and Val. But there was someone else, too, a man who was sitting in a chair with his back to me. Indeed, the others seemed to be looking at him curiously, as if they were staring at a circus freak. Raines crouched in front of the seated man, his hands on the man's shoulders as he looked deeply into his eyes.

I stood stock-still as Raines began to speak to the guest. "You are relaxing," he said. "You are so relaxed. It's as though you are lying on a great green lawn somewhere, the greenest of green lawns, and you are looking up at the perfect blue sky and there are clouds up there, like when you were a child, and now you're starting to roll down that green hill, you're rolling and rolling and rolling, and you feel no fear . . . you feel free, very free and you are perfectly happy and relaxed, and you're rolling along . . . like a child. Do you see?"

The man whose back was to me nodded slowly, and it was obvious that he was already in some kind of trance.

"Now you're starting to slow down. You're at the bottom of the hill," Jeremy said. "You're rolling slower and slower, and you feel relaxed, so very relaxed, and you're asleep but you can still see the green grass and hear my voice clearly. Isn't that right?"

"Yes," the man in the chair said. I knew his voice. I knew it only too well. And as I walked toward them and around the side, I could now clearly see him in profile, and suddenly, I couldn't breathe very well. Those slightly rounded shoulders, that shock of black hair. The man in the chair was my father.

I gave out a short little shocked laugh. It was bad enough that I had fallen into ill-repute with crazy Raines, but now my own father was being turned into some kind of hypno-slave by this lunatic.

I stormed around in front of my poor hypnotized father's chair with the full intention of breaking things up, when I saw a sketch pad and pencils just behind Raines. What the hell was this all about?

I didn't know and I wasn't going to wait to find out, but

as I started to speak up, Val put her lovely forefinger on my lips, and Raines turned briefly and winked at me.

"You feel wonderfully relaxed, Mr. Fallon," Raines said. "You feel so good, so deeply in touch with your own heartbeat. Can you hear your heart beat, Mr. Fallon?"

"I can," my father said in a monotone, looking up and smiling like a sweet, trusting child.

"Yes," Raines said, stroking my father on the head, like a pet. "Yes, of course you can. You have never felt so wonderful, so deeply in tune with yourself. It makes you want to express yourself, isn't that right?"

"Yes," my father said, "yes, it does. I feel . . . I feel . . . so fine. Excellent, actually, Jeremy."

He smiled happily and put his hands on Raines shoulders. Again, I wanted to break it off, but then I remembered hearing somewhere that if you messed up a hypnotic session, the subject might become unbalanced and be unable to return to the conscious world.

I was helpless. Whatever madness Raines had in mind I was powerless to stop.

Now Raines moved back a little, moving slowly, like some dream dancer, and he showed my father the sketch pad and pencils.

"You feel so fine that you would like to draw something. Wouldn't you very much like to draw?"

"I would?" my father asked in a small, innocent voice.

"Indeed you would, Jim," Raines said sincerely.

"What would I like to draw?" my father asked, taking the pencil in his hand.

"Whatever you wish," Raines said. "It's up to you."

My father smiled again happily, trusting, and I felt a chill go through my body. This could not be happening. I'd smoked too much hash and was dreaming the entire thing.

"Whatever I wish," my father said. "Whatever . . ."

Then he picked up the pencil and began to draw. He started tentatively at first, a light brush stroke, but then he slashed a bold stroke across the canvas and another and another. And we watched as he drew a picture of a young and beautiful girl with great black eyes and a long, haunted face. Eddie and the Babe made a sound, "Oooooooh," and Val grasped my hand hard, and Lulu smiled at me, and I felt tears coming down my face and I turned and looked at Raines, who reached out and put his right arm around my shoulder.

"That's my mother when she was young," I said, choking on my words.

Everyone was quiet, and Val held my arm tightly and shed a tear herself.

"Is this okay?" my father asked, in a soft, trusting tone.

It was all I could do not to break down and I said, "Oh, yeah, Dad, that's fine, just fine."

Later, after Jeremy had brought him out of it, my father stood with me on the front porch. We drank vodka and grapefruit juice and looked out at the dark front yard.

"You feel okay, Dad?" I asked.

"Yeah, I feel fine. First time I've felt fine for three days."

"You've been sick?"

"You might say that," he said. "Heartsick."

It was so unlike him to confide in me I didn't know what to say.

"Your mother has left me," he said, and his voice was flat and toneless as a dying man's.

I heard the words come out of his mouth, but I couldn't register them emotionally. After all, I could barely believe what I'd just seen, and this new piece of information seemed like one more fantasy.

"Come on," I said lamely. "That's not possible."

"Left me for a guy in her sculpting class," he said. "They're getting married, moving to Virginia."

"Jesus," I said, remembering my mother's sudden interest in sculpting, an interest both my father and I had found amusing.

"I don't blame her," my father said. "I couldn't live with a guy like me either."

A tear rolled down his face, and I wanted to put my arm around him but didn't dare.

"Maybe she'll come back, Dad," I said. "I'll have a talk with her."

"Don't waste your energy," he said. "Twenty-five years we been together. She wouldn't leave if she planned on coming back."

"Just the same," I said, feeling spooked, "I want to try. Where is she living?"

My father rolled his eyes and sighed deeply.

"In a motel out by Howard Johnson's," he said. "A place called the Black-Eyed Susan."

"Oh, Jesus," I said. "I know that place."

My father looked at me in a jaundiced way.

"Oh, really?" he said. "And how are you so familiar with it?"

I wish I'd kept my mouth shut. The Black-Eyed Susan was infamous when I was in high school. It was a place kids could go to have sex and nobody asked them for I.D.

"Well . . ." I mumbled. "I mean I don't know it personally. I just heard that it was a good place."

"Uh-huh," my father said. "Hey, look at that."

He ran down the steps and looked at the old tire hanging off the oak. I walked down behind him, and before either of us knew what was happening, he had sat down in the tire and I was pushing him into the starry night sky.

"Why did you let Jeremy hypnotize you?" I asked.

"I don't know. I was waiting for you and we just got to talking. I didn't tell him about your mother, but somehow I got to telling him about how I used to draw and paint and he brought it up. I mean, ordinarily I wouldn't have done anything like that, but since three days ago, I feel like I'm up for all kinds of new things. They say that's what happens to you when you're having a nervous breakdown."

"*Are* you having one?" I asked, pushing him higher and feeling myself recede farther into a state of shock.

"I think so," my father said. "I can't sleep. I can't eat. I told Jeremy all about that, and that's when he suggested he try hypnotizing me."

"I can't believe you let him do it."

"Neither can I," my father said. "But I feel great. Maybe Jeremy is right."

"Right about what?" I asked suspiciously, pushing him toward the moon.

"That a nervous breakdown is just what I need."

"Oh, God," I said. "I hate that kind of crap. Of course it's not."

"I don't know. I'm not happy like I was. Hell, that's obvious. Maybe your friend is right. I have to let in all kinds of new things. Push me a little higher, son."

I did as he asked and watched him kick into the dark night.

"Dad," I said, "do you think that you might want to paint again?"

"I don't know. I don't know if it's that simple. I didn't stop for a simple reason."

"No," I said, pushing him higher still. "But you're so damned good at it, I think it would make you happy."

He came down then and used his legs to brake himself. When he had stopped swinging, he turned to me and put his right hand on my arm.

"I wasn't any Hopper, Tom," he said. "I was just a guy from Baltimore who painted."

"You were good," I said. "You never found out how good."

He looked at me with such kindness and charity that I turned away. But it lasted only a second, then the old hardness came back into his face.

"Ahhh, what do you know," he said.

229

He gave me a faintly patronizing smile, and I felt something breaking inside my chest. He must have sensed it, because he softened his scowl and slugged me on the arm.

"You know," he said, "maybe it's not so important what I do. Maybe it's important *you* find what's right for you. You used to talk about writing. I remember you even won a couple of awards."

"Yeah, Dad," I said. "They gave me a silver pen in the seventh grade for a short story I wrote about Mr. Tooth Decay in health class."

He smiled and nodded his head.

"Are you going to pursue it or not?" he asked.

"I don't know if I'm any good," I said.

"So what?" he said, and there was the old toughness in his voice, but I felt somehow that he meant it in a loving way.

"I've been trying a little, Dad," I said. "Keeping a journal."

"Your friend Raines, he wouldn't be afraid," my father said.

I didn't know what to say to that. It felt a little like a dagger slipped into my side. But, of course, he was right. Jeremy, I thought, was afraid of nothing.

"Well, I'm not Jeremy," I said, and my voice was truculent, childish, and I wanted to immediately suck back in the words. But it was too late.

"No, of course not," he said. "Just as long as you don't regret not trying. Believe me, son, there's nothing worse than that."

He gave me a little half smile, turned, and looked at the huge Baltimore moon.

It was very late when my father left.

In shock, I staggered back up the front porch steps and up to my room.

THE KING OF CARDS

In the bedroom, Val was waiting for me. She was naked, sitting in the cane chair by the window.

"Hi," she said. "I think your dad's great."

"Yeah," I said and slumped down on the bed across from her.

She put her arms around me and smoothed back my hair. "What is it?"

"He came here to tell me that he and my mother are getting divorced."

"Oh, God, Tommy. I'm sorry."

"Hey," I said, "it's what I've been saying they should do for the last five years. Man, I can't tell you how many times I would say to my mother, 'You don't have to take this crap, him staying in the toilet all night. Go ahead and leave.' You know what she used to say?"

Val didn't answer, she just kept running her hand through my hair.

"She used to say, 'You think you're so smart, hon. But you don't know how you'll feel if I ever did it.' Yeah, and I used to laugh at that and yell, 'Hey, Mom, if this is like some deal where you're staying together for my benefit, don't bother, 'cause I'm not getting a damned thing out of it.' And I meant it, too. I really did. So how come I feel like somebody just tied me to a couple of horses and had them ride off in opposite directions?"

"They're your parents, Tom. Of course you're going to be hurt by it."

I got up from the bed and felt the tears roll down my face.

"No," I said. "I shouldn't feel anything like this, 'cause we're the new people. Hey, we don't believe in jealousy and we're freeing ourselves from the old inhibitions and like only squares could feel bad 'cause a bourgeois marriage broke up."

"So you're a square," she said, standing up next to me and holding my face with her hands. "But you're a lovable square. And both your mom and dad know that."

"Shit," I said. "Shit."

231

I fell into the bed and curled up next to the wall in the fetal position.

She wrapped herself behind me and put her head on my back.

"God," she said, "families."

I pulled her to me and held her and shut my eyes and thought of my mother's speech a week ago. Suddenly it occurred to me that her story about the Hargroves had not really been about staying in Baltimore at all. No, she was telling herself that tale as a last-ditch effort to resist leaving my father.

"Leave Baltimore and a lion will eat you right up, hon."

Those were the kinds of stories her mother, Mamie, had told her and, as far as I knew, had been passed on in our family from generation to generation to keep people in their place as a magical talisman against wanderlust or adultery.

I laughed at myself now. What a fool I'd been not to see it. In the past six months my mother had told one of those stories at nearly every family get-together, and what she was really saying was, "Somebody notice me, somebody listen to me, or I'm going to blow out of here whether the lion eats me or not!"

But we never heard her. All we did was laugh at her. Good ole Ma telling her ridiculous folktales again. Good ole Ma, entering a dumb radio contest.

It had never occurred to either my father or myself to ask her what lay beneath those stories. And now she was gone. My mother, gone with another man. I still couldn't believe it.

I sat up and looked at Val.

"I'm going out to see her," I said.

"Tommy, it's late."

"I don't care," I said, reaching for my jacket. "This is wrong. It's crazy. They can work this thing out. I mean, you saw my father tonight. He's hammered by this. But this could be just the thing to wake him up. A good shock to his system."

"Tommy," Val said, "it's not really your business."

"Oh, really," I said, my voice dripping with sarcasm. "Well, who's business is it then? This is my family. And I'm not going to just let them sit by and die. Can I use your car?"

"Of course, but . . ."

"No 'buts,' " I said on my way out. "I know I can do something here. And I gotta give it a shot. I'll see you later."

She tried smiling at me when I left, but I could see the pain in her face. I knew what she was feeling. My pain, my sadness, but I couldn't accept that from her.

"Don't give me a patronizing smile, okay?" I said. "I don't need that from you. I know exactly what I'm doing."

I gave the bedroom door a little extra slam on the way out.

I was only about a block away from the Black-Eyed Susan Motel in Towson when it occurred to me that I should have called my mother before I came. She might not even be there, or she might be asleep. It could have waited until tomorrow. But I felt such an urgency. My father needed me. He hadn't said it, but I could see from the dead look in his eyes that he wasn't going to do that well without her around. Sure, he felt okay tonight, but that was just Jeremy's temporary magic. He needed my mother. I was certain of it. And she needed him. After all, they'd been married for twenty-five years. You couldn't just throw an entire lifetime down the drain for some complete stranger.

It was up to me—the only sane voice in the family—to straighten them out.

I pulled into the parking lot and looked up at the huge neon flower sign. The Maryland state flower, a symbol I'd always liked for its down-home beauty. But now the steel petals looked like some kind of lewd obscene joke. I thought of my mother living here and shuddered.

I went to the manager's office and looked inside. The place was lit like some kind of pink cave, and there was a paperback novel open on the desk, a thriller that pictured a girl in a string bikini riding behind some jet skis, but there was no one there, so I took a peek at the guest book and found my mother's name. Ruth Fallon—Room 27. I walked outside and took a couple of steps up to the second landing. It was then that I noticed that the place had scrolled flowers all over the place, on the walls and on the iron handrail grating—steel flowers that looked like musical notes stuck on a black steel staff—and again I was struck by the motel's seediness. How could my mother be staying here? It occurred to me then that she must be suicidally depressed to make such a desperate move.

I came to her door, room 27, and started to knock, but voices stopped me. Happy voices, laughter.

"Oh, Larry," the voice said. My mother's voice.

I stopped my hand in midknock.

"God, Larry," the voice said this time.

"Ruth . . . You are so good to me, Ruth," a man's voice said. A husky voice. Drenched in sex.

"No," my mother said. "You're the one that's good."

"To hell with it," the man's voice said. "We're both good."

"Could you hand me a beer, hon?" my mother said.

"Don't mind if I do," the man said.

I felt dizzy, breathless, and staggered back from the door.

"Your program is gonna be on the TV soon, hon," my mother said.

"Oh, yeah," the man said, laughing. "But on the other hand, the program can wait."

"I'll have a little drink to that," my mother said.

Then I heard them both laughing again. I didn't stay for any more. I walked very quickly down past the black-eyed susans, took the steps three at a time, and headed for the car.

Miss Kissable Lips, I thought. Miss Kissable Lips has finally found her man.

234

THE KING OF CARDS

> ➤

It was 3 A.M. when I got back to Chateau Avenue. I'd stopped at the Hollow and had about twenty beers and in a moment of pure perversion I'd gotten into an argument with an out-of-work plumber over who was the greatest quarterback, Johnny Unitas or Y. A. Tittle. All my life I had worshipped Unitas but tonight I made my case for old Yelberton Abraham and in the process found myself taking on the entire bar. The "debate" had quickly declined into a name-calling contest, and finally the plumber had told me I was a "cheese-eating daddy-jacking son of a bitch who didn't know jack shit about football." I had told him to stick his ratchet up his ass, and there had been a pushing and shoving battle, which poured out into the street. He'd finally landed a little punch on my head, which raised a small welt. It wasn't big enough to assuage my guilt, but it would have to do.

My parents were breaking up. The little fiction that I told myself, "They really loved one another in spite of all their troubles," was a lie. I had known it was a lie for a long time, and yet, I still clung to it and I felt like a fool.

I climbed the steps to my room and saw Val lying there asleep. She had been right. There was no point in me going out there, none at all.

I looked at the desk across from the bed and saw my journal. And thought of the lie I'd told my father about it.

In the last week I'd barely touched it.

I sat down heavily in the cane chair by the window and stared up at the moon.

I thought of Raines guiding my father's hand, my father kicking out his swing to the stars, and the sound of my mother's sexual laughter, which made me cringe. Yeah, I was a new man. Nothing could bother me.

I picked up my journal and a pen.

And sitting there, by the moonlight, I began to write.

That night I wrote for four straight hours, wrote scene after scene, snatches of dialogue, fragments of my life at Chateau Avenue. I felt possessed of some strange energy; language, pain, laughter, and sex all met in one great confluence of my mind and heart. Whether it was any good at all, I had no idea, but I knew I had to get it all down, and I had to keep getting it down from then on.

Finally, around seven, I decided to get up and go downstairs for coffee.

I walked down the steps, half asleep, still buckling my Levis, when I was shocked by the sight of a stranger in the living room.

He was a pillow-fat man with a head like a huge olive. His hair was piled up like black whipped cream, and he wore a tan raincoat as big as a tarpaulin and five-inch-high Cuban heels. In his hand was a cigar about the size of an oar. At that moment, the Babe came walking out of the kitchen. She had on a green see-through off-the-shoulder peasant blouse and the tightest pair of red short shorts known to man.

"Excuse me," she said. "Can I help you?"

The fat man took a great long look at her, blew a black puff of smoke in her face, and shook his head.

"Raines around here?" he grunted.

"Upstairs asleep," the Babe grunted back in a parody of his guttural voice. "Wish you would put out that cigar."

The fat man looked at her hard then. The playfulness disappeared from his little pig eyes.

"Oh, you do, do you?" he said.

"Yes, I do," the Babe said. "Sorry, but I'm just not into them."

"Oh, really," the fat man said. "Well, what is it you are into? 'Cause from the looks of things it ain't business."

I was going to intervene at that point, but Eddie walked in from the kitchen. He took one look at the fat man, and grimaced.

"I don't know who you are, mister," he said, squinting

his eyes like a gunslinger. "But this is our place, and since you walked in without ringing the bell, it would be wise for you to do as she says and put out the cigar."

The fat man said nothing but simply stared at Eddie with an insolent little smirk on his face. It was as though he were a scientist investigating a bug.

"Sorry, I didn't send youse an invitation," he said. "Name's Johnny Martello. Maybe you know of my employer, Mr. A."

"No," Eddie said, "I do not know of your employer, but I do know that that cigar is choking the Babe here, so I'm asking you one last time . . ."

"Ah, that's all right, Ed." I heard a voice from behind me. I looked up and saw Jeremy coming down the steps. His cowlick stood straight up on his head like a rooster's crown, and he was wiping the sand from his eyes. But when he saw Martello, he snapped to attention.

"Johnny," he said in a voice that was thick with insincerity. "Johnny, my friend, don't mind Eddie and the Babe. They're just being a little overly sensitive. Come in, and I'll have Lulu cook us up some breakfast."

He turned and pointed to Lulu Hardwell, who was trailing down the steps behind him in a shockingly revealing blue nightgown with so many ruffles she looked like a walking curtain.

Martello squinted and looked up the steps.

"Innaresting," he said. "But I don't got no time for innaresting. The truth is I got a check for you, but first I wanta' see your setup."

Jeremy looked as though he was going to squirm out of his pants.

"Yes, of course, the setup," Jeremy said. "And ordinarily we could do that. But today I have clients out in western Maryland, and I'm running late."

"No see, no money," Martello shrugged. "See you all of a sudden."

He laughed, flicked a huge ash on the floor, and started to leave.

"Ah, Johnny," Raines said. "Don't run along. We'll make time."

He tried to give the words a devil-may-care spin, but there was terrific tension in his voice.

"Good. And, by the way, who are these dudes?" Johnny Martello said.

There was a long and terrible silence, and I had to restrain Eddie by grabbing his stump.

"Well, as a matter of fact," Jeremy said, "this is some of my staff, and there isn't a better one around."

Martello looked at Jeremy Raines and shook his head.

"I heard you was a put-on artist," he said. "So I'll go along with you. Yeah, this is your staff. Right."

He cocked his huge head and looked at us with a sly and knowing expression.

"Hi ya', staff," he said, then gave a short little contemptuous laugh.

I felt something breaking inside of me. My breath came up short, and I suddenly had an overwhelming desire to grab Johnny M. by his throat.

Martello looked carefully at each of us and then a dull light came on in his eyes.

"Hey, you're like serious?" he said. "These people *are really* your staff? Well, we'll see about that."

There was another long silence. Then Raines signaled Martello to come follow him to the kitchen and down the crumbling cellar steps to the Hole.

I stood waiting with Val, Lulu, Eddie, and the Babe and the quiet was like five blindfolded prisoners waiting for the first shock of the firing squad.

"That guy needs a new asshole," Eddie said.

"You said it," the Babe said. "I can't believe we're gonna be working with him."

"Don't worry," I said. "Jeremy will charm him into submission."

"Don't count on it," Lulu said.

She started for the kitchen.

"I don't think he wants you to go down there," I said.

"Bullshit," Val said, "Jeremy needs all the support he can . . ."

She never finished her sentence, for that second we heard Jeremy and Johnny tromping up the cellar steps.

The five of us stood there in the living room as still as statues.

Johnny looked at us and shook his head.

"I know what you all think," he said. "You think I am going to make a speech about how lame this organization is. You think I am going to do a whole number on the complete lack of professionalism, what a shithole the cellar is, but you are completely wrong. I'm going to say only this. You got a note due in five days. First installment on the loan Mr. A. so generously laid on you. If you do not have the payment, then this company becomes part of the Rudy Antonelli Corporation, from which day forth it'll be run right, so I wish you good luck."

He started to turn and stalk out, his big belly bouncing in front of him like the prow of a battleship. Eddie Eckel could stand no more. He moved in front of Johnny and glared at him with pure hatred.

"You are a complete and total asshole," Eddie said.

Johnny said nothing. Instead, he reached into his pocket.

"Better get outta' my way, stumpy," he said in a reptilian hiss, "or I pull my hand outta my pocket and then you ain't gonna need either hand."

For the longest time the two men stared bullets at one another. Then, finally, Eddie moved aside.

"Five days, beatniks," Johnny said, then turned and waddled through the front door.

We stood in complete silence. I felt a helpless rage rolling inside me, and I looked at Jeremy, who slumped onto the steps.

"All right, the guy's a goombah, so what? Five thousand is no problem," Jeremy said. "We finish Catholic University today, and they owe us seven grand."

"Great," I said, "And then what? We've still got this jerk coming around here every day. Listen, Jeremy, I know I'm

not an expert in business, but something just struck me.
Mr. A. wants us to fail so he can take over the business."

"That's crazy," Jeremy snapped. "You're paranoid."

"Am I? You told him all about the potential of the card
business. He's no dummy. He knows we've got a shaky
scene here. He figures he pressures us a little, we either go
under or sell out at some low figure. This is just the beginning. No matter what we do, they're going to be hounding
us from now on."

There was a long silence, then Jeremy jumped up from
the steps.

"That's bullshit. He's not Al Capone. He has some assholes working for him, but believe me, if we come up with
the bread, he'll lay off. Now let's stop spinning these paranoid fantasies and get to work."

"I don't know," Eddie said suddenly. "I think the prof
might be right. You saw that guy. These are pricks, Jeremy.
I say we give 'em their money back now, find some other
way to raise the dough."

"Oh, really," Jeremy said. "Well, what do you have in
mind, Ed? Because I'm happy to entertain any brilliant fi-
nancial solution you have."

There was a real edge of mockery to his voice. It was the
first time I'd ever heard him speak that way to anyone, and
I knew in my heart that he was scared now, scared to death.

"Don't talk to Eddie in that way," Babe said.

"Hey, he didn't mean anything," Val said, jumping in.
"What's Eddie, a sensitive little lamb?"

"You shut the hell up," Eddie said. He moved toward
Val and thrust his finger in her face.

"Hey, watch it," I said, moving in front of her and pushing my face a half inch from his.

We were one second away from punching one another
when Raines spoke.

"Listen to you all," he said. "Listen to you! We've made
it through worse times than this. And we're going to be
fine, fine. Here's what we are going to do. We'll get a few
more colleges to buy our cards, then when they pay us we

will pay off Rudy A. and find other more legitimate investors. Relax, and remember, we're family."

That shut us all down. I stared at my shoes, as did Eddie.

"I'm sorry, man," Eddie said.

"No, it's nothing. We're all just tense. Forget it."

He pat me on the shoulder, and when I looked across the room, Val and Babe were hugging one another. But it didn't feel good, not good at all. And when I turned to look at Raines, he gave me a forced, painful smile, and I knew that he was as worried as the rest of us.

Still, though Martello had shaken us all, we refused to panic. Now, more than ever, we were determined to save Identi-Card from ruin. I placed a tense call to the development lab and found out that the latest batch of pictures had come out perfectly. That buoyed our spirits considerably. Now all we had to do was make certain the right pictures went with the proper names, laminate each card with plastic, pull a massive all-night embossing stint, and roll over to Catholic U. on Friday, cards in hand. They'd pay us, we'd pay Rudy, and for another month, at least, we'd stay alive.

Two days after Martello had come into our lives, the weather changed. The first signs of real winter were in evidence and the falling brown and orange leaves blew up and down Chateau Avenue, covering the steps, the sidewalk, and the parked cars. Jeremy wore an old green corduroy jacket with leather patches on the sleeves and a pair of oversized khakis and had an ancient battered but rakish green plaid scarf wrapped around his neck. He was never without his black plastic wraparound sunglasses. The total effect was that of some bizarre hybrid, part Maryland horseman-gentleman and part downtown hipster.

As we walked toward the Nash, Jeremy kicked through the leaves happily, like a sweet-natured child.

"We'll surprise Mr. A., my boy," he said. "We're going to bring home the proverbial bacon."

"Where are we headed, Chief?" I asked. "Out to some new colleges?"

"Not yet," Jeremy said, smiling. "We've got to make a little trip to Larson-Payne first."

I couldn't believe my ears.

"Now?" I said. "With Rudy A. hanging over us?"

"You worry far too much," Jeremy said. "Relax, I have to do this now. While I feel inspired. Business can wait."

In a white room, with only a stool inside, Billy McConnell sat stock-still. Jeremy, Dr. Hergenroeder, and I looked at him through the one-way mirror.

"No progress at all," Dr. Hergenroeder said. "He hasn't budged one inch."

"Maybe this sounds like a stupid question," I said. "But have you ever considered Billy's problem might be physiological?"

"No, it's not a stupid question," she said, running her hands down the lapels of her lab coat. "Of course Billy's been completely checked out, and from everything we can tell, physically he's completely normal."

"Okay," Jeremy said. "Today is the day. It's going to happen. Count on it, friends."

Dr. Hergenroeder shook her head and sighed. It was obvious that she felt badly that Jeremy was going to be disappointed again.

"Did you get the paintings?" Jeremy said.

"Yes, he brought them in yesterday. They're very good."

She walked behind her great steel desk and brought out a painting, though it was impossible to say what it looked like because it was covered with old newspaper.

"What's this?" I said.

Jeremy smiled at me mysteriously and took the painting from Dr. Hergenroeder.

"The audio ready?" he asked as he slowly unwrapped it.

"Yes," she said. "We're all set up."

"Good," he said. There was something very strange going on. As he unwrapped the painting, he smiled at me.

"What have you done now?" I asked, feeling an uneasiness in the pit of my stomach.

Then he tore off the last of the paper, and I gasped. The picture was a beautifully drawn watercolor of a high castle and a deep blue moat. Looking down forlornly from the castle window was a handsome little boy, a boy who looked exactly like Billy McConnell. There was such longing in that face, such loneliness. It was as if he was silently waiting for someone to come cross that castle moat and unlock his heart.

"That's my father's work," I said, astonished.

"Yes, sir," Jeremy said, smiling and putting his hand around my back. "Painted it in three days. Did a brilliant job, too."

"It's good," I said, stunned. "I mean look at that. How many times did you have him in here to see Billy?"

"He never saw him. I showed him a photograph."

"You're kidding. How'd he pull this off?"

Jeremy nodded and smiled at me.

"Maybe he knows about some other kid who was locked in a castle."

Ordinarily I would have jumped all over such an obvious psychological interpretation, but the sadness and compassion in the painting rendered any such protests beside the point. I felt a lump form in my throat, and suddenly I was turning my head and coughing hard.

Then I noticed that there were other paintings on the floor, still wrapped, but when I reached for them, Jeremy grabbed my hand.

"All in good time, my boy," he said. "All in good time. Now Dr. Hergenroeder, let's get this show on the road."

In a room warmly painted with Mediterranean blue walls, the floor of which was covered with a rich, thick blue carpet, Billy McConnell sat in an old-fashioned overstuffed chair—the perfect listening chair. At his side was a little table and lamp, and on the table was a glass of milk and a plate of chocolate chip cookies. And on the wall in front of him was my father's painting of the boy in the lonely castle.

We sat in the adjoining room, watching through the two-way window. Billy sat completely still. He seemed not even tempted by the cookies. His blue eyes were as vacant as any store dummy's, and his mouth fell open. The room went dark for a second, but then suddenly from the ceiling there was a blue light that beautifully illuminated the painting.

Jeremy moved to the microphone that he'd set up in our room. He spoke in a deep, soothing voice.

"Once upon a time," he said, "there was a young prince named William who lived all alone in a castle. It was a beautiful and safe place, made of heavy stones, but it was lonely because of the moat in front of it. And in that moat was a horrible moat monster who would eat anyone who tried to come see Prince William. Oh, this monster was ugly. He had huge, gaping teeth and a mouth that could stretch so wide that it could eat an entire horse. All day Prince William sat by himself in that tower, and he felt deeply, deeply alone. More than anything in the world, he yearned for a friend, but no one ever dared visit the castle for fear of the moat monster. Until one bright summer day, a kindly old shoemaker came walking out of the woods."

As Jeremy said these words, the light went out on the first painting and a second painting was lit. In this one we could clearly see the old shoemaker, with his white beard and little wooden box. He looked up at the boy in the tower

244

and he seemed to be doing a little jig. Jeremy continued with the story:

"Prince William was happy. At last a friend had come to visit. The old man was so happy, for he too had been lonely. He felt so good that he performed a happy little dance and sang a song:

> My name is Joe the Shoemaker.
> I'm happy as can be.
> For at last I have a friend
> To share my life with me.

"As he sang, Old Joe the Shoemaker started to wade across the little moat. Little did he know about the dangers of the horrible moat monster. Prince William, the lonely little boy in the tower, was terrified. He knew that unless he yelled down to Old Joe, he would be eaten by the horrible moat monster. He tried to yell, tried with all his might, but he hadn't spoken to anyone in so long he couldn't get the words out of his mouth. What in the world could he do? If he didn't yell 'Watch out!' Old Joe would be eaten by the horrible moat monster! Oh, he wanted to warn Joe, he really did, he *had* to find the courage to yell. He just *had* to!"

The lights went out in the room, and we watched as Billy looked at the illuminated painting. I said a silent prayer, "Lord, let him respond. Please." I looked over at Jeremy, who bit his knuckles and whose eyes bore a hole through the window.

We waited for a minute, two . . . three . . . five, but there was no response. Billy sat as still as a corpse, his face registering a great, gaping blank.

"I'm sorry," Dr. Hergenroeder finally said. "I'm afraid it's just not going to happen today."

"Let him stay in there for a while," Jeremy said.

"But he has to get back for his medication," Dr. Hergenroeder said.

"I don't care about that," Jeremy said. "He's hearing it.

I'm sure of it. Let him sit there. Take him back in fifteen minutes. Please."

She sighed deeply.

"I have already broken my back in order to get you permission to try this," she said.

"I know, Margaret," Jeremy said, pressing her hand. "And I have one more request for you. Play the tape of the story over again tomorrow at the exact same time."

"I don't know if I can," she said.

"Please," Jeremy said. "Once more, tomorrow."

"All right," the doctor said. "I'll make it happen somehow. I promise."

"Good," Jeremy said, hugging her and kissing her forehead.

"I'm sorry," I said. "I know what this means to you."

"Yeah," Jeremy said. "But it's going to happen. You can count on it."

On the way back to Chateau Avenue, we nearly ran into the back of a streetcar.

"How in the hell did you ever get my father to paint those pictures?" I said.

"Easy. I paid him," Jeremy said.

"Out of what?" I said. "We're just about broke."

"Right," Jeremy said. "That's why I paid him out of your salary."

"What?" I said. "Did it ever occur to you that I have to live off of that pathetic sum?"

"Now think about it," he said. "What expenses do you have? I mean you get all your food and chemical supplements at the house. Hell, you can live for free practically."

"You are impossible," I said. "A total meddler. I swear to God. It's impossible to deal with you. Completely impossible."

I shook my head and looked out the window, then thought of my father's drawings, of the loving detail in them—the castle, the lonely boy. Back at the hospital, Raines had been suggesting that my father's inspiration came from my own loneliness, a sweet thought, and maybe it was true. But the boy in the tower might have just as well been my father himself, waiting by the dock on old Pier 1 for his rough and tumble old dad, Cap, to sail home from the Chesapeake Bay. Yes, I thought that was the Fallon legacy from father to son, we gave birth and we loved one another, but only at a distance, never up close. I must have let out a long sigh, for Raines turned and looked at me expectantly.

"I was just thinking," I said. "Marriage didn't work for my father, but I don't know how he'll make it being single either."

"He's going to be okay," Raines said. "Look, he's already painting again. He's ready for change. I don't see that as so awful."

"No, of course not," I snapped. "It's not your family breaking up. You know I get pretty sick of your glib answers to things. 'Change is good.' 'Let's be happy.' Well, are you fucking happy? Racing around like a maniac? Trying to be goddamned Jung and Freud and Rockefeller all rolled into one?"

Raines put a large hand on my leg and squeezed.

"Yes," he said, "I'm happy. But you should know something. I didn't get here by being a superficial asshole. Okay? I've got my scars, too, Tom. I've earned it."

"Yeah? Well, how? You know all about my past, about my parents. But you don't tell me one damned thing about yourself."

"But you haven't asked," Raines said. "And as for the past, I don't find it that inviting. You can assume it's been filled with all the usual tragedies."

"That's a cop-out," I said. "You're just trying to create some kind of mystique. The man of mystery."

"So what if I am?" Raines said. "Maybe that's what interests me the most, reinventing myself."

I growled at that, but Raines laughed.

"I'll tell you this much, Tom, I don't believe you get to know a person by all-night confessional sessions. I think the personality unravels like a strip of plastic cards. Different faces, different names at different times. I mean the whole idea of having one self, having to be one person, is insulting. Still, if it really matters to you, someday I'll tell you about the Raines clan. Meanwhile, let's just keep moving. We'll discover whatever's important along the way, huh?"

"Sure," I said. "If we're not wiped out by our charming new partner."

"Don't worry," Raines said. "We have the Catholic University photos in the bag and two more schools lined up— Western Maryland College and Goucher. We'll be able to pay off Rudy A. And Billy is going to come around, I know it."

"You really think so?" I said. "You know there are some things you can't just manipulate and will into being. You realize that, don't you?"

He smiled very sweetly and shook his head. "No," he said, "I don't. Now let's get back to the house. We've got cards to deliver!"

He punched me in the arm in a conspiratorial way, and once again I found myself unable to be mad at him. "Right," I said. "Let's go."

We smelled the burning plastic as we walked up the porch steps.

"Oh, God," I said.

"Hurry, my boy."

We ran through the living room, crashed into each other as we both tried to open the cellar door, and half fell down the steps.

There in the Hole we were witness to a terrible sight.

THE KING OF CARDS

The laminating machine had been left on for far too long and had overheated. There was a smouldering, noxious chemical smell and the entire room was filled with a great twisted, snakelike swirl of half-melted plastic, inside of which were burnt and charred cards. And even as we watched in horror, there were stacks of other cards that were starting their way through the two steaming, smoking rolls of melting, bubbling plastic that awaited them.

Sitting sound asleep on the chair next to the laminator was none other than that reliable, pipe-smoking professional, Tim Donnolly.

"Jesus Christ Almighty," I said, rushing to wake him up. "What in God's name have you done, Donnolly?"

As I rushed toward him, I heard someone coming in upstairs and made out the excited and hysterical voices of Eddie and the Babe. A second later, I heard them running across the floor and down the cellar steps.

"What happened?"

"Oh Jesus . . ."

I walked closer to Donnolly and the twisted, plastic spitting laminator with its smoking cards. I pushed my hand down on the stop button, and with a great groan, the machine ground to a halt. I looked down at the still sleeping Donnolly.

"Donnolly, you asshole, wake the fuck up! Do you hear me, you idiot? Wake up!"

My mouth was now only inches away from his face. He half opened his right eye and looked up at me with a confused gaze.

"Hey, hey, hey," he mumbled in a happy stoned way. A little spittle formed on the side of his mouth.

It was then that I saw the prescription bottle. It was sitting next to him on the floor. I reached down and picked it up and saw the magic words. Percodan . . . 20 capsules . . . 50 milligrams.

I wrenched off the cap, pulled it open, and shook the pills into my palm. There were only ten of them left.

That's when I slugged him, knocking him backward, head

over ass, into the mass of curling, smoking plastic that lay behind him.

"You worthless fucking junkie!" I screamed. I fell on him and started hitting him in the face and would have beaten him unconscious if Eddie and Jeremy hadn't pulled me off.

I pushed them both back and screamed again, this time at Eddie.

"The guy's a junkie. And you knew it! You knew it and you hired him anyway!"

Eddie looked furtively from side to side, then opened his palms.

"He swore to me he'd cleaned up," he said. "I was giving him a shot. I'm sorry!"

"Sorry?" I said. "Sorry? You've finished us. Don't you see that? Get him out of here before he O.D.'s."

I reached down and pulled the nodding Donnolly to his feet.

He looked at me with crossed eyes and gave a happy baby gurgle of joy.

"Look at all the cards," he said. "Look at all the cards . . ."

It took all my restraint not to kick in his head.

"Get him out, now!" I screamed.

That's when I turned and saw Val, Lulu Hardwell, and Johnny Martello standing at the foot of the steps.

There was a long, long pause as Johnny surveyed the surrealistic writhing snake of smoldering, twisted plastic that covered the entire moldy basement.

"Hey, look at what we got here," he said. "Looks like somebody was sleeping onna job."

"What happened?" Val said.

"A little accident," Jeremy said, but his voice was for once not filled with optimism. It was the closest to true despair I had ever heard from him.

"A little accident?" Johnny said. "You guys are very, very funny. This is the end, finito. You don't get the money from Catholic U., which means you jerks don't meet your payment. From now on we own Identi-Card and believe me, assholes, *we* will run it right!"

250

I said nothing, for there seemed to be nothing left to say. As much as I hated the fat, balding toad-faced Martello, what he said seemed to be the truth. We were finally, irrevocably finished.

I looked over at Jeremy. Val looked over at Jeremy. Lulu Hardwell looked over at Jeremy. Eddie and the Babe looked over at Jeremy.

He stood stock-still, looking over the smoking wreckage. Then he smiled and looked at me.

"My boy," he said. "Are you with me?"

I felt my heart both leap and die simultaneously. What last-ditch madness was he going to try?

"You know I am," I said.

"Good, because we need to make a little phone call. Right now."

Hello, Catholic University, Dean's Office."

"I'd like to speak to Mother Superior please."

"May I tell her what this is regarding?"

"Yes, of course. This is Thomas Fallon. I'm calling from Identi-Card in Baltimore. It's *very* urgent."

"I'll put you right through."

There was a long pause, and I turned and looked at the others who were watching me with great eyes, while next to me Val held my hand. In the background, I was aware of the little green pea eyes of Johnny Martello, looking on with smug satisfaction, waiting as his kind were born to do—for others to fail, so that they might refresh themselves by dining on the corpse.

"Hello?"

"Hello, Mother Superior? This is Thomas Fallon of Identi-Card Products. I'm afraid we have some bad news."

"Yes? Is it regarding the cards? Because it's essential we have them, Mr. Fallon."

"Yes, ma'am, of course it is. You know we here at Identi-Card are absolutely dedicated, even fanatical, about getting the cards to their owners on time. But I'm afraid this time out we are going to need a little reshoot."

"A reshoot? Why on earth? Mr. Fallon, I must tell you that if you do not get the cards here on time you are in breach of contract."

"I'm aware of that, Sister, and I would just like to say that I can offer no excuses. Mr. Raines wouldn't like it if I did, and I feel that we must carry on in the spirit that he has established."

There was a slight pause.

"What do you mean, Mr. Fallon? What's happened?"

"I am afraid I don't know what *you* mean Mother Superior."

"You're speaking of Jeremy, Mr. Raines, in the past tense. Has something happened to him?"

"No, of course not. He's, ah, still with us."

"Still with us? Now listen, Mr. Fallon, Jeremy Raines happens to be a personal friend of mine as well as a business associate."

"Well, I know Jeremy wouldn't want to worry you, Mother Superior."

"But I demand to know if something *untoward* has happened to him."

"Well, I want to tell you. I really do. But his last words to me when they were taking him away in the ambulance were . . ."

"Ambulance? My God! Tell me—is he—"

"His last words were 'Get the cards to Catholic U. on time. We can't disappoint Mother Superior!' "

I could hear some heavy breathing now, *very* heavy breathing.

"Now listen, Mr. Fallon, I understand that you gave your word, but as a representative of the Holy Church, I *command* you to tell me what has happened to Jeremy Raines."

"I don't know what to do. On the one hand there is my

THE KING OF CARDS

oath to my friend and employer, who this minute awaits an
operation on his brain, and . . ."

"On his brain! Now no more nonsense, Mr. Fallon. Tell
me."

"Well, seeing as you are a representative of the Church,
I suppose it wouldn't be too terribly bad if I broke my
confidence. It happened out on Route 40. Jeremy was on
his way in our new Identi-Card truck with his load of cards
for you, when this drunken Oriole fan, a redneck well digger
from down in Marlboro, a guy named Dwayne Spiggot,
came careening across the center divider and hit him head
on. You know it's so ironic. There was supposed to be
another driver this morning, but Jeremy felt such a special
bond with you that he insisted on driving the cards himself
and now he lies there in the hospital awaiting a massive
brain operation. An operation that may never come!"

"Never come? Why on earth not?"

"Funds, Sister. Jeremy has plowed all our profits back
into the business, so we're cash poor, except for the Charity
Fund, which he won't let us touch."

"What of medical insurance?"

"I'm afraid he let it lapse. You know how it is. He's so
busy thinking of others that he barely has time to pay attention to what he considers such mundane details."

There was a long pause.

I felt pins and needles coursing through my arms.

"All right, young man. Will you assure me that you'll get
the cards reshot?"

"Yes, ma'am, but I don't follow your train of thought."

"My train of thought is as follows, Mr. Fallon. I will
release to you the seven thousand dollars that Catholic University owes your company, so that Jeremy can have his
operation. But you must never speak of this with anyone
and all the cards have to be reshot this weekend."

"Sister, I must confess something to you. I am not a
religious man, but this act of faith and generosity will make
me take stock of my spiritual situation, I assure you."

"That's good to know, Mr. Fallon. I'll send the money to you via messenger, and I want you to know that this evening the sisters here at the university will be saying a special novena for Mr. Raines."

"God bless you, Mother Superior!"

We hung up the phone simultaneously, and when I turned around and faced my friends, a huge cheer resounded around the room. Val hugged me so hard around the neck she cut off what little airway I had left, and I slumped heavily into the big chair next to the embosser. Perspiration dripped off my face as though someone had put a sponge on my head, and I heard my heart beating triple time through my drenched shirt.

Jeremy's face loomed in front of mine and he kissed me on the forehead. "My boy," he said, "you've done it. You've saved our lives!"

"For which I will probably die in hell," I said. "I'm afraid I'll never match the master."

"But you did," Jeremy said. "You snatched victory from the clenched jaws of defeat, so to speak."

"Yeah," I said, laughing in pure relief from anxiety, "but underneath I'm still a guilty liberal."

"Well, John-boy," Lulu Hardwell said, "looks like Identi-Card is still in the hands of the good guys."

"Why don't you shut the fuck up, you big-titted dyke cunt?" Johnny said most ungraciously as he leaned on the laminator.

This put a damper on the celebration, and Eddie Eckel slammed his hand down on the embosser.

"You know?" he said. "I'm getting real tired of you, fat boy. *Real* tired."

"That so?" Johnny said. "Well, what inna' world you going to do about it, you hippie shithead?"

Eddie's eyes went red and without saying a word, he rushed Johnny, but Johnny was quick, much quicker than I would have believed possible, given his size. He stepped back, pulled out his gun, and in one smooth motion brought it down on the back of Eddie's head.

THE KING OF CARDS

I had never seen anything like this. I suppose none of us had, except on television or in the movies, and this was much different than those feeble exercises in fantasy. This was ugly, personal. I could actually feel my friend's bones and vessels turning to bloody mulch as he fell hard on the basement floor.

Johnny waved the gun around the room now, and there was pure madness in his eyes. He stood amidst the swirls of plastic that coiled at his feet on the floor, like some crazed, technological serpent. Indeed, standing among the ruined, twisted coils, it was difficult to determine where the cards ended and his greasy flesh began.

"I'm sick of the lot of you damned beatniks. I don't care if you do make this payment. You're all loafing scum and I'm taking over this here operation as of now, and if anybody don't like it, I'll blow their brains right out their fucking ears."

I looked into the chamber of that big .38 and I felt the most serious fear I have ever known. Val gripped my hand, and I watched Lulu and Babe shrink before my eyes.

Then, there came a strange sound. It was the grinding of the laminator. Jeremy had hit the switch so casually with his right hand that none of us had noticed.

The laminator growled, spat, and chugged, and suddenly Lulu Hardwell hit the switch to the old iron ore machine, which groaned and clanged like some old dying ghost locomotive, and it was then that I noticed panic in Johnny M.'s eyes.

"Hey," he said, "what in hell's going on? You turn off 'ose machines."

He aimed his gun right at Jeremy's head.

"I'm warning you," he said.

There was a terrible tension in the room. Then, suddenly, hardly aware of what I was doing, I picked up a box of cards and threw it at the rotund thug.

Miraculously, I made a direct hit on the side of his head. His gun went off, fired wildly into the floor, and then Johnny fell right into the great sheet of boiling, steaming, melting plastic that had once again begun rolling furiously out of the laminator. And as he went down, he hit his large, dark head on the side of the cast-iron embosser. He got a stunned look on his slab of a face and made a little sound, the sound of a small animal being run over by a barreling semi. Then he disappeared into the great, swirling, rolling folds of burning plastic that coiled themselves like a great, fiery serpent around his neck, nose, and mouth.

I suppose one of us could have done something. The switch was nearby; it was only a step or two to turn it off and save him, and it wasn't as if we actually wanted him to die. No, later when we spoke of it, all of us had serious regrets that we hadn't moved.

But it was as if some unseen hand held us back, some great secret identity in the sky who held us in thrall at his own handiwork, for I knew then that the coiling, circling serpent of plastic that mummified sleeping Johnny was indeed another being, not our creation, not Jeremy's, but the creation of the Great Blankfaced I.D. Being above us, who moved in the famed Mysterious Ways, who laughed and chortled and was occasionally even moved by our wild little embroilments in the row house city by the Chesapeake Bay.

In any case, we did not move and we watched impassively as the unconscious Johnny Martello was ensnared in the melting, twisting I.D. cards. We watched as the great stream of plastic wrapped round his legs, his fat hands, bending his right one grotesquely behind his neck.

His body flipped and flopped like a harpooned whale. Right in front of our eyes this fearsome hoodlum was becoming a mummy from his oversized, ugly head to his pasta-bloated stomach, right down to his five-inch black-and-cream Cuban heels.

And only after he was sealed as completely as Ramses II did Jeremy turn off the laminator.

"I think," Val said quietly, "we're all murderers."

"No," I said, "I killed him. You're clear, Val."

"I want Lulu, and I want her now," said a voice.

That made us all stop again. Slowly, fearfully, we turned

around to face the steps. Had Mr. A. sent another of his
goons? If so, we were dead meat. But God had been mer-
ciful. There, standing at the foot of the steps, was none
other than a greasy, hairy man with a Big Cat hat on and
a crowbar in his hand.

"Dan the Trucker!" Lulu screamed.

"One anda' same," he said. "What's wrong with 'ot guy
'ere . . . 'onna floor. Is this one a' those happenings I seen
on the news?"

All five heads nodded "Yes" at once.

"Of course," Lulu said, walking toward Dan with a hip-
swaying bounce. "That's exactly what it is, Dan."

Dan's gorilla eyes darted back and forth to each of us,
and then he stared with a confused gaze down at the her-
metically sealed gangster.

"I dint know 'ey had happenings in Bal'mere," Dan said.
"I thought that was jest something 'ey did up in New York."

"Oh, no," Lulu said. "They're very big in Baltimore now."

"But 'at guy dere, he looks kinda dead," Dan the Trucker
said.

"Which is the whole point, Dan," Lulu said. "We're making a statement here, a statement about, ah . . ."

Here she seemed to run out of lies, and I found myself
moving shamelessly forward, as big a bullshit artist as Jeremy Raines.

"A statement about the increasing plasticization of our
culture." I said, my knees shaking as I spoke.

I quickly moved to the very dead Johnny and picked up
one limp, plasticized arm.

"You see the way the I.D. cards are melted onto his arm?
Well, that's our way of saying that the . . . government is
reducing us all to nameless drones and that none of us has
any real individualism left. Because of the encroaching
spectre of plasticizing Communism."

"Damn, that is 'zactly what I beleef, too," Dan said. "This
happening stuff could be okay after all. But you sure he
ain't *really* dead. I mean he ain't breathing in there, is he?"

"Well, no," I said, unable to stop myself. "Because he

isn't real. That isn't a real person at all. That is . . . a puppet.
A wonderful lifelike puppet."

Oh, God, I thought, thank you for visions of the Evil
Hand Puppet.

I picked up the very dead Johnny's arm and let it flop to
the ground. It was already becoming quite stiff.

"A puppet," Dan said. "Damn. Looks like a real guy to
me."

"Realism," I said. "There's nothing like it!"

"You all are too weird," Dan said, taking off his Big Cat
hat and scratching his balding head. "Come on, Lulu, let's
you and me go over to the Harford Road and get us a chicken
potpie atta' Hot Shoppe. These people are too darn weird.
And by the way, I know none of you is really priests. You
was jest putting me on. Now come on, Lulu."

Lulu shot us a parting look. There was no arguing with
him.

"Be right with you, Dan," she said. "As soon as I finish
some business with Jeremy here. You wait upstairs, okay?"

"You ain't gonna run out on me again are you? Ain't no
use. I love you and you are mine and you got to get away
from this place . . . and this here damned plastic puppet."

We all smiled like madmen. Dan shook his head and
walked slowly back up the steps.

"I'll get him out of here," Lulu whispered. "And don't
worry, he won't say anything."

"You think he bought the puppet thing?" I said.

"Maybe," Lulu said. "God, I must have been horny to
ever hook up with him. But he's not that bad a guy in bed.
Anyway, I'll keep him busy for a couple of weeks, until this
all blows over. Then I'll be talking to you."

"You're a princess," Jeremy said. "But are you sure you'll
be okay?"

"Don't worry about me, sweety," Lulu said. "But what
in the hell are you going to do with the puppet there?"

"No problem," Jeremy said. "I know just the place for
him. Well, good luck old girl. And keep in touch."

"You're aces Jeremy," she said. "The King of Cards."

Then she turned, winked, shook her Ripleys one last time and headed up the steps.

Feeling a little under the weather?" Jeremy said.

"That's an understatement," I gasped as we drove out the York Road toward the beltway. The elms and oak trees hung out over the road, and their limbs looked like the waving arms of starving children. I was holding my stomach, which felt as though there were nails inside.

"Jesus, I can't believe this. The goddamned guy weighed a ton. I was sure somebody was going to walk out on their back porch and see us carrying him to the car."

"It would have been a great deal easier if we could have gotten him out of the plastic, but it seems to have embedded itself into his skin. Gives him a weird sheen, don't you think? He looks healthier, really."

"Ha, ha," I said. "Cut the shit. You're as scared as I am. Ask me how I know?"

"Okay, how?"

"Your hands are shaking and your knees are knocking. And you're rubbing your nose and chin. Also, you're drooling even more than usual."

Jeremy sighed deeply.

"This is true," he said. "Yes, this is very true, my boy. I'm feeling a modicum of anxiety. But never fear. I have the perfect place for this lad, the place where he'll never be found."

"Really?" I said. "And where might that be?"

"Well," Jeremy said, "I've always wanted you to see the old family mansion. Tonight's the night."

"We're going to your house?" I said, my heart in my throat again. "What in the hell are you talking about? Jeremy, this has all been too much for you. You're out of control."

"Relax," Jeremy said. "You're a student of history, and hey, there's a whole world of history there."

He laughed then in a way that was more than a little mad and stepped down on the accelerator.

The Raines family home was a great stone place on the Severn River at Cape St. Clair. I had driven by the turnoff to the cape a hundred times on my way to Ocean City. I even remembered asking my father what it was like. The name had a kind of special allure for me: It sounded exclusive, mysterious. My father's typically blunt reply was that it was a place where rich assholes sat around flattering each other. So I had never been down that dark road, and it seemed strange to me that I had at last made it, with a body in the trunk.

Now as we drove toward Jeremy's old home, I opened the window and smelled the country, that old sweet honeysuckle vine, and heard the sounds of crickets. In the pitch country dark, I could make out the shadows of great oaks and tall waving sawgrass. Nature only the rich could enjoy.

"No houses around here," I said in a small voice, which I barely recognized as my own.

"Right, because my father wouldn't sell. He didn't want any more development."

"You mean you own all this out here?"

"We used to. There's a kind of legal battle over who owns it right now. Deeds, wills, all very boring stuff."

"Oh, right. Very dull."

I wanted to say more, make him tell me the story behind all the mystery, but suddenly we rounded a bend and turned down a narrow dirt road, and the old Nash bounced wildly up and down. I hit my head on the roof top and felt the shock down my neck and back. I gripped the armrests and braced my knees under the glove compartment. Then, just as suddenly, we were out of the dark woods and headed up a circular driveway big enough to stage a track meet. And in front of us was an expansive brown-shingled house, three stories tall, with a classic screened front porch. I gave a little shudder of a laugh because although the place was the quintessential WASP home, it also perfectly reflected Jeremy's character. That is, it seemed to sag a little on one side, and the proud high turret sat off at a jaunty, cockeyed angle, like Jeremy's cocked head itself. Now that I looked closer, even the magnificent front porch was a little higher on one end than on the other, and I thought of a house I'd seen in a children's book when I was a kid. This was a place called the Crazy Mirror House, which was at the end of a maze in a town called Tooneyville, where all the citizens looked like insects with top hats, waistcoats, and knickers. And sitting in my row house bed, I was frightened by the looming insect faces on those eighteenth-century clothes.

And now, God only knows why, I thought of Dr. Spaulding, and he seemed that way to me. Like a waistcoated insect, perhaps a giant ant, with a top hat and a monocle, and I nearly laughed from the absurdity of it. God, what would he think of me now? How would he regard my potential as a gentleman and a scholar now that I was a murderer? Jeremy pointed to a light in a second-floor window, and I felt my stomach tighten into knots.

"Christ, there's not someone here, is there?"

"I doubt it. There's only Farlow, the caretaker. But don't worry, he's about five hundred years old and deaf as a doornail," he said.

"That's very, very reassuring," I said. "Too bad he's not blind too."

"We better establish just where he is, though," Jeremy said. "We don't need any more ugly little surprises tonight. Let's go in for a second."

"Heck, yeah," I said. "Say, we'll fix us up a crab feast, invite in some of the neighbors. Hey, we could even prop Johnny up at the table."

Jeremy smiled and pretended to hit me in the stomach.

"You know, as a cynic, you just don't make it," he said. "Just stay the sweet guy you are and you'll do fine."

I wanted to slug him then. I was that wired, but he had already started up the rickety steps toward the old house.

Inside, the place was a museum. Half of the furniture was covered with dustcovers and the other half looked like pure Chippendale. There was an ottoman with gold brocade, an ancient grandfather clock, and a rose-colored fainting sofa, which somebody had carted back from Imperial Russia. The rug was a faded Indian print with black dancing Kali goddesses on it, and on the walls near the grand piano were pictures of men with pith helmets holding a great gutted rattler above their heads.

Jeremy pointed to a small muscular man who held the head of the serpent in his hands.

"My uncle Steve," Jeremy said. "Wonderful man. He spent his life traveling, making the world safe for democracy. Got a commission from Teddy Roosevelt and ended up with a chest full of medals. When I was young, I adored him. Then I found out he was behind the B and O scandals of the 1940s. Cost most of their little investors their life savings. The shit."

He laughed and wandered through the cavernous room and then came to the great, winding staircase.

"Farlow," he shouted through cupped hands. "Farlow, where are you?"

His voice echoed eerily through the empty house, and as it grew fainter, there was a greater air of desperation to it. Finally, he turned around and came back to me.

"He's not here. He does that more and more. Just doesn't show up. Who can blame him? There's no reason to be here anymore. My uncle uses the place a couple times a year, that's all. I tell myself I keep Farlow on because he's attached to the place, but the truth is once a place is in disrepair, servants and caretakers can't wait to leave. It's the owners who need to feel their servants still want to be here."

There was a great sadness in his voice then, a kind of longing for something unnameable. He walked over to the wall and looked at the photographs.

"Over here's my father," he said in a casual way.

I walked to the photo. Of course, I'd always wanted to meet his family, and now, in spite of the plastic-coated corpse in our trunk, I found myself unable to resist.

He pointed to a lithe strong man with Jeremy's own crooked nose, even the cocked head. In the picture his father was shaking hands with Mayor Edward Mareno in front of City Hall.

"Your father really did know the mayor?" I said. "He must have been a very important man."

"Yes," Jeremy said. "He was. Until they chopped him down."

"Why?"

"Well, it was simple. Mareno wanted to build highways, tons and tons of them, and it just so happened that he was also the silent partner in a concrete company. My father was treasurer on the city council, and he found out about the sweetheart deal. The mayor offered him money and position to keep quiet about it. But my father wasn't tempted by such things. He decided to go public with the story. But he had a lousy sense of timing. Because of their friendship, he warned the mayor first. I suppose he was giving him one last chance to drop the plan. Mareno said he'd think it over. Meanwhile, he divested himself of all his holdings. In the end, he made it look like my father was the crooked one and said he was stealing money to pay for a girlfriend."

"Was there a girlfriend?"

"Probably. My father had a certain weakness for younger women. But there was no stolen funds. He didn't need to steal."

"What happened to him?"

"He went to jail for three years. When he came out, he wasn't the same."

"You mean jail broke his spirit?"

"No," Jeremy said. "That was the curious thing. In a sense jail *gave* him his spirit. He had a religious conversion. All the old life of wealth and power now seemed utterly meaningless to him. Empty. He said that all that mattered in the end was 'seeing through the screen.' You should have heard him, Tommy. It was like he was possessed when he said it. 'You've got to see through the screen. That's all that matters, son. Don't let them tell you any different.' Then he would laugh; it was like the laughter of some holy man. Of course, our friends and the good old family shrink thought he had gone round the twist, and maybe it was true, but if it was, it was a kind of divine madness."

"Seeing through the screen?" I said. The phrase sent electricity through me. It seemed to somehow be the very embodiment of Jeremy's mercurial personality. "Did he ever explain that to you?"

"Not in so many words," Jeremy said. "But he was absolutely intent on it. He became obsessed with charity work, visited terminal patients in hospital wards. He grew a long dirty beard, and he let his fingernails grow until they curled at the ends. To others he seemed quite mad, but for the first time, he began to pay attention to me. He would smile at me, say that I was his little miracle. I remember him looking down on me as I lay half asleep in the hammock out in the yard and he said, 'All along I've thought that whatever was miraculous was out there, but it's not so. It's right here. We have to make people know that, son.' "

"How did that make you feel?" I said, fascinated.

"Pleased, but embarrassed, I guess," he said. "I know now that Father was having a kind of vision. Either that or a complete breakdown, but at the time I was only twelve and I remember how weird it was when he had to come speak to the headmaster at Gilman about my unruly behavior."

"Where was your mother during all this?"

"On her way out. Mother couldn't bear the social disgrace, which was odd, because she wasn't from our rarified little social set. No, she was a dancer on Broadway when they met in a absurd little play called *Jelly Bellies*. Father always had many women; before the jail term they would call him at all hours here, and Mother would cry and go off into that room."

Here he stopped and pointed to a small library to my right. The books were still sitting in the shelves, but they were covered with a fine, golden dust.

"She would sit in there and read thrillers. Father always hated that. He was a bit like you, my boy, always big on moral and spiritual uplift. He wanted her to read the Bible, the Upanishads, and she would scream, 'You liar, you hypocrite, you talk religion but you're screwing every woman at the club.' "

"But it wasn't true."

Raines smiled sadly and sat down heavily in a rattan chair.

"No, not anymore. I mean I don't know for sure, but I think that after he had his breakthrough he wasn't any longer interested in the flesh. In that way we're very much alike."

"Oh, yeah," I said. "You're a real saint. What were you doing in your room with Sister Lulu?"

"Spiritual instruction," Raines said, smiling. "Oh, we had sex a few times, because she wanted me to, but I was trying to find out about her experiences in the nunnery. You see, I thought if I talked to someone who had had a religious conversion, someone who understood miracles, I might be able to . . . well, it didn't work out that way. Lulu was more interested in the simpler delights, and of course, she'll be better off for it in the end. No doubt."

There was such sadness in his voice, such loss, and I felt that cold night, as we talked in that abandoned old house, that I was at last beginning to peer into the complex heart beneath his whirling, scheming mind.

"Mother smoked Luckies," he said then. "She wore

Chinese robes made of raw silk. She was exquisite looking. God, when they were young and walked into the Chesapeake Restaurant, no one could eat. I mean people simply stopped and stared, and I would be walking in front of them and I would think we were royalty, we were magic. But in reality it was their youth and their love that gave them the magic. In the end . . ."

He stopped, and for a second I thought he might break down, but he only smiled at me wanly and walked toward the front door.

"In the end, father wanted to start a church," Jeremy said. "He wanted to go into the wilderness, out in West Virginia, and he actually got some right-wing lunatics to put up the money."

"Do you think he was mad? I mean, why would he?"

"Well, there's a line in one of Ginsberg's poems," Jeremy said. " 'America, you hurt me into wanting to be a saint.' Maybe that was it. Or maybe it's in our blood, Tom. Wildness, great designs. Father told us we were descendants of the kings. In the end, all such things are always mysteries, aren't they? In any case, Father had his followers, even then. Of course, Mother didn't think so. He would say, 'There are people who count on me, Louise,' and she would say, 'Yes, if you count all the sex-starved bitches.' But he would never get angry, just look at her as though she had clubbed him, and I would stand there and think, if I don't move, if I don't move a muscle, it will all go away and be like it was."

"Like Billy McConnell?" I said.

"You're becoming far too smart," Jeremy said.

"Did he really move to the woods?" I said.

"No," Jeremy said. "The day before he was to go, he had a vision of lightning and rain, and he became convinced that he had to take his boat out on the Chesapeake and sail to Mayo down on the Eastern Shore. There he would meet someone who would show him how to finally 'see through the screen.' He left, and we never saw him again. The boat ran aground somewhere down near Betterton, but there was no trace of Father. Mother left after that. She went back to New York for a while with some vague plan about making a stage comeback, but, of course, she was too old. She died three years later from pills. They found her in her room at the Gramercy Hotel curled up with her Erle Stanley Gardners and thirty-five Seconals."

He turned and looked at me with such pain and longing in his face that I could not help myself. I put my arms around him and hugged him tightly.

"Jesus God," I said.

He said nothing, but we stayed that way for a while, and then he gently pushed me away.

"There's one family we can still save," he said. "Come with me."

I followed him out the door and I got a terrifying feeling. Yet it wasn't from the fact that we had to drag Johnny's cold body across the dark earth to the flowing Severn River behind his parents' home. And it wasn't really because Rudy would be coming around to find out what happened to his associate. No, rather it was that I had come this far—killed a man—and only now did I begin to understand Jeremy and my own heart. Yes, now I saw clearly that I had hoped in my own naive, romantic way that Jeremy Raines was somehow a man born without a history, a man who had whole cloth invented himself. Oh, it was clear to me now, as we dragged that dead bully Martello toward the old shell beach, that in my own folly I needed to believe in Raines as a man who had defied all history, who was a product of nothing, who was pure legend, like Daniel Boone and Ben Franklin. I had, of course, from time to time, wondered who he really was but not very often and not very deeply. Maybe I didn't really want to know, for I suppose somewhere in my own crossed heart, I knew that his history would be tragic, as sad or sadder than my own. Now, even as I shuddered from the night wind and the fear in my stomach, I saw that Dr. Spaulding had been right, that all was truly irony, for this man, this hero I had created, who I had believed owed no man, was as tied to his own history, society, and family as all the rest of us. Indeed, he seemed to me now *more* a product of his bizarre family than I was of my own. Yes, Jeremy Raines was the creation of that classic American whipsaw—money and religion—and it made sense to me at last why the King of Cards had to create a desperate business that was in reality a church, a church with himself installed as pastor, keeper of the flock and the flame, the bright flame lit all those years ago by his own mad father.

And it also occurred to me then that I had been wrong to not want to know about his past, for knowing didn't lessen him in my eyes. No, he was picking right up from his father's work, which was the work of the true America, Wall Street, Madison Avenue, the High Flying Eagle on the Legendary American Greenback. In his own mad way, Jeremy was taking it all to some new place, where the dollar bill and the longing heart would be forever united. There would be no difference between them. He had even said it to me, "There's time for poetry and time for money," and I knew that in Raines's mind, they would be the same time and they would bind us where love, blood, and kin had failed.

Oh, it was a dark, chancy dream; both poets and businessmen would scream equally loud that such a thing was impossible. To the poets and the thinkers like Dr. S., Jeremy would be one more Babbit, taking the bad road to philistinism, and to the businessmen he would be "unprofessional," an "amateur."

But in his heart, Raines thought it could work. Like his father, he had founded a church, but not in West Virginia and not one of renouncement.

It was the High Church of Fast Times, Easy Money, and Friends for Life, and if it was absurd, it was no more so than the very promise of America itself.

THE KING OF CARDS

>

Y̶ou're quiet," he said as he lifted Johnny's arms and walked over the earth backward to the river.

"The son of a bitch is heavy," I said, telling a white lie, because I was not ready to let him in on my thoughts. I had seen him in some new and radically different light, and I didn't know what to make of it, how to talk to him, only that now everything between us had forever changed.

I was older now, I thought, as old, and wise as I was ever going to get. He had shown me everything he had and in some new way, we were really partners, each other's brothers, each other's fathers, both lost and found here on the dark shores.

And of course I was scared, scared shitless, as we finally threw Johnny's fat deadweight body down on the brown sand by the dark, flowing Severn.

"Get stones," he said. "Lots of them. I've got an old anchor here, over by the boat house."

"We ought to get these cards off of him," I said, "in case he ever comes up."

"He won't come up," Jeremy said.

"Still . . ."

"All right. Be my guest."

I reached down to the gangster's ice-cold skin and found the melted plastic on his bloated bluish cheeks. Words can't express my horror as I dug into Johnny M.'s cheeks, trying to pull the melted plastic from his face. My stomach lurched, and I gagged. Jeremy reached down and handed me a pair of rusted garden scissors.

"Use these," he said. "It'll go quicker."

"Thanks," I said, gasping for air.

Then I dug in and really got to work.

It was a good forty minutes before I'd gotten most of the damnable plastic wrapping off of Johnny, and it took us another hour to row out into the brackish waters of the Severn. Finally, there under the brilliant ice blue stars, we threw his body into the drink and Johnny Martello sunk quickly, without a trace.

"Nice, isn't it?" Jeremy said, lying back on the bow of the old rowboat. "When I was young, Mother and Father and I would spend whole afternoons out here fishing. Mother pretended she hated it, but she didn't really mind. In those days, it didn't matter what they were doing as long as they were together. I never saw two people more in love."

"What went wrong?" I asked, not believing we were having this conversation as Johnny sank to the bottom of the Severn, his toes being bitten by crabs, trout, eels.

"That's the great mystery," Jeremy said. "That's the question without an answer, because it had gone wrong way before Father's jail troubles. The Raines men have always had too much appetite for life. Maybe insatiability is the worst crime. We burn people out. Hell, we burn ourselves out."

He laughed a little sadly and took the oars in his hands.

"There's always a formula for success," he said quietly, "but there's never any blueprint for tragedy. Well, what say we head back to terra firma?"

And so we did, headed back to the dark land under the brilliant St. Claire moon, like two college friends out on a nighttime fishing trip.

But as we rowed back into the dock, that illusion was shattered forever. Someone waited for us, a huge, hulking man in a long dark coat.

"Christ," I whispered, "it's Mr. A."

"No," Jeremy said. "It's only Farlow, our housekeeper."

"Do you think he saw us?"

"I don't know, but it'll be okay. He's very loyal."

We rowed to the dock and tied the boat up as the old man moved over the creaking warped boards toward us. He was tall and stoop shouldered and had a great gray walrus moustache. His eyes were cast downward, which made him look like a huge hound.

"Jeremy," he said. "It's you. I almost called the police."

That sent another chill through me.

"No need for that, Mr. Farlow. Just showing my friend here the delights of the river at night."

"You could get swept away by the current out there," Farlow said. "Damned crazy for you to go out there."

"Now you know I know the river like the back of my hand," Jeremy said. "Things going well for you, Farlow?"

"Well as can be expected. Nobody's been here for weeks. Why don't you come in and have a drink or a cup of warm tea. I could brew it in a jiffy."

"Can't. Have work back at the hospital. Hey, if any of the doctors call up for me, I wasn't here. Playing a little hooky, Far."

Farlow smiled and put his arm around Jeremy's shoulder as we walked toward the lopsided shingled house.

"Haven't your secrets always been good with me, son?" he asked.

"Of course," Jeremy said.

"When he was young, we played hide and seek out here," Farlow said, turning to me. "He thought he was a clever boy, but I could always find him."

"That's right," Jeremy said. "That's right, Far. You were the only one who could."

"We had us some fine times," Farlow said. "We had us some high old times."

"I'll call you," Jeremy said. "Next week. Maybe we'll open the old place up again. Have a crab feast."

Farlow's eyes flittered in the moonlight.

"Could we?" he asked, sounding suddenly like a child who has been made a promise he dare not believe in.

"Not only could we," Jeremy said, squeezing his old arm, "but we shall. Next week. We'll show that there's some life left yet in the old place."

Farlow said nothing then, but his face turned to joy, and he suddenly hugged Jeremy tightly, like a father would a son, and I felt such emotion well up in me that I had to turn my head.

When I looked back, Jeremy was shaking hands with him.

"Good to see you, Jeremy," Farlow said. "I'll wash out the crab pots."

"And don't forget to make the stewed tomatoes, Farlow," Jeremy called as we walked away. "Can't have the feast without your stewed tomatoes."

"I'll make them," Farlow called after him and then he waved, and we left him there alone, standing on the starry, moonlit dock.

As we drove out the dark St. Claire road toward Baltimore, I stared at the great tall oaks, which formed a canopy over the road. While we had been disposing of the body, I had lost myself in speculation, but now the full horror of what we had done came back to me and I felt numbed, shocked, as though my brain had been covered over by layers and layers of the plastic that had wrapped itself around fat Johnny. I took deep breaths in order to keep the rising panic inside me down, shut my eyes as Jeremy drove too fast down the bumpy, spooky roads, and remembered my youthful fantasies of the Cape. I recalled sitting in the back of my parent's Studebaker at the age of twelve, thinking that the Cape must be the very essence of the highly advertised Good Life of the Chesapeake Bay, which had been drummed into my head in American history classes all through elementary school. Here came the old Catholic colonists who escaped the persecution of the cruel British High Church. Here on these gentle shores under the shade of broad-branched magnanimous trees, our forefathers ate giant plates of oysters and crabs, which were so plentiful, came from waters so bounteous, that they must have felt they lived in a waking dream, a dream of plenty, a dream that must have been to them like some new Eden. How our forebears must have loved their lives, these rough men with their powdered wigs, bright knee stockings, muskets, horses, and tobacco. And their women. I pictured them all as beauties in bright hoop skirts, long, flowing hair framing their pale white faces, and behind them on the veranda, a veranda very much like Jeremy's family porch, perhaps there was a lively string band playing some Scotch-Irish aire that rang over the salt marshes and out into the great blue gull-filled Chesapeake Bay. Yes, that was the dream of Olde Maryland, and one I'd entertained from time to time.

If by some miracle I could ever get my hands on just a little money maybe I could have a home down here on Cape St. Clair. I'd even thought, not more than ten days ago, that armed with my new money and my new artistic sensibility that Val and I could settle down near here. At first she would think it square, lame, but the place would win her over in the end, and we would at last have the place that all orphaned children want most of all—a true and loving home.

Now, however, as I drove the dark, leaf-strewn lane with Jeremy Raines, it was as though those delightful fantasies were the absurd, naive speculations of a foolish child. And when I thought again of Dr. Spaulding, I began to laugh bitterly. All his hushed talk, all his academic babble, that was all beyond me now. Yes, whatever sensibility I had, whatever potential, it was now wiped out, smeared over with human blood.

For we were killers—it was that simple, that terrible. We had dropped a man into the kind, bubbling river not two miles from here, and I thought, as we rolled mindlessly along under the uncaring trees, that in this one violent, absurd moment, I had moved from boyhood innocence to something dark, something so strange that I had no name for it. Looking over at my friend, I actually thought, *So this is it, so this is what it's like to* really *know things*. It seemed as though a great weight crushed down on my shoulders, a stone of a thousand pounds. I laughed sadly to myself and thought of those same genteel pilgrims who had founded my great home city, and I remembered that all their civility and gentle Chesapeake life was itself bought and paid for in blood. It occurred to me that Jeremy and I were in our own strange way closer to our forefathers now than I had ever been before. Yes, tonight I had touched and known some dark secret that all conscious men shared, that no effort was free, that no yearning for refinement or class or love itself was achieved without deadly struggle, like those sweet Puritan colonists who bought their bounteous harvest through righteous slaughter.

Though I said none of this to Jeremy, I knew without a doubt that he understood what my long silence meant, for when we finally stopped the battered Nash in front of our Chateau Avenue house, he smiled sadly, looked at me, and said, "You know things now, my boy, you know things, but remember, as good old Johnny Unitas told Raymond Berry, in order to make the catch, you have to keep your eye on the ball."

And that made me laugh, for I knew he was right, knew it in my deepest bones, he was dead-on right. There was no other way to get through this. I had to keep my eye on the ball and nothing else, but still, my laughter didn't stop the chill that lay just beneath my skin.

I opened the door to head up to the house, but as I did, Jeremy reached over and grabbed my left arm.

"Wait a second," he said and there was a deep weariness in his voice. I turned and saw the exhaustion in his eyes.

"What is it?" I said.

"I'm not going in," he said.

"No?"

"No. I have to get over to D.C. by 9 A.M. and then hit Virginia by noon."

"Virginia?"

"Ah, yes, my friend, I suppose in all the confusion I neglected to tell you. We have interest in our cards from three schools in the good old Blue Ridge Mountains. So I'll be gone for three days."

"You look like you're ready to drop," I said. "You need sleep."

"Who says I do?" he laughed.

"Me," I said. "I say it."

He smiled his crooked smile then and boxed me on the arm.

"You think you can tell me how things are now? Is that it?"

"That's it," I said darkly. "After tonight, I think now maybe we're really partners. After all, isn't that what you wanted?"

He nodded his head and ran his hand through his cowlick.

"As I told you the first day, it's destiny, my boy," he said.

That stunned me a little, but in a second we both laughed again, a strange hollow sound, like the laugh of a child lost in a fun house.

"Only one thing, Tom," he said. "You're still a lousy businessman."

"No worse than you," I said.

We both smiled at that.

"What would you have me do?" he asked. That caught me off guard.

"Really?" I asked.

"Really."

I wasn't sure what he meant, but my answer surprised myself.

"You should heal," I said.

"Like I healed Billy?" he said.

"Billy's not your fault," I said.

"Oh, well, maybe like I *healed* Johnny then?"

"You're forgetting, I killed Johnny," I said.

Jeremy sighed deeply and shook his head.

"No, it was me. It was me all along. I dragged you into this. Are you sorry you've come?"

"No," I said. And in spite of everything, I meant it.

He ran his hand through his cowlick and wrapped his fingers around the steering wheel.

"You know," he said, "I have always known that I was destined for something. I have always felt it, deep inside.

But, it's still just out there, just barely beyond my grasp."

"On the other side of the screen?" I asked.

"You're getting way too bright," he said.

I stared at his face and for the first time felt as though I had pierced the mask of charm that he wore so effortlessly. I reached out and patted his shoulder, then gripped it tight.

"We're going to make it," I said.

He looked out at the first morning light.

"Do you think so?" he asked softly.

"I know so," I said, but there was a crack in my voice, and there was just the slightest flutter of his eyes before he switched on the ignition again.

"I have to get on the road, Tom," he said.

"Call later," I said.

I opened the door and got out. When I looked back in, he was smiling at me and there was such a tired, beat tenderness in his voice.

"You'll love Farlow's crabs," he said. "Believe me, it's going to be one hell of a party."

I started to answer him, but Jeremy had already slammed the car into reverse and bashed into the Chevy behind him. Then he ground the gears into first and drove off into the morning.

When I got back to my room, I found a note from Val.

Have gone to my own place to think. Call me later.
                                              Love, V.

I thought I understood. What had happened last night was like a bad dream, and now in the light of a new day, the dream should have ended, but it hadn't. None of us were ever going to be free from this night. It would mark us all forever, whether or not Mr. A. found out.

Even so, I was dead tired and fell asleep within minutes. My dreams were ghoulish in nature. I saw fish eating a human face until there was nothing left but half a nostril and one staring eye. I saw a giant crab moving toward the Baltimore harbor and men with cameras being swallowed by his great gaping mouth. I heard the sound of flashbulbs and the pop of revolvers and saw fish-faced men in black suits chase two children down a maze of cobblestone toward a crooked house.

Then the phone rang, once, twice, and I felt a rough hand shaking my shoulder, and looked up and saw Eddie standing above me.

"Tommy, phone for you."

"Who?"

"Don't know, man. Weird call."

I pushed my way out of the bed, then grabbed a T-shirt and hustled downstairs. The dreams were still rolling on inside me, and I felt a fear in my stomach as bright as a one-hundred-watt bulb.

I picked up the phone and sat down on the old couch.

"Hello."

There was a long pause, then I heard a small, childish voice: "Watch out. Please watch out."

"Watch out?" I asked, confused and dream ridden. "For what?"

The voice came again, small and fearful. It sent chills down my neck.

"Watch out. Please watch out for the moat monster."

I felt my breath come hard, and it was a long time before I could speak.

"Billy," I said. "Billy. It's all right. You've done it. The prince is going to come down from the castle. You see? He'll open the drawbridge and he'll make sure that his friend is safe."

There was silence.

Then the voice came again, small but insistent through the line, "Watch out. Please, watch out . . ."

My throat was dry, parched. Then Dr. Hergenroeder came on the phone.

"Mr. Fallon," she said. "It's a miracle."

"Yes," I said, too shocked and moved to go on. "Yes, it is."

"He's still a little disoriented," she said. "He needs to hear the story back in the context Jeremy set up. Can he come out here?"

"Jeremy's in Virginia," I said. "He had some work to do. He won't be back for a couple of days. Will Billy be okay?"

"Yes, I think so. He's awake. He's able to talk a little, but he's terribly concerned with the outcome of the story. Of course, I could improvise an ending, but it would be better if he heard it from Jeremy."

"I'll tell him when he calls in, Dr. Hergenroeder," I said.

"That would be fine. Give him my love."

"I will, Doctor," I said. "Good-bye."

I put the phone down and fell back on the couch. I looked around the living room and thought of that day only four months ago when I'd first come to this house.

Though the room was practically the same—there was even the same old *Time* magazine on the battered barber chair—everything now seemed entirely changed.

Now it seemed to me, more than ever, the house on Chateau was an oasis, where life was lived at a pace and at an emotional intensity that existed no place else and that I knew could never be sustained.

I shut my eyes and heard Billy McConnell's words again in my head: "Watch out. Please watch out." And melodramatically I thought that he was speaking not to the picture at all, but to me and Jeremy and Eddie and the Babe and Val. Lord, watch out for the moat monster, all of you. Please, watch out.

THE KING OF CARDS

I slept fitfully on the couch until ten o'clock, then called Val. We agreed to meet at Monty's for lunch at noon. Before we hung up, I told her about Billy McConnell's breakthrough, expecting her to be as excited by it as I was, but the enthusiasm in her voice was forced. Indeed, it occurred to me as I hung up that she sounded strained and burned out, and that worried me. I didn't go back to sleep again.

I arrived early and was surprised to see four white guys with Beatle haircuts practicing rock 'n' roll licks on the same bandstand where the poetry readings were held. I watched them for awhile; they were doing an electric version of "See That My Grave Is Kept Clean," an old folk song by Blind Lemon Jefferson, a blues singer Eddie had turned me onto. It sounded forced and loud to me, all the subtlety and quiet desperation was gone from it. Instead, these four guys sounded like they couldn't wait to die ignoble, brokenhearted, and anonymous, that their fondest dreams were to be placed in a shallow grave on some burning hot pine grove highway in Alabama.

I listened to their frantic black face interpretation until Sam Washington came in and leaned at the opposite end of the bar. I remembered that first time we met, months ago, and took up a stool at the opposite end.

But apparently he remembered as well, for he walked toward me and leaned his big belly on the bar.

"White boy, how you making it?"

"Okay," I said. "What's with the rock 'n' roll band?"

"New thing, man. Monty's only doing poetry ever other week. Rock draws bigger crowds of rich white folks."

"I didn't think Monty's was about big crowds," I said.

He smiled and put out his big palm, and I touched it lightly with my own.

"Tommy," he said, "you suffering from an advanced case of young."

"Last time I saw you, you were with two great-looking girls," I said.

"Yeah, the Glitter Twins," he said. "They was some very nice chicks. We had us a lot of good times of a very short duration."

"And then what?"

"And then? Hey, they move on. You know how it is, people come, people go."

He smiled as if he had just described a process as unchanging as the patterns of the sun and moon, and I shook my head.

"Tell me this, Sam. Doesn't anybody ever stay anywhere?"

"Not in this world, baby," he said easily. "But you don't really want to go back to the old one, do you?"

I didn't answer that but quietly sipped my beer. Then, from the back of the bar, Val came in, and again I was knocked out by her beauty, her black leotard, her red turtleneck, her ballet shoes.

"Hang loose, baby," Sam said.

He winked at me, turned, and headed toward the jukebox.

Val came toward me, and I put my arms around her. She hugged me back, but there was no joy in it, more like a child forced to hug a distant uncle.

We ordered a plate of mussels and two National Bohemians, and I whispered to her that we had disposed of Johnny.

"Where?" she asked.

"You don't need to know," I said.

"But I *want* to know," she said.

"I know you do but forget it, 'cause I'm not telling you."
She shook her head and patted me on the hand.

"You're noble," she said, "protecting me from the *mob*."
She said it with the right flourish of melodrama, and I
had to laugh.

"I was only half kidding," she said. "You *are* noble. You
have a streak of true Southern nobility. And I like it very
much. Only . . ."

She stopped and twisted her forefinger through her red
hair.

"Only what?"

"Only, I'm not ready for nobility, Tom. I'm not ready for
you."

"Oh," I said.

"I'm leaving, Tom. Going out West."

"Why? What the hell for?"

"I don't know. Because it's time, I guess."

"Really?" I asked. "Oh, because it's *time*. Well, that explains everything. I mean with that explanation I can fully
accept . . ."

"I love you," she interrupted. "You know that. That's one
reason I'm leaving, so that we don't regret anything."

"Well, I'm going to regret it," I said. "I'm going to regret
everything. You can count on that. We could make it work,
Val. We're both writers. We can offer each other support,
help each other."

She laughed and took my arm, then reached with her free
hand into her purse. She took out an envelope with the
Poetry Magazine logo on it and shoved it across the table to
me. I opened it and pulled out rejection slips from *Poetry*,
Contact Magazine, *The Paris Review*, and six or seven others
I'd never heard of.

"I'm sorry," I said. "How long have you been sending
these out?"

"For over two years. And I've never had one published."
I held her hand tightly.

"That's rough," I said. "But that's all the more reason
you need me. I can help you through this period."

She shook her head.

"I have a confession to make, Tom," she said.

"What?"

"I read your journal the other night. I wasn't trying to find out anything, I was just curious. I'm sorry . . ."

"It's okay," I said.

"No, I shouldn't have. But I have to tell you something Tommy. There was more real life in your writing—as rough as it was—than in any of my poems."

"Oh, bull," I said. "That's rubbish."

"No," she said. "No, Tom. It's you. I could really hear *you* in your work."

"Yeah," I said, "Timid, overly intellectual, cautious, not knowing who the fuck I am from one minute to the next . . ."

"That's right," she smiled, "but it was you. I mean, it's you trying to become yourself, and it was exciting to read. As for me, well, I had a kind of epiphany. It's a funny thing. I'm always reading about epiphanies in literature, that one clear moment when you really know reality, when you see the naked truth about your life. And I always imagined when I had mine it would be this glorious shining insight. I would be doing something completely banal, like taking a bath, and it would come to me. I would see I was destined for greatness. Well, I finally had it. I went walking down the docks last night and I looked out and saw the boats and the blue and yellow lights from the harbor, then everything seemed to recede, and I felt that I was deeply, deeply alone in a tunnel somewhere, and presto, like *that*, I realized who I was. It seemed unbelievably simple to me. I was just this fucked-up neurotic girl who thought she had talent because she was so fucking lonely."

"That's crazy," I said, reaching for her hand.

But she shook her head, fighting back the tears.

"No, Tommy, let me finish. I knew, I mean I *really* knew, I have no talent as a poet. You know it yourself. I'm just an imitator. So I'm throwing all this out."

I sat there stunned. She had delivered it all with such

weight that her decision seemed irrevocable. Still, I couldn't let her go.

"You don't mean it. You're just upset," I said, not knowing if I was lying to her or not, "after what we've been through."

"No, I do mean it," Val said. "I know this is going to hurt you, but you're moving, Tommy, and I am too. We're together partly because of Jeremy. I owe him so much but not enough to watch him go down. I can't stay around and see that."

"He's not going down," I said.

She said nothing to that, only sipped her wine.

"Where will you go?"

"San Francisco."

"With Hogg?" I said. "That English twit?"

"No," she said. "He asked me, but I don't want to live with anybody. I've been dependent on men too long, Tom. Like Garbo, I 'vant to be alone.' "

I ignored her self-conscious little joke. My hands were clammy, and I felt my heart racing wildly.

"Listen, I'll quit school," I said. "We'll go together."

"Quit school?" she said. "No way. You *love* school, remember? I don't want that on my head."

"Wonderful," I said. "The last of the sentimental romantics moving through the silent night alone."

She looked at me dead-on then and nodded sadly.

"I guess that's me," she said. "It's not very original, but it's what I want."

"I'm sorry," I said. "Christ, I envy you your courage. And I love you."

"I love you, Tom," she said, but there was a finality in her tone that broke my heart.

"When will you leave?"

"Soon."

I said nothing to that.

"We have tonight, Tommy," she said.

"Great," I said bitterly. "Fine."

"If you want it," she said.

"Sure," I said curtly. "Meet me at the house at seven."

I barely got the words out, then quickly got up from the table and walked toward the door.

Back at the house I staggered into my room and fell on the bed. I wanted to sleep and forget it all, but there was no chance of that. Only weeks ago I had told myself that this was my real home, that these people were going to be my family, and now, now all of it was evaporating in front of my eyes.

I got up, walked to the window, and looked at the cracked swimming pool outside. Leaves had collected in the deep end, under the board, and two pieces of patio furniture floated in the shallow end. I couldn't believe it. Val was going away. I wouldn't see her anymore, wouldn't be able to hold her. The thought was inconceivable.

Then there was a knock at the door, and for a second I thought it was Val, but instead the Babe walked in.

"Hi," she said.

"Hi. How's Eddie's head?"

"He has a concussion," she said, then lay down on the bed. "I was scared, really scared. I told the doctor he was drunk and fell down the basement steps."

She stared up at me. She had on a pair of powder blue short shorts, and her chubby pink legs were spread wide open.

"What were you just thinking about, Tom?" she said.

"Nothing much," I said.

"Yes, you were," she said. "You're thinking about Val and how much you're gonna miss her."

"You know she's leaving?" I said.

"Yeah. It's a shame, Tommy. I liked you two together. I mean I knew it was a fucking disaster from the jump, but I liked it anyway."

"You knew it was a disaster?" I said. "Well, I wish to hell you'd told me."

"Would it have made any difference?" she asked.

"No, I suppose not," I said.

"No. You'll be sick for a while, but you'll get over it," she said.

"Thanks."

"I wanted to show you something," the Babe said.

She sort of slithered around on the bed, and for a second I thought she was going to suggest we have a conciliatory fuck. Instead she pulled something from her back pocket.

It was a paperback book. Henry James's *The Ambassadors*.

"You're reading that?" I asked, completely surprised.

"Uh-huh," the Babe said. "And I *really* like it. I just want to say I'm glad you moved in here, Tom. You really have brought the whole level of the place up a couple of notches."

"Thanks," I said, not knowing what else I could possibly say.

"The thing is," the Babe said, "I wanted to ask you a question about the way this story is told."

"The point of view in *The Ambassadors*?" I mumbled, dazed.

"Yeah. See in the introduction of the book James says he sees everything through this guy Strether's eyes, but I read a lot of chapters where old H.J. seems to be sort of cheating on his technique."

"He does?" I asked, flabbergasted. Only a few hours ago I had dropped a body into the Severn and now I was having a literary discussion on point of view in Henry James with a hillbilly sex queen from Glen Burnie, Maryland.

"Sure he does," she said. "I've seen a lot of scenes in the novel that old Strether couldn't have known anything about at all, so ole Hank James cheats, huh, Tom?"

"Yeah," I said as if I was talking to a spaceman, "I guess he does."

"I gotta tell you, Tom, it sorta shocks me," the Babe said. "I mean I know everybody cheats. I just didn't think great artists did. I mean I guess I sound like a hick and stuff, but they're not supposed to, are they?"

It was the "are they" that got me. It was so damned sweet.

"No," I said, "they're not supposed to."

"Oh, well," she said as she got up from the bed. "Another illusion shattered. I guess in the end everybody pulls whatever shit they think they can get away with."

She put her arms around me in a sisterly way.

"Listen to me going on about all this when you're still upset from us offing that scuzzball and Val leaving. Geez, I always did have a lousy sense of timing. Anyway, I love you, Tom, and if you want to go out and get shitfaced 'cause your heart's broken, just let me know, okay?"

"That sounds great," I said like a man in a trance. "Terrific. I will."

"Cheer up, Tommy," she said as she walked toward the door. "Ole Baltimore's filled with pretty girls, and they all love artists."

She winked at me and started for the door, then turned, looked at me, and slapped herself in the head.

"I almost forgot," she said. "Rudy Antonelli called today. Around ten."

"He did?" I said, and my voice cracked a little.

"Yeah, but relax. He just wanted to know where Jeremy was. I told him he was in Virginia looking for potential customers. I thought that would cool him out."

"Did it?"

"Sort of. Though he wanted to know exactly what schools Jeremy is trying to get to buy our cards. I mean, I loved that 'our' stuff. Like are we really in business with him?"

We are, I wanted to say. Oh, brother, are we. But I didn't bother with it.

"Did you tell him the names of the schools?"

"Yeah. Didn't see that I had any choice in the matter. It was okay though. He sort of calmed down after that. You think these little calls are going to be a regular thing from now on, Tom?"

"Until we pay him back," I said, trying to sound optimistic.

"Boy," the Babe said, "let's pay him back quick then. I gotta tell you this whole connection has been kind of a bummer. That guy Johnny, whoooo. Very nasty."

She shook her head and shut the door.

Right, I thought, a bummer. Murder. Yeah, I guess that would classify as a major bummer. But even though she annoyed me, I marveled at the Babe. In her world, all experiences had a kind of democratic equality, the same emotional weight: dead goombahs, busted hearts. To dear old Babe it was all light fare, and I knew that whatever happened here, she and good old Eddie would survive. Somehow that cheered me, for they were true downtown Glen Burnie Baltimoreans. They had grown up in used car lots, served time in Pentecostal churches, gone to rotten schools, been busted by moronic sadistic cops, the list of their abuses was endless, but they were saved from emotional ruin by their deadeyed knowing slant on it all.

They expected nothing, and they had each other, though it was sentimental bullshit, I envied them a little. They wouldn't fall on the ruin of their own oversized expectations, like Val, Jeremy, and me.

Val arrived at six, and when she did, what was left of my confidence crumbled. She looked so breathtakingly beautiful, as though she had made herself up with just a little extra effort so she would be sure to really break my heart. She wore a bright red Spanish blouse with ruffled sleeves and a scooped neckline, pink ballet shoes, and tight black capri pants, which showed off her fabulous muscular calves. Her red hair was clean and shimmered, and her face was shining and bright.

Seeing her looking that good just about killed me and badly threw off my hastily improvised game plan.

I had fantasized that we would spend the entire evening, night, and morning in bed making love and that I would convince her by my sheer Lothariolike prowess that she should stay with me forever. But now that she was here I found myself absurdly trying to act cool. So I watched the local news on the old battered black-and-white TV and drank a jelly tumbler full of Wild Turkey.

"You want a drink?" I asked, staring at our local black news anchor, dapper Ralph Murray.

"No, I'll have a joint," she said.

"Very, very hip," I said with a childish malice in my voice.

"Well, *I'll* have a drink *and* a joint."

I smiled in agony as Murray talked with a woman reporter at a downtown street fair.

Val smiled right back at me.

"Well, I'll have a drink and a joint and some speed," she said with a poker face.

"Oh, really," I said. "Well, I'll have some speed, a drink, a joint, and five bottles of codeine-laced cough syrup."

Val nodded sagely and shook her head. Her hair was so alive it caused a pain in my crotch.

"Okay, Mr. Hipster," she said, giving me a killer smile and flashing a little thigh. "I'll have all of the above and throw in massive electric shock."

This was not how I planned it. I wanted soft music and whispered nothings, but I couldn't back down. I stared at the TV as Murray took us to Glen Burnie to show us a stolen-car ring.

"Okay, okay, okay," I said. "I'll plug right into your electric shock and add land mines and self-immolating flame-throwers, not to mention the joint, the whiskey, the cough syrup, and a whole bottle of biphetamines."

She said nothing for a second to that, and I smiled thinking I had topped her in our little self-destruction contest.

"You give up?" I said.

But she said nothing else, only stared at the television.

THE KING OF CARDS

"Hey," I said, "earth to Val. You still here, honey?"

"Oh, my God," she said. "Oh, Jesus."

I looked up at the television set. Ralph Murray was talking with a remote reporter named Ned Meyers. Meyers was wearing a trench coat and was standing by a riverbank somewhere. Behind him were divers in wet suits; behind them there was a corpse being hauled out of the water.

I heard Meyers's commentary as if I were underwater myself: "The body was found by amateur scuba diver Earl Sands this morning around 9 A.M., as Mr. Sands and his son scuba dived down on fashionable Cape St. Claire. Tell us about it, Mr. Sands."

Earl Sands weighed about three hundred pounds, and he wore a battered Baltimore Oriole hat, a ratty terry-cloth short robe that didn't quite cover his huge belly, which hung over dark shorts with little white hard crabs on them. "Well, my family was out here inna houseboat, which I bought and fixed up inna '58. Got me a real good deal on that sucker, too, down Ochun City!"

He smiled and Meyers nodded and pointed to the body that was now being laid on a stretcher just behind the two of them.

"The dead man, sir?" Meyers said. "Could you tell us?"

"Oh, yeah, him," Earl said. "Well, he is real dead. That's for sure. Way it happened was my son Earl, Jr., and me was diving a little, heard there might be some old sunk British ships down in this part of the river. Even heard there might be treasure. You heard that, have you?"

"I don't know about treasure, sir," Meyers said. "The body? Could you please tell us about the body, sir?"

"Heck, yeah. See, uh, Earl, Jr., he was down on the bottom looking, always dives faster 'n me. Anyways, I submerge to say thirty feet and he's all excited, pointing and a jumping up and down, and damn, I look down there and there is this real honest-to-God dead guy down there. Just like old Mike Nelson would find on "Sea Hunt." Hell, this guy was all messed up. Had a big anchor round him. Some mess, I'll tell you."

289

They cut away from him then and move over to the gurney, where two police officers were pushing a white-sheeted Johnny Martello into an ambulance.

Ned Meyers came back on the screen. He looked sincere, grave.

"Police say that the dead man is Johnny 'Hands' Martello, a known soldier in the crime family of local underworld figure Rudy Antonelli. It's not known at this time how he died, but Police Chief Don Hoffman tells us that it looks like a gangland slaying. This is Ned Meyers for 'Action News.'"

I fell back in my chair and felt my heart pound through my chest.

"What time did they say they found Johnny?" I said.

"Nine this morning," Val said. "We better call Jeremy."

But I wasn't hearing her anymore.

They found Jeremy's car charred black in a deep ditch just outside of Fairfax, Virginia. The Virginia State Police said that the driver must have fallen asleep at the wheel and gone over the embankment. The car had rolled at a high speed down a steep hill and hit a grove of oak trees at the bottom. There it had turned three or four times and burst into flames. There was a gasoline explosion. A farmer named A. C. Deal had heard it a mile away, but by the time he had called the police (he didn't bother to look himself; a man had his chores), there wasn't much to work with.

They knew it was Jeremy Raines because they found his burned and still-smoldering I.D. card, which said simply Jeremy Randall Raines, president, Identi-Card Products, Baltimore, Maryland.

THE KING OF CARDS

➤

Val fell apart when the police came with the news. It was a subtle thing though, no screaming or crying or gnashing of teeth. Instead she just became smaller. Her voice was tiny, she hunched her shoulders so badly that she looked almost comical, and in bed she regressed into the fetal position. She didn't say much, only that she wouldn't be going to the funeral and that she didn't want to talk about it.

Which was all right by me. I was busy getting blind drunk with Eddie and the Babe, a three-day bender, which up to a point made me somehow seem more sober, more awake, and agonizingly clearheaded. It was as if I had actually achieved what Jeremy's mad father had raved about—I'd seen through the screen to the opaque, clear, brilliant white space.

My friend was dead. Raines, Jeremy Raines, was dead. There had never been anyone like him, no one more brilliant, no one more energetic, more greedy, more generous, no one loved life half so much, no one was more confused, no one was more manipulative, no one was more of a liar, more of a saint, more fun, more impossible. I guess I babbled all those things to Eddie and the Babe and to Val when she would stagger down from her room and join us, sullen and bleary-eyed. The old white kitchen table at Chateau Avenue became some kind of liquor-filled, joint-smoking altar, and one by one, we all testified to Jeremy's sheer shooting-star intensity.

And it occurred to me through my stoned haze that he was both disease and doctor, purveyor of the all-American bullshit of hype and slayer of it as well, Jeremy Raines, flak maker, flak killer.

Oh, drunk and in mortal agony, I probably made him out to be a combination of Christ and Lucifer rolled into one, though that was surely overdoing it.

But what better person to overdo it about?

He was like no one else I had ever met, and even then, I knew that I would never meet anyone who was as fully alive.

Among the million things I was wrong and confused about, I was right and clear about that. No one *has* ever come close.

I remember calling my father, crying like a baby, and crawling out to the front yard, where a naked, loaded Lulu Hardwell was swinging into the cloudy Baltimore moon.

And I remember an endless discussion of how he died. Was it an accident? After all, he was exhausted and was the worst driver in the free world. Or was it possible that Mr. A. had gotten to him, pushed him over the edge?

There was even talk that it wasn't Jeremy in the burnt wreckage. After all, the body was too charred for identification, and his aunt—his only living relative, as it turned out, and the first one notified—had his remains prepared by the undertaker and placed in a closed coffin, so an autopsy was impossible.

Through her tears, Val talked of going to the police, but quickly saw the folly of that. We had no proof of any misdeeds, and if we opened that can of worms, there would be a very nasty little investigation into the disappearance of one Johnny Martello and all of us could end up serving time down at the "Cut," Jessups Prison.

I had one other thought, which I shared with nobody. I kept seeing Jeremy's haunted eyes the morning that we'd come back from his estate and I kept hearing the questions he'd asked me: "What would you have me do?" and his other words, spoken in such a small, unsure voice, how he had always known he was destined for something, but that it was still out there, just barely beyond his grasp. And that final look he'd given me, naked, lost, as he pulled the battered Nash away from the curb. And I thought, did he know that it was over? That the party had ended and he had to follow his father to the other side to finally see all the way through the screen? Did he, in some exhausted, impulsive moment of weakness, twist the wheel just enough to miss the curve and go plunging down the embankment?

But of course I would never, ever know.

No, in the end we were like all mourners in the face of tragedy—desperate, lost. All we had was one another, and though it didn't feel like anything close to enough, we somehow staggered through those first horrible days. And in the end Val decided to go to the funeral after all.

The day was bright and sunny, a perfect afternoon to sell a few cards, hustle a few drinks, get stoned, get laid, but it was a lousy day to watch my best friend get put into the earth.

Still, as it turned out, Jeremy had one final joke to play.

The funeral was held in St. John's Church in fancy WASP Roland Park.

In this great stone church, with its deeply recessed naves, towering cupolas, and statues of the Virgin, two distinct sets of mourners were present and sat on opposite sides of the main aisle. On the right side was a gray-suited, bereaved-looking Farlow. He accompanied Jeremy's aunt, Alice, who wore a black satin mourning dress and a black lace veil. And behind them, in row after row, were all the WASPS from Jeremy's past, the men dressed in their perfect pin-stripes, the women in expensive plain dresses. Seated with them were various old shifty-eyed Baltimore politicians, ancient, gray-haired and gray-faced deans from many of the local colleges, including our old friend, A. Taft Manley, of Johns Hopkins University. Outside, when we were all milling around, he noticed me and said, "Well, Whirley, isn't it a terrible, terrible thing." And it was all I could do not to burst into hysterical laughter.

Also sitting there alone on the WASP side of the church was Dr. Spaulding. He wore a blue pinstripe suit and a blue-

and red-striped rep tie, and he seemed so composed that he looked like a statue.

There were so many things I wanted to say to him, apologies I wanted to make. God knows, I had been wrong when I made that terrible outburst in his office a month back.

And yet, I still felt some inner fury at him, some deep-seated and twisted emotion that I couldn't translate into sentences, so I merely nodded to him as I took my seat.

On the other side of the aisle were Jeremy's friends, the four of us who lived with him, Sam Washington and the suddenly reappearing Glitter Twins, jazz musicians from Monty's, poets, artists, Sister Lulu Hardwell and her trucker friend, Dan, dressed in his green uniform and wearing a Big Cat hat, which Lulu took from him at the door. This crowd was dressed in their wildest duds for the occasion. Val wore the tightest dress imaginable; she said that Jeremy wouldn't want her there looking sad and sexless. Babe wore a flapper's dress she had found at a thrift store, and Eddie was resplendent in an old double-breasted gangster suit from his father's closet that made him look like Nathan Detroit. Sam was dressed in a sneaky brim hat, a fire engine red sportcoat, and two-toned hustler shoes, while the Glitter Twins were dressed in skintight sequined sheaths and four-inch fuck-me high heels. The other artists and beats were covered with hair and paint, and there was one man I had never seen before dressed completely in a black rubber suit. I made it a point to avoid him; I was too wasted to hear his story. Also on our side of the aisle and in the rear of the church was Dr. Hergenroeder and five staff psychiatrists from Larson-Payne, all dressed conservatively, but they had brought with them a special caravan of mental patients, about nine or ten of those who loved Jeremy. One of them, Jimmy Crabtree, aged 67, walked around in circles and sang "Mary Had a Little Lamb" three times in a high-pitched, childlike voice. Another, a hugely fat paranoid, named Horace, sat on the end of the row and mumbled, "They're looking at me. They're looking at me. THEY THINK I'M A

FUCKING QUEER!!!" about a hundred times. Jeremy would have approved.

And in the very back row was a black-shades-wearing Rudy Antonelli and three of his goons. They arrived late and sat down with a swooping flourish. I could feel their eyes boring into my neck as the Episcopal bishop spoke.

His name was Dr. Taylor Scott. He wore long black robes, and he gave a dull, predictable speech about the "tragic loss of one of Baltimore's rising young businessmen, a beacon of light and optimism . . . a man whose career and fate seemingly knew no boundaries . . . now cut down like so many visionaries in the prime of his youth." The WASPS mumbled agreement, Jeremy's aunt cried silently on old Farlow's shoulder, and a few of the stoned hipsters from Monty's laughed out loud. They thought that Jeremy was a put-on artist, that pretending to do business was his own triple hip way of laughing at the establishment, making a mockery of all that was holy in the straight world.

They annoyed me more than the WASPS, because I felt that they should have known better. But I tried hard, through my own clenched teeth as I stared at the closed coffin, not to come down on any of them. That was *my* problem. Jeremy was beyond all that. Businessmen, artists, cons, teachers, shrinks: In life, he accepted them all and even loved them all. As we sang an old hymn that Farlow said was his favorite in church as a boy ("Holy, Holy, Holy"), it occurred to me that this was his real legacy.

With Jeremy Raines there were no wasted moments, and I swore to myself, as I held Val close to me, that I would waste not one more of my own, not one in guilt, not one in remorse, not one in wasted sadness, not one in self-pity. I would live life, by God, to the fullest, take up where he left off, feel his spirit inside of me, pushing me on.

In the graveyard old Farlow reached down and elegantly touched the edge of the coffin, and that pretty much finished me along with everyone else.

And perhaps that was the way it should be, for bankers, university presidents, hipsters, poets, mental patients, shrinks, and even murdering gangsters wept as one, wept for their dear departed friend, he who burned brighter than any of them. And it occurred to me that this is what Jeremy wanted more than anything else. That all the world would become one loving brotherhood.

But this could just have possibly been bullshit. I was too wasted and emotionally drained to really be sure. He may have just wanted money, sex, and a good time, but at least in that, he excluded no one, which was more than I was capable of. For as I left that sward of lawn, I stared with pure hatred and a little fear at Rudy A. who caught my glance and came toward me. Alone.

"Walk with me," he said.

I looked at Val and told her to wait for me by the car. Then Rudy and I strolled away from the departing circus of mourners, out among the white gravestones.

"I want you to know I'm very sorry about your friend," Rudy said. "He was a great guy. Colorful, you know?"

"Yeah," I said, "wasn't he?"

"But a very bad driver."

"Yeah," I said, "very bad."

"You think I killed him, don't you?" he said.

"Why would you do that?" I said.

"You tell me? I wanted to do business with him. He was going to make me rich."

I said nothing to that, but I understood what he was telling me. It was his dead solid perfect alibi.

"Maybe you think he had something to do with the death of Johnny Martello," I said.

"Why would I think that?" he said. "I know who killed Johnny."

He reached into his cape pocket and pulled out a battered envelope. Grabbing my right hand, he poured the contents into my palm. Four perfectly shaped four-leaf clovers. For a second I was stunned, uncomprehending. Then I nearly laughed out loud. Jeremy must have copped them from his desk that first day we had struck our deal with Mr. A. I hoped it wouldn't mean trouble for Bobby Murphy; I'd have to call him soon and explain.

"These came in the mail. The Irish assholes did it," Rudy said. "We'll have to settle with them. Soon."

I looked into his eyes for a sign that he was lying or playing with me. But there was none, which still didn't mean he wasn't putting me on.

"What do you want?" I said.

"You're a smart boy," Rudy said. "Smarter than the others. Now that Jeremy's gone to his reward, you and I are in business together. I want you to stay on, run things. Jeremy was a genius, but he was a lousy administrator. Will we be partners?"

"I don't know," I said numbly. "It's too soon to say."

"Of course," Rudy said. "But I thought I should put my cards on the table. You go get drunk, get laid, then you come tell me, say, day after tomorrow? Okay?"

"Okay," I said.

"One more thing," he said. "Since I now own the business, the house on Chateau is mine. You and your girlfriend Val are welcome to stay as caretakers, but the rest of that herd moves on out to pasture, like tomorrow? Got it?"

I said nothing to that at all.

Then he reached up and pinched my cheek hard.

"You're a smart kid. Just cause your friend blew it don't mean you can't make some bread, huh?"

There didn't seem to be any answer to that either, so he

turned and walked off. He didn't have to go far. His limousine had been trailing us the whole time, and he only had to take a couple of steps before the door flew open, and he ducked inside.

I walked back toward the parking lot and my friends, and I saw someone talking to Val. At first I thought my eyes were playing tricks on me. It didn't seem possible. But after a few more steps, I saw that it was no illusion.

It was my father hugging my girlfriend.

"Hey," I said, walking toward him. It wasn't really what I had in mind, but it was all I could get out without choking up.

"I'm deeply sorry, son," he said.

Then he put his arms around me and squeezed me, and that was all she wrote. I felt great shivers come through me, shock waves after an earthquake.

"Dad," I said. "He's gone, Dad."

He held onto me and said the words I hadn't heard since I was a child: "It's all right, Tommy. It's all right, son."

And then Val joined us and Babe and Eddie and Lulu and even—God love him—Dan the Trucker, and we stood there holding each other like some lost chiefless tribe who'd gotten split up in the deep woods and found one another at last by some sweet, still blue pond.

There was a party down at Monty's that afternoon, crab cakes and jazz and hashish and people telling stories, funny, sad stories about mad Jeremy, but I was all storied out, and I told Val I was exhausted and heading back to Chateau

Avenue to sleep. She held me, and she said she understood and that she would be along after a while and that I shouldn't worry.

And I didn't, because I knew she'd be there. Whatever there was between us, it was never cloying or dead, and I thanked God for that.

But I had told her a white lie, because though I was so tired that I could barely stand, I drove out to leafy, beautiful Charles Street and took a right at the winding road that led to Larson-Payne. It was about four when I got there, and in the shifting afternoon sunlight, which cast moody, elongated shadows of the great brick buildings across the lawns, I went inside to find Billy McConnell.

He was sitting up in his bunk when Dr. Hergenroeder let me in. He was as handsome a child as ever, but now there was something in those eyes, a confused but very obvious curiosity. He gave me a shy smile, which seemed to say that he knew me from somewhere, but that he could not name the time or place.

"Billy," Dr. Hergenroeder said. "This is a friend, Tommy Fallon."

Billy looked at me and smiled wider. But he said nothing.

"Let's go for a little walk, Bill," I said.

Billy looked at Dr. Hergenroeder eagerly.

"It's all right," Dr. Hergenroeder said. "But just a few minutes. And you have to bundle up. It's chilly outside."

Billy didn't move. He only stared straight ahead, and for a terrible moment I thought he had slipped back into the dark hallway from which Jeremy had rescued him. Then slowly he was up and putting on his brown corduroy coat.

Outside the wind whipped through the trees, making a sound like howling wolves.

We walked down the long hill, and I felt a twisting pressure in my stomach. What was I going to tell him? It seemed to me that given the circumstances, the short time we had together, that every word I said to him should contain some grain of eternal wisdom, something that he could hang onto when the darkness threatened to descend on him again.

But as we walked farther and farther away from the great red brick walls of the hospital, no such words came and I felt a sinking sensation. Oh, God, if only I were Jeremy, if only it were me that had died out on that lonely Virginia road. Better, better by far that it had been me, for what the hell was I, a failed lover—my girl was going to move 3,500 miles away, a failed friend—I never gave as much to Jeremy as he did to me. I was headed down the path my father had plodded on all those years as surely as the moon ascended in the troubled sky. I would be a no-show like the old man, afraid to try at all, hiding behind my second-hand critical judgments as he hid behind his cynicism. And now, as we walked down the hill, I was failing again, failing to provide one whit of insight, philosophy, Christ—even companionship for young Billy, who needed it so desperately.

I was utterly paralyzed, and as we walked silently on toward the dark woods it seemed to me that this small boy, lost in his own well of fears, was really my twin, the two of us locked in some deep, mute blackness.

Then ahead of me I saw some white wooden lawn chair and a pile of old dead leaves.

And without knowing why or even what in God's name I was doing, I patted Billy on the head and took off at a wild pace toward them.

I could see the breath blowing from my mouth, and I could hear twigs snapping beneath my feet and I ran faster and faster, and leaped into that pile of leaves, something I hadn't done since I was twelve years old.

And I was filled with a sense of lightness and joy and felt—God knows I know it sounds sentimental but even so—felt that Jeremy Raines had propelled me across that green grass and I looked back at Billy, and he was still standing there, yes, but he was leaning, leaning toward me like a sprinter on the starting blocks, and I yelled to him at the top of my lungs:

"Come on, Billy . . . Come on!"

He looked up at me, and there was fear in his face.

"What about the Moat Monster?" he said.

Of course, I thought . . . what a fool I've been.

"He's gone," I said. "It's okay. Come on . . ."

I opened my arms, but he shook his head.

"How did he die?" Billy said.

Oh, God, I had to think of something fast.

"The knight," I said. "This knight came by and his name was Sir Jeremy and he had a great silver spear that he used to kill dragons, and he told the boy in the castle to stand back . . . and then . . . then . . . he threw the spear up right next to the boy's window, and it stuck in the wall. The boy pulled it out, and Sir Jeremy shouted up to him, 'The next time the Moat Monster shows his ugly head, you shut your eyes and you think of me, your friend, Sir Jeremy, and then you throw it with all your might.' The boy listened and fairly soon, the Old Shoemaker tried to cross the moat and sure enough, the Moat Monster raised his head, and bellowed up at him. Listen Billy . . . he was a horrible looking monster with a huge, ugly mouth. He had double rows of the sharpest teeth and the sound he made was awful. But now the boy was almost ready. He shut his eyes and thought of his friend, Sir Jeremy the Knight, and then with all his might, he threw the spear, down toward the moat."

"He did?" Billy McConnell said.

"Yes, and it was a perfect strike. He stabbed the Moat Monster right in the jaw. The Moat Monster flipped and flopped and turned this way and that and made a horrible moaning sound and finally died belly up in the blood-stained waters."

There was a slight smile on Billy's handsome face.

"He did?" he said.

"Yes," I said, madly improvising. "Yes, and then the Old Shoemaker was able to cross and he and the boy lived together, as friends, happily ever after."

Billy listened, and I felt my heart pounding. Then he looked at me and said quietly:

"But what happened to the knight?"

My throat caught then and I found it hard to continue . . .

"He . . . he kept going on . . ." I said, "to another world . . . to help other people . . . because that's his job."

"And did the boy ever see him again?" Billy asked.

I didn't know what to say. I was afraid of any answer I might give . . . and yet . . . yet . . . I knew better than to lie.

"No," I said. "No, he's gone on. But every time the boy shuts his eyes, and thinks of his friend, then it's like they're together again. You see, some people, Billy, you only need to know for a short time and they'll be your friends forever."

"Is that true?" he said.

"Yes," I said. "That's true. Now come here . . . come on . . . Run . . . Run."

But Billy still hesitated. So I picked up a great armful of leaves, and threw them in the air, and let them settle on myself, and laughed wildly. He smiled shyly and leaned forward, but it was as if he was glued to that patch of ground. So I did it again—threw the leaves in the air, and leaped around like a madman, and gave out a crazed whoop. I was so mad I didn't even realize what I was shouting. And then I realized it wasn't my voice at all . . . but Jeremy's . . . and he was saying through me: "Come on, my boy, time's a-wasting now." And it was then that Billy started to run. He ran toward me with all his might and his little red face was smiling and he gave out a little shy cry of joy. And I began to laugh like a lunatic, and threw the leaves up in the air again . . . and then he leaped feet first into the pile with me, and he gave out a high-pitched cheer and I cheered with him, and covered him with leaves, and he tossed them back on me, screaming and laughing and we

302

were like two mad idiots out there on the great wide hospital lawn.

And when we were finished and walked back, I didn't have to say any priceless Words To Live By, because I knew we had all the time in the world.

In fact, all I remember saying to him, as I gave him back to Dr. Hergenroeder in the marble vestibule, was:

"Be a good boy and don't worry, because I'll be here Tuesday. I'm your friend and I'm never going to leave you. Ever. You can count on that."

"You won't?" he said. "Promise?"

"Promise."

Tears came to his blue eyes, and he looked up and hugged me, and I knew that this was it—I was in with Billy for life. And as I walked across the great lawn in the gathering dark, I felt that Jeremy was smiling down on me, and then it occurred to me that maybe mad Jeremy Raines had planned even this—and I laughed and looked up at the darkening sky, and said:

"Okay, Jeremy . . . okay, my boy . . . what else do you have for me?"

And the answer came three blocks away, as I maneuvered Val's car over the old streetcar tracks on the York Road.

I didn't really have to tell Babe and Eddie that Rudy A. wanted them gone. They were packing by the next morning, throwing things into their old Chevrolet.

"We're heading to the West Coast with Val," Babe said. "You oughta come with us, Tommy. Tell you the truth, we've been dying to make it out there for some time, but out of loyalty to Jeremy, you know . . ."

"What's so great about it out there?" I asked. "I don't get it. You guys don't even surf."

Eddie slapped his stump into his forehead.

"We're not going to surf, man. We're headed to Haight-Ashbury. There's a whole new thing going on out there. I got a card from a guy I met in Tangier. He said it's a meeting place for hippies. It's wild."

"Hippies?" I said. I didn't like the sound of the word. It sounded soft, disposable.

"Guys like us," Eddie said. "You know how in Baltimore we're like freaks. Well, it's like everybody in every state who is a freak is going to live out there together."

"And secede from the nation?" I said.

"Maybe," Babe said. "Tell you the truth, I'm about as cynical as you are about it, but what the hell, it'll be an adventure."

"It's going to be a lot more than that," Eddie said. "It's going to work. You sure you don't want to go, Tom?"

"No," I said. "I'm not sure, but I have things here I want to do. You guys send me your address. You can never tell when I might want to roll out."

Val came out of the house then, carrying a lamp from our room and a giant fern.

"I thought I was living without material things," she said. "But we already have enough to rent a damned U-Haul truck."

"You'll be glad you have some of your own stuff when you get there," I said.

Then I stopped and shook my head: "Christ, listen to me," I said. "I sound like your father. 'Take your rubbers, children. Don't accept any ice cream from strangers.' "

That got a small laugh that died in all our throats. I turned away from them then and began to cough. When I turned back, Eddie and Babe were already behind the wheel of the Chevrolet.

Val was waiting for me on the front steps. She was dressed in her tightest Levis, white tennis shoes, and a form-fitting black T-shirt. I could barely look at her.

She handed me a green sheath tied by a red bow.

"My poems," she said.

"I won't take them," I said. "Not unless you have copies."

304

"I do have some of them," she said. "But it doesn't matter, Tom. I wasn't kidding. I'm through with all of that. I only want to live day to day. You know, it's funny. Babe and I were talking about it this morning. I liked to write but I never read as much as I should have, not like a writer should. You're the reader. I bet you turn out to write some great books."

"Sure," I said.

"Maybe someday you could write about me," she said, putting her arms around me and kissing my cheek.

"I don't want to write about you," I said. "I need you here. I still love you."

"I love you too, Tommy. But I've got to go. You know that."

I kissed her again on the cheek, and then as if some gentle hand were guiding us, we both turned and looked up at the house.

"Oh, God, Tommy," she said.

She held on to me then and wept openly, and I knew that I had lost her the second Jeremy died.

"You'll be fine when you get out there," I said. "You're right. You need to put some distance between yourself and all this."

"He raised me, you know," she said.

"I know," I said.

And then she kissed me one last time, broke away, and got into the car.

On the way out, just for old times' sake, Eddie ran into an Impala that was parked in front of him. He left a good-sized dent and honked three times, then they were gone.

The memories of all that was lost those many years ago swirled through me. Like some native on an African plain, I could feel the spirits inside me. Babe and Eddie, Jeremy and Val. It was as though they were small animals trapped beneath my skin.

I stayed on the old back lot near the garages until it got dark, then made my way out of there, navigating my rented car over the used condoms, the broken wine bottles, the hypodermic needles. It was nearly dark, and there was no sense tempting the fates. I could have gone back up Chateau for one last look at the old sight, but there seemed no point in that. Remembering all of this was just about all I could take anyway. I felt limp, exhausted, old, very old, and as I drove out toward Calvert and my room at the Sheraton I thought of something Jeremy had said to me once when we were both stoned and wasted one wild weekend as we drove across the twinkling winter city to sell his magic cards.

I had asked him if trying to do so much, trying to *be* so much wasn't going to wear him out. I think in my ultraliterary, way, I had misquoted Fitzgerald from *The Crack Up:* "Life is lived most successfully if looked through only one window." Jeremy had punched me hard on the arm and said, "Never say that, my boy. That was in the old world. We're not like that. We don't have merely one self, so to look at life through one window would be just cheating us of our possibilities."

And I had laughed at that and said, "You are a hopeless romantic and a complete bullshit artist." He had looked hurt then and said in a tense, sincere voice: "No, Tommy, it's not bullshit, I mean it. We really are new men. We're capable of anything."

I had laughed at that. But I was wrong. For he had meant it, and in his mad, scrambling way he *had* lived all his selves to the hilt.

In my hotel room, I lay on my back and thought about dropping in on my father. He lived in a two-bedroom apartment now not far from Calvert, and I had told him if I got in on time, I'd see him. If not, we'd get together after the ceremony.

Now, I almost acted impulsively and made the short trip to his apartment, but as I got up to throw on my sportcoat, I realized that I'd had about all the pain I could take for one day. Our relationship was better, sometimes I thought it had gotten better ever since the night Jeremy hypnotized him. (Was that really true? Or was that merely wishful thinking?)

Still, I thought, when my mother had left him, *he had* changed his life. In fact, not long after Jeremy had hypnotized him, he had taken up painting again. He had even had a couple of one-man shows in local galleries, and they had been reviewed favorably. Which is not to say he was the secret, stymied genius I had hoped for.

No, I'm afraid not. He had lost too many years of development for that. Yet, he was a good, solid realist painter with a surprising tenderness in his work. I even had one of his oils on my wall, a beautifully rendered painting of the watermen at Crisfield on the Eastern Shore. I also had him do the cover of my last book, *The Black Watch*. It was eye-catching, fine.

To that extent, he *had* reshaped his life. Had it come from the shock of my mother getting up the courage to leave him? Had Jeremy's magic had something, *anything*, to do with it? Had my own life, my own gathering seriousness, somehow had an impact on him?

Perhaps it was all of these. All I knew was that he was better, happier, and I thanked God for it.

But sadly, one thing hadn't changed. Retired from his hated computer job at Social Security, he still spent most of his life in the bathroom, washing, slicing his boils, applying his salves. And it still drove me crazy.

That was why I didn't go over to see him that night. Feeling as melancholy and wasted as I did, I couldn't have taken one of our old adolescent scenes in the bathroom.

Lying in my bed, half drifting off to sleep, I began to

giggle in a kind of mad way. I could just see it. Myself, a forty-five-year-old man, hunched up against the bathroom door as he washed himself again and again and again: "Dad . . . I got the honorary degree, Dad."

The sound of running water obscures my voice.

"Dad . . . I have seven novels out now, Dad."

The sound of the running water is now joined by the jolly sound of the flushing toilet.

"Dad . . . Are you proud of me, Dad? Do I get a little fucking credit, Dad? Can't you come out of the fucking bathroom for this one fucking night, Dad?"

And now I'm kicking at the door, feeling this monstrous rage and screaming, "Look at me, Dad. Come out of there, Dad. I don't give a fuck about your boils, Dad; I don't give a fuck about your hemorrhoids, Dad; I don't give a fuck about the Baltimore curse, Dad. Just talk to me a little, you selfish, fucking lunatic."

No, no, no, I thought as I fell into sleep. There wouldn't be any of that, some James Dean tearjerker scene out of *East Of Eden*. No, I had learned something Jeremy hadn't taught me, but that those of us who survive must learn in the end.

Cut your losses.

My father was, in his own way, thriving. He was painting well, and I loved him and was happy and proud for him, but I would never stay overnight in his home again.

What can I tell you of the doctoral ceremony? There was good old "Pomp and Circumstance." There were seven hundred seniors in the graduating class, and I had to stand in the foul Baltimore heat wearing my black woolen robes and watch them all receive their diplomas. My mother and the silent sculptor Joe came. She wore a snappy blue suit with three big white buttons. She was well tanned, had lost weight, and, except for her Baltimore Oriole earrings, looked like she had become a Floridian. Joe wore a lime green suit and a tie with a large mouth bass on it. He walked with the help of one of his own creations—a cane made of a large piece of polished oak that had been carved to look like a coiling serpent. To be perfectly honest, it was pretty damned good work in a folksie kind of way. They sat together and held hands, and I was happy to see that whatever else had happened in their lives, they had found true love. My father, on the other hand, was ten minutes late. He looked old and had a red patch over his left eye from where he had washed himself so often that the skin had dried out and left a rough patch of dried-out tissue.

Ironically, he sat next to my surrogate father, the man I had yet to make up with, Dr. Spaulding, who himself looked so old, so frail, that it frightened me. Yet, he carried himself as always ramrod straight, and his snow white hair was neatly combed.

And as I sat on the lectern, in the great amphitheatre in the Dell, I suddenly felt a little fearful. What were the two of them talking about? Was it me? As absurd as it may sound, I was afraid that they would start comparing notes, laughing at my pretensions, that the two of them would team up against me and suddenly stand and point at me and say, "You're not worthy of this. You're a fraud, a phony. You left your hometown, you left your family. You're not even a Baltimorean anymore."

I almost gave way to a feeling of despair and utter darkness. I suddenly had an impulse to walk off the stage and go straight to the parking lot.

But, of course, I did nothing of the kind. I sat there and took a deep breath, concentrated on the speakers, and thought of Jeremy Raines, smiling and hanging off the porch, talking to us in his inspirational way, as I have done ever since the days at Chateau.

You see, in memory, Sir Jeremy had continued his magic. He was a talisman for me, my own mental gris-gris stick, from which I shook off the ghosts and mad, screaming bugaboos of my family.

Is it right to use an old friend like that? I've often wondered, but I think Jeremy would approve. He meant to preach, to inspire, to make us all move up, up, up, and out of our own dying skins. Yes, I think he would approve.

And there was one other thing that kicked me out of the blues.

There in the back of the VIP crowd, sitting alone, I saw Billy, Billy McConnell, with his black Italian suit and long blond hair. That was one promise I had kept all these years. I had helped pay his way through college, dear old Calvert, of course, and after school he had come to work in New York. I was able to introduce him to photo editors at various magazines and publishers and now he was doing quite well as a professional photographer. Billy kept a small apartment in Chelsea. We saw each other constantly. Indeed, the affection between us had grown steadily since that first walk outside the hospital so many years ago. Sometimes late at night my eyes would fill up in gratitude as I realized what a blessing he was, for he had become, to my astonishment and endless delight, my own son.

Now, I thought, if only Val, if only Jeremy, would come walking through the door. But no need to get into all that.

Finally, after every senior had received his diploma, my time came. The dean of the Humanities College, dignified Dr. Moss, came forth and said kind words about my novels, their spirit of humanism, how I had taken a popular form, the thriller, and used it to investigate the moral corruption of our time. (And even as the audience applauded, I wondered, had I? Had I written anything worthy at all?)

Finally, it was time to make my speech and I stepped forth, took the microphone in hand, and began. Though I had told myself in New York that no one ever listened to commencement speakers, I wanted badly to say something that they could take with them out into the dark world. Haunted by memories, I felt like some half-crazed version of the wedding guest, and I wanted my words to carry the weight for all those beaming, naive young faces. And more than that, I wanted my words to redeem the dead themselves. Of course I failed miserably. The first half of my speech was about my own generation, how we lived for passion and wildness and how, even though we failed in some of our goals, I felt proud, deeply proud of all we had said and done. We had protested against the war, and I believe to this day that we were right. We had tried to live passionately, erotically. At our best, our lives had been a religious journey, a quest of the spirit, and in spite of everything, I felt that many of us were still trying to live it.

I stopped and looked at them all. I wandered up and down the stage like some sad Beckett clown, and I suddenly wanted to tell them all about Jeremy and Val and Babe and Eddie. Yes, I wanted them to know, to feel, to understand that there was some holy kernel of youthful truth and beauty that we experienced that they too must find for themselves. I even started in with the tale but then abruptly broke off, smiled, wandered back across the stage, then gave up and fell back on the old time-worn clichés. I told them to "live passionately," "fight for your community," "live in the imagination," and I ended with a cautionary note (just what happy graduates don't want to hear).

"I am now in my forties, and looking back I can't say I wouldn't have done some things differently, but basically I am happy with my generation—even their excesses—and I know one thing for certain. We won't be like the suburban generation of the 1950s, who looked back into their lives midway through and found that they hadn't lived."

I finished thinking that I had failed. God, there was more, so much more that I wanted to say. I wanted to say that friendship is the most holy of all things and the hardest to sustain, that they must fight to keep the sweet-natured spirit of youth, that everything in the culture will conspire to sap it out of them. I wanted to become some mad Jonathon Edwards warning them of jealousy, mad materialism, and the death of passion.

But instead I simply put down the mike and bowed my head to show them I was done. There was a long moment of silence, then they rose as one and gave me a standing ovation, polite, measured; I doubt they heard a word of it.

Professor Moss came forth and thanked me and shook my hand, and I stumbled back to my seat and laughed as I thought of Jeremy. What if he had given the speech? He would have kept them there rapt for hours, and by the end, half of them would be working for Identi-Card and the other half would be lining up to be investors. Yes, I thought, as I walked into the great reception room and hugged my father and mother and Billy, there was more I should have said, there was more I must write, something that captured the true spirit of Raines and those mad days, or I wouldn't be able to live with myself. I couldn't bear to be a mere professional, even one with a New York apartment, money, and a new Ph.D.

The reception was held at Turf Country Club out in Green Spring, Maryland. As I drove my father through the gates, I thought of how far I'd come. This place was strictly off-limits to me as a boy. The only people I ever knew who went to dances here were guys who parked cars for the rich. Now, when I no longer cared about it, this world had opened up to me, and I commented on it to my father, who I was certain would appreciate the irony. After all, he had spent his entire life despising the rich and their private little reserves, but he was having none of my cynicism.

"You know, Tom," he said, smiling at me, "you shouldn't knock the Turf till you try it. The food here's really good, and they have a great swimming pool and nice golf course."

I looked at him astonished.

"How the hell do you know?" I said.

" 'Cause I been out here quite a few times," he said.

"You have?" I said, astonished. "For what?"

"To meet with my clients," he said, sighing in a slightly

exasperated way as if this was a well-publicized fact. "There's a couple of people I know real well. They've bought several of my paintings, and we have lunch here every once in a while."

I rode by the red stables and saw a beautiful black-haired woman working out a reddish brown horse, a magnificent-looking animal.

"Why you old phony," I said. "All your life you lambasted these people."

"Right," my father said. "But what did I know? I mean, yeah, the rich screw people, but individually, a man can get along with anybody. Hey, besides, I been poor and under-appreciated all my fucking life, son. I like 'em making over me a little, even if they are bastards."

He laughed at this in a hearty way that I hadn't heard in years.

"I know what you mean, Dad," I said, laughing myself. "I know exactly what you mean."

We pulled up to the clubhouse, and a young tuxedoed valet ran up to open the door, while another helped my father from the car.

"Hello, Mr. Fallon," he said. "Nice to see you again."

"Hi, Jimmy," my father said, winking at me. "Nice to be seen."

The room was filled with reporters from the *Sun* and a couple of television crews. There was even somebody from a Washington TV station, and I found myself again giving interviews, mumbling the same half-baked stuff I'd said in my acceptance speech. In between I ate a couple of perfect Maryland crab cakes and downed three or four drinks. My mother got me aside for a few minutes and looked over at my father, who was holding court with a couple of his new rich friends.

"Doncha' just love that?" she said. "Eugene Debs cashes in."

I laughed, and she waved her hand as if to dismiss her bitter thoughts.

"You know what I hate about Florida, hon?" she said.

"No, Mom, what's that?"

"I hate it that people don't read. In Balmere every one of my old girlfriends likes to read mysteries, but down there people think you're acting like an old person if you read. 'Es woman downa street, she told me that I should be out riding onna motorcycle. Her husband rides one everyday, and they go down and play shuffleboard with all the other retirees. But personally I'm like you. I mean I am a person who has to have the life of a mind, like you always used to say."

"So what does this mean, Mom?" I asked. "You and Joe moving back to Baltimore?"

"I think so, hon," she said. "When I left here, I thought I was done with the place, but you never really are finished wif Balmere. When you come right down to it, I think that's the main problem with all those people in Florida."

"What's that, Mom?" I asked, holding her sweet old hand.

"They aren't living where they grew up," she said. "I found out a person needs to be where he grew up, or else he don't have any touchstones."

I smiled at her and thought about what a rage such sentiments might have inspired in me years ago. When I finally did leave Baltimore, I was dead certain that I was through with the place forever. I wasn't going to be trapped like Dad. I wasn't going to get pushed into some trivial little life on the row house block. And I had made it, made it in the big town. But I would never get the place out of my mind. The difference was that now I no longer wanted to forget. Quite the opposite: Since I had finally let my memory run riot, I found myself hoarding every little detail, for they all seemed precious and dear.

314

THE KING OF CARDS

I was talking with Billy when Dr. Spaulding took my arm. He did it so casually that it shocked me. He had certainly never done anything like it before. The only time we had ever touched at all was to give one another stiff handshakes. Yet, here he was leading me away from Billy, toward an isolated corner of the room.

Finally, we were out of earshot, standing by a trash can filled with the remains of old crabs.

"Congratulations, Thomas," Dr. Spaulding said.

"Thanks," I said.

I wanted to go on. I fully intended to finally say what I hadn't said all those years ago, that I had been young and, well, a jerk, but before I could speak, Dr. Spaulding smiled at me warmly: "I enjoyed your speech, Thomas."

"You don't have to be polite," I said. "I know it was a bunch of disjunctive babbling, sentimental garbage."

"Well, I see one thing hasn't changed," he said in a suddenly stern tone.

"What? What's that?"

"You're still ridiculously hard on yourself."

"Not hard enough," I said. "I still haven't reached my true potential, you know."

Though I meant it, I tried to say it with an ironic twist, and he laughed and took off his glasses and tapped them on his palm. Seeing the old gesture made me feel such a tenderness for him that tears nearly came to my eyes.

"You sound like the characters in James's story *The Real Thing*, you remember that one, don't you?"

"Yes," I said. "I remember it. The story about the man who looks and looks for his real, true destiny, then finds when it's too late that it's love, and it's been right under his nose all along."

"Well, it's a good deal more complicated than that," he

Robert Ward

said, "but essentially, yes, that's it. The story is about a mind that is confused by ideas, by 'ideas about excellence,' and 'destiny.' You have a marvelous gift, Thomas. Why don't you relax and enjoy it?"

"You read my books?"

"Of course, all of them."

"That's nice to know," I said. Then I cleared my throat.

"Professor," I said, stumbling and feeling suddenly like a schoolboy again. "Remember . . . years ago . . . the last time we quarreled. I said a lot of things that day, stupid things, unforgivable things, and I'm sorry. You were the best teacher I ever had. It's that simple."

I felt choked up then, it was that kind of day, so I sipped my bourbon and faked a little cough.

"Well, I was quite furious with you at the time," he said. "I thought about running you out of school. I don't think I've ever been quite so mad at a student before."

"I wouldn't blame you if you had," I said. "I was dead wrong."

He sighed and shook his head.

"No," he said. "You were dead right. What you said was tactless and thoughtless and filled with the self-righteous anger of youth, to be sure, but there was no denying it, you were right. I was not the man I wanted to be, and to be honest, I had met Jeremy Raines the year before and had lunch with him down at that place."

To say that I was astonished to hear this would be a gross understatement.

"You?" I said in a voice so low that it came out a mere whisper. "You were down the old Chateau Avenue place?"

"Yes, I was," Dr. Spaulding said. "He invited me to come by for lunch, so I did, and, well, at first it was all very pleasant. He and the girl you went with, Val Jackson, made me lunch, fried crab cakes and stewed tomatoes, and we sipped white wine."

A cloud passed over Dr. Spaulding's face.

"What happened?" I said.

"We got into an argument, something about art versus

316

life, and I'm afraid I took the old classicist's view that there was nothing new under the sun, that the artist's job was to pass on what was of value of the old culture to the younger generation. Of course Raines took the same tact you did, only, and I hope you won't be offended or insulted, he did it with a great deal more subtlety. He said that there were new things, new ways of being, that the world was so filled with change—new technology, new invention—that the entire idea of identity itself would change in a very few years. Of course, I turned up my nose at such thoughts. I reminded him that he wasn't the only Utopian ever born. I suggested that he was uneducated, even in the Utopian ideas from his own tradition, that he should do some reading before he passed off such stuff as original."

"You did?" I said, and my voice sounded very much like that of a fifteen-year-old. Still, the very thought of the two of them in such a discussion amazed me. God, what I would have given to have been there.

"What did he say to all that?" I asked.

"Well, it was strange," Dr. Spaulding said. "He smiled at me and agreed with everything I was saying. He admitted that his education was spotty and that this was a great failing and he hoped that I would help him get acquainted with Utopian writings. He said that he wanted us to become great friends."

Now Dr. Spaulding stopped and shook his head.

"It was very strange. As you are no doubt aware, I have always consciously kept a certain formality, a certain distance between my students and myself. For many reasons, first and foremost being that I believed, still believe, for the most part, that neither student or teacher is well served with excessive chumminess. The teacher's job is to bring his brain and sensibility to class and to use whatever talents he has to elucidate works of art. He is not a therapist or, really, even a friend, and so ordinarily I would have been offended by such a rude offer, especially by a student who knew the rules and seemed to be deliberately overstepping the implied agreement."

"But you weren't," I said suddenly. "Instead you felt that you might actually like to know him better. In fact, I bet you felt that if you didn't become Jeremy's friend, you would be passing up something magical, something that might send your life careening off into some wild new direction."

He looked at me and laughed, and I felt shy again, shy and embarrassed for putting my words into his mouth. But he wasn't offended by it in the least.

"That's right," he said. "I sensed it at once. I know this sounds absurd but I remembered reading about Paul Verlaine meeting Arthur Rimbaud and feeling this kinship, this astounding capacity for friendship, and for something else, too, for a kind of vision that really is beyond words. But Raines seemed to have something, seemed to *know* something, something I couldn't know and was too afraid to find out. It was made all the more palpable by the fact that he never disagreed with me at all. No, he simply smiled at me, and then he said the most curious thing. He said, "Professor, I wish your back would stop hurting. Why don't you let me hypnotize you? Then you could sleep at night."

I could say nothing to this. I was dumbstruck.

"He was right," Dr. Spaulding said in a whisper. "I had a bad back, but I had never said anything about it to anyone. Perhaps he could tell from some way I was leaning. Perhaps I had unconsciously rubbed my back with my hand. I don't know, but he was also right about my not sleeping as well."

"Did you let him hypnotize you?" I said.

"No," he said. "No, I did not. I told him that my bad back was from lifting furniture around my house when I was moving into my apartment, but he knew this wasn't true."

"You lied to him?" I said. "But why?"

"Because he scared me, Thomas. Though I have never told anyone about this for fear of looking foolish, I will tell you that your friend Raines knew that my back was sore from nerves. He also knew I was lying; I left soon after that, and I was never so glad to get away from any place in my

318

life and yet . . . yet, when I thought back on it, nothing had happened. Nothing and everything."

"And your back," I said, breathless.

"Oh, it still hurt for months. I'm not suggesting he had those kind of powers, and yet, I've had dreams of him. All these years, Thomas, and I still dream of his eyes, his voice. Anyway, he frightened me. He seemed to live beyond the rational. And when I heard you were living there with him, that you had taken him up on the invitation I had refused, I felt such a mixture of things, fear for you, real fear, for what if Raines used whatever charismatic powers he had for evil ends? I liked you, Thomas, and I knew how young and, well, *needy* you were, and I didn't want anything bad to happen to you. But I also felt jealous, jealous that you would have the courage to go where I feared to tread."

I smiled and put my hand on his arm.

"It wasn't courage, Doctor," I said. "It was pure naïveté, believe me. I had no idea what I was getting into when I moved into Raines's house."

He shook his head violently and held my forearm.

"No," he said, "it's time you understood something about yourself. You were brave then, and you are brave now—braver than me—and I deeply cherish the fact that you were one of my students. I only wish there were more like you and Jeremy. The last couple of generations that have come through old Calvert have one goal in mind, to become good little members of the middle class."

"So I understand," I said.

"Anyway, Tom, I am proud of you and I think what you said about your generation is true. You weren't afraid of the irrational like I was, though we had our reasons. Not to make excuses, Tom, but my generation had just seen some serious irrationality with Hitler and it had frightened us off the whole concept, but in my old age I know there is something else, inside, some place where the poems come from, some place where Freud and Joyce came from, some place that can use the unconscious to heal and create. I think

319

your friend knew that. And what is even rarer, I think he
understood how to harness it."

"Yes," I said, and now tears did come to my eyes.

"You still miss him, don't you, Tom?"

"Yes," I said. "It's funny, but as I get older, I miss him
more."

He nodded and squeezed my wrist slightly. "And what
of the girl?" he said. "Do you ever see her?"

I smiled then.

"Val? No, but I've heard tales. When she left Baltimore,
she moved to the Haight, then she ended up in Vegas
dealing Keno, and for a short time, she went with a
gangster."

"My Lord," Professor Spaulding said, but he looked
interested.

"The guy used her for a punching bag though," I said,
falling into my noir voice, "so she left and ended up in
Paris, where she married a deputy mayor. Now, I hear she
has a terrific apartment near the Champs-Elysées and two
children. I understand she's quite content. I almost called
her last Christmas when I was promoting my last book for
my European publisher. But at the last minute, I chickened
out."

Dr. Spaulding nodded and sipped his drink.

"If you wouldn't mind a little advice," he said, "call her.
Don't let your old friendships die. Is there a girl in your
life?"

"There have been girls," I said, "but no marriages. Maybe
now, though, I'm ready. Maybe it's time."

"If you're ready," Dr. Spaulding said, "you mustn't let
the past drag you down, though I understand your obses-
sion with it. There is nothing ever quite like one's first dear
friends. Keep in touch, Tom, okay?" He squeezed my arm
lightly, then smiled and turned away.

THE KING OF CARDS

>

When it was over, Billy drove me to the airport. He was excited over the award and kept laughing and calling me Dr. Fallon, which was charming of him. But then I found most things he did charming. He had, after all, become my son, as surely as I had become Dr. Spaulding's, and I was happy he was here and happier still that he could drive the car, for I was no longer sure I could navigate the streets. So much had come rolling back to me that it was hard for me to see the great oak trees flashing by on Charles Street, hard to see the mansions in Roland Park, hard to see Johns Hopkins University as we sped toward downtown.

And as we drove down funky, strip-joint Baltimore Street, I thought I saw Jeremy standing with a group of winos in front of the old Two O'Clock Club.

Oh, yes, I was gone, gone once again into the past, and I thought of the old 1940s movie flashbacks, which showed the past through a haze, and I thought the Hollywood boys had it exactly backward. The past is always lit under a nova of white light, it's the present that's a whirling cloud of mist, it's the present where one stumbles one yard at a time, barely able to see daylight, trying to avoid the flying bodies.

I thought of Dr. Spaulding and Jeremy at their lunch. That was too wild. My two spiritual fathers, those who had taken me through ice and fire, had finally met one day, and though they were not destined to be friends, it was as though they had recognized something in each other. What was it? Something they both needed yet lacked?

In Raines, an architectural intellect, the crucial ability to make a plan and see it through?

In Dr. S., magic, pure spirit, a spirit he had lost somewhere in the darkness of the war?

Oh, that was pure schematic bullshit, writerly jive and yet, it was hard to resist, for wasn't I their symbolic child?

321

Yes, I knew that somehow I had carried on as well as I had these past twenty years because of them and, to some degree, *for* them.

For them and for dear, selfish Dad and for my mother, and more so for my memories of Val and Eddie and Babe, too, whom I never saw again the day that they left me in front of the house on Chateau.

Billy drove us on, out past the gleaming rebuilt city, a place that now advertised itself as Charm City, and maybe it was true, but for me, all the real charm was in the past and unlike my mother, I knew I would have to live with my new jerry-built signposts in other towns, in my adopted world in New York. For I couldn't come back home, not with all these smiling, yacking ghosts walking around.

As we headed into the airport parking lot, I shut my eyes and I remembered that last night long ago. No, I hadn't told the professor or anyone else about that. That was my own little sweet, sad secret. Now, as the big planes floated over my head, I recalled myself standing there as Babe and Eddie and lovely, sad Val drove away, leaving me alone, feeling like some abandoned lover on the long blues highway.

But also knowing that there was no time for sadness, no time at all, for the second they were out of sight I knew what I had to do. It was as though Raines himself were alive and guiding me and as I got into my father's car, I heard myself talking to him.

"Is this what you want?" I said. "Tell me straight. That's all I ask. Tell me straight, okay?"

And as I drove aimlessly out the York Road, over the old dead trolley tracks, I heard him clearly.

"You know the game plan, my boy. You know very well."

Of course, I was more than a little mad, though at the time it didn't seem like madness. No, it really was as though we were doing this together, Raines and I, and I got the kerosene and the rags and I laughed and said to him: "If you had lived, you lunatic, if you had lived, what would you have done? Tell me, what would you have fucking done? Would you have become a gangster or a governor, a doctor, a dictator, a thief, some crooked saint guru who breaks old women's hearts down on tony Charles Street? What would you have done, dead boy, dear, crushed friend?"

It was impossible to say of course, just a mad little game I played in my grief and pain and loss and also, I guess, to keep me from being afraid when I walked down into the basement where the wild King of Cards and I had first met, that crazy blue morning when the old house shook from the iron ore machine.

It was just about midnight when I got back to our old home and walked down into the Hole. I sat there for a long time in the half light of the old overhead bulb looking at the embosser, the crazy, murderous laminator, the great streams of plastic, the piles of Daliesque cards with one ear, one nostril, an unblinking eye.

And I thought, yes, it was true, this *had* been my own home, my best friend's home, and whether I saw any of them ever again or not, it was a sacred place, and it must never, ever fall into the hands of Rudy Antonelli.

So I threw the first little Molotov cocktail right into the middle of the cellar. It ignited almost at once on some old yellowed *Evening Suns* and then on the curling plastic strips; the flames shot out and crackled and gave off the rotten odor of burning chemicals.

I took my time, watching everything like a camera, impartially, with no feelings at all. I just wanted to record it all, keep it inside me, so I would never forget any of it.

Solemnly, I dowsed the steps behind me as I went upstairs. Then I dropped a match on the landing and watched the entire stairway ignite below me and I felt both fearful and mightily glad all at the same time.

As I backed out of the house, I thought about throwing

one more bottle in the living room but I was afraid the curtains would catch and that the fire trucks would get here in time to save the place.

I sure as hell didn't want that. All the salvation had already taken place; this little church had done its job and now it would close its doors to saints and sinners alike.

I should have gone right away. After all, they'd be coming soon, but I stood outside for a while, just down the street, watching as the flames from the cellar started to catch the first floor.

It was going to be a good blaze, a perfect blaze. There would be nothing left. No jacks, no jokers, no princess or prince, and no merry olde king.

I walked three blocks to Winston to where I'd parked my father's car and started the engine, just as I heard the first sirens wail.

As I drove out past the blinking, flashing bar signs on the York Road, two more fire engines came streaming by me, their sirens screaming. I sucked in my breath and kept on driving, and suddenly, he was there riding shotgun beside me, Mad Jeremy Raines, his wild cowlick sitting straight up like some silent movie comedian, and I could almost hear him say, "Looks like it's going to be a very hot night, my boy, wouldn't you say?" And I laughed out loud and shook my head as we headed off together for one last wild adventure in the dark Baltimore night.